Praise for The Transmigrant

The Transmigrant is brilliant in its simplicity of style, an inspired narrative and vibrant living tapestry that humanizes Jesus in a sensitive and delicate way, the likes of which we have not seen in religious literature since Hermann Hesse's tale of the Buddha, Siddhartha, or Kahlil Gibrann's The Prophet. Well-researched and backed up with an insightful closing note from the author, this exquisite book, like the long lost scrolls of Russian explorer Nicolas Notovitch, places "Yeshua" in India during the eighteen "Missing Years," offering a detailed alternative history for the open-minded reader.

—**Paul Davids,** writer/producer/director of *Jesus in India*
(NBC Universal)

Kristi Saare Duarte's vivid narrative deploys the methods of fiction to get at a truth about Jesus that history too often ignores. He was raised within the land and traditions of Israel, and became the central figure in the worship of the Church, but Jesus' horizons were broader than Judaism or Christianity. Jesus felt, explored, and articulated connections between humanity and the divine, and among human beings, in a way that has never been matched. By de-centering the geography of Jesus' development, *The Transmigrant* uncovers the emotional substratum of religious genius.

—*Bruce Chilton,* author of *Rabbi Jesus: An Intimate Biography*

To those who are passionate about historical literature, the Transmigrant will transport you to that ancient cosmos of biblical times with such searing vividness, you will swear the story is unfolding before your very eyes, you will swear that you are witnessing a cinematic event. And to those who are passionate about one of the greatest mysteries of all times -- the lost years of Jesus' youth -- your questions and thoughts and ruminations will finally be answered in a plausible and convincing manner. *The Transmigrant* is much like Jesus' own saying about "man not living on bread alone," for the journey of this unforgettable story truly satisfies the reader on both a physical as well as spiritual level.

—**Luis Gonzalez**, author of *Luz*

The Transmigrant

The

Trans

migrant

KRISTI SAARE DUARTE

Maps and Author's Note may be found at the back of this book.

This is a work of fiction. Names, characters, places, and incidents are a product of the author's imagination. Locales and public names are sometimes used for atmospheric purposes. Any resemblance to actual people, living or dead, or to businesses, companies, events, institutions, or locales is completely coincidental.

The Transmigrant/Kristi Saare Duarte. -- 1st ed.

Published 2017
Printed in the United States of America

ISBN-10: 0-9971807-0-6
ISBN-13: 978-0-9971807-0-1
eISBN: 978-0-9971807-1-8

Library of Congress Control Number: **2017907781**

For information, please contact:
Conspicuum Press
PO Box 231
New York, NY 10027

Cover design by Alexander von Ness at Nessgraphica.com

For my mum and dad,

PIIA and SIIM SAARE

Thank you for teaching me to question everything, not to believe everything I read, and to think for myself.

I miss you every day.

In the beginning was God alone, and with him was the Word, his second. He contemplated and said, "Let me send out this Word so that she will produce and bring into being all the worlds."

—Tandya Brahmana, Sama Veda (17th Century BC)

In the beginning the Word already existed; the Word was with God, and the Word was God. From the very beginning, the Word was with God. The Word was the source of life, and this life brought light to people.

—The Gospel of John (1st Century AD)

CHAPTER ONE

Capernaum, Galilee, AD 1

Flap. Flippety-flap. Flap. The yellow butterfly fluttered its black-tipped wings in desperation against the synagogue ceiling, unaware of the open window only a few feet away. On a mat below, five-year-old Yeshua lounged against his father's shoulder, squeezed in between the other Yehudi men of the village. His gaze wandered to the women's side of the dividing curtain where his mother sat cross-legged with his younger siblings. They were still too small to understand the words of God. Not like Yeshua. No, God and Yeshua were already the best of friends.

On top of a wooden pulpit at the front, flickering oil lamps danced in the breeze and the scent of incense filled the snug meeting room with magic. Yeshua tried to keep pace with the grown-ups who swayed back and forth, chanting monotonous words of praise. He longed to one day be just like the rabbi who leaned over the pulpit as if he carried the conscience of the entire world on his shoulders and read out loud from the Torah scrolls in Hebrew, the priests' own language. Yeshua would stand in front of all the neighbors and, with a steady voice, teach them the true words of God. Words of wisdom.

The rabbi brushed his wrinkled hand through the remaining wisps of gray hair on his head and lowered his tasseled head scarf onto his shoulders. When he spoke, the ambience changed like an evening sky, shifting from blazing orange to purple and pink. It became warm and vivid, as if angels had touched everyone's heart.

"Esteemed men—children of the Lord!" the rabbi exclaimed in a voice that could have awakened even the deadest corpse from eternal slumber. "Do you not see how he loves you more than your fellow villagers? And still, you cannot—*should not*—ignore his commandments. For you, he created Sabbath as a day to rest, not hurry. Forsake your worries today and revel in the divine. Ah, what a magnificent day to celebrate in God, to enjoy silence and seclusion. To sit still and hear his voice speak to us…"

Yeshua's chest filled with a tender glow. With paradise. And just like the graceful butterfly above, he remained oblivious of the invisible chains that bound him.

But Sabbath came only once a week. On other days, a sleepy Yeshua rose before sunset and followed his father to the workshop around the corner from their home where he spent his days filing corners of tables and doors with an iron rasp until his hands burned with blisters. That's what boys did; they adopted their fathers' trade. It didn't seem fair: filing wood was for babies. But his father said only big boys could use the fun tools like the saw, the plane, and the chisels. Yeshua peered through the window at the black-headed gulls that soared across the sky, free to go anywhere they chose. And he drifted into daydreams.

One day, as Yeshua was helping his father unpack a delivery of cedar logs for a tax collector's table, two impossibly tall white-robed men staggered into the workshop. They had to bow their turbaned heads to enter.

"Water," one of them croaked in broken Aramaic, his eyes bloodshot with thirst. He slumped onto the floor. "I please beg of you. Water."

The log in Yeshua's arms fell to the floor with a bang. God said to always help the needy. He squeezed his way between the giants, and ran out the door and around the corner to their house, where his mother was baking bread in the courtyard. "Ama, Ama! Two men—foreigners.

Come quickly! And bring water."

"Who has come?" She frowned but didn't move.

"Come! They need water!" Yeshua pulled her hand with all his weight. "Hurry!"

Without haste, Ama cleaned her hands, filled a jug of water from the vat, and pulled her head scarf across her face. Yeshua stayed close behind her as they entered the workshop, then crouched in the corner while Ama served the men cool water in ceramic cups. He had seen men like these before, from afar. Fascinating men, straight out of legends, they passed through Capernaum in caravans of hundreds of camels along the trade route between Damascus and Alexandria.

Ama dripped lavender oil onto the strangers' palms and necks and told them to rub it in with a circular motion until their breathing had resumed a normal rhythm.

"Now, good men, what else may I do for you?" Abba said, and gestured to his wife to leave. Yeshua leaned against the wall and tried to make himself invisible. He was transfixed by these intimidating men with wide-bladed daggers hooked to their belts and fingers heavy with golden rings. And yet there was a kindness, an almost loving presence, about them. One of the men, his eyes like a burning sunset, caught him staring and grinned. His white teeth glistened against his swarthy complexion. Yeshua relaxed; these were respectable men after all, honest travelers. The men unfurled a heavy linen scroll that revealed a circular chart with scribbles of stars, moons, crosses, and triangles. The man who had smiled at him pointed at the chart and spoke in chunks of Aramaic peppered with peculiar words Yeshua had never heard before.

"We come looking for…a ray of light… And three hundred years ago, Prophet Zarathustra… Praise be to God for your help… Planet Jupiter and stars in the sky show the way to us…and there will come…next prophet soon…" The man stopped midsentence and pointed at Yeshua. "This your son?"

Abba nodded.

"Come to here, boy." The man reached out his enormous hand, grasped Yeshua by the chin, and stared into his eyes as if searching for something. His intense gaze made Yeshua faint with fear, but he couldn't look away. Nearby, his father breathed heavily, nervously. Yeshua swallowed. Time seemed to have stopped. And then the man burst out laughing. Thick, short bursts of laughter. Yeshua wriggled free and ran to safety behind his father, where he watched the strangers chuckle and clap their hands. Their cackles echoed around the room.

Why were they laughing?

The man who had grabbed his chin beamed. He mumbled something to his friend, and then turned to Abba.

"Your son, one day, great man. Prophet. What you call it—Messiah. The world waits long time for him, his message."

"No, no…" Abba shook his head, his voice in shards. "No!" he said again with more determination. "Forgive my insolence, but that's nonsense. My son is a carpenter. Enough of this foolishness. Why does everyone wish for a Messiah to come and solve all their troubles?" He rubbed the spot between his eyebrows. "Those are the ignorant dreams of victims, of desperate men."

The strangers rolled up their scroll and smoothed their robes. The discussion was over. The man who had spoken reached into his pouch and retrieved a yellow scarf tied into a bundle, which he placed in Abba's palm, closing his fingers around it.

Then the strangers disappeared into the dusk as abruptly as they had arrived.

"Abba, Abba, what did they say? What did they give you?" Yeshua couldn't hold back any longer.

Still shaking his head, his father patted him on the head and untied the yellow silk scarf. Folded inside was a shiny golden ring with a large turquoise stone, a clump of fragrant frankincense, and a jar of myrrh oil. When Yeshua reached to grab the ring, Abba slapped his hand.

"No touching!"

Tears stung Yeshua's eyes. Why was his father angry?

Inside their home, Abba threw the bundle at his wife.

"Look, Maryam. Behold what they gave us. Gifts for a nobleman. A king!" He covered his eyes with his hands. "They spoke of a prophecy. Their charts depict that an extraordinary child has been born hereabouts. But I didn't understand where. In Galilee? Maybe Judea? The Roman Empire?"

"And?"

Yeshua put his arms around his younger brother Yakov for comfort, shielding him from the serious discussion.

"They search for him. That's what they do. They make charts of the stars and planets, decipher them, and then scour the world for this child."

"And that's why they gave you these presents? To help look for the child?" Ama squatted next to her husband, baby Iosa suckling her breast.

"No. They reckon it's—the large one."

Ama glanced at Yeshua.

He hugged his brother closer. What did it mean, the *large one*?

"Who are they?" she asked.

"Zoroastrian seers. Devotees of a prophet called Zarathustra, from Persia." Yosef pressed his knuckles together. "They wish to educate him about their faith. They will return when he's grown."

"Oh!" Ama pulled her nipple from Iosa and placed the protesting infant in his cot. "Did you tell them we are Yehudim?"

"Forget it, Maryam. Let's just forget this." He tied up the gifts in the yellow scarf and hid it in a hole under the stove.

Yakov squirmed out of Yeshua's embrace and snuggled up into his father's lap, but Yeshua couldn't move. Why had the men laughed? And why did they bring gifts for a king? And who was the large one they spoke about?

Could it be him—Yeshua? Was it possible?

Capernaum, Galilee, AD 3

In the years to come, Yeshua observed the foreigners who passed
through the Capernaum market. They came from Syria and Cappadocia,
from Egypt and Cyrenaica, from Mesopotamia and Persia, and even
farther east. He learned that if he sang for the merchants traveling in
caravans of heavily laden camels, they often flipped him a copper coin
or handed him a piece of fruit. The pilgrims and holy men, dressed in
threadbare robes, were more reserved and offered him nothing but
smiles. He always kept watch for the men who had visited his father's
workshop, scanning the face of every tall white-clad man, crowned by a
white turban, but the mystics never appeared again.

Once Yeshua had mastered Greek, the universal language, he
approached every traveler who passed through his hometown, ravenous
for information about the world. The wealthy traders told fascinating
stories about the countries they had traveled, brutal bandits who had
stolen their cargo, and women they had seduced. The holy men spoke
only about their gods, each of them convinced that his method of prayer
was the only right way and everyone else was mistaken—as if Yahweh
would have multiplied and changed his rules for each part of the world
just to cause confusion. Like with the Tower of Babel. Why would God
do that? Wouldn't God prefer that everyone agree on a single manner of
devotion?

One day, a red-cheeked Buddhist monk with a shaved head and glittering eyes handed Yeshua a leaf as if it were an invaluable gift. "It's from the Bodhi tree," he said, and wiped his hands on his tattered saffron robe. "From Gaya. In the Maha-Meghavahanas."

Yeshua inspected the simple coarse leaf. "What is it? A healing plant, this Bodhi tree?"

The monk laughed so hard, his belly shook. "It's from the Bodhi tree, the one Lord Buddha sat under when he reached enlightenment."

Yeshua twirled the leaf between his fingers. It looked like any ordinary leaf.

"What's enlightenment?" he asked.

"Nirvana."

Yeshua frowned. What could one possibly reach while sitting under a tree? A shadow? Perhaps an itching ant bite?

"Nirvana is a state of mind, when you become so wise you don't need to be born again. You overcome suffering. Nothing worries you; nothing angers you. You awaken."

Awaken. Somehow, Yeshua understood the word, even though he did not understand it. Eager to learn more, he pulled up his legs and squatted on the ledge next to the monk. And right there, in the thick of the chaotic Capernaum market, the monk with vibrant eyes told him about his life and how he had left his parents at the age of five to begin spiritual training, dedicating his life to studying the teachings of an enlightened nobleman. Yeshua's heart raced, and he leaned in to hear more. Were there many other children like him who had left their parents to serve God?

The rabbi insisted that Yahweh was the one and only God, and that the Yehudim were his chosen people. But if that were true, were all those holy men traveling the world to spread their message wrong? Had they misunderstood the word of God? Or was the rabbi mistaken? How much did the rabbi know, anyway? He spent most of his days shaping clay into pots, and devoted only one day a week to teaching God's words.

The more Yeshua spoke with travelers from faraway lands and the more he compared their beliefs with the teachings of the Torah, the more confused he became. He sought answers in the synagogue. He stalked the rabbi after the Sabbath sermon, hoping the teacher would help him find answers to the questions that multiplied within him day by day.

"How was Moses able to split the Red Sea? And why did God kill the Egyptians who chased them? Why didn't he simply close the sea after the Yehudim had passed? What if the Egyptians also wanted to repent and serve God?"

The rabbi continued cleaning up the pulpit. He picked up the scrolls, furled them tighter, and stored them in a trunk.

Yeshua continued. "And why should we treat other Yehudim better than we do gentiles? Aren't we equal in God's eyes? Didn't he create us all?"

The rabbi didn't look up as he answered. "We are God's chosen people. We made a covenant with God, and he with us. We're not perfect, but we must keep together as a people to keep our promise to God."

Yeshua scratched his head. "But…"

The words died in his mouth. The rabbi had walked away. Yeshua followed him out the door and back to the rabbi's house. "Why did God want us to destroy the Canaanites and the Amalekites? Isn't He supposed to be kind and compassionate?"

The rabbi sighed and turned back to face Yeshua. "Oh, child, wherever have you learned this foolishness?"

"It's in the commandments, the mitzvoth."

"Yes, yes, but why do you challenge the commandments of God? You're far too young to understand. Forget about the Canaanites and Amalekites. They had their own destiny. Your only duty is to be a good boy and obey the commandments. Now, go home; I'm closing the doors."

At home, Yeshua bombarded his father with more questions. "Why should we fear God? And why do we have to criticize sinners? Shouldn't we help them instead, show them the right way?"

When Abba stumbled on the answers, Yeshua realized that no one in the world knew everything, not even his father or the rabbi. They only pretended to be wise. They read the scriptures and followed the traditions without ever questioning whether they were right or wrong.

Yeshua tried again with his mother. "Ama, why do we have laws that tell us what to eat? Why does God care? And what happens to those who don't follow those laws, like the Tarsians and the Romans?"

His mother explained that the rabbis made sure the slaughtered animals were healthy. Some sea creatures might carry diseases. The Yehudim were holy and therefore needed a special diet. But she could not say why meat and milk could not be eaten at the same meal or why only animals with cleft hooves were acceptable as meat.

His brother Yakov laughed at his constant pursuit of certainty. "You're so silly," he said. "You think you can change the way the rabbi thinks?"

But Yeshua didn't feel silly. There was something odd about the laws, the way they contradicted each other. On one hand, there was love, but on the other hand, this love could not be shared with all their neighbors. And if the Yehudim were so special, wouldn't they all be rich and live in fancy homes like the Romans? God seemed to have chosen them over the Yehudim. After all, the Romans ruled, whereas the locals picked up the scraps of work their rulers didn't want.

That was probably why the rabbi always spoke about the coming Messiah. Well, *everyone* was talking about him: the Warrior King who would come real soon and throw out the Romans and give Palestine back to the Yehudim. He fantasized about fighting side by side with the Messiah and helping him kick out the oppressors. They scared him. And they frightened his mother. She, the bravest of all, became so petrified at the sight of a legionnaire, she would pick up her children with the strength of Goliath and run in the opposite direction.

If only Yeshua knew what the Messiah looked like, he would go search for him right away.

Capernaum, Galilee, AD 6

Yeshua waited all year for Yom Kippur, the Day of Atonement, when he could spend the whole day praying. No one bothered him with petty work or chores. This year, he would put his entire soul into the prayers to make sure God answered all his questions. Because whenever he kept absolutely still, God seemed to be right there with him.

Two days before the holy day, Yosef took his sons for a walk around Capernaum to ask their neighbors' forgiveness for offenses given in the previous year. Like all good Yehudim, Yeshua offered God's love to friends and foes alike, as if God had granted him the power to erase sadness and ensure a future free of hardships. He knew his blessings didn't actually change anyone's life, but that brief glimmer of hope in their eyes made him warm inside.

The next morning, Yeshua's father gathered his wife, four sons, and two daughters in the courtyard to practice the Kapparot ritual. Everyone received a newly stitched cotton handkerchief and two coins. "Tie the money into the handkerchief and swing it—like this!"

The children watched wide-eyed as their otherwise stern father swung the bundle over his head like a monkey. Even their mother giggled behind her scarf.

"Accept the coins, Lord!" Abba called up into the sky. "Gather them from me as payment for my sins."

The children whirled their bundles with frenzy, especially Yakov, whose coins flew out of his hand not once but three times. And when they all agreed that God had accepted their plea, they walked through the town to offer their coins to someone in need.

Ama and Abba both gave their coins of atonement to the widow next door, as did the well-behaved toddlers, Iosa and Shimon. When nine-year-old Yakov wanted to offer his coins to the miller, Abba's face turned beet red and his hand rose for a slap. Yeshua quickly pushed his way in between his father and Yakov, who had huddled down to wait for the impact.

"Why in the name of Abraham would you waste your offering on a lousy drunkard?" Abba's voice rang sharp.

Yakov shrugged. "He needs the money."

"He squanders his money on wine!"

Yakov stood tall on his toes and stared into his father's eyes. "He's got to eat too, Abba, just like us."

Yakov could stare down anyone, but Abba was tougher. What would the neighbors say if he allowed his son to waste his hard-earned money on someone who drank all day and then cried on the streets at night because he had nothing to eat?

At last, Abba broke his stare. "Very well, son, it's your choice. I do not condone it, but God has awarded you the right to select your recipient."

Little Miriam, who always did whatever Yakov did, also gave her coins to the miller, then watched in sadness as the miller rushed off to the inn. Their coins would be gone in a heartbeat.

Yeshua thought long and hard. Who deserved his money the most? Salome, his angelic little sister, pushed her long hair out of her amber eyes and squeezed his hand. She glanced toward the house where a one-legged soldier lived, but Yeshua shook his head. Their parents would draw the line at helping a Roman. Instead, Yeshua steered his family toward the outskirts of town, where the lanes merged into fields. He stopped in front of a run-down shed with damaged window shutters. A soiled blanket covered the entrance. From inside came moans and sighs.

"Let us return, Yeshua, it's not safe." Ama spread her arms in front of her family to block their way.

At that moment, a leper stumbled out of the house. A torn robe shrouded his skeletal body, and a scarf covered his mouth, exposing only his blistered cheeks and forehead. His cloudy eyes rolled back in his head like those of a rabid animal.

Yeshua released Salome's hand and gathered his courage.

"May God bless you, my friend. Happy Yom Kippur," Yeshua said as he held out the handkerchief with the coins. The leper snatched at the bundle like a viper, before Yeshua could change his mind.

Salome shifted her weight from one leg to the other, staring at her feet. She clutched her coins so hard that her knuckles turned white.

Yeshua gently unwrapped her fingers and took the money from her hand. "Is it all right with you?"

When she nodded, he dropped her coins into the leper's palm, not even flinching at the finger stumps the disease had left behind.

"May God's light always shine on you," the leper said, gushing with gratitude.

Yeshua's heart bubbled with happiness. But when he stepped forward to embrace the leper, Abba yanked him back.

"Enough!"

As they walked away, Yeshua turned and waved to the leper. He had made the right decision; this poor man had been the most deserving of them all.

During the prefasting dinner that night, as they sat on mats around the platters of food, Abba blessed the bread and asked his children to explain the reasons for their decisions. Yeshua listened as the others spoke, but couldn't get one thought out of his mind. "Abba, why do lepers have to live like that, in hiding?"

"In hiding? They merely live outside the center. It is the town rule, a manner of managing disease. Elsewise, we might all be contaminated."

"But why can't people just leave food for them? You know, outside their house? They're hungry. I've heard they don't even die from leprosy; they starve to death."

"That's not true, son. Many families grant them weekly provisions and food. You know very well it's our obligation as Yehudim to help others."

"Then why does the rabbi say lepers need to show the world how impure they are? They're not impure, Abba; they're sick!" Yeshua couldn't sit still any longer. His stomach cramped at the thought of those lepers suffering. They hadn't done anything wrong. "And who says they have to rip their tunics and destroy their garments like that? And grow their hair long? Why can't people let them live in peace?"

"No one wants to fall ill, agreed? It's a means of protecting ourselves."

"But how would you feel, Abba, if you had to wear your disease like that? Don't they suffer enough? Of course they'll stay away; they won't want others to suffer as they do. But they should be treated like men, not animals."

Ama cleared away the food, avoiding another heated discussion.

Yeshua clenched his mouth shut. His father was the man of the house. He might be wrong, but he deserved respect.

Abba turned to his oldest daughter. "And how do you justify your charity?"

Salome raised her head like a proud heron and straightened her back. "Everyone needs to eat. Like the miller, even if most of his money goes to drink." She glanced at Yakov. "But the lepers, they can't work. At all. They need us to help them, and that's why."

Abba smiled and patted her head, ignoring Yeshua. He took another helping of soup and looked at his children. Yeshua sighed, relieved. Once again, sweet Salome had saved him. She always knew how to mellow her father's rage.

Hearing that the bickering had subsided, Ama returned and sat next to her husband so he could light the oil lamps and recite the blessings for the holy day to begin.

At dawn, Yeshua woke with a grumbling stomach and a heart filled with excitement. Yom Kippur had arrived at last! It didn't matter that he wasn't allowed to eat or drink anything until sunset; he could weather the hunger. He pulled the blanket off Yakov and Iosa, who were sleeping beside him, and together they tiptoed into their parents' room to wake them; time to go to the morning service.

Moments later, Yeshua sat cross-legged in prayer in the synagogue. Beside him, his three younger brothers struggled to sit still in silence. And before long, they were all pinching one another as hard as they could while trying their best not to laugh and squeal.

This year, Yeshua had warned his brothers not to touch him. His father had promised that if he behaved, he would finally teach him to read. But that wasn't the whole truth. Yeshua longed for quiet reflection, yearned to spend time thinking about the deeper meanings of the scriptures. The rabbi always said that every action or thought was returned manifold. A kind act could turn the meanest bully into a lamb, and God would punish any misbehavior. The Buddhist monks he met said that all sentient beings—animals and humans—had equal rights to happiness. It made sense. Because God loved everyone, not just the Yehudim. What had the Hindu trader said? "Why would there be a reservoir when there is flooding everywhere?" That had to be the truth.

He closed his eyes and turned his attention to the singsong of the rabbi's voice. A warm feeling enveloped him, and he drifted into nothingness. Into love. And in his mind, a light flickered, and a soundless voice spoke to him: *My son*, it said. *Your holiness is the redemption of the world. You will spend your life serving me and teaching others about salvation.*

Yeshua blinked awake and looked around. Who had spoken? His brothers? No, they still tumbled around, teasing one another. All the grown-ups swayed in prayer, their eyes focused on the rabbi. Yeshua shrugged; he must have been dreaming. He sat up straight and caught up with the chanting. He knew the verses well.

> *Adonai, the true Lord, may you always be*
> *with us;*
> *Manifest your presence.*
> *You created our spirits and guide us in the*
> *light;*
> *And we praise you. Amen.*

By the end of the day, Yeshua's brothers were asleep on the carpeted synagogue floor, exhausted from a long, tiresome day of prayers and from having to behave. Yakov whined in his sleep; this was his first year of fasting on Yom Kippur. Yeshua was hungry, too, but in a different way. His stomach was empty, but his spirit was filled with light. The rabbi's sermon on forgiveness and charity had inspired him, and his dream had given him hope. Yom Kippur marked a new beginning: all past sins were forgiven, and their names were inscribed in God's Book of Life with the promise of a good year ahead. Oh, how Yeshua loved the Yehudi traditions!

When the ram's horn blared to mark the end of Yom Kippur, Yeshua woke Yakov with a shove, and they chased each other back to the house, where platters of food awaited them in the courtyard. Without pause, Yakov and Yeshua stuffed their mouths with olives, bread, horse beans, meats, and fruits.

"What is this?" Abba slammed the gate behind him. "Is my house invaded by beasts?" Yeshua and Yakov put their food down, laughing nervously as they backed away, then watched their father sit down to eat, showing them how it should be done. With dignity. With presence. With gratitude. Relishing every bite.

Capernaum, Galilee, AD 8

The year Yeshua turned twelve, he joined his parents on his first pilgrimage to the holy city of Jerusalem to celebrate Pesach. The temple had filled his daydreams for years; in them, he wandered around its holy grounds and knelt down in prayer at the altar. He couldn't believe the time had finally arrived to visit the source of his dreams.

Yakov, as always, made fun of him. "Hey, it's just a building, you know. Stones and mortar, that's all it is."

Yeshua ignored him.

"It's no different from our synagogue—and you go there every Sabbath." Yakov laughed. "They've even got the same rabbis, the same prayers, the same offering tables."

It wasn't the same at all. Yeshua twisted his brother's arm as hard as he could, but Yakov just grinned and pulled away.

"You think some kind of magic will happen when you're there? That God will reach down and touch you?"

Yeshua's cheeks burned. That was exactly what he hoped. He wanted another sign from God that he was special, that his dream had been real, that he had a purpose in life. He wanted the priests to notice how wise and devoted he was and tell him he should teach the word of God even though he hadn't been born into a priestly family.

"You're a fool," Yeshua said, and walked away. He left the house and went around the corner to the workshop, where he picked up an ax and hit a piece of almond wood over and over, until the floor was covered with splinters. Were his dreams just fantasies? What if he went to Jerusalem and everyone treated him like any other ignorant Galilean boy? But no, surely the high priest would notice him in the crowd and understand how special he was. Wouldn't he?

On the day before the journey, Yeshua's grandmother arrived to tend the younger children at home while Yeshua and his parents traveled to Jerusalem.

"My little wonder boy," she said, and hugged Yeshua so hard he couldn't breathe. She was old and thin but stronger than many men. "How you've grown, Yeshua. You're almost a man now."

Yeshua straightened his back. Almost a man!

"Yeshua wants to be a priest," Yakov cried out with a mock-serious face.

"No, I don't!"

Yeshua kicked Yakov's shin, but his father, quick as an adder, grabbed the kicking leg.

"Children, behave. This is a celebration. I do not want to hear another quip from either of you tonight. Understood?"

Yeshua pursed his lips. No one seemed to understand him. He took a seat next to his father and ate in silence as the grown-ups continued their boring conversations about who had gotten married and who had died, gossiping about people in his mother's village he had never met.

Early the next morning, Yeshua and his parents set off for Jerusalem. The roads were crammed with families making their way south. Antlike rows of people approached from every direction across a panorama of dusty hills. Here and there, weathered pilgrims paused to enjoy a meal or take a nap before they continued to the next village. And far too often, they passed a group of fools gathered around a self-proclaimed prophet who filled their minds with strange ideas about the coming Messiah. Abba rushed his family past them, afraid their false teachings would stick to them like a rash.

They walked all day with only a break for lunch and stayed at inns at nights, rushing through Galilee and Samaria to reach Aunt Elisheba's house in Judea before the beginning of Pesach. On the way, Yeshua made friends with Aaron and Levi, two boys from a village on the western shore of Lake Kinneret who were also on their first pilgrimage to Jerusalem. They were excited about seeing the temple, but they were even more eager to become men and get married. They went on and on about girls, changing their minds at a whim about which girl they would choose. When Yeshua tried to discuss important matters with them, like the true meaning of Pesach, their eyes glazed over. And when he asked them why they thought God saved only the Yehudim firstborns from the plague and whether all babies wouldn't be innocent, Aaron threw a ball at him and laughed. Yeshua felt nothing but relief when their ways parted.

In a village just outside of Jerusalem, Aunt Elisheba and Cousin Yochanan welcomed them with hugs and kisses, praising God they had made a safe journey. When his parents excused themselves to rest, Yochanan dragged Yeshua up to the roof.

"You and I are going to sleep here!" Yochanan pointed at a couple of sleeping mats. "It will be great. We can spy on all the pilgrims coming through the village and bombard them with pebbles."

"Pebbles?" Yeshua had never met his cousin before, but he seemed wild. His cousin's hair hung long and unkempt as if it hadn't been combed for months. But his clothes were clean, and despite everything else, he had a pleasant freckled face.

"Small stones." Yochanan punched Yeshua's shoulder and laughed. "I'm just joking, cousin. Let's just look at all the pretty girls."

That sounded a lot better, because Yeshua didn't want to cause trouble. The worst thing that could happen now was if his parents forbid him to visit the temple.

Downstairs, the front door slammed.

The color drained from Yochanan's face. "Uh-oh. It's Abba!" He gulped, eyes wide. "We must go downstairs. Now!"

In the dining room, Uncle Zekharyah greeted Yeshua's parents with the customary "Peace be unto you."

Yeshua shuddered as he approached his uncle. Piercing black eyes peered out from the many wrinkles of his face, and an oversized nose formed a beak over his scowl. How could this menacing man be a servant of God? Yeshua forced a quiet "Peace be unto you" and returned to safety behind his father.

Aunt Elisheba bid them to sit on plush cushions around a low table covered with an embroidered golden cloth in the dining parlor. Tall oil lamps cast a warm light over the many platters of food and on the colorful tapestries on the walls. In front of every seat was a plate with food that Yeshua knew represented their ancestors' flight from Egypt.

Uncle Zekharyah filled a silver goblet with wine and recited the kiddush blessing to sanctify the first night of the Seder. In unison, they raised their glasses of wine and sipped. Aunt Elisheba proceeded to circle the table and pour water over everyone's hands to symbolize ritual purification.

As the youngest members of the family, Yeshua and Yochanan took turns asking questions about the story behind Pesach, and the grown-ups replied by reading from the Haggadah. By the time the meal started, Yeshua's stomach was growling with hunger. He devoured his serving of grilled lamb, egg, unleavened bread, and figs. The wine numbed his mind and Yeshua relaxed, no longer frightened of his uncle.

With their bellies stuffed, Yochanan and Yeshua were asked to search every corner of the house for the hidden bread, and when they found it, they all welcomed the spirit of Elijah into the house.

After the fourth and last ceremonial glass of wine, Yeshua crawled up to the roof to sleep. He lay on his back and watched the moon move in circles. If he closed one eye, it stopped for a moment, and then it started rotating again. His stomach felt queasy, but the exhaustion from walking for four long days had caught up with him, and within moments he was fast asleep, snoring like a little field mouse.

Hours later, a dog barking in the distance woke him. He tried to sit up but failed miserably. His pounding head dragged him back down, as if someone were squeezing it in a vise. Bile rose into his mouth, and he had to swallow several times to keep it down. His whole body felt embalmed, like a buried pharaoh. He wanted to die. Surely death would be kinder than this.

On the mattress by his side, Yochanan peered at him. When he realized why Yeshua was moaning, he scampered downstairs and returned with a jar of goat's milk. "Drink this. And then you've got to sleep some more. You'll feel better."

By the time Yeshua awoke the second time, the sun had passed the horizon and his headache was gone. He crawled out from under the sheet and sauntered down the stairs, steadying himself on the wall.

"Oh, there you are!" His mother greeted him with a cautious, worried smile. No doubt, Yochanan had told them of his condition. "Here, have some lentil soup. It will restore your spirit.

Yeshua sat at the table and ate a few nourishing spoonfuls under the watchful eyes of his mother and aunt.

After the meal, it was finally time to make their way to Jerusalem, where Abba and Uncle Zekharyah were waiting. Across the hills, they passed vendors pulling carts of produce and women balancing jars of water on their heads. In the far west, vultures circled over large wooden crosses where crucified revolutionaries hung dead, like ready meals for the birds of prey. And there, at last, the sacred city spread out on a hilltop before them like a patchwork of sand-colored cubes in a hundred different shades.

Yeshua gasped.

High up on the mount stood King Solomon's temple, blinding white and begging to be adored. Even grander than he had imagined, its pillars and glistening alabaster walls reflected the rays of the midmorning sun. And in the center rose the gold-rimmed sanctuary, the heart of God. Yeshua started running, his cousin close behind. He couldn't wait another second. They scrambled down the muddy paths through the olive orchards and all the way up the hill and through the town gate. They rushed through the labyrinthine streets, pushing their way through the masses. The place hummed with chaos, a melee of pilgrims and merchants, all moving toward the same destination. Yeshua's heart pounded as he ran along the wide paved temple road through a bazaar flanked by craftsmen's stalls: tailors, potters, weavers, and silversmiths. Everything imaginable was on sale, even the unblemished lambs and pigeons reared specifically for sacrifice. It was hectic, messy, and loud— and absolutely wonderful.

His mother and aunt had fallen behind, but Yeshua couldn't stop now. After all these years, the temple was finally within his reach.

With Yochanan right behind him, Yeshua climbed up the wide stairs to the mikvehs, the cleansing baths outside the temple, and past the pilgrims who rested outside. He paced in place as he waited in the long line of older men. Once it was their turn, the boys skipped down the steps as if God didn't have time to wait, quickly splashed water on their heads, and jumped out, wringing their tunics as they ran up the final steps. Yeshua could hardly breathe. The walls of God's own house towered above him. No matter how many times the temple had been looted and desecrated, it remained, holier than anything else in the entire world. It justified everything his rabbi had said: the Yehudim were the chosen people, and Yahweh's temple belonged to them.

"Where might you think you are heading?" A Levite blocked the temple gate with his staff.

Yochanan rolled his eyes. "The temple."

"I see that. But what—"

"Pesach. Eh, don't you know my father, Zekharyah? The priest?"

Yeshua wanted to sink through the ground. His cousin was so rude. "We've come to celebrate Pesach, like honorable Yehudim," he said, and shoved Yochanan in the ribs.

The Levite grunted but accepted their shekels. When he stepped aside, Yeshua rushed inside, fell to his knees, and kissed the holy ground.

The Court of the Gentiles, the largest square he had ever seen, bustled with thousands and thousands of people. Groups of worshippers sought shade from the relentless sun under the colonnades that surrounded the plaza. Yeshua slithered through the crowd and climbed the stairs to the men's court. Inside, a crowd of priests tended the sacrificial fire, which devoured the offered animals with insatiable hunger. The stench of burning carcasses blended with the sweet scent of frankincense and spices. Yeshua pinched his nose to keep from gagging. And then he looked up. In front of him stood the most magnificent structure of all, the Holy of Holies. Adorned by columns and crowned with a row of golden triangles, the tall building held the inner sanctuary, where only the high priest was allowed entry. Yeshua's knees weakened. One day, he promised himself, he would be invited inside.

Yochanan grabbed his hand and pulled him to the side. "It's time," he whispered.

"Time for what?"

A group of lyre-players had appeared on the stairs in front of the Holy of Holies. When they struck the first chords, dozens of singers joined them, and the courtyard filled with a heavenly chorus. The large doors of the Holy of Holies opened, and the stately high priest Ananus emerged in the doorway. His white beard glistened in the sun as he raised his hands above his bejeweled turban to announce his arrival like a young and powerful Abraham. When he descended the stairs, his shoulders crouched under the weight of the heavy purple gold-trimmed cloak and the hefty breastplate that hung from his neck. The crowd fell into silence. Yeshua held his breath.

Ananus fingered the twelve jewels of his breastplate, as if reminding the crowd of the twelve tribes of Israel. He drew a deep breath, cleared his voice, and then spoke. Divinity seemed to flow through him across the worshippers who had gathered. Yeshua's entire body trembled and his eyes filled with tears; this man had been ordained by God. He closed his eyes and drank in every word. What a privilege to be here in Yahweh's own house with God's own shepherd.

Every morning after that first day, following prayers and breakfast, Yochanan and Yeshua stole away to the temple. For hours, they listened to the temple priests speak with other pilgrims and marveled at their guidance on how to conduct their lives and how to best serve God. Yeshua loved the stories about the Messiah who was supposed to arrive any day now. How he longed for the day when the savior would return the rule of Palestine to the Yehudim and restore their dignity and freedom.

Every now and then, Yeshua ventured a question.

"I've been wondering, how will we recognize the Messiah when he comes? What exactly will he look like?"

The priest stroked his beard in thought.

Yeshua continued: "How can we tell if he's a true prophet? If people don't believe he's the Messiah, they will kill him, won't they?"

"We will simply know," the priest said, although he sounded anything but convinced. "God will open our eyes."

"But what if the Messiah is afraid of being stoned to death? The law says to stone false prophets, doesn't it?"

He continued questioning. He asked why the law required the burning of a city that had turned to idol worship. Why couldn't the priests explain why it was wrong instead of hurting the poor people who lived there? Didn't God realize that innocent women and children would lose their homes, too? The priests laughed at his eagerness, and Yeshua flourished in their presence. He could tell they respected him, perhaps even admired him. He belonged here, among all the other teachers. He decided right there and then that he would devote his life to studying Yehudi law and literature, and learn all there was to know about the traditions. One day, he promised himself, he would come back as an equal, as a priest. God had asked him to, hadn't he?

When the day came to return to Capernaum, Yeshua embraced his cousin with all his might. Yochanan was the most interesting person he had ever met, the only other person his age who knew anything about the scriptures and was willing to engage in philosophical discussions, pondering the relationship between reason and revelation and how the different thoughts complemented each other. Yeshua had learned more in this one week than in his entire life. He felt older, wiser, and more mature. And he had fallen in love with Jerusalem. There was no other place like it in the world.

Uncle Zekharyah held Yeshua at arm's length to bid him good-bye. A crooked grin spread across his face.

"What I hear, young man, is—you would like to study the scriptures?" His voice cracked, and his dry tongue licked his lips.

Yeshua nodded, glowing with pride.

"What do you say: would you like to become a priest?"

Yeshua blushed. "Well, yes, I'd like to, very much—"

Uncle Zekharyah burst into a hearty laugh. He clapped his hands and roared, "That will be the day, my boy. That will be the day!" He wheezed for air and continued his ugly laughter until it ebbed into coughs. Then he pulled Yochanan to his chest. "But this boy, my dear Yeshua, he will be a priest. Like me. Like my father. Because this boy was born of the priestly order of Abijah. And you?"

Yeshua stared at his feet. He could feel his father's eyes drill through him, embarrassed.

"And you, boy, are a carpenter."

Yeshua heard Abba clear his throat. Tears burned behind his eyelids. He bit the inside of his cheek to keep them from falling.

"Of course. I am a carpenter. Like my father. And like his father." Yeshua wanted to run out the door and never come back. What if all the priests in Jerusalem were like his uncle? What if they viewed him as nothing more than a simple carpenter? Yeshua couldn't bear it. His head pounded, and the blood rushed to his ears.

When Abba apologized for his son's vanity, Yeshua wanted to disappear into the morning fog.

"I have packed you some meat and vegetables…" Aunt Elisheba said, trying to lighten the mood, but her husband's ridicule hung heavy over them all. Abba, Ama, and Yeshua had been put in their place. They were the poor Galilean relatives visiting the high and mighty Zekharyah.

Yeshua forced a smile. He refused to let his uncle see his weakness.

Capernaum, Galilee, AD 8

Back home, memories of the temple occupied Yeshua's thoughts night and day. He knew he belonged there, no matter how many times his father told him priesthood was not for him. What did they expect him to do—work as a carpenter the rest of his life and forget about God? There had to be a way.

He lived for the rare moments when the rabbi let him read a passage during the Sabbath service and basked in the praise that his neighbors showered upon him. Whenever that occurred, the long days at the workshop making doors, benches, and window shutters changed into opportunities for contemplation. The quiet work allowed him to think about God and ponder questions to ask the rabbi the next time they met. In time, his reading in Hebrew improved, and soon, rumors of the well-spoken child spread to the villages around Lake Kinneret and the synagogue filled with strangers. Yeshua's faith sprouted again. Perhaps he could somehow convince Abba that priesthood was his true calling after all. Maybe he could find a way to bypass the rules.

But all hope was shattered the day a neighbor, with his wife and daughter, knocked on their door.

Abba perked up.

"Come, Yeshua, greet Mr. Iakobi," he called. "You are familiar with the stonemason, are you not?"

Yeshua politely wished him peace and crunched his nose. The triple-chinned stonemason reeked of sweat, and the smile on his meaty lips was more fake than a Roman's vow. Yeshua sat next to his father as his sisters brought out trays of grapes and cheese with goblets of wine for the men.

At the other end of the courtyard, Mrs. Iakobi and her daughter chatted with Ama. The girl's blue eyes glimmered with admiration as she gawked at Yeshua from the distance.

"I've heard you in the synagogue." Mr. Iakobi's words stumbled in a lisp over a lazy tongue. "Such eloquent speeches. Quite perceptive, you are."

"Thank you, sir."

"And are you as clever with your hands as you are with the word of God?"

Yeshua hesitated, racking his brain for the right words. He wasn't a very good carpenter. Mediocre at best.

Abba elbowed him.

"Woodwork, it's an art," Yeshua said at last. "He who works with his hands, head, and heart is not merely a craftsman; he's an artist. And when I chisel a door or a bench, I think of God."

The mason nodded.

"A bench is my creation. As we are all God's creations."

When Mr. Iakobi clapped his hands, Yeshua knew he had found the right words. He hadn't lied, merely evaded the question.

And so the evening proceeded with questions and answers, wine and food, laughter—and resounding claps from Mr. Iakobi's flabby hands. By the time he formally presented his dewy-eyed daughter, Yeshua was light-headed with both wine and pride.

"Come, meet Chava, my daughter. She's nearly twelve, wouldn't you believe. Next month. Isn't she lovely?"

At closer look, the girl was as plain as a doll made of clay. With a plump face covered with pimples, the only pretty thing about her were soft blue eyes that radiated with anticipation.

"I'm honored to meet you. My name is Yeshua."

They stared at each other, a few feet apart, aware that their parents hoped to see sparks flying. There was not even a flicker. The chemistry was stillborn.

"What do you reckon?" Abba asked Yeshua after the guests had left.

"I guess he's a fine man. But he's so fat, he couldn't even fit onto one single cushion." Yeshua laughed.

"No, silly boy, the young lady."

"She's a girl," Yeshua said, and shrugged. "But did you see her mother? She didn't take off her veil all night long."

Abba walked over to the vat to wash his face. "He's an affluent man, one of the wealthiest in Capernaum. Even Galilee." He looked straight at Yeshua to make sure he was listening. "You do understand that Chava would be an exceptional wife for someone like you. You could chisel your doors to pieces and still never be poor."

Wife? His father wanted him to get married? But he wasn't yet thirteen.

"I'm not sure, Abba," Yeshua tried. "Maybe I'm not the kind of man who gets married."

"Nonsense! What drivel is that?" Abba slapped his face so hard it burned. "A man who has no wife lives without joy, without blessing, and without goodness!"

Of course the Lord wanted all men to be married, but he just couldn't marry a girl with a face like an overripe apricot. He would rather wilt and die.

"Every man needs a woman to clean and cook for him."

Yeshua shrugged away, but Yosef yanked him back.

"You plan to reside with us the rest of your life, is that so? Have your mother work off the skin of her knees for you? Or would you like your sisters to serve you as well? You do realize that your sisters will marry one day, and your mother and I will not live forever? What will you do then? Prowl the streets like a beggar?" Abba slammed the bedroom door behind him.

Yeshua fought back tears. He escaped up to the roof to ask the stars for guidance. His father was right. He would have to marry one day. But not yet! Tomorrow morning, once Abba had calmed down, Yeshua would ask to wait another year or two. He would still be young at fourteen or fifteen. There would still be girls left to marry, wouldn't there?

He lay on his back and counted the stars until his eyelids grew heavy. As he was drifting to sleep, a shooting star raced across the sky. Yeshua pushed himself up on his elbow and giggled. A sign from God!

"Thank you, Lord," he whispered, "for always being by my side. I know I can rely on you to help me grow and learn more so I can be in your service. That's all I want. And when I'm ready, I'll trust you to bring me the right woman to be my wife. But please, only when I'm ready."

Despite his prayer, the days and weeks that followed saw the house overrun with visitors from around Lake Kinneret offering up their daughters. Every man within a day's travel and with a daughter of marrying age knocked on their door. Some girls were pleasant, others intolerable. Some were beautiful, others homely. Some families tried to buy his father's approval with fancy gifts, whereas the wealthier families offered only their own company. The house filled with jars of wine, flowers, fruits, and pastries of every kind. Yakov joked that they would all grow fat before their father selected the most profitable match, but Yeshua didn't laugh. He didn't want to marry any of them.

Aware of his father's impatience, he pretended to contemplate the offers. "Yes, maybe this one," he said every now and then, only to withdraw his approval a couple of days later. "I think I made a mistake. I've heard bad things about her."

With every new prospect, Yeshua's panic grew. One of these days, Yosef would make a decision, and his dream of becoming a priest would be over. There had to be a way out of this.

One day, when Yeshua visited the local tool sharpener in the market, he noticed a childlike monk in a mustard-colored robe resting on a ledge by a watermelon cart. Yeshua approached him with an open smile.

"Shlama," he said in Aramaic, a greeting of peace most pilgrims understood.

"Shlama, brother," the monk answered. He raised his hand to shade his eyes against the sun's glare. "Please sit down and share my cup of water."

Yeshua had to blink twice. He had never met a traveling holy man who spoke Aramaic before. He sat next to the youth and accepted a sip of the muddy water.

"What brings you to Capernaum?"

Yeshua learned that Dhiman, the monk, was almost exactly the same age as he, and equally devoted to a spiritual quest. "I can't be a priest, though," Yeshua said with bitterness in his voice. "I know every scripture almost as well as our local rabbi, but he's not really a priest, he's a potter. He serves God only on the day of Sabbath."

"That's quite foolish, isn't it?" the young monk said.

Yeshua hesitated. It was difficult to explain. He barely understood it himself. Why would God choose specific families to be priests when others might be more suitable? Wouldn't God prefer someone dedicated, like Yeshua, to spread his word to the masses?

"In my culture, anyone can be a monk," Dhiman said. "I was only a baby when my father left me in a monastery."

"And you can be the highest monk one day?"

Dhiman laughed. "Yes, with years of study and devotion, I could be the highest monk. But that is not important."

Yeshua swallowed. Where was this place?

"I come from Sindh. Far away." Dhiman pointed in the direction of

Mesopotamia. "Very different too. A pleasant land, many green mountains and dry mountains, a hot-hot desert, and a cool blue sea that stretches on and on until the end of the world. And more forests and rivers and fields than you could ever count. Everyone is very kind there." Dhiman's eyes shone when he spoke about his country. "I'm on my way home now. I mean soon—tomorrow."

Dhiman radiated with anticipation, but Yeshua pouted. He wished his new friend could stay a little longer. They had so much in common.

"You want to come along? With me?" Dhiman asked.

Yeshua's jaw dropped. Could he really? Then he remembered his father's plan. "No, I can't," he said. "I'm sorry. My family…"

His family what? His family expected him to stay and work and marry a rich girl. But couldn't his brothers also marry into wealthy families and work in his father's shop? What if he left Palestine? Maybe he, too, could become a monk? In his mind it seemed impossible, but in his heart the decision was already made. He couldn't imagine anything more wonderful.

"Absolutely out of the question!" Abba said when Yeshua revealed his plan. "Are you some kind of scavenger rat searching for a new home? Do you want to roam the world like the madmen preaching in the fields? You will remain here and wed." He grabbed Yeshua by his robe and dragged him into the workshop. "I will not tolerate such disrespect," he muttered as he bolted the door from the outside.

Yeshua stared at the door. He tried to push it open, but it wouldn't budge. In despair, he fell to the ground, curled into a fetal position, and wept like a child. How could his father be so selfish? Didn't he know this was his last chance for happiness? He *had* to go to Sindh. It was his destiny. He was meant to serve God as a monk, and now Abba had ripped his future away. Yeshua screamed and pounded his fists on the thick door. He swore and begged and called for his father to open it. But it stayed shut.

As the sky changed into a watermelon pink and the birds tweeted their morning calls, Yeshua knew he had lost his chance. Dhiman's caravan was leaving at dawn. Yeshua would never find him again. His fate was sealed. Time had run out, and marriage was unavoidable. If he couldn't go to Sindh and he couldn't be a monk or a priest, he had to find a wife, work as a carpenter, and suffer through his life like any other laborer. What was the point of studying if it could never lead to a better life?

Yeshua slammed an ax into the first piece of wood he found. He hacked and slashed until his arms ached and he couldn't find another log to kill. Then he sighed and kneeled at the pile of wood chips he had created. What did God want with him?

"Use me then, Lord," he prayed in resignation. "If I can't serve you as a priest, show me what to do. Use me for a purpose greater than myself."

Three days later when Abba released him from his prison, he made it clear that Yeshua had lost the right to consider any further prospects. He was told to select one of two girls, both from respectable families. But Yeshua didn't like either of them.

"I don't care," he said. "You choose."

Abba broke into a broad grin and announced that at last they could start planning the betrothal feast of their firstborn son.

Capernaum, Galilee, AD 8

A wife had been chosen and a date set for the wedding. Soon Yeshua would have a family to support. He tried not to think of the dream he had surrendered. If God wanted him to be a carpenter, that's what he would be.

Every morning thereafter, he rose before dawn and worked until long after the sun had set to improve his skills. He might never be a master, but he now aspired to be adept. His angles still never came out quite straight, and somehow he always managed to chip off part of a rose petal or palm leaf by mistake, but the harder he tried, the more he improved. The day his wife moved into their house, he would be ready. He resolved to make his father proud.

That's why he couldn't believe it when several weeks later, he saw Dhiman sitting on a ledge by a fruit cart in the same corner of the market, as if time had stood still. Yeshua rushed to his friend and flung his arms around him. "What happened? Why are you still here?"

"I fell very sick," Dhiman said. "My stomach turned all the way upside down. I couldn't get out of bed for many weeks. I had to stay until I recovered."

"You should have called for me. I could have helped you," Yeshua said, before he remembered what he had gone through since they had last met.

He told Dhiman how his father had locked him up and then forced his engagement. "He's a good man and all, but he thinks everyone should live like him, in peace and quiet, fearing God. He's happy if he makes enough money to feed his family after he's paid his taxes. He simply doesn't understand why I yearn to serve God."

Dhiman smiled knowingly. "Why don't you come with me? I'll be on my way in three days."

"I can't. I'm engaged now." Yeshua thought his heart would break. Dhiman was offering him a last straw of hope, and he had to turn him down.

He waved a sad good-bye as he left Dhiman behind and returned to the coolness of the workshop. A tabletop needed finishing before day's end, and when that was done, the planks for a tax collector's door had to be measured and cut. Still, a tender seed of optimism incited him to run, escape, delve into the unknown. His dreams were within reach, if only he could muster the courage. He picked up the scraper to smooth the surface of the tabletop. Abba would never survive the humiliation if he broke the engagement. He just couldn't let his family down. Hadn't he caused them enough trouble already? No, there was no way he could leave.

Three sleepless nights later, Yeshua woke with a stomachache. In only a few hours, Dhiman would embark on his journey home, leaving him behind. Outside the narrow window, the stars twinkled at him, as if urging him to go. Should he? Without thinking, Yeshua slipped out from under the blanket he shared with his brothers, grabbed an extra tunic, and rolled it into a bundle. Salome grunted in her sleep but didn't wake. He cast a last look at his brothers and sisters and stole out of the room. He must leave now, before he changed his mind. Before it dawned on him that from now on his life would continue without his father and mother, without sweet Salome. And without Yakov, his brother and best friend. Who else would make him laugh so hard he got the hiccups? But his brother belonged right here, in Palestine. Yeshua wiped away his tears, lifted the crossbar off the front door, and pushed it open slowly, making sure it didn't creak.

He stopped short. What was that sound?

Behind him, someone moved. Someone was watching him. Yeshua held his breath, but his heart beat so loudly it even blocked out the chirping crickets. Materializing from the shadows, Ama held out a bundle to him, smiling sadly. Yeshua wanted to apologize, explain, embrace her, but she motioned for him to go. Quickly.

"I'll be back, Ama. Soon. Before winter—or maybe a little longer. But I'll return."

He looked back only once before he closed the door behind him. Tears blinded his vision. In the bundle, he found dried fruit, almonds, flatbreads, and the golden ring with its turquoise stone, the gift from the Zoroastrian priests. Carefully, he placed the ring in the pouch that hung off his belt and ran toward the market. It wasn't rightfully his; the ring belonged to the Messiah. But what else did he own of value? Perhaps it would save his life one day.

"You made it, my friend!" Dhiman said when Yeshua caught up with him in the deserted market. "I knew you would come."

Yeshua shivered with excitement. He hugged his new traveling companion. And then they ran. They had to make it as far away as possible before dawn, because surely Abba would come chasing after him. In a day or two, they would join a caravan, but only once they had made sufficient headway. Yeshua smiled on the outside, but inside he wept for the pain he had caused. Could he ever forgive himself?

The night was dark and quiet and frightening. Yeshua trembled as they climbed the Gawlana hills and passed through high grass along the road to Damascus. In the distance, a hyena laughed. Behind a tree, a lion growled as it ripped the flesh of its prey.

Dhiman squeezed Yeshua's hand. "They don't like how we smell, you know. Other animals are much tastier than we are. Don't worry, we're quite safe."

When at last the sun peeked over the eastern mountains and the nocturnal creatures had retired, Yeshua and Dhiman paused by a stream to take their first well-deserved rest.

"Here, take this." Dhiman handed Yeshua a mustard-colored robe, identical to his own. "Wet your hair in the water, and I'll shave it for you."

"Shave it?" Yeshua hesitated. Yehudi law forbade men to shave the head or beard. He might be on the run, but he was still Yeshua bar Yosef, from Capernaum.

"Come on, don't be such a faintheart." Dhiman laughed. He showed Yeshua what a child's game it was by stroking his shaving knife against his own head. "Look, it doesn't hurt at all."

Yeshua flinched. "It's against the law," he tried.

"What law? The one that says you can't be a priest because you hail from a family of carpenters? Why do you obey a law that makes no sense to you?"

Dhiman's words stung, but his expression was soft. "Sit here. And trust me, your God won't be angry. He's not upset with me, and I shave my head every day."

Yeshua frowned. Dhiman might be right; he had traveled the world, and apart from a few days of illness, God had protected him from harm.

"Look, we have to disguise you somehow. If not, you'll be on your way back home before you know it, married to some girl who burps and farts in her sleep." He poked Yeshua, teasing a smile. "Besides, monks get free food, even from the most penny-pinching merchants. And you don't want to go hungry, do you?"

Reluctantly, Yeshua dipped his head in the river, then kneeled before his friend and succumbed to Dhiman's knife. He watched his dark brown locks fall, one after the other, to the ground. The wind swirled around his bare head and a sense of freedom surged within.

He beamed at Dhiman, pressing his palms together as he had seen the other monks do.

"Kehro haal aahei!" Dhiman said, answering his friend's smile with a bow.

"Kehr— what?"

"Kehro. Haal. Aahei. It's hello in Sindhi."

Yeshua practiced his first Sindhi greeting over and over again as he walked around Dhiman with his head lowered and his palms pressed together. He had to get the part right if he was to pass as a monk.

"Now teach me something else," Yeshua said, all smiles, when he had mastered the phrase.

Yeshua's legs ached from the tiresome journey, but excitement put a spring in his step. Within two days, they reached the Roman city Caesarea Paneas. Dhiman suggested they stop there to wait for a caravan, but Yeshua begged him to continue; Abba might be close behind. He couldn't go back now. His life was on the road, like Abraham, Joseph, and Moses, who had wandered from place to place accompanied by God. Still, every night before going to sleep, he asked to be forgiven for the shame he had caused his family. And despite his enthusiasm, he cried himself to sleep, knowing he might never see them again.

Four long days after leaving Capernaum, they finally reached the southern gate of Damascus. Tall poplars and sweetly scented apricot trees lined the colonnaded streets in the busy city that heaved with people on their way to somewhere else. A hot wind pushed Dhiman and Yeshua toward the Temple of Hadad in the city center. Yeshua recoiled with terror when heavily armored Roman legionnaires in horse-drawn chariots drove past them at full force, and exhaled with relief when they disappeared out the arched gateways without even glancing at him.

Dhiman found his way with ease through the narrow side streets to a field outside the temple where a half-dozen caravans had paused to sell their merchandise. The traders came in all shades of brown, from the blackest soil to the pale hue of tanned leather, and wore garments in every color of the rainbow, from vibrant purples, dull greens, and faint yellows to reds as dark as blood. The women who passed them hid their faces behind veils as thin as onion skins or scarves of the thickest wool. Yeshua could have spent days mingling in the crowd, looking at the people, and learning everyone's stories and hearing their dreams.

Dhiman and Yeshua put their bundles down in the shade by the merchants' post, and Dhiman fished out two wooden bowls from his sack.

"Sit here," he said. "Place the bowl on your lap, close your eyes, and imagine it filled with breads and oranges, whatever your heart desires."

Yeshua's mouth watered at the thought of freshly baked flatbreads and olives. The food his mother had given him was long gone. If only someone would have mercy on them and give them a morsel to eat. He peeked through half-closed eyelids and saw a man passing with a cart full of grapes. His heart fluttered, but the vendor didn't stop. Nor did the next one, or anyone else. Yeshua's stomach pinched with hunger. If he didn't eat soon, he would faint.

Dhiman urged him to be patient. "Remember what I told you," he said. "If you train your mind, you can do anything."

Yes, Yeshua remembered. Being a monk meant liberating yourself from suffering by reaching a state of nonattachment or peace. And if he accepted his hunger as a pain that was not real, he would not feel it. Dhiman claimed some monks spent months in caves praying—or meditating, as he called it—without eating. And they survived. Yeshua wasn't sure he believed him. If his body cried with hunger, how could his mind overcome it?

With no other choice, he pressed his tongue against his palate and centered on a full stomach after a sumptuous dinner of grilled tilapia. And within moments, the pangs of hunger dissipated.

Yeshua was about to tell his friend of his astonishing accomplishment when a man paused in front of them. With his white turban, robe, and flowing beard, he looked exactly like the Zoroastrians who had sought him out when he was a child. Yeshua tried to hide behind Dhiman, but the man looked straight into his eyes as he dropped a roll of bread and a slice of salted mutton in each of their bowls.

"Taudi! Thank you!" Dhiman yelled after him, and Yeshua joined him, relieved. There was no need to be afraid. No one would recognize him in this clothing. He relaxed, and they fell to eating like starved wolves. Moments later, a Mesopotamian merchant placed a piece of cheese and some figs in their bowls. Their luck had changed.

But when Yeshua looked at the food, his heart sank. "I can't eat this."

"What?" Dhiman laughed and peeked into his bowl. "What's wrong with it?"

"I can't eat the cheese. I just had meat."

"Just eat it, sheep. If you want to survive, you've got to forget your laws. For now. Pretend it's not cheese. Look, it's an apple."

"What do you mean, survive? Didn't you tell me that monks can spend months in a cave without eating?"

Dhiman picked up the piece of cheese and stuffed it into Yeshua's mouth as he was talking. "See? Not bad, right? Let's see if your God punishes you. Then you can go back to eating only meat or only cheese. Agreed?"

Yeshua chewed while he thought about how to answer.

Dhiman chuckled. "You'll see: when you are hungry, when you are traveling, your God doesn't care about what you eat. He only cares whether you're kind and friendly and generous—that sort of thing."

Yeshua was too exhausted to argue. And that salty cheese had tasted so good. It had already passed his lips; how much worse could it get? His stomach was full, his body nourished, and his soul filled with gratitude.

Perhaps Dhiman was right: when you stop searching for a solution, problems simply resolve themselves.

Just before nightfall, a caravan on its way east pushed into the field: a hundred camels and dozens of mules, all staggering under heavy bundles of merchandise. Dhiman sprang up to greet the traders as they secured their animals to the cattle posts. Yeshua watched them from a distance. Some of the men looked like Dhiman, with heavy eyelids and skin the color of honey. Others were short with round faces and mere slits for eyes. And then there were the tall, near-black, reed-like men with long hair and full beards.

Dhiman approached the leader of the convoy, a burly man with baggy pants, long black mustache, and an aloof attitude. Not too friendly. Yeshua shuddered. He wanted to call him back, ask him to please wait for the next caravan, but his friend was already in deep negotiations.

Dhiman returned with his hand stretched out: "The ring. I need the ring."

Instinctively, Yeshua's hand went to the pouch that hung from his belt. "No, it's mine."

"Come on, give me the ring." Dhiman tried to grab the pouch, but Yeshua dodged out of the way. Dhiman shrugged. "Very well, Yeshua. You stay here. Or go back to Capernaum. Whatever you want to do."

Yeshua wavered. What if the caravan leader was a crook and deserted them at the next village? Or worse, what if Yeshua needed the ring to return home one day? But Dhiman's face was unrelenting. He had to give up the ring or return home. Warily, Yeshua unfolded the yellow silk scarf and took a last look at the golden ring before he handed it to his friend.

May God help him.

"Tomorrow," Dhiman said with a victorious grin. "We're leaving at noon."

The boys spent the night with the slaves and the camels, next to the inn where the merchants were staying, grateful that their new traveling companions had lent them sleeping mats and blankets for cover.

The camels kept Yeshua awake with their throaty grunts and snores. He looked up at the endless skies above and wondered what adventures lay ahead. Tomorrow, their route would turn inland toward Mesopotamia, even farther away from home. For the first time, Yeshua wondered if he had made the right decision to leave. He had no money, no guarantees. He missed his parents. And Yakov—oh, how he wished his brother were here!

Yeshua closed his eyes and recited the evening prayer Ama had taught him:

> *Hear, O, Israel, the Lord is our God, the Lord is One.*
> *Blessed be the name of his glorious kingdom forever*
> *and ever. I shall love the Lord my God with all my*
> *heart and with all my soul and with all my might. And*
> *I shall teach of him to my children, and speak of him*
> *at home, and think of him when I walk outside, and*
> *when I lie down and when I rise...*

Damascus, Syria, AD 8

The splatter of a camel urinating next to his head jolted him awake. Startled, Yeshua jumped up from the mat, yelping so loud he woke Dhiman.

"He was peeing on you!" Dhiman laughed, rubbing the sleep from his eyes. "You're the camel's latrine!"

Yeshua punched him, pretending to be upset, but soon enough his frown turned into a grin and he doubled over laughing. What an adventure this was going to be!

Although the sun wasn't up yet, some of the inn's patrons were already stirring. Yeshua and Dhiman rolled up their mats and went to watch the market unfold. The fruit and vegetable vendors were the first to arrive, followed by the meat and egg vendors, along with the bakers selling flatbreads. The foreign traders set up stalls of perfumes, bundles of fine fabrics, ornately woven mats, and golden jewelry right next to the tall Mesopotamia Gate covered with blue mosaic tiles.

Luck remained on Yeshua and Dhiman's side. Almost every merchant they passed gave them something—a handful of nuts, grapes, bread, or dried strips of beef—enough for them to pack some food away for the next leg of their journey. Yeshua had already learned that no meals were guaranteed, and for the first time in his life, he understood to appreciate everything he received.

In the coming days, the caravan escorted Yeshua and Dhiman through Syria, Mesopotamia, and Bactria. They rested from the midday heat under tall date palms in the oasis town of Palmyra. They paused in the capital city of Seleucia by the river Tigris, where the merchants traded pearls and Eilat stones for yards of Han silk and statues made of bronze. They idled in the city of Rhagae while the men entertained themselves with harlots in the shadows of the Gebri castle. They hurried through Balkh, where Prophet Zarathustra's followers stalked them in narrow alleys between whitewashed houses, and sighed in relief when they left the town behind.

Between cities, the road led through barren landscapes, over mountains, across rivers, and past fertile oases. They passed tented nomad settlements and tiny villages with clusters of mud huts. They suffered through blinding sandstorms and days of unbearable heat in the deserts, and endured violent snowstorms as they trudged through deep snow at the higher altitudes. Every now and then, bandits on horseback attacked the caravan to steal their merchandise, but the caravan's swordsmen always reigned superior, and along the way dozens of horses were added to the cargo.

In every commercial center, a few merchants departed and others joined; the caravan expanded and compressed like a school of fish with an ever-changing shape and composition. Prostitutes were bought and abandoned a few miles later. Holy men walked along for short stretches, seeking protection from wild animals and thieves. Youngsters tagged along in search of excitement, only to find that life on the road left them hungry, worn, and covered with dust.

Yeshua and Dhiman grew closer with every step. They bonded as outsiders beside their wealthy comrades and their slaves, and became graceful receivers of any leftovers. Although the caravan leader appeared hostile, he always made sure Yeshua and Dhiman stayed warm during the harsh winter months and found sufficient cover during the storms. And when their sandals wore thin, a new pair magically appeared by their mats as they slept.

Yeshua's olive complexion had darkened and dried from months in the sun, wind, and frost, and by now he looked like any other nomad. Along the way, the boys adopted each other's phrases and gestures, and soon their accents merged into one. They earned their keep by assisting the cooks with chores like chopping carrots and onions and helping the slaves unload the cargo animals at local markets. At night, they told stories by the bonfire. Yeshua spoke of the heroes of his tradition: Abraham, Noah, Moses, and Elijah. Dhiman recounted tales about the wise Buddha. In time, their epics blended to the point where the boys no longer knew whose story it had been or where it had originated.

As much as Yeshua revered his Yehudi patriarchs, he was intrigued by the Buddha.

"He was born a prince in the mountain kingdom of Sakya," Dhiman said and closed his eyes, as if visualizing the story before him. "Before his conception, his mother dreamed that a white elephant offered her a lotus flower and entered her womb, which meant she would give birth to the purest of beings." Dhiman opened one eye to check if Yeshua was listening, then continued. "When the baby was born, all wise men predicted he would grow to be a great master and dedicate his life to serving the needy. But the child's father, the king, wouldn't hear of it. In fury, he bolted the castle gates and wed his son to a pretty maiden."

Yeshua heard himself gasp. The Buddha's father had acted in the exact same manner as his own.

"The prince grew up in ignorant happiness within the palace walls, enjoying all its luxuries. That is, until the day his parents allowed him to go outside for the first time. The prince was horrified by what he saw: a man sick with the plague, a wrinkled old beggar—even a corpse. No one had told him that health and youth were fleeting. However, the next time he left the palace, he befriended a blissful monk who had given up all his possessions to teach others how to be peaceful and kind. The prince became so deeply impressed that he left his wife and child to embark on a spiritual journey. He escaped at night, donned a robe, shaved his head, and set out in the world carrying only a beggar's bowl."

Yeshua stared at his friend. Was he making this up?

"Along the way," Dhiman continued, now with both eyes open, staring into the fire, "the prince studied with many teachers and learned how to meditate. He practiced every day. Yet it bothered him that despite their immense knowledge and wisdom, no one knew the answer to ending suffering, aging, and death.

"The prince and the five monks who accompanied him concluded that the only way to complete wisdom was absolute austerity. For six years, they fasted, slept on beds of thorns, and let the sun scorch their skin. When this, too, failed to bring enlightenment, the prince gave up. He left his fellow monks and, in despair, sat down under a large fig tree to meditate. He vowed to stay in the same position until truth found him. On a full moon night, the prince had a vision: a demon offered him an abundance of magnificent gifts, including his three beautiful daughters. When the prince politely declined, the demon attacked him with lightning and storms and an army of monsters. The prince struggled to ignore the interruptions and stay in meditation. He sat up straighter and relaxed his mind, and slowly the visions faded. At the light of dawn, the demon finally gave up. Like a poof of smoke, he shrank away and disappeared into nothingness. And when the prince opened his eyes, he had become the Awakened One—the Buddha."

A shiver ran down Yeshua's spine. He, too, was on a spiritual quest. He, too, had fled his home at night and had embarked on a journey to become a wise man.

"When the Buddha woke from the dream that had been his life, he understood the causes of suffering," Dhiman continued. "He knew how to avoid a life of misery. How to be free."

Yeshua nodded, urging him to continue.

"The Buddha reviewed the memories of his previous lives and understood how everything in life is subject to cause and effect, and how everything we do—good and bad—always comes back to us." Dhiman took a deep breath. "He recognized that every living being goes through a cycle of life and death."

"So we're born again to amend what we did wrong in another life?" Yeshua asked.

"Not quite. The Buddha said we're born, decay, and die at every moment of our lives. We change all the time, renewing ourselves, learning and evolving."

Dhiman reminded Yeshua of his rabbi in Capernaum and wondered why his teacher had never mentioned the Buddha. Perhaps he hadn't heard about him?

"The Buddha meditated for weeks and weeks until he had absorbed all the knowledge of the world. Then he set out to teach anyone who wanted to listen that we all can become enlightened. He traveled the world for years to share this knowledge with both men and women, rich and poor, the ignorant and learned——"

"Like you?"

Dhiman blushed. "But I'm not the Buddha. I know nothing. I want to learn, but…maybe I'm still too young. The Buddha," he continued, "taught for forty-five years. He handed out alms, healed the sick, performed miracles, and showed people how to achieve enlightenment."

"How did he heal them? With oils?"

"With hands, I think."

"My grandmother does that, heals with her hands. But she also uses herbs and potions."

"When the Buddha died, the trees burst into full bloom and flowers rained all over his body, for he was the greatest soul that ever lived."

Every night, no matter how exhausted they were after a day of walking, Yeshua begged Dhiman for more stories. There was so much to learn.

His friend embodied everything Yeshua admired: compassion, humility, and awareness. Yeshua was still caught in the material world: he envied the merchants who could purchase a whole grilled lamb for dinner. He angered when someone took his sleeping spot. And despite Dhiman's warnings about pride, Yeshua still yearned to be the wisest leader the world had ever known. And, once in a while, he still cried himself to sleep because he missed his family. Detachment seemed impossible.

From their first days together, Dhiman and Yeshua cared for each other like brothers. On the hottest nights, they slept almost naked under the stars, and they huddled by the side of a camel on nights so bitterly cold they weren't sure they would survive until morning. They laughed together, prayed together, sang together, and told each other countless stories. They learned each other's languages and any other language they came across. They shared their thoughts, dreams, hopes, and fears, and even touched on forbidden topics, like girls and sex. When Yeshua woke from his first wet dream, Dhiman calmed him and explained how the male body works. When Yeshua fantasized about prostitutes in the markets or when they spied on merchants copulating with fallen women, Dhiman assured him arousal was natural and that with mind training and practice, he would be able to control his lusts.

But it wasn't until they were somewhere between the fertile slopes of the Hindu Kush mountains and the valley of Kabul, after more than ten months together, that Yeshua asked Dhiman to share his meditation technique.

"Breathe in and out," he said. "Feel your breath and follow it from your nose into your lungs and down to your stomach. Notice how your belly sinks in as the breath leaves it completely empty. Touch each breath and experience its energy. Really feel it."

"What's so special about breathing? I want to know how you practice, not how you breathe."

"I sit, I walk, and I eat."

"Everyone does that. That's not meditating."

"But when I sit, I know I'm sitting. When I walk, I know I'm walking. And when I eat, I know I'm eating. It begins with breathing."

"How?"

"I'm always present in what I'm doing. When I eat, I chew each bite mindfully. I think of the wheat that made the bread. I think of the sun, rain, and soil that nourished the wheat. I think of the water from the stream that was added to the dough. I think of the woman who kneaded the bread and the fire that baked it."

"You think a lot then?"

"Being conscious of what I'm doing stops my mind from drifting. It calms me."

"We also eat in silence. In Palestine," Yeshua added as his mind traveled to his family meals. "Do you also thank God for your food?"

Dhiman laughed. "We're grateful for what we have received, but no, we don't thank God. How many times must I tell you? We don't believe in a god."

Yeshua opened his mouth to argue, but stopped himself. There was no convincing his friend.

"Come, try the Om, why don't you?" Dhiman said. "It's powerful."

Dhiman crossed his legs and put his hands on his knees, palms up. He took a deep breath and on the exhale let out a monotone "Ooooooommm."

Yeshua crinkled his nose. His friend was odd sometimes. But there was no harm in trying.

"Ooooooommm," Yeshua copied Dhiman. He chanted the word over and over until the sound vibrated through his entire body. A warm light filled his chest, and a channel expanded at the crown of his head.

"Dear Moses, what was that?" he asked, startled.

Dhiman explained that a long time ago, a man from Sindh discovered the sacred mantra and found that chanting the word helped expand the mind.

After that day, Yeshua practiced meditating every chance he got— before breakfast, during the midday break, and before going to sleep. Several days passed before he was consistently able to quiet his thoughts and relax his mind, but gradually, the flashes of calm extended and his sense of awareness increased. He also practiced what Dhiman called a walking meditation by focusing on a point in the distance, like a snow-covered peak or a waterfall, while he walked, filling his body with a sense of perfect bliss.

"God talks to me," Yeshua told Dhiman early one morning, shivering, as they awoke on top of a slab of stone with only a thread-worn blanket for cover. They had crossed the narrowest part of the Khyber Pass in the Hindu Kush mountains the previous evening.

Dhiman laughed, as he always did when Yeshua confessed his innermost thoughts. "That's splendid, but what does your god say?" he asked.

"It's not my God. It's our God: our Father and Creator. The source."

"Calm down, Issa. Just tell me what 'God' says to you."

The caravan leader had renamed him Issa after a harlot in Rhagae had mocked him and said that Yeshua was a woman's name. Issa was a solid name. It would do for now.

"God tells me all sorts of things," he said. "When I agonize about the shame I brought on my family, God tells me not to worry. And when I grow angry because someone grabbed a bigger share of the meal, leaving less for everyone else, God asks me to forgive them. He says anger and worry only hurt me; they don't change anything."

Dhiman laughed. "That's not God speaking; that's your inner voice."

But Yeshua knew the thoughts weren't his; God was teaching him how to become a better and happier person.

Sindh, AD 9

The weather grew warmer as the caravan descended into the Indus Valley. Lush meadows and pine forests replaced arid mountains and dusty plains. In Rawalpindi, an important trading center, Yeshua and Dhiman bathed in the river and scrubbed the dust off their bodies. They laundered their robes that had turned a dirty brown. From here on, the two would travel south while the caravan continued east. Teary eyed, Yeshua and Dhiman thanked the merchants for their protection over the past year and for the food, woolen blankets, and water they had shared.

As they descended the first hill out of the town, they heard the smatter of hoofs galloping behind them. "Hold it!" someone called. Yeshua spun around to see the caravan leader on horseback emerge through a cloud of sand.

His heart stopped. What had they done?

With a crooked grin, the leader tossed a bundle at Yeshua. His teeth glistened through his black beard. "This belongs to you."

Then he turned his horse, his saber held high, and disappeared back into the dust.

"What is it?" Dhiman nudged Yeshua to open the parcel.

Inside was the golden ring they had offered as payment for the journey. Yeshua clutched it close to his heart. "Thank you," he said, addressing the man who had left—and God. Once again, he had something of value that might help pay for his return home someday.

On the southern road, Yeshua and Dhiman trailed the fertile riverside and nourished their bodies with juicy melons, ripe bananas, and fresh fish. They made friends with the local men, who wore their hair and beards long and wrapped colorful scarves around their heads, and who shared fanciful epics about the local gods. They spoke about Shiva, a four-armed god who always destroyed the universe only to re-create it. And Varuna, a god of the sky and earth, who ruled the ocean and night demons, and Vayu, a god of the restless wind, who delivered the sweetest perfumes. At first, Yeshua thought they were teasing him with silly stories only to fool him, but the more he listened, the more it made sense. Why shouldn't God show more than one face?

The Sindhi people prayed to murtis, oval rocks that were placed in simple roadside shrines and represented their gods. They rang a bell to announce their arrival and smeared the murti with red paste as a mark of honor. Then they offered the murti food and flowers, recited a few mantras, and bowed to the rock with their palms pressed together.

"This way, Shiva knows to look after me," one of them said.

Yeshua couldn't resist. He picked a flower from the side of the road and offered it to the murti.

"Have you gone mad?" Dhiman snickered. "You think a stone will protect you?"

"But why can't God be in everything?"

"And you think your god is in a stone?"

"Of course not. But this murti represents Shiva, and he's an aspect of God."

Dhiman was not listening. In his world, there was only one way— Lord Buddha's way. God and deities had no relevance. What mattered was to see through the delusion of life and comprehend true reality. They walked on in silence. Yeshua would tell Dhiman later that he thought the Lord Buddha could also be an incarnation of God.

After the bland meals of the desert, the foods of the Indus Valley made their mouths water: deep-fried fish fritters rich with the flavors of garlic, ginger, chilies, and coriander; chicken biriyani sweetened with cardamom and cinnamon. Yeshua's favorite was rogan josh, a peppery lamb stew that set his throat on fire.

But the first time Yeshua entered a Sindhi marketplace, the locals no longer appeared so friendly. A screaming merchant chased him through the market, lashing after him with a belt. Yeshua ran as fast as he could between the stalls, knocking down piles of mangoes and baskets of spices, to avoid being whipped. When at last he stopped, out of breath, and looked back at the merchant, the man stared at him with hateful eyes.

"I don't understand. What did I do?" Yeshua called out.

The merchant tipped a cauldron full of lentils onto the ground. "This is what you've done, you ignorant donkey. You looked at my food."

"Looked at your food? But what—" Yeshua pressed his palms together. "I'm so sorry. I didn't know." His eyes filled with tears. The man had lost a whole pot of food because of him. "Can I make it up to you somehow? I have no money but—"

"Just stay away from me. And never, ever look at anyone's food, you son of a demon." The merchant stabbed him with his stare before he disappeared back into the market. There was money still to be made.

Immediately, a throng of children appeared and threw themselves on the ground to scoop up the lentils with their bare hands. Yeshua, too, rushed forward, but by the time he got through the crowd, only soggy earth remained. His stomach ached with hunger, but he knew he had no right to benefit from the merchant's loss. And it pleased him to see the famished children lick their hands to savor every last bit.

"Do not worry, my friend."

Yeshua turned to look at a young boy in a yellow turban.

"One rich man lost a little money, a few coins, but not to worry. Watch those children, their tummies full. Very good karma."

"I don't understand what happened. Why was he angry?"

"A nonbeliever's eyes can poison the food of true believers. But praise be to Shiva, the more deserving gained a good and proper meal."

When Yeshua entered the market again, he kept his eyes on the ground. He heard clanking as merchants covered their pots wherever he went. Yeshua followed the rich scent of hot foods and stopped when he detected freshly baked bread. Without looking up, he greeted the merchant. "Namaste, my good sir. Do you have it in your heart to spare a piece of bread for a pilgrim?"

Gratefully accepting half a naan, Yeshua pressed his palms together in gratitude and recited a prayer in Aramaic to bless the generous baker. The baker chuckled with delight and waved him off with a friendly "Namaste." People here always appreciated a blessing in a foreign language more than familiar mantras. His gaze still cast down, Yeshua found a stall that smelled of curried meat. "Blessings, my honorable man. Can you please spare some food for a poor pilgrim on his devotional journey, his yatra?" In this manner, morsel by morsel, Yeshua filled his stomach and shared benedictions among the people of the Indus River Valley.

The day they finally reached his village, Dhiman fell to the ground on his knees, as if to kiss the earth in gratitude. But then he rose, pressed his palms together in front of his heart, reached them over his head, and lowered them back to his heart. Again he knelt, placed his palms on the ground, and walked them forward until he lay flat. Rising, he took a step forward and repeated the movements over and over, approaching his home like a centipede while mumbling mantras of devotion. Yeshua followed close behind, reciting the prayer he had altered over the course of his journey, "The Lord is my God, the Lord is One. Blessed be his glorious kingdom forever and ever. Every day, in every moment, I love the Eternal One with my entire mind, with my entire body, with my entire soul, and with all my might…"

The villagers gawked as Dhiman and Yeshua passed, and children gathered behind them in a long line. Some ran from house to house, calling for one and all to come see. Together they walked through the village center and crossed a small hill on the road leading out of town until, finally, the monastery appeared before them. Dhiman's home. A rectangular mud-brick temple with a straw roof stood in front of a ring of low huts. Its steeple rose like a pile of flatbreads toward the clouds.

Inside a low wall covered by blossoming vines, dozens of monks went about their business, sweeping the grounds or sitting cross-legged on blankets, cleaning stones out of grains or shelling pistachios. One by one, they noticed their long-lost brother at the gate. The murmur grew louder and spread like a wave, and they rushed to greet him as one. They huddled together in a tight embrace and covered his face and hands with kisses.

The chatter flowed in torrents as they asked him where the road had taken him and what he had experienced on his journey. Yeshua removed his sandals, took a seat on the low wall, and waited patiently. Dhiman had been away for three years; his friends were ecstatic at his return.

The monks entered the temple, leaving Yeshua outside. As the sun descended and disappeared behind the blue hills, Yeshua listened to their endless monotone chant. Faint with hunger, he had no other choice but to wait. He crossed his legs, turned his palms toward the sky, and observed his breathing. The soft wind caressed his soul, and the scent of incense painted the landscape with magic.

"Issa!" The voice reached him from another dimension. "Let's eat."

Dhiman's cheeks flushed with elation as he grabbed Yeshua's hand and led him to a large brick building that served as the dining hall. A monk handed him a bowl full of steaming hot beans, rice, and vegetables. They sat on a woven straw mat and ate in silence, using only their right hand, as Dhiman instructed. After months of traveling and begging for scraps, it seemed strange to be offered food without asking for it. Yeshua suppressed an urge to stand and recite a blessing of thanks in Aramaic. No one had uttered a single word since they had entered the hall, and he was well aware that if he wanted to stay here, he would have to follow their rules. Would they ever invite him into the temple to join their chanting? His heart sang at the thought. For now, though, the best thing in the world would be to get some sleep.

Dhiman and Yeshua rinsed their bowls in a vat of water and sat down, still in silence, in the courtyard. After all the other monks had gone to bed, Dhiman led Yeshua to a cluster of huts behind the dining hall to find a place to lie down.

"Here," Dhiman said. They entered a small round hut with a pointed straw roof where a single monk was asleep. "But hide the ring. Valuables are not allowed here."

Yeshua tied the golden ring into the corner of his head scarf, unrolled his sleeping mat, and was asleep before his head hit the ground.

The clanging of a cymbal shattered his sleep. Yeshua was about to curse whoever was making the noise when he remembered where he was.

"Morning prayer. Come." Dhiman was already up and by the door.

Morning? It was still dark outside. Fearful of offending his hosts, Yeshua rolled up his mat and wobbled out to the temple on sleepy legs. The moon stood high above, and the stars sparkled in the boundless sky.

"Morning meditations are the best, you know," Dhiman said. "Your mind is not awake yet."

Yeshua shook his head. Had no one told them the meaning of the word *morning*? It started when the sun rose above the horizon. But enough of the grumpiness: he wanted to learn, and learn he would. He followed Dhiman into the rectangular temple building and sat behind the monks, facing the teacher, his mind at peace. The temple embodied all he had dreamed of, a place where he could learn and grow and be respected as an equal among like-minded men. He joined the chanting as best he could, repeating each mantra again and again, but without sound so he wouldn't distract the others. A few of the monks turned to smile at him. They, too, had been novices once.

The session seemed to go on forever. Yeshua's legs ached from sitting still, and his mind wandered. But he was too self-conscious, too embarrassed to move. Instead, he focused on remembering the words and tried to disconnect from the pain. When the prayers finally came to an end, his legs were so stiff he could barely walk.

"I'm so happy I came here." Yeshua played with some flat stones, piling them up, one on top of the other, under the shade of a banyan tree. "I think I love him, you know—the Buddha."

"You're not supposed to adore him. You're meant to find the Buddha within."

"Well, that's what I mean."

Dhiman knocked over the pile of stones. "You're such a sheep sometimes. The Buddha is our inspiration, not a god. He was a man who found enlightenment, and because of him, we have a set path to end suffering. But you can't just sit under a tree and meditate for a few days and expect to become enlightened. First, you learn to control your mind. It takes time and a lot of effort to even get close. Are you sure you want to do this?"

Yeshua nodded. He was ready.

"Well, my sheep," Dhiman said, laughing, "let's start with the morning prayer."

Dhiman explained the ritual. The first part of the prayer served to protect the world from negativity. The next part reminded the monks to detach from all material matters—the essence of Buddha's wisdom.

"It's important," Dhiman said, "to memorize the prayer, because only then can we contemplate the meaning of the words and develop our natural wisdom. At the end of each session, we, the younger monks, praise the elders for keeping the Lord Buddha's teachings alive. And then we all stand and bow in silent prayer before the service ends with a gong."

Yeshua's eyes stung from salty drops of perspiration, and the sun scorched his skin as he and Dhiman washed the monks' robes in large vats. They beat the clothes with pipal tree branches and rinsed them in the cool river. Yeshua toiled with passion. What a blessing to work in the monastery among like-minded seekers! He scrubbed until his hands were red with blisters, and his shoulders and arms throbbed with pain from the intense physical effort, but he did not stop. This was his only means of repaying the charity from strangers. Miraculously, he had been fed every single day, and now he wanted to prove to God that he was a worthy recipient.

At last the meal gong sounded. The boys trailed the other monks into the dining hall, received their bowls of food, and sat on a mat to eat in silence. After a few weeks, Yeshua had adjusted to monastery life. Dhiman had taught him to eat slowly and mindfully. He paused a moment to contemplate each bite, repeating the mantra he had learned.

"Thank you for this meal, this gift from the earth, the sky, the sun, and all who have labored to provide it. I accept my meal with humility, hoping I have truly earned this bowl of food. I take each bite with compassion. I thank all plants and creatures that have been offered as food, and I will eat only what I truly need. I accept this meal as nourishment for myself, for the community, for our village, and for all living beings."

"Why do we say 'creatures'?" Yeshua asked. The monks never ate meat.

Dhiman smiled. "Didn't you see me eat beef and mutton and fish during our journey?"

Yeshua knitted his brow, considering, but nodded slowly. "But in here, in this community, we haven't had meat for weeks. I assumed—"

"You're right. But the Buddha said that we must be thankful for what we are given in our bowls, whatever it is. And we may eat pure fish and meat, if the animals haven't been killed for the purpose of feeding a monk. We should never eat a creature slaughtered just for us."

Before resuming chores, the monks were called to class in the temple. A monk almost as tall as the sunken straw ceiling led a chant about compassion and repentance. The men swayed and bowed, reciting the verses over and over. Light-headed, with his heart open and his mind cleansed, Yeshua returned to washing clothes with fresh enthusiasm and renewed spirit, despite his aching limbs.

At nightfall, Yeshua and Dhiman hung the last robes to dry on the low bushes and walked back to the temple. The large hall was dense with the smoke of incense. An oil lamp cast a faint glow over the rows of monks sitting cross-legged, palms pressed together in front of their hearts. Yeshua slipped into meditation, but instead of drifting into nothingness, he drifted into sleep. He shook his head and started over again, only to awaken a moment later from his guilty conscience. What a relief when the chanting started!

One of the oldest teachers, a monk withered like a dried rosebush, raised his hand for silence, smoothed out his mustard-colored robe, and spoke in a voice as soft as churned cream:

"The Buddha said that a monk who speaks without knowing, who says, 'I have mastered this wisdom,' speaks from a place of selfishness, of greed and anger. He holds himself too dear. He is like a poor person who talks about his riches, or a man who speaks about owning properties that he does not own, and when the day comes and they need to present the commodities or the silver or the gold, they have nothing to show." The teacher chuckled to himself. "A wise man admits he does not know yet, that he is learning. Never let your mind be corrupted by evil longing to know it all, to know better than others."

Yeshua shifted in his seat.

The teacher continued: "To learn, you must come from a place of humility, of openness. Because when you share your knowledge, what is it you share? Before you can teach even the little beetle or the proud cobra, you must accept that your knowledge is like a drop of the entire ocean. You can teach *something*. I can also teach you *something*. But none of us can teach anyone everything."

All the monks laughed, recognizing that they were still far from mastery.

"In fact, if you try to be perfect, you can only harm yourself. We can aspire to be good, yes, but it is not easy to do only what is beneficial to others all the time.

"That's why the Buddha said one should always remain compassionate with oneself and with others. A man who ignores the teaching of the Buddha and the bodhisattvas is a fool, and like the bamboo, can produce only fruits of self-destruction. Because purity and impurity come from within; no one can purify another."

Yeshua listened, trying to absorb it all. Suddenly, he missed the rabbi at the Capernaum synagogue, the simple potter who spoke with the same clarity and wisdom.

One after the other, the monks proceeded to ask questions.

"How will I know if I'm ready to teach?"

"The students will come when you are ready. Until then, keep learning. And remember, someone else will always know more than you."

"But how can we possibly harm ourselves? Why would we?"

"By greed and pride, or guilt and shame. Those sentiments are not healthy. Treat yourself as you would treat a dear friend or teacher: with respect, compassion, and forgiveness."

"If purity depends only on me, what can I learn here at the monastery?"

"At the sangha, we help each other to improve. You study the Buddha's teachings that show you the way, and we encourage each other because mastery is nearly impossible to achieve on your own. However, *you* are responsible for putting the knowledge into practice. No one else can do it for you."

Too tired to eat, Dhiman and Yeshua went straight to bed. Before falling asleep, Yeshua whispered to his friend, "This is heaven, Dhiman!"

Yeshua was impatient to absorb everything he could about Buddha's teachings—dharma, as the monks called it: the four noble truths, the eightfold path, the five precepts, and the many suttas. He learned the daily chants and mastered inner stillness at meditation. He immersed himself in chores: he dug latrines, prepared food, swept the grounds, and washed robes, staying present in every moment. He made meal offerings to the Buddha and posed questions to the teachers. Little by little, he was accepted into the sangha community as one of their own, but much to his chagrin, he was constantly reminded that he was not allowed to teach anyone, especially outside the monastery walls.

"If selflessness is important, why do the elders hold themselves above us?" he asked Dhiman as they were sweeping huts.

"You're still a beginner. You've barely started the eightfold path, and—"

"And what? We taught the merchants when we were traveling, didn't we? Surely I know enough to teach the villagers, don't you think?"

"Issa, don't be such a pigeon. You know nothing. The elders have studied dharma since they were little children. They're masters. They've learned the right view, the right intention. They use the right speech, the right action. They're probably right on the cusp of enlightenment——"

"I might be, too!" Yeshua said, and banged the broom into the doorpost, sending the dust flying right back into the hut.

"You?" Dhiman laughed with the empathy of a loving father. "Oh, Issa, you may be clever, but you've barely been here two months. You haven't even mastered the first steps. You think you understand the Buddha's teachings? It takes many, many years."

"Why should I spend all this time studying to be a monk if I can't teach others what I know? How's that any different from working with my father and studying at the synagogue on the Sabbath?"

"It takes time, Issa. Every moment of practice is necessary. The Buddha said it takes many drops of water to fill a jug. You'll be a teacher one day. But you must be patient."

"You think I'm going to work as a slave my whole life so I can teach when I'm too old to care?"

"Think of the Buddha. It took him many years to reach enlightenment."

"What if I'm the Buddha reborn?"

Dhiman walked away, shaking his head.

But what if it was true? Yeshua understood the suttas better and grasped the lessons faster than most of the monks. In Palestine, he had discussed the Torah with the temple priests many years ago. And on the way to Sindh, he had spoken to men of every faith and impressed them with his wisdom.

Yeshua slung the broom as far as he could. It crashed to the ground with a bang.

"Your anger proves that your desire to be a master makes you suffer."

Dhiman had returned, and handed Yeshua the broom. He put his arm around him and squeezed his shoulder. "When you try to preserve your self, you raise yourself higher than all others. But you're no better or worse than anyone else. We are all one."

Reluctantly, Yeshua had to admit Dhiman was right—he yearned for recognition. Still, what if he really was Buddha reborn?

From that day onward, Yeshua worked hard to detach himself from everything he previously had thought important. The Buddha had said an enlightened being recognizes his own self in all beings, all beings in his own self, and looks at everything with an impartial eye. Yeshua tried to absorb the lessons with an open mind, aware that the teachers were perfect in their imperfection. The less he tried to control his life, the more his days passed without worry. And once he gave up seeking permission to teach the locals, the people of the village approached him with questions whenever he left the monastery. Thus he shared his lessons in secret.

Teaching was invigorating. When he sat with a group who drank in his every word, he felt complete. Most villagers didn't know much about the Buddha, and were curious to learn about the wise man from the East. In return, they taught Yeshua about Surya, Indra, and Mangala, the deities of heaven, and Saraswati, Vishnu, and Lakshmi, the gods of earth. They shared stories from the Vedas and epics from the Smritis. The more Yeshua learned, the more he understood the connection between the teachings of the Torah, the lessons of the Buddha, and the wisdom of the Vedas: the goal of all three was to reach Nirvana, oneness with God. Soon he looked for any excuse to leave the monastery and spent less time doing his chores and attending his daily lessons.

In the end, Dhiman was the one who sent him away. "They know you've been teaching outside the monastery," he said, his eyes cold.

Yeshua looked at his friend, stunned. "I was just speaking to some people in the village. I didn't really teach them..."

"Yeshua, you know the rules here. You agreed to obey them."

"But it didn't lead anywhere. I wasn't progressing."

"You're such a fool. I brought you here to learn, to reach a higher consciousness. And you threw it all away."

Yeshua's stomach cramped. He had become arrogant, had considered himself better than the elders, thought they would never find out. But just like in Palestine, some laws could not be broken.

"I'll never forget your kindness," he called after Dhiman. "I'm sorry. I am. But perhaps the Buddha is calling me." Yeshua kicked a stone and sent it rolling down the path. "I want to follow in his footsteps."

Dhiman turned around. "You still don't understand, do you?" His voice was soft with compassion. "His message, that's what's important, not where his body moved. Perhaps your father was right; perhaps God's work is not for you. Go home. Be a carpenter. Do what you were born to do."

Yeshua stepped forward to embrace Dhiman, but his friend turned his back and walked away. Dhiman shut the gate between them, leaving Yeshua outside.

Tears rolled down Yeshua's face as he slung his belongings onto his back and walked up the hill, away from the monastery.

Satavahana, AD 10

Loneliness haunted him on his aimless walk across the hills. Dhiman had been his companion day and night for over a year. The always kind, laughing monk had taught him more than anyone else in the world, and now Yeshua was alone in a foreign land with no one to comfort or guide him.

The first few days, he struggled with direction. He couldn't return to Galilee. Not yet. He wasn't ready to marry, give up his dream of becoming a priest. Should he really follow the Buddha's footsteps? If only he had begged Dhiman to let him stay. Surely he would have been forgiven if he had promised to change his ways.

What would God want him to do?

Gathering courage from his meditations, Yeshua decided he might as well continue his search. He set off toward Jagannath, a place the villagers had told him about, where the sea was endless and the air heavy with fervor, and where the mystical White Brahmins resided.

As soon as he left Sindh, he disposed of his monk's robe and reverted to his Galilean tunic and mantle, stirring up laughter from the children as he passed. He had grown significantly since he left home, and the short tunic and tight mantle made him appear like a poor vagrant compared with the immaculate locals in their colorful robes and turbans.

At first, he struggled to communicate in a mix of Sanskrit and Sindhi, but soon enough he captured the essence of Prakrit dialects. And thus, he was rarely alone for long periods of time. Even the poorest of families invited him to stay for the night and offered him their best sleeping mat in a room shared by several generations with hardly an inch of space between them.

The farther he walked from the tolerant region of Sindh, the more apparent the disparity in social standing between men.

"My esteemed friend," a priest said, while scooping up spicy chana masala with fingers like fat sausages from their shared bowl, "I could not help but observe that you were speaking to a builder earlier. And I must tell you—it is not clever for a man of your position to communicate with Shudras. It will do you no good at all. These craftsmen are simple-minded, if you must know, filthy and ignorant. Their only use is serving the twice-born, like you and me."

Yeshua almost choked on his stew. Of course the priest could not know that Yeshua was a craftsman by birth. Because of his lighter skin, although darkened from the sun, everyone assumed he belonged to the priestly caste.

Yeshua couldn't resist provoking the priest. "How can you be sure they haven't been born before?"

The priest laughed so hard, his belly fat bounced up and down and bits of food burst from his mouth. By now, Yeshua was used to being laughed at. He lowered his head and joined his hands in reverence. He didn't mind being ridiculed as long as people answered his questions.

"It's in the Rig Veda, as you surely must know. Primal man was divided into four castes: His mouth became the Brahmins, and that's why we Brahmins are able to speak of wise matters. His arms became the Kshatriyas; that's why the soldiers and kings can fight so well. His thighs became the Vaishyas; see how strong the merchants and landowners are. But the simple craftsmen and servants, the Shudras, were made from his feet. And you know how dirty and smelly feet are. They step on everything. Feces, spit, fish heads—any kind of rubbish. And that's why we know they have never been born before."

"Of course, of course," Yeshua said. "And the others?"

"What others? There are no others." The priest scratched the stubble on his chin.

"The ones who work behind closed doors in the markets, the ones who never speak to me. The untouchables; is that what you call them?"

"You must never speak to them, Issa!" The priest sputtered with contempt, his fists clenched white. "Dirty rats, they are. Meat-eating filth!" The priest leaned away to distance himself from Yeshua as much as the narrow room allowed. "You haven't spoken to them, have you? Haven't touched them? Eaten their food?"

Yeshua smiled his sweetest smile. "Of course not," he said. "Why would I ever do that?"

But he had spoken to them. They just hadn't answered. Every time Yeshua approached, they fled. It wasn't until Yeshua learned they could get killed for simply talking to a Brahmin that he stopped trying to befriend them.

The priest explained that speaking to, touching, or eating food prepared by the untouchables would pollute the higher castes to the extent that they could lose their status in society and become untouchables themselves.

While crossing the Shipra River on a raft, the boatman asked if Yeshua was headed to Ujjayini, a town upriver. "You mustn't miss it. Oh no, you most certainly will regret it for the rest of your life if you don't see this magnificent town. Only one day's walk north, not very far at all."

Yeshua looked in the direction up the lush riverbed where the boatman was pointing.

"You see," the boatman said, "many years ago, when Ujjayini was the capital of the entire Avanti kingdom, there came a time when the demigods felt weak and powerless. They approached Lord Brahma for advice on how to restore their health. Lord Brahma told them to churn the milky ocean to obtain the nectar of immortality. But the demigods were so frail, they had no choice but to ask the demons for help with the churning. In turn, they promised to share the treasure. The demigods and demons took turns agitating the ocean, until one day, a pot filled with the sweetest nectar rose from its depths. When the demigods saw this treasure, they no longer wanted to share it, because what would happen if the demons grew too fierce and overpowered them? A fight ensued between the demigods and the demons. During the battle, a few drops of the sacred nectar fell on four towns, one of which was Ujjayini. That's why it is one of the most sacred places in the world."

By now, Yeshua was used to hearing fantastical stories. He didn't even blink.

"I'm sad to tell you," the boatman said as he pulled the raft onto the shore. "The most sacred Kumbh Mela festival ended a few days ago. You would have enjoyed it. Not to worry—you won't regret it if you go. There is no other place quite as enchanting."

The boatman was right: Ujjayini did not disappoint. Serenity radiated from the very earth. Few voices were heard, and the people who did speak lowered their voices to mere whispers. Both men and women smiled his way and, more important, smiled at each other. Everyone walked slowly, scanning the ground before planting their next step as if afraid to hurt the soil. Goats, cows, and elephants shared the streets with humans, and children gently steered them away from the market stalls with friendly pats and kind words. And he had never before seen a place so clean. Abba would have loved it.

This was paradise.

Exhausted from the suffocating heat, Yeshua rested in the shadow of a temple painted in cheerful greens and pinks. The passing locals wore either pristine white or colorful robes or walked around completely uncovered. Yeshua blushed at the sight. He had only ever seen Dhiman and his brothers naked before, and here unclothed strangers paraded in front of him without shame.

"Welcome to Ujjayini, brother," a white-clad, barefoot monk said through the white mask that covered his mouth.

Yeshua pressed his palms together. "Namaste."

"Come. Let me show you our most magnificent temple."

"Yes, it's extraordinary."

"Oh heavens, not this one. You must never enter the Mahakaleshwar

Jyotirlinga, my brother. It's a most dangerous Shiva temple, you see. No, what I will show you is something *truly* breathtaking—the temple of Jain."

Yeshua had never heard anyone refer to Shiva as evil, but he accepted the invitation out of curiosity.

As they walked, the monk swept the ground in front of them with a brush of twigs. "I'm gently removing God's small creations, the insects, to not harm or kill them."

Yeshua tried to step in the monk's exact footsteps, careful not to offend his beliefs.

At the Jain temple, a whitewashed structure with a pointed steeple, the monk removed his white robe, entered a shallow mikveh pool for purification, and gestured for Yeshua to follow suit. The water burned, almost as hot as the air. Yeshua washed himself quickly and wrapped himself with a fresh white robe that the monk handed him. By the temple door, the monk dipped his finger into a bowl of saffron-colored paste and smeared it onto his forehead. With a content grin, he reached out and smudged the space between Yeshua's eyebrows.

"A clean body helps the mind enter a spiritual dimension," he said. "Like cleansing bad karma."

In the cool inner sanctum of the temple, Yeshua sagged to his knees from heat exhaustion, no longer able to stand upright. His head swirled from dehydration. He closed his eyes to stop his head from spinning and focused on his breath, trying to think of nothing. Nearby, he heard the monk shuffling around.

When his heart rate had slowed and the feeling of panic had subsided, Yeshua opened his eyes. The white walls of the sanctum had been decorated with symbols: a red cross with its four arms bent at right angles and a hand with a wheel drawn in the middle of the palm. At the front stood a marble statue of a man sitting cross-legged, his palms facing upward and a peaceful smile on his face.

The monk nodded when he saw Yeshua had regained his energy. "I'm Harikesh. Most welcome to our temple."

"Issa." Yeshua rose to greet him. He motioned to the statue. "I see you follow the Lord Buddha."

"Oh no, not the Buddha. It's Mahavira. He lived a long, long time before the Buddha. In fact, he was perhaps one of the Buddha's best teachers."

Yeshua suppressed a smile. It didn't seem likely.

"And like the Buddha, Mahavira was a prince who left his home at thirty years of age, achieved enlightenment, and soon thereafter died."

"Died?" That seemed like a tragic end for someone who had just found what he was searching for.

"Yes. He was quite an ascetic, bless his soul. He gave up eating and died from starvation. Thus he was liberated from the circle of rebirth."

What a waste of life. Wasn't the purpose of life to learn, grow, and share your knowledge—not suffer and die? Still, he was intrigued by the man who had died for Nirvana.

"You believe in reincarnation?" Yeshua asked.

"Yes."

"And karma?"

"Certainly."

But Harikesh's understanding of karma was different from what Yeshua had learned before.

"Karma is like a delicate substance," Harikesh said. "It attaches itself to your soul and grows and diminishes, depending on what you do, what you say, and what you think. Although you can't see it, it stays with you for the rest of your life—and all your lifetimes—until you have eliminated the bad karma by good deeds and purification."

"You believe in souls?"

Harikesh motioned him to silence. He handed Yeshua a clove from a bowl in front of the Mahavira statue, then pressed another between the ring fingers of each hand, pointed the head of the clove toward Mahavira, and bowed to the statue. He chanted: "I bow down to Arihanta. I bow down to Siddha. I bow down to Acharya. I bow down to Upadhyaya. I bow down to Sadhu and Sadhvi. With these five bows, I destroy the sins among all that is auspicious."

The prayer offered respect to the enlightened souls on earth, to those already free from reincarnation, and to all spiritual leaders, teachers, monks, and nuns.

"Namo namaha," Harikesh chanted, over and over, before he paused to explain that the words meant "I salute you," a pledge to release the karma that bound his soul.

Then Harikesh bowed again and asked his spiritual masters to guide him on his path.

In the days that followed, the cool temple became a welcome refuge from the intense heat. Between prayers, Yeshua and Harikesh rested in the garden under the shade of the fragrant neem trees and discussed the Buddha and Mahavira. Both prophets had taught that nothing good or bad happens without reason. A person's karma is either inherited from actions in a past life or carried over to the next life by anger, violent thoughts, and immoral actions.

Yeshua loved the pleasant harmony of Jaini life. Like the Sindhi monks, the Jains believed you could become a perfect soul by overcoming desires, attaining the right perception and the right knowledge, and refraining from harmful behavior. Whoever mastered his thoughts conquered the cycle of birth and death. And yet the Jains denied the existence of God. They believed the universe had always existed and regulated itself through the laws of nature. No God appeared to offer help in distressful situations; everyone was responsible for their own fortune. Yeshua thought they were wrong, of course. God had always been his companion, and without God, he would be lost.

As the weeks wore on, the Jains' extreme commitment to nonviolence began to bother him. He had to wear a mask and filter his drinking water several times through a stretched fabric to avoid harming any insects. Walking anywhere took hours because of the constant sweeping before each step. And when a dying cow screamed in pain all night and Yeshua begged the monks to release the poor animal from suffering, they refused. A creature's agony is part of its karma, they said, and thus the cow had to die on its own to avoid reincarnation. When Yeshua argued, the Jaini monks reminded him that his mind was still tainted. They told him to practice forgiveness. Yeshua had to cover his head with his traveling sack to muffle the shrieks of agony.

One night, Yeshua dreamed that Buddha and Mahavira took him by the hand and led him toward a rising sun where thousands of people were waiting. "Tell them the good news," they said. "Share your wisdom."

During early morning meditation, Yeshua contemplated the dream. The two enlightened teachers had suggested he leave Ujjayini and continue his journey east. And although the message confused him, something about the dream felt real. Like when he was a child and God spoke to him during Yom Kippur. Ever since he could remember, he had dreamed about Moses and Abraham. But this dream had been different. Mahavira and the Buddha had spoken directly to him, as if their message held considerable importance. Even now, completely awake, he felt their presence. What would God want him to do? Was it time to continue his journey?

Yeshua looked at the white-clad meditating monks around him, all deep in trance. Staying at this temple with such wise and humble teachers had been a gift, but he didn't belong here. With his mind made up, he decided to wait until the day got cooler and then quietly leave. Harikesh would probably remind him that having doubts was natural and would ask Yeshua to wait. He'd say that in time Yeshua would feel better.

But Harikesh seemed to have anticipated his departure and made no fuss about it.

"I always knew this was not your final destination, my brother. But always remember, Issa," he said in parting. "The sense of your importance is only an appreciation of your self by yourself."

Satavahana, AD 10

That night, Yeshua slept in a shallow cave on a hillside. The road from Ujjayini had petered out into a field, and he had not come across a single person who might offer him accommodation. Although it was a blessing to sleep alone, away from the stirring of others, the familiar human noises were replaced with the frightening sounds of the jungle. Crickets and frogs competed in a dissonant choir. Tigers growled in the distance. Somewhere, an animal screamed. Flying squirrels swooshed by and occasionally brushed against the branches he had used to close off the cave. Yeshua shivered, anxious about what the night held. What did a young man like him know about surviving in the forest? He stared at the cave entrance and prayed that God would keep him safe.

When he dozed off, his sleep was deep, and he didn't hear a panther slink in between the foliage covering the cave entrance. The giant feline walked up to him, sniffed his face, and left as quietly as it had entered. But in the morning, he did notice something strange: a breach between the branches. A flying squirrel must have crashed into the foliage with enough force to leave an opening, he thought. He promised himself to be more careful in the future.

Yeshua pushed his way through the dense forest where the sun filtered through the treetops just enough to cast shimmering specks of gold on the ground. The jungle was alive with buzzing insects, distant growls, croaks, and squeaking branches. All around him, monkeys chattered and birds tweeted in a hundred different languages. Animals drifted close but remained out of sight. Only the mosquitoes kept him company until Yeshua smeared his skin and hair with crushed lemongrass to repel them.

To still his doubts, he focused his thoughts on God. He couldn't give up now. God wouldn't have led him this far only to be bitten by a venomous snake or eaten by a tiger. He convinced himself that no spider in the world could poison him, no snake would attack him, and no leopard would eat him. Surely with God's protection he was safer here than he had ever been at home. He brushed the fear from his mind and trudged on.

When a drop of water hit the tip of his nose, he didn't react. He had grown used to condensation splattering around him. But when a second drop and a third and a fourth struck his head, he looked up. Was he being attacked by a flock of birds? Above him, the sky had turned as dark as night. His heart stopped—surely it couldn't be rain. He had ignored the stories about monsoons, the violent seasonal rains, assuming it never rained in the humid south. But the increasing frequency of heavy drops proved him wrong. And before he could find cover, a deafening crack of thunder shook the ground and the rain gushed down like a waterfall. The sky blazed with lightning. Yeshua crouched under a teak tree and pulled a wide leaf over his head.

He no longer felt safe.

Within minutes, Yeshua was as soaked as if he had been swimming in Lake Kinneret. Why had no one warned him about rainstorms? Or maybe they had and he hadn't listened? Yeshua weighed his options. He could stay under the tree and hope the storm would abate in time. Or perhaps he should turn back. But no, he had been walking for more days than he could count. How far ahead was the next village? Which way should he go?

A blanket of dark clouds had turned the forest into a pitch-black tunnel.

What if the rain didn't stop for days?

He was hungry and wet and miserable. He had survived on berries for the last few days, but if the rain continued like this, he might get stuck in the mud and starve. What if he died here? Would they find his body and make up stories about him, saying he had died in a quest for salvation? Or turn him into a god like Mahavira after he died of starvation? Perhaps they would place his statue in temples and make offerings of flowers and incense. Maybe even ask him for protection. Yeshua laughed out loud, despite his misery. He chuckled as he forced his way forward, pushing branches and leaves out of his way, shaking with giggles and chills until his chuckles drowned in sobs. He didn't want to become a deity that people prayed to. And he wasn't ready for salvation. He was too young; he had so much to do and to learn, so much to see. He had to survive this. He *had* to survive.

Yeshua took off his sandals. His bare feet felt steadier on the ground, allowing him to walk faster. Well trained by the Jains, he placed his feet down with care to avoid stepping on the copulating frogs that had appeared from nowhere. At least in this torrential rain, the insects and serpents had disappeared into hiding. Even larger animals would be sheltering somewhere. Only toads and inexperienced Galileans would venture out in a storm where Indra, god of thunder and master of skies, ruled.

The rain seemed endless. Yeshua moved ahead, guided by the moss that grew on the north side of the trees. He drank fresh water that accumulated in hollow leaves, chewed on bamboo shoots, and sucked on tiny sour white berries. And when his legs buckled beneath him, he curled up and slept in fits under the leaking canopy of cascading ashoka tree leaves.

Several days rolled into nights before he finally noticed a light flickering in the distance. Could it be a house—with people? The wet cloth of his tunic clung to his legs, making every step an effort, but the hope of shelter propelled him forward. How he longed to be inside a dry room with a cup of hot water and perhaps a bowl of rice.

His heart beat faster.

The light came from a window of an isolated hermitage enclosed by a high brick wall. Yeshua drew his wet mantle closer as he knocked on the gate. In a few moments, he would be inside, warm and dry. He would have something to eat, and then rest. Yet he couldn't shake the feeling that something was wrong. He heard no footsteps. No one spoke. In a spiritual refuge, a monk usually stayed close to the gate in case someone needed help. But this place was so far away from anywhere, what guests could they expect?

Yeshua knocked again.

No response.

He banged on the wood.

Nothing. Not a sound from inside. Perhaps the monastery had been abandoned. But no, he *had* seen light from inside. Someone was in there. He walked around the wall to see if there might be another opening or a lower section he could climb over, but they had built the wall high and smooth to keep out unwelcome visitors.

He returned to the gate and resumed banging.

"Namaste!" he shouted. "Please let me in. I come in peace."

At last, he heard footsteps. Thank heavens!

"Who is there?" A child's voice.

Could this be one of those ashrams where people left their children to be educated in the sacred scriptures?

"My name is Issa," he called. "I'm a pilgrim. Please, please let me in. I am tired and cold and hungry. Please, I need a place to sleep tonight."

"Are you a man?"

Yeshua frowned. What kind of question was that? Would they let him in only if he were a child? "Yes. I'm a man. Please let me in. I promise to leave at dawn, before anyone awakes."

"I can't let you in."

Was this child out of his mind? It was pouring. No one had ever turned him away before. Wherever he had gone, he had been invited in, whether the people were poor or wealthy. And in this horrible weather, what kind of person would leave him to suffer?

"You don't understand," he tried. "I'm a pilgrim. I'm on a yatra. I'm a monk."

"I can't let you in, Baba."

"Please! I'm soaked and I'm hungry. I need a place to sleep. I beg you!"

Not a peep from the other side. Was the child still there?

"Please!" He choked back a sob. "Can you bring an elder or a monk? May I speak to a grown-up?"

Silence.

Was he talking to a wall, or was the child still there? He collapsed to the ground and surrendered to his tears. He would die out here tonight. He had used his last bit of energy to reach this place; he couldn't move another inch. He was exhausted and frightened. He pulled his mantle over his head and sniveled.

Screech.

The gate opened beside him.

Yeshua peered up at a tiny creature completely wrapped in a white sheet with only her face showing. A woman. That explained everything: this wasn't a monastery—it was a nunnery.

"Come this way." She gestured for him to follow.

Yeshua rose on shaking knees and bowed as deeply as he could without falling over. "Thank you, Sister," he said between clattering teeth. "Thank you so very much."

Without a word, the delicate nun led him to a hut at the back of the yard and pulled its curtained door aside. Yeshua flinched at the stench of mold and feces. A chicken coop. He pinched his nose and entered. At least the hut was dry, and the birds kept the space warm. He smiled gratefully at the nun and thanked God for guiding him here. Then he settled into the hay to sleep.

He would have slept all day, but the rooster had other plans. At the first light of dawn, he started crowing, as if yelling, "Wake up, you lazy people! Can't you see it's a new day?"

Yeshua stuck his fingers in his ears, but they barely muted the sound. Finally, he rubbed the sleep from his eyes and sat up. Only a few feet away, the rooster pranced back and forth among the hens, shaking his colorful tail feathers. In one quick swoop, he grabbed a hen by the neck and gave her all his love. Of course, Yeshua had seen sheep, camels, horses, and many other animals mate before, but this was different. For the first time, no one saw him watching. He couldn't take his eyes off them. In a way, he was like the rooster—the only male in a hermitage of women. But the nuns didn't care about his tail feathers; they had sworn to celibacy. Still, he couldn't help wondering: what if he pranced around like a rooster and grabbed any woman he wanted? He felt a stir between his legs and stroked his groin as he watched the rooster grab another hen by her neck. The act was over in a few heartbeats. Afterward, the hen ruffled her feathers and walked away, content.

What would it feel like to touch a woman? Yeshua thought of the harlots along the caravan route with their painted faces and perfumed hair. They grunted and squealed with delight while making love, but sometimes after the act was over, they spat at the man who had just had them. Dhiman said all women were like that, hot and cold, but Yeshua never believed him. He had heard his parents make love under thick blankets when they thought the children were asleep. He had heard Ama giggle and whisper to Abba that she loved him. He had hated hearing them moaning like animals. What an innocent boy he had been! Yeshua's thoughts returned to the girl from last night. Would she like him to touch her? He lay back in the hay, closed his eyes, and fantasized about her naked body until he dozed off into deep sleep.

"Baba, I've brought you some food."

Yeshua woke with a start. Where was he? The sound of the rain and the odor of the henhouse brought him back to the present. When he opened the curtain, the girl was gone, but she had left a bowl of vegetable stew and a cup of hot water under a cover outside. Yeshua gulped the bland stew down, too hungry to eat mindfully. He licked the bowl clean and peeked out through a crack in the wall. How many nuns lived here? Were they all young? But he couldn't see anyone outside. And now the rain had slowed to a drizzle.

It was time to leave.

He stuffed his belongings into his traveling sack and left the dishes outside the hut. The muddy courtyard was deserted. Not a soul in sight.

No one to thank for their kindness. He contemplated leaving them the ring as a token of gratitude, but decided he might need it later. Besides, they already had a place to live and vegetable gardens to feed them. Better keep it for insurance.

He had almost reached the gate when rumbling shook the ground. Before he could blink, the sky turned black and released a new torrent of rain. As fast as he could, Yeshua ran back to the chicken coop and dove into the warm hay. He would have to stay put until the storm abated. The nuns would have to forgive him.

But the rain didn't stop. Yeshua meditated throughout the day and slept through the night. The next morning, the rooster woke him again at dawn and started his flirting rounds, but this time Yeshua didn't find it amusing. He was bored with no one to talk to and nothing to do. He stared through the crack in the wall, hoping one of the nuns would walk by or at least bring him food, but for hours no one moved anywhere. Yeshua crossed his legs to meditate again, knowing there was nowhere else to go. He entered a quiet place of detachment from everything and lingered in a state of bliss in the presence of God.

When he drifted back into consciousness and blinked his eyes open, he found a girl sitting by his side in the hay. The young woman had let down her veil to bare her shaven head. She stared at him, frail and innocent like a baby antelope with enormous brown eyes. Despite her baldness, Yeshua had never seen a prettier girl in his entire life. He couldn't take his eyes off her. She had a perfectly oval face and a mouth that begged to be kissed. But her skin was dull, and the bones protruded through her skin. Her nipples… Yeshua gasped when he noticed the pointy dark circles under her thin white robe.

She looked down at her lap with a demure smile.

"I'm Issa." He forced his gaze away from her chest. "I'm a pilgrim."

The girl raised her eyes to peek at him, and then lifted her veil to cover her face. "My name is Ramaa."

Yeshua tasted the name between his lips. "Ramaa. What a lovely name."

They sat in silence for a while, not sure how to continue.

"Are you a nun?"

"Yes."

"Have you lived here long?"

"No."

"Who do you worship here?"

"I should go." Ramaa got up.

Yeshua grabbed her hand. "Please don't."

She hesitated for a moment, and then sat down again. "If the elders find me here, they will kill me."

"They won't kill you."

"You don't understand. They *will* kill me. I'm a widow, don't you see?"

Yeshua sat back and studied her. How could such a young woman already be a widow? And why was she here?

"I know you mean well"—Ramaa's eyes filled with tears—"but you don't understand."

"Then tell me!"

Ramaa tried to get up again, but Yeshua was quicker. He grabbed her by the shoulders and shifted her to face him. The veil fell from her face. His eyes wouldn't leave hers. "Please. Tell me."

She shook her head.

"No one will find you here."

Ramaa hesitated for a moment. And then she told Yeshua her story. She had been born into a Brahmin family, the youngest of five daughters. Her father, distraught over having another girl, never spoke to her. At the age of ten, she was married to the oldest and wealthiest Brahmin in town. Before her wedding, Ramaa had not known what men and women did behind closed doors, and her husband had made her perform all kinds of erotic acts that she was still too embarrassed to even think about.

One morning, after four years of marriage, her husband didn't wake up. She shook him and slapped him as hard as she could, but his eyes remained closed. She wasn't sure why he had died, but it meant her life had come to an end. Becoming a widow was a great sin in the Satavahana Empire. Her family disowned her, and her in-laws beat her up and threw her out of their house. They blamed her for her husband's death, calling her a witch. She was given the choice of dying on her husband's funeral pyre or joining a nunnery. And that's why she had come here.

"All the nuns here are widows—everyone?"

"Yes. All of them."

"I'm happy you're here," Yeshua said. He yearned to reach out and caress her cheek.

"I'm not. I wish I were dead."

Ramaa told him the mother nuns who ran the hermitage were traditional widows who made sure everyone suffered in their grief. They wailed from morning to night over their dead husbands, but it was all an act. Some of the husbands had been dead for over thirty years and their wives had never even loved them. But they believed that making others suffer would bring them good karma.

"They refuse to let us eat well. We grow enough vegetables to feed ourselves and a small village, but they insist that all food must be watered down. Did you not notice? "

Yeshua nodded. Yes, the food had been horrible.

"They're all waiting to die. They cry and pray and sing those dreadful devotional songs all day long, and they force the rest of us to join them."

"So what are you going to do?"

"Nothing. This is my fate. I only pray that in my next life I will be born as a man."

Ramaa stared at the ceiling, blinking her tears away. Yeshua wanted to take her into his arms, but after months of living among men, he no longer knew how to treat girls.

"I really must go now." She darted out before Yeshua had the chance to stop her or ask her to return later.

Heavy clouds still shadowed the courtyard, but the rain had ceased for a moment. Yeshua gathered his things and threw his sack over his shoulder, pausing for a moment at the doorway. Where had Ramaa gone? How he wished she could come with him. They could pretend she was his wife. But a married man would not go on a pilgrimage with his wife. And a nun would not travel with a man, even if he were a monk. Perhaps she was right: she had to stay here and atone for sins committed in previous lives to ensure her next life would be better.

Yeshua shook his head. There was no point in staying.

Satavahana, AD 10

Yeshua shut the gate behind him and took one last look at the impenetrable walls of the nunnery. His tunic smelled faintly of mold and feces, but at least his clothes had dried in the warmth of the coop. And the clouds had scattered—somewhat. He checked the position of the sun and examined the moss on the nearest trees to determine the direction he had to go. The jungle to the east looked even thicker and gloomier than the forest he had come through.

"Sriman—wait!"

A grandmotherly woman bundled in layers of yellowing fabric waved him back to the gate.

Yeshua hesitated. He prayed she wouldn't ask about Ramaa. He would rather cut off his tongue than get the girl in trouble.

"Yes?" he asked, fidgeting, trying to avoid her eyes. *Please don't ask about Ramaa.*

"More rain is coming." The old woman's voice scratched like a rusty chisel against a dry whetstone. "The closest village is five days away. You might not make it there alive."

He shook his head. "I really should go."

"We do have room. Stay a week…two. The monsoon will have passed by then."

Yeshua looked from her to the darkening sky and back again. A warm hut or a wet jungle?

The nun showed him to a proper room in a building by the gate with an actual hay mattress and a bowl of water for washing. And no animals. "It's not much, but it's all we have."

Yeshua wanted to weep with gratitude.

"We'll bring you some food and milk; you must be starving."

She ducked to leave through the low doorway, but paused and turned back with a grin. "Perhaps later, you will tell us a story?" She lowered her scarf, revealing layers of wrinkles, and licked the lips of her toothless mouth.

"Yes, of course. I would like that. Very much."

He smiled. To think that perhaps the women were glad he had come. The monsoon almost guaranteed no one would ever find out he had stayed here. He might be their only chance for male company, perhaps for the rest of their lives.

Compared with the chicken coop, this room resembled a palace. And soon he discovered that the food improved also: stew with large chunks of vegetables, freshly baked naan, and warm milk. The only thing missing was Ramaa.

Later in the day, a middle-aged nun brought him to a hall where women of all ages sat cross-legged, facing a stone murti. Some were so old they had to be carried in; others were mere children. With their bald heads, sunken eyes, and malnourished bodies, they all resembled monks more than women.

Yeshua took a seat beside the offerings of flowers, vegetables, and fruits. Morose faces observed him with listless interest. They had no reason to trust him. After all, men were the reason they were forced to live in this miserable place.

"You're a Brahmin from the far west, isn't it so, Lord Issa?" The speaker was plumper than the others with healthy red cheeks and clean nails. "I'm assured you can tell wonderful stories."

"Mai, please," Yeshua said, using the proper address for an older woman. "I'm not a lord, just Issa. And I'm not a Brahmin. Well, not by birth, but in my heart, yes."

A murmur of surprise went through the hall. Sparks of interest lit their eyes and, here and there, hints of smiles.

"I come from a land far away," he continued. "It's called Palestine. We have no tigers or elephants. We have cheetahs and donkeys and lambs. And we eat fish every day because we live by the lake. We don't pray to deities like Vishnu, Shiva, Krishna, or Soma; we have only one God, and he is the almighty one, the creator of the world and everything in it."

"Like Brahman?" a child asked. An older nun elbowed her to shush her.

Yeshua shrugged. "Not quite, but similar, I guess. God is all-powerful and protective, whereas your Brahman exists in everything but leaves all the action to the deities." He looked around and noticed Ramaa in the back among the younger nuns. She smiled, and his heart jumped. She looked like a goddess. He bowed to the murti to collect himself before he continued.

"In my land, instead of telling stories about gods, we talk about our ancestors and the prophets who came before us. Like the Buddha. Do you know the Buddha?"

The women nodded. They had all heard about Lord Buddha.

"My people, the Yehudim, are the sons of the very first man on earth, Adam. We're descendants of Abraham, the man who first knew there's only one God and made a covenant with him. Before Abraham, my people were like you: they prayed to murtis and worshipped the sun and the wind." Yeshua picked up a pink lily from the offerings and twirled it between his fingers. "Many years ago, my ancestors lived in exile in Egypt, a country far from Palestine. The king of Egypt—he was called the Pharaoh—was a horrible man. He hated the Yehudim and enslaved them. But then a Yehudi child called Moses was born, and everyone believed he would be the next powerful prophet. When the Pharaoh heard about this child, he became frightened that Moses one day would call all his slaves to revolt. And he ordered that all Yehudi baby boys be killed."

The women gasped. Content that he had caught their interest, Yeshua continued.

"Moses' mother, of course, was terrified. To save her son, she took him to a big river, placed him in a basket made of reeds, and watched him float down the stream. But Moses' sister, afraid the baby would fall into the water and drown, hid in the tall grass and followed his journey down the river. The basket washed ashore close to where the Pharaoh's daughter was taking a bath with her maids."

Another gasp. Some of the nuns cried, remembering the children they had lost.

"No, please don't be sad." Yeshua scrambled up from his seat. "It's a happy story. Listen!" And so the nuns learned how the glorious prophet Moses survived and grew up to save Issa's people from slavery and led them to the Promised Land.

The women wanted to know everything about Moses. What did he look like? Did he marry? How did he know the voice speaking through the bush was God? Was it perhaps Agni, the god of fire? How could God tell the difference between the Yehudim and the Egyptians? Did they wear different colored clothes? And how exactly did God divide the waters of the sea? Did all the Egyptians drown, or did some of them swim away? Why did Moses and his tribe kill almost all his fellow Yehudim after God gave him the Ten Commandments? Wasn't Moses forbidden to kill? Why did they have to wander in the desert for forty years? And so on.

Yeshua was dizzy with fatigue and glee when he sauntered off to his room to sleep. He had laughed more than he had for months and ended the night by thanking them all for saving him from the storm.

He fell asleep with peace in his heart.

The rain would not stop. Every morning, Yeshua joined in the nuns' songs devoted to the supreme spirit Brahman. It was the only way, they said, to free themselves from their karma. They wailed with heartache and desperation, and Yeshua hummed along to relieve himself of the anguish he had caused his parents.

After their one daily meal, which he now shared with the women, he spent the remainder of the afternoon telling stories from the Torah. The ladies especially enjoyed the story of David and Goliath. They reciprocated with stories of how they had been cast out of their homes and what they would have done if they had had a slingshot. The nuns howled with laughter and slapped their knees at the images they created, each of them telling a better story than the previous one.

Soon enough, the women forgot that Yeshua shouldn't be there. The elders spoiled him with tamarind fruits meant for the Vishnu murti. The young girls spread petals of fragrant ylang-ylang flowers on his bed. The adolescents peeked at him when they didn't think he was looking and stole past his hut in pairs, giggling. And yet, Yeshua couldn't embrace them. Or kiss them. He struggled to sleep at night, fantasizing about them all, but especially about Ramaa. They hadn't spoken since that first time, but she always caught his eye and, whenever she passed, let her body brush against his. Yeshua yearned to meet her alone somewhere, but always found her surrounded by others. He tried to silently beckon her, hoping she might read his mind. It seemed an impossible dream, and soon his chance would be gone. After the monsoon season ended, he would have to leave.

One night, a peculiar scratching sound jolted Yeshua awake. Mice? Or was someone in his room? He fumbled to cover his naked body and blinked to adjust his eyes to the darkness.

"Who is there?"

No reply. He could barely make out the shape of a person standing in the corner. White eyes. White teeth. White robe.

"It's all right. Come talk to me." His voice sounded hoarse with sleep and desire. Oh, how he hoped it was Ramaa. "Don't be afraid. I won't touch you."

He meant it. He wouldn't touch her. Unless she wanted him to, of course. "Please, sit." He patted the mattress beside him.

The girl sat down and uncovered her face. Yeshua squinted in the dark and looked into two perfectly shaped brown eyes. Ramaa. His heart almost stopped.

"I shouldn't have come."

"I'm so happy you're here." His voice trembled.

"I should go." She didn't move.

Yeshua could hardly breathe. "I've been waiting for you," he said, caressing her hand with his little finger.

"I know."

He placed his hand behind her neck and guided her face toward his. He hesitated for a moment, feeling her hot breath close to his mouth. But he couldn't wait; he pressed his lips against hers. At last. Her lips were soft and wet against his, with a sweet taste of vanilla.

She pushed his face away.

"I'm sorry, I didn't mean to…" Yeshua's cheeks burned.

"Don't apologize." She sounded like a little girl.

His lips ached with the hunger to kiss her.

Then she leaned in and let her mouth meet his. Yeshua had to grab the mattress with both hands to keep from tearing her robe off. He kissed her over and over, sucking her, savoring her very being.

"Oh, darling, my princess, my love…"

Ramaa shushed him and pushed him down on his back. She let the white robe fall from her shoulders and straddled him, rubbing her naked body against his. Her small breasts heaved and sank with every movement. He groaned and let her take control.

She guided him into her warmth, her wetness, and moved her body back and forth, first slowly, and then faster and faster. Yeshua grunted, every inch of him tingling with ecstasy. She swung her body, thrust her pelvis forward, and threw her head back with pleasure. And right when Yeshua would have climaxed, Ramaa rolled off and lay down beside him, panting.

"Not yet," she whispered, and ran her hand through his sweaty hair. "Hold on a little longer."

Yeshua breathed heavily, wild with lust and confusion. What was he supposed to do now? He looked into her innocent but oh-so-mature eyes, his heart almost bursting with love.

Ramaa kissed him again. Then she grabbed his thighs, turned him over and pulled him on top of her. She guided him with a steady grip until he understood how to move in an even rhythm. Bodies glued together, they rocked and swayed faster and faster until Yeshua groaned and exploded into her. Unexpectedly, he started laughing.

"Shh, someone might hear you!" Her teeth glistened in the dark.

But Yeshua had just made love to the most wonderful woman in the world, and he wanted everyone to know. He held Ramaa, his angel, in his arms and kissed her forehead, her eyes, her lips.

"I love you." Yeshua held her even tighter.

Ramaa closed her eyes and smiled. "Thank you," she said.

"For what?"

"Loving me. And giving me faith. I think I can survive here now."

"Are you out of your mind? I can't leave you here." Yeshua pushed himself up on his elbow. "I'll marry you. I could never live without you."

Ramaa shook her head. "I can't marry you, Issa. I'm a widow. I'm marked."

"Don't talk like that. I will marry you. I'll bring you back to Galilee, and we can live there happily, without worries. I'll work as a carpenter again, and you...you can take care of the house with my mother and sisters."

"You don't understand. We won't even make it three days from here. With my shaved head, everyone will know what I am. I'll shame you."

"I don't care!"

"I do. They'll kill me, and probably you too." She shrank away from him. "I won't let that happen."

Yeshua took her face into his hands and forced her to look at him. She was crying freely now. "Ramaa, I love you. I'll protect you."

"No, Issa. I'm sorry. I can't. I've got to stay here."

Yeshua stormed up from the bed. "But I can't leave you! I'll take care of you, I promise."

Ramaa looked at him. She had made up her mind.

"Please come with me."

She picked up her robe and wrapped it around her. "I'm sorry, Issa."

Yeshua looked away. He held the curtain open as she ducked under the low doorway and stepped out into the pouring rain. And then he crumpled up and cried. He wept for the loneliness in his heart and for the sorrow he had caused his family. He cried for his mother's embrace, for Yakov's laughter, and for knowing he would never kiss Ramaa again. He buried his face in the hay and let the tears flow until they had all dried out.

On the other side of the courtyard, the rooster announced the dawn of another day. Yeshua picked up his belongings and let the curtain fall behind him. This time no one asked him to stay when he walked out the gate.

The rain had weakened to a drizzle. Soon the skies would clear and the sun would come out.

Satavahana, AD 10

Yeshua trudged through the soggy jungle, up slippery hills and through flooded valleys. The rain had submerged entire villages, leaving only rooftops protruding above the water, like islands. Young men and boys dressed in nothing but loincloths paddled around in hollowed-out tree trunks to help move families onto drier land.

At last the big rains stopped. In a matter of days, the earth would absorb the water, and the nature would begin another cycle of life. He passed villages where silly little girls played berry catch on the riverbanks and men's voices rang with irritating merriment as they tilled the moist earth and prepared the fields for sowing.

Yeshua paused a few days here and there to help with the farmwork, but he couldn't rejoice over the clear skies and new beginnings with the others. Heartache had made him somber: his smile had faded, his posture sagged, and the stories he told on his journey had become serious. He despised the sound of people's laughter, the hope that shone in their eyes. How could God be so cruel? How could people flaunt their happiness when he crouched in pain? He turned down meals because he wasn't hungry, and only pretended to meditate while his mind was crying out in chaos. He had left a part of himself behind with Ramaa. Only half of him continued.

Behind the veil of depression, Yeshua carried on like the benevolent pilgrim he had once been. He faked a smile and continued to share goodwill, blessings, and stories about Abraham's people. During sleepless nights, he wondered whether this journey had been a mistake. Life as a simple carpenter in Capernaum no longer seemed so bad. He could have married, had children, and worked beside the rabbi in the synagogue as his parents had advised. But as soon as morning broke, he was convinced once again that he was exactly where God had led him. He had gathered more stories for teaching others, tales about the Buddha and the Hindu deities, his travels, and people he had met. Like Ramaa.

Yeshua's heart twinged at her memory: the scent of her flesh, the taste of her skin, the sound of her voice, the loving look in those antelope eyes. He should never have left her. They could have been close to Ujjayini by now. They could have stayed in the peaceful town until her hair grew out; no one would have known she was a widow. A hollow, lonely sigh escaped his chest. Deep inside, he knew Ramaa had stayed because she had not wanted to come. Her place—her fate, as she called it—was to repent for her karmic debt in that god-awful hermitage. Yeshua shook his head, tears burning his eyes. She was so wrong. One day he would go back to save her. He would pretend he was her husband's brother or something, and the old widows would have to let her leave. One day, they would be together again.

"When your senses touch certain things, you experience cold or heat and pleasure or pain, but you will soon learn that these sensations are always fleeting."

Yeshua woke from his daydream and looked up at a gangly Brahmin with a moss-like long beard who had sat next to him in the shade of a mango tree. His amber eyes radiated with kindness.

"Feelings come and go, my son. You will have to bear them with patience."

Yeshua frowned. How had he known?

"It's from the Bhagavad Gita: Lord Krishna's advice to Arjuna."

Yeshua's face lit up. He had heard of Krishna.

"Only those who are not affected by feelings, who remain untouched by pleasure and pain, are ready for immortality."

"Is that also from the Baga…? Baga-what?"

"Bhagavad Gita. The story speaks of yoga, philosophy, rebirth, liberation——a moral code for life." The Brahmin slipped his hand into the folds of his dhoti robe and produced a piece of cheese wrapped in cotton. He offered it to Yeshua. "From the Mahabharata. You've heard of it?"

Yeshua nodded. Of course; the Sindhi villagers had mentioned the holy scripture of the Hindus.

"The Gita, as we call it, recounts the discussion between Lord Krishna and the warrior prince Arjuna before they entered into battle. Arjuna at first refused to go to war because he would have to fight his own cousins. Thus, Lord Krishna taught him about the nature of God and explained to Arjuna his duties as a man, warrior, and prince. I can recite you the verses, if you'd care to listen."

A kernel of excitement sprouted within Yeshua's dulled heart. This was why he had crossed the Satavahana Empire: to learn and discover.

"I've got all the time in the world," Yeshua said, and bit into the creamy cheese. It melted on his tongue.

Despite the many strange names, Yeshua lost himself in the story, watching the powerful drama unfold before his mind's eye. He devoured every word, oblivious of twilight turning into night and the moon rising to greet them. A cool gust of air and the shriek of waking bats brought him back from his trance. Limping on legs stiff from sitting too long, they walked to the Brahmin's house, where the narrative about Krishna and Arjuna played out until the early hours of the morning.

That night, Yeshua dreamed about Lord Krishna. The blue-hued prince danced around him on light feet, his eyes bright and beckoning. "Come!" he called. "I'll show you the way." And in the dream, Yeshua followed him, enchanted by the melody of Krishna's flute. "Come!" Krishna kept calling as he disappeared into the horizon. And although Yeshua couldn't see him any longer, he traced the steps of the blue deity, convinced he had been shown the right direction.

When the Brahmin asked Yeshua to stay longer and study the Bhagavad Gita with him, Yeshua declined. The Gita lessons and the dream about Krishna had reawakened his passion. He knew what to do now, why God had guided him here. He had to continue east to

Jagannath, where the White Brahmins, a large community of Krishna's followers, lived.

"Lord Krishna will escort you, like he brought you to my house," the Brahmin said, and he handed Yeshua a parcel of food for his journey. "And perhaps one day you will find he has always been with you."

Although the hilltops obscured his view, a fresh wind scented by surf and seaweed confirmed that Yeshua was closing in on the coastal town of Jagannath. Day after day, he climbed up and down peaks, hoping he would see the ocean at each rise, but every time he was disappointed: only more hills, more fields, more forests. Then one afternoon, as he sat on a cliff's edge because he couldn't take another step, his eyes caught the reflection of glittering waves in the distance. His heart surged. Was his long journey coming to an end? He couldn't wait to bury his feet in the sand and immerse himself in the cleansing water. He yearned to take long swims in the weightlessness only a sea could offer. Perhaps there would also be grilled or salted fish for sale in the village. His mouth watered. Yeshua jumped up and hurried his steps. The horizon appeared and disappeared until, finally, the full spectrum of the ocean opened up before him. His weary legs carried him downhill, past two-story caves inhabited by naked Jains and through emerald fields. He met turbaned merchants riding on fully packed elephants and women balancing vats of gigantic fish on their heads. At last, he saw the settlement of houses perched on the shoreline. Hundreds of simple mud houses with thatched roofs circled a larger complex. Could it be the temple of the White Brahmins? Yeshua's heart beat faster. Jagannath! The place where his destiny would blossom.

"Namaskāraḥ," Yeshua said in Sanskrit to a passing adolescent who was towing a reluctant goat with great difficulty. "Is this the way to the temple?"

The boy bowed all the way to his toes and pressed his palms together. "Swāgatam. Welcome, Brahmin. Yes, it's right there—just down the road. Pass the tannery—you will smell the stench from far away—turn left, then right, and then left again, and there you will see the temple."

Yeshua tried to remember the directions, but instead he shrugged and said, "Let me help you with the goat. And you can show me the way."

Together the boys pulled the goat through the outskirts of the village into the town center, where their roads parted at the boy's house, not far from the temple.

But the temple could wait. Straight ahead, at the horizon, the deep-blue ocean blended with the evening sky. The view connected with something deep inside him, as if the answer to every question lay in the waves that kept coming, one after another, changing the perspective with their every motion. He removed his sandals and let the sand massage the soles of his feet before he stepped into the refreshing sea. He waded until the water reached his waist, and then he dove. He swam under the surface until his lungs wanted to burst. When he couldn't hold his breath any longer, he shot up into the air and inhaled the pure essence of life. He laughed. He cried. He hadn't felt this alive since he'd left Ramaa.

Once fulfilled, Yeshua returned to the beach to observe the theater of Jagannath life. Local fishermen in rickety boats returned to the shore before sunset, just like at home in Capernaum. Impatient buyers balanced woven baskets on their heads and walked into the ocean to meet them, striving to get there first and buy the fish that would keep their family fed another day. One man rode his camel out to the farthest boats. The animal kicked and fought, his muzzle barely reaching above the surface, as his master negotiated the price of the merchandise. Women, children, and the elderly waited on the beach. A scrawny boy sold pieces of coconut; others hustled bananas, flatbreads, sandals, and cotton scarves.

As night embraced the shore, the scene died out, and the villagers retired to their homes, leaving behind a pile of discarded fish heads and entrails. Yeshua rolled up his traveling sack under his head and pulled a thin cotton cloth over his body. In the morning, he would visit the temple. And if he was lucky, they would ask him to stay. If not, well, he wasn't quite sure what he would do. He couldn't go home—yet. Perhaps he could retrace his steps, fetch Ramaa, and start a new life somewhere as a teacher with her as his wife.

Yeshua's stomach cramped at the thought. God had sent him into the world to teach, but wherever he went, no one wanted to accept him as their true teacher. To the crowds, he was nothing but a clever young man who could entertain them for a day or two. The only way he could possibly support Ramaa was as a carpenter, and in this part of the world a carpenter would be treated as a third-class citizen without the right to even contemplate the scriptures. Ramaa would never want him. If the White Brahmins rejected him, he would have to keep going. Somewhere, someplace, they would want him to stay.

When the first light tickled his eyes and a soft breeze tousled his hair, Yeshua woke well rested. The sun had already begun its journey into dawn, painting the clouds with downy strokes of soft purple and gold. In the distance, a murmur of prayers approached, a toneless mantra repeated over and over again. Yeshua propped himself up on his elbows and watched a group of men stride into the waves. Their chants grew louder as they scooped water over their heads and lifted their faces to the sky. Yeshua hesitated for a moment before he approached them, stopping a few feet from the group. He closed his eyes and mimicked their movements and Sanskrit words:

> *Om. Oh God, the Giver of Life,*
> *Remover of pain and sorrow,*
> *The provider of happiness,*
> *Oh! Creator of the universe,*
> *May we receive your supreme light,*
> *May you guide our thoughts in the right direction.*

Yeshua's heart opened wide as he centered on the mantra and absorbed the calming energy of the prayer, becoming one with them all. Through the slits of his eyes, he noticed a group of bearded Brahmins in white robes and turbans nearby. One Brahmin, a young boy, tugged at his turban that kept sliding down over his eyes. Yeshua suppressed a laugh: these men around him were the White Brahmins, the ones he had been searching for. Oblivious of his dreams of belonging, they had fulfilled his ultimate wish. He closed his eyes again and chanted at the top of his voice, a smile playing at the corners of his mouth.

Afterward, he followed a few paces behind the White Brahmins as they returned to their temple, but paused outside the gate. Was he allowed to enter? Did they have rules, like in Jerusalem, where nonbelievers who entered the temple would be punished by death? What was the worst that could happen? Would they throw him out? Kill him? But he had come this far; he had to take his chances. He removed his sandals and entered through the gate. A cluster of fig trees encircled a pool of water in front of the main temple building, a square construction made of red clay with a pointed palm frond roof. Behind the temple stood a couple of long, rectangular mud huts dotted with carved-out windows and doorways.

Yeshua hesitated. How should he approach them? What should he say? His admission to the temples in Sindh and Ujjayini had been relatively easy, but now that he wanted nothing more than to stay, he was terribly nervous. God didn't appreciate if you wanted something too much, just like the Buddha cautioned against attachment. Yeshua straightened his back and brushed his doubts away. He had to let go of his desire to stay in this temple. He had to trust God to guide him. If he wasn't supposed to stay here, he would find another place to fulfill his destiny.

He sat down next to the gate, took a deep breath, and sank into a profound meditation, convinced that everything would fall into place.

Jagannath, AD 10

"Brahmin!" A spry voice jolted him from his trance. "Brahmin!"
Yeshua wriggled his toes and fingers, returning his awareness to his body.

He shaded his eyes with one hand. A boy dressed in a white turban and a loincloth, and a cloth slung over his shoulder, stood before him. With an arched nose that dominated his narrow face, he resembled a determined bird. He squinted at Yeshua with unfriendly eyes.

Yeshua scrambled to his feet and sidled toward the gate.

"Brahmin. Where are you going?"

Yeshua stopped short. What did he mean? Hadn't the boy just shown him he wasn't welcome?

"You are hungry? We have breakfast soon. Let's go."

Instinctively, Yeshua raised his face and hands to the heavens in gratitude. God was indeed his shepherd. He did not need to worry.

Vasanta, the bird-boy, served him a spicy vegetable stew on top of a folded sal leaf. Around them, hundreds of bald, white-clad men of different ages ate in silence. Some were bearded, others bare faced, but all had smears of white paste across their foreheads and chests. The air vibrated with tranquility. Yeshua absorbed every moment. Despite his long, tangled locks and sand-colored tunic, nobody paid him any attention. This place was exactly what he had been looking for, where God, Krishna, the Buddha, and Mahavira had guided him. If only they would ask him to stay.

After the meal, Vasanta showed Yeshua around the grounds. Each Brahmin was given a tiny cell in the long mud huts for praying and sleeping, a space so tight that a grown man could not possibly stretch to full length. A devotional life was not supposed to be comfortable.

"Brahmin Issa," Vasanta asked as they took a seat on a low wall, "where do you keep your Upanayana threads?"

Yeshua cocked his head. What was Upanayana?

Vasanta held out the thin string of interwoven threads that hung over his shoulder and diagonally across his chest. Yeshua had noticed the strings on others before but had assumed they were nothing more than adornment.

Yeshua shook his head.

Vasanta's mouth fell open. He lifted Yeshua's tunic to look. When he didn't find any threads, he slapped his hands against his cheeks. "But you are a Brahmin——how can this be?"

"It's not a tradition in my land." Yeshua smoothed out his tunic and brushed back his hair. "What's it about, anyway?"

"Initiation to education." The boy stared at Yeshua, his black eyes wide with disbelief.

"You see," Yeshua said, "I'm from very far away, from beyond Mesopotamia and Bactria. And our Brahmins don't initiate us with sacred threads. But please, tell me more about this tradition."

"The most important day in a boy's life is the Upanayana. And only after the ceremony may we study mantras with our guru. It's not allowed before." Vasanta stopped as if he had been struck. "You at least have a guru?"

Yeshua shook his head.

"And you're so old! Hai Ram, you should have had your Upanayana when you were little. Uh-uh." Vasanta pulled on the corners of his eyes like he was going to cry. "You cannot stay here if you have not been initiated. It is a big problem." He dug his nail into Yeshua's shoulders. "What shall we do?"

Yeshua wasn't sure why initiation would be so important. It hadn't mattered anywhere else. Surely Vasanta was exaggerating.

"Maybe we could say I lost my threads on the journey. After all, I've come all the way from behind the River Indus."

Vasanta poked his finger into Yeshua's chest. "They will know. The teachers, they will see right through you. You cannot stay here. Impossible." He chewed on his finger. He clearly wanted Yeshua to stay but couldn't figure out how.

Then, as if struck by a brilliant idea, Vasanta jumped off the wall. "Wait here. I will talk to High Brahmin."

Overcome by worry, Yeshua leaned against the fig tree that grew beside the wall and watched his friend hurry back to the temple building. If only the High Brahmin would say yes.

That evening, the High Brahmin introduced Yeshua to Kahanji, a scraggy guru with soft walnut eyes that held a universe of wisdom and made him resemble an owl. Yeshua trembled with anticipation when he understood that Kahanji was one of the most revered teachers of the temple; all the other Brahmins bowed low as he passed. But before Yeshua could begin his lessons, he must first be initiated in the sacred thread ceremony.

Kahanji waited in the pool in front of the temple, his white robe flowing on the surface of the water. The ghee lamps emitted a buttery smell and tinted the surrounding Brahmins with a golden hue. Elated, Yeshua stepped into the water to meet his guru.

Kahanji welcomed him to the order and tapped Yeshua's forehead to release any evil spirits. Yeshua bowed his head and shivered when the cold steel of the guru's sharp blade scraped his head and released his locks into the water. Around the pool, hundreds of Brahmins chanted as Kahanji removed Yeshua's robe, unfastened his loincloth, and swabbed his body with a soft white cotton cloth. A fresh breeze caressed Yeshua's naked body, and he inhaled the aromatic scent of burning incense. His heart filled with love. He was in Jagannath at last, in the temple of the White Brahmins, and he had met his very own guru.

Kahanji pushed his head under the water and held it steady under the surface. Yeshua steeled his body and fought the instinct to push his guru's hands away. They wouldn't let him drown, would they? His lungs pounded against his chest. He couldn't move, shouldn't move. But like bubbles, his life was slipping away into numbness, darkness. When Kahanji finally released his grip and raised him by the chin, Yeshua coughed, spluttered, and gasped for air. Another moment under the water and he would have panicked. He would have embarrassed himself in front of all these Brahmins he wanted so desperately to join.

Kahanji's grin proved that it had been a test and he had passed. Once out of the pool, still naked, Yeshua hesitated a moment before he fell to his knees and touched his guru's feet with his hands to signify his devotion, as Vasanta had instructed. He could almost hear his father's voice, warning him that a Yehudi should never bow down to others. But Yeshua no longer cared. He needed to do this.

The chanting grew louder as the Brahmins dressed Yeshua in a fresh white robe and tied a head scarf around his head to free him from any negative karma. Yeshua glowed, as if he had been born anew.

At the ceremonial fire that night, Kahanji lifted a jar of ghee over the flames and dripped a few drops into the fire, where they sizzled and burned. Yeshua took the jar from Kahanji and recited the sacred Gayatri mantra, contemplating the meaning of each word.

> O, Master of the Universe, our protector and
>   giver of life,
> Self-existent, free from all pains, who frees the soul
>   from all troubles and fills us with happiness.
> O, Creator and Energizer of the whole universe, who
>   glows with divine illumination,
> Cleanser of all imperfections and Giver of divine
>   virtues and strengths,
> I meditate upon you to activate and enlighten me.

Kahanji twisted a long piece of white thread between his hands, doubled and tripled the length of the threads into a long string, and tied it with knots. He placed the sacred threads over Yeshua's left shoulder, pulled one end under his right arm, and tied them around Yeshua's right thumb. The Brahmins chanted faster and faster until Yeshua could no longer distinguish the words. Kahanji placed his palm on Yeshua's chest. Once again, Yeshua knelt and touched his guru's feet, then stood to face him. A Brahmin covered both their heads with a shawl, and together Kahanji and Yeshua repeated the mantra until they were united in the same rhythm. In halting Sanskrit, Yeshua vowed to recite the Gayatri mantra every day at dawn, noon, and dusk, to study the Vedas, and to serve his guru. When the shawl was removed, all the Brahmins showered Yeshua with rice and blessings.

Yeshua grinned with pride and presented Kahanji with his golden ring—an appropriate gift for the invaluable knowledge he would receive—and then his guru smeared Yeshua's forehead with red powder. The ritual had come to an end. At last Yeshua was a White Brahmin of Jagannath, a worthy student of Krishna's teachings.

In the following days, Kahanji and Yeshua went for long walks along the shore where Kahanji taught Yeshua how to focus on his breathing and how to chant the Vedic mantras to release their divine power. The chants strengthened the connection with Brahman and freed his mind from negativity. When one recited them with genuine devotion, one could control emotions like fear and anger, and—according to Kahanji—cure any illness.

They studied Kundalini, the life force that runs from the base of the back all the way to the brain.

"When awakened," Kahanji explained—and with his stick he drew an image of a body in the sand—"Kundalini activates the seven chakras, centers of divine consciousness along the spine that serve as passages into the soul and regulate primal needs." He ran his stick along Yeshua's spine. "The chakras control expression and passion. They influence the digestive process and intuition. At the base of the neck, quite logically, is the chakra of communication." Kahanji put his thumbs on Yeshua's neck and covered his ears and throat with his fingers to demonstrate the connection. "And the third eye"—he knocked at the spot between Yeshua's eyebrows—"helps us see everything as sacred and holy. Finally, at the top of the head, right outside of the body, is the crown chakra that connects to the highest state of enlightenment."

Kahanji showed him how to calm his mind, slow his breath, and center his attention on the third eye chakra until he could visualize its pulsating indigo light. But as much as Yeshua loved his guru's lessons, he hated his technique. As soon as Yeshua relaxed and let his body hunch, Kahanji hit him with his stick.

"Keep your spine straight! How can the Kundalini move through a crooked path? Sit up!"

Yeshua raised his head and relaxed his shoulders. He pressed his hands down on his thighs to straighten the curve of his spine and focused his mind on the energy center between his eyebrows until a warm flow of white light filled him up.

One day, after his lesson, he saw flashes of gold and indigo sparkle in the nothingness around him and asked Kahanji what they were.

His teacher didn't want to hear it.

"Why are you rushing? What is the hurry? Bah! Be grateful you can sense the light. Much too advanced for your age."

When Yeshua blushed at the praise, Kahanji hit him again. "No, no, no, no, no! Poisonous pride has no place here."

Vasanta was right: the teachers could see right through him.

Kahanji waited until the flush had faded from Yeshua's cheeks before he continued.

"You see, the blue light belongs to the most highly evolved saints and deities. And the golden light, young Issa, is the vibration of enlightenment. But as Krishna teaches us, we must think of the work, not the outcome. Never strive to reach higher levels; aim to solidify your connection with Brahman. That, my friend, is all that matters. If you have ears, hear me."

Yeshua assented, although he didn't agree.

"Forget about enlightenment; it may take many lifetimes. It's hard work. Look around. Most Brahmins here are far older than you, and they still haven't accomplished what you aspire to. What makes you think you're unique?"

"What about the Buddha?" Yeshua asked, his nostrils flaring with indignation. "He reached enlightenment in one lifetime, didn't he?"

Kahanji's lips twisted into a grin. He chuckled to himself, turning to stare at the blazing sun outside the high window.

Yeshua bit his tongue. When was he going to learn to keep his mouth shut? He heard his guru draw a deep breath before he returned his piercing gaze to Yeshua.

"You think you are like the Buddha, do you, Issa? Has it never occurred to you that the Buddha was born an enlightened soul? He was a reincarnation of Brahman, like Krishna."

Yeshua clenched his jaw. He knew the story well. The Buddha didn't start seeking enlightenment until he left his palace later in life. It took him years to find the way. But he found it. And so would he. Yeshua swore he would find the right path.

Despite his disagreements with Kahanji, Yeshua loved his life at the temple. The White Brahmins were more devoted than anyone he had ever met. Their day started with a bathing ritual at dawn, they meditated until noon, and they studied the sacred scriptures in the afternoon. In the evening, they earned a living by healing people from outlying villages with herbs, prayers, and the laying on of hands. Kahanji claimed that once someone was initiated to receive the pure healing energy of Brahman, their mere touch could cure. A true healer could even restore someone to perfect health just by looking at them.

The Brahmins committed every waking moment to devotion, leaving no time for idle chats. During the first weeks, Yeshua had sneaked into Vasanta's cell at night to share his thoughts about everything he had learned, but as the weeks went on, the urge for trivial gossip abated. His connection with God filled all his needs. All his questions were answered in meditation.

Every afternoon, all young Brahmins assembled for their daily lesson. With a voice like honey and an aura of peace, their teacher Arcahia could open the hearts of the toughest men and fill their souls with eternal light. Yeshua soaked up his every word and imagined the Buddha must have been just like him—incredibly friendly and infinitely wise.

He treasured the days when they discussed the meaning of the

Bhagavad Gita and how its lessons could be implemented into the Brahmins' lives.

"Never fear what's not real, never was, and never will be," Arcahia said. "What is real always was and cannot be destroyed. What do you think this means?"

Several young Brahmins offered their opinions.

"We shouldn't be afraid of anything because nothing exists?"

"Master, I'm afraid of snakes. Are you saying they don't exist?"

"But everything can be destroyed, can't it? Maybe Krishna meant to say, 'Fear not what cannot be destroyed.' Am I right?"

Arcahia encouraged them to dig deeper. Yeshua knew the answer, but his Sanskrit was still weak, and he had never before spoken up in class. He waited until everyone else had run out of ideas before he gathered his courage and cleared his throat.

"What we see isn't real," he tried, at first stumbling to find the words. "It's a product of our imagination—what we have learned to see." He paused. "What we want to see. The only thing that's real is God, and only God. That's why there's no point in being afraid, because nothing real can be destroyed. I mean, God can't be killed. And if nothing else exists but God, we don't have to be afraid of anything—because nothing unreal exists."

Yeshua looked down at his lap to avoid the stares from his fellow Brahmins. The words had flown from his mouth, and they made sense. At least to him. But what if he had been wrong?

"Yes, yes, that's it," Aracahia said. "Nothing unreal exists, and therein lies the peace of Brahman."

A few of the other Brahmins shifted in their seats. They still didn't understand. "Master, what do you mean only Brahman exists? What about me? What about my brother here? And you? And this room?"

"Yes, we do exist. But we are all part of God, of Brahman. We have nothing to fear, because only our bodies can perish; we cannot. We are real, but our bodies—they are illusions."

"My body exists. Look: it hurts when I pinch my arm!" The boy squirmed with pain, and the whole class laughed.

Arcahia laughed, too. "You believe it hurts only because you have been taught that pinching your arm will hurt. Now, if you go into a deep meditation where you are connected to Brahman and pinch yourself again, you won't feel any pain, because you are no longer connected to this body that is not real."

The students understood this point. In meditation, of course, they all knew they became one with God.

Another boy, quoting a passage from the Bhagavad Gita they had discussed earlier, said, "People will find numerous ways to separate God from the world. And although everything in the world is perishable—including your body—you should remember that everything is pervaded by the Imperishable Supreme Divine, which is Me."

"Quite so. Quite so, my dear Angada."

Yeshua exhaled with relief when the attention turned to someone else, but his cheeks still betrayed his pride. Arcahia observed him with kindness. Krishna said pride and arrogance belonged to those of demoniacal nature, and Yeshua wanted nothing to do with demons. But he had learned that the first step in becoming enlightened was to be conscious of the mistakes you made—and to learn from them.

In the late evenings, Yeshua studied Ayurvedic medicine with his guru. Kahanji taught him that everything in the universe consisted of five elements: earth, water, fire, air, and space. All diseases were caused by an imbalance of those elements or by suppressing natural urges, like yawning, sneezing, farting, or even ejaculating. Kahanji claimed that those who lived according to natural laws would never fall sick.

At first, it seemed impossible to remember how different foods affected health: vata foods caused gas, pitta foods generated bile, and kapha foods produced phlegm. "The body is like a lute, Issa," Kahanji said in his raspy voice. "When the strings are too loose or too tight, the instrument is out of tune, and the man becomes sick."

He insisted that Yeshua participate in yogic exercises to strengthen his body and release stagnant energies. He showed Yeshua how to use a small twig to clean his teeth and taught him why eating meat is harmful to spiritual development—because a man's soul absorbs the fear and suffering of the animal that was slaughtered.

"Perfect health comes from balancing the mind, body, and spirit," he said.

During visits to the village, Yeshua practiced healing under Kahanji's watchful eye. They treated fever with a potion made of cumin seed and ginger, cough with honey and ground lotus seeds, and diarrhea with a porridge of buttermilk and whole grains.

Some ailments were more severe, even horrifying. The first time Yeshua saw a man with seizures, he thought a demon had possessed him. The man's body shook so violently that his torso rose from the bed, his eyes bulged, and white froth gathered at the corners of his mouth. Yeshua was terrified, but Kahanji ordered him to hold the patient down while he slit open a vein in the patient's temple to release the poisons. Together, they chanted a mantra and massaged a paste of herbs onto the patient's scalp, hands, and chest. As the spasms eased, Yeshua smeared the ointment into the nose and onto the eyelids. Their chants silenced to whispers as the man changed from a raging monster into a dozing, perfectly sane human being.

"You understand now, Issa? A healer is someone who can inspire faith. That is all it is," Kahanji said as they walked back to the temple. "The mouth may speak to human ears, but souls are reached by souls communicating with other souls."

The seasons changed from summer to monsoon season to winter and back to summer. As younger initiates joined the temple, Yeshua was no longer the new boy; he spoke Sanskrit with a mere hint of an accent, recited the Vedas by heart, and flexed his body in challenging yoga postures like any native Brahmin.

With increased enlightenment, time seemed to stretch at will, and he always found an hour or two to spend with Vasanta discussing Brahman, the scriptures, and sometimes even women, because the memory of Ramaa had never left him. After going through stages of hating her, blaming himself for her indifference, and crying himself to sleep with longing, he had come to accept what had happened. Although he still missed her, he knew their romance had been doomed from the beginning. Their relationship would have impeded his spiritual development and stalled his journey toward becoming a guru. As the Gita taught, "The senses have been conditioned by attraction to the pleasant and aversion to the unpleasant: a man should not be ruled by them; they are obstacles in his path."

The only cloud in the otherwise clear sky was Kahanji. The old guru was never content with anything Yeshua did.

"Issa, keep your mind on the now," he said, and banged his stick so hard on the clay floor that it cracked. "Stop living in your dreams. Forget about enlightenment; it will never happen."

Some nights Yeshua tossed and turned on his thin mat, worried he would grow old and die before learning enough. All he wanted was to go out into the world and teach, fulfill his promise to God, and with Kahanji, that day might never come.

He studied the gurus around him and wondered how they had succeeded. It couldn't be just that they were older and had studied longer. If there was no death and everything around them was an illusion, wasn't age an illusion too?

What was he doing wrong?

Jagannath, AD 14

One evening, in the middle of supper, Kahanji staggered up from his seat. He swayed like a drunk man, his eyes rolled up in his head, and before anyone could react, he collapsed to the floor. The other Brahmins rushed to help him, but Yeshua couldn't move. He watched in a daze as the others left their meal and helped carry their esteemed guru to the infirmary while he just stood there. Empty of feeling. What was going on? Why was he crying?

With a jolt, Yeshua shot up from his seat. Without thinking, he ran out of the deserted canteen, through the courtyard, and to the infirmary. He pushed his way through the other Brahmins and fell to his knees next to Kahanji, who lay on a bed of mats. Yeshua stroked his teacher's wrinkled hand, barely noticing the others, who chanted sacred mantras to guide the guru's spirit to the other dimension.

"Don't leave me yet, Master," Yeshua whispered. "I'm not ready. There's so much more to learn." But his guru lay unconscious, oblivious of his words. Yeshua's tears spilled through his long beard and onto his lap as he wept in silence. Kahanji had taught him so much.

One by one, the other Brahmins left, leaving Yeshua alone with his guru.

"Go to sleep, Issa," said a Brahmin who had come to prepare Kahanji's body for his passing. "There's nothing more you can do."

But Yeshua didn't want to go. He leaned against the wall and watched the Brahmin smear Kahanji's limbs with herbal ointments, smudge holy ash on his forehead, and trickle holy water into his mouth.

Yeshua's eyelids grew heavier, and when he no longer could keep his eyes open, he dozed off into restless sleep.

"Tell Issa not to worry about enlightenment." His master's voice was raspy and thin. "Tell him Krishna's soul is alive within him." Yeshua sat up straight. Was he dreaming? He leapt forward to embrace his teacher, but Kahanji was already gone.

A desperate wail surged from the bottom of Yeshua's throat as he shrank back and wrapped his arms tightly around himself, shivering. Kahanji had been like a father to him. Strict but fair. And Yeshua had loved him. He had loved him so much.

Moments later, the Brahmins laid Kahanji's body on a cot in front of the temple gate, placed ghee lamps near his head, and lit incense around him. The High Brahmin tied a scarf around Kahanji's head, and bound his thumbs and then his toes together. The Brahmins believed grieving could hinder a soul's transition into heaven, but Yeshua couldn't help the tears running down his cheeks. He had just discovered how much he loved his guru, and with Kahanji's last breath, learned that his guru had loved him, too. At last, Yeshua understood why he had been so hard on him: he wanted Yeshua to learn all there was to know before he passed away. Perhaps it was true after all: when the student is ready, the right teacher will appear. Only sometimes the student is too arrogant to realize it.

Could it be true, though, that Krishna's soul lived within him? Yeshua covered his mouth with his hand before anyone noticed his smile. He *had* to overcome this ridiculous sense of self-importance.

The Brahmins washed Kahanji's body, removed his clothes, and draped him in a white cloth. Yeshua picked up a handful of rice from a bowl and walked around the corpse three times before stuffing the rice in his guru's mouth to nourish him for his journey. The cold skin of his departed master made the back of his neck prickle. Only the shell remained. Then he recalled the words from the Gita: "The soul is a spirit a sword can't pierce, fire can't burn, water can't melt, and air can't dry."

Together, the Brahmins placed the corpse onto the funeral pyre and walked around it three times in a long line. The High Brahmin passed a ghee lamp over the corpse.

"Oh Agni, god of fire who knows all our deeds, lead us to bliss and protect us from the deceitful attraction of sin. We offer you our devotion again and yet again." He scattered orange flowers on Kahanji's head and torso.

Yeshua wiped the tears from his eyes when they lit the pyre. He sat in silence with the others and watched his master's remains disappear in the flames. The fire consumed the cloth in moments; it took much longer for the skin and bones to burn to an unrecognizable pile of ashes and bones.

Someone grabbed his hand. Vasanta.

"Come," he said. "It's time to wash away our sorrows."

They bathed in the ritual pool, where Yeshua's tears blended with the tepid water. In a daze, he helped clean up Kahanji's hut and dispose of his belongings, preferring to keep busy over letting sorrow overwhelm him.

Vasanta placed something in Yeshua's palm and closed his fingers around it. The cold metal burned his hand. He didn't have to look to know what it was: the golden ring Yeshua had presented to Kahanji on the day of his Upanayana.

"Keep it, Issa. It will remind you of everything he taught you."

Jagannath, AD 14

Kahanji's passing changed the rhythm of Yeshua's life. When he no longer had to study Ayurveda or visit sick villagers, his afternoons and evenings allowed for independent study. But the freedom made him restless, and he found himself yearning for someone to tell him what to do.

On the tenth day after Kahanji's passing, the day his soul would join the gods of his ancestors, Yeshua and Vasanta sneaked out of the compound to explore the town of Jagannath. The boys walked in silence until they reached the market with its stalls of mangoes and palm fruits, cotton fabrics in all colors, hot lentil curries, and chai. Yeshua tingled with excitement. How he had missed the sounds of shouting, laughing, bargaining, and swearing in the four years since he had left the real world!

But the poor people ducked away from them. The women hid behind their veils to avoid polluting the passing Brahmins. Vasanta clutched Yeshua's arm. "Krishna teaches that we're all equal, doesn't he? That we shouldn't discriminate between saints and sinners, the good and bad, or friends and enemies."

"Of course."

"Then why do these women fear us? Don't they know we're good fellows?"

Yeshua put his arm around him. "Perhaps they can't see through the veil of illusion. They judge us based on our work, the color of our skin, and our education, because that's what they've always been told to do.

Only those who live every moment in Brahman understand this. Like you."

An idea was born in his mind, a faint echo of a dream he had suppressed.

That night, after their evening meal, Yeshua knocked on the door of guru Arcahia's cell.

"Master, forgive the interruption." Yeshua bowed as low as he could before he entered the cell. "I'm well aware that there's a lot more to learn, and of course I'm a mere beginner of Vedic studies. But can't we perhaps go and speak among the villagers? Teach them what we know?"

Arcahia nodded in deep thought, seemingly unsurprised by the question. He looked Yeshua deep in the eyes and blasted him with a love so strong, Yeshua almost lost his balance.

"Let me speak to the High Brahmin," he said. "I'll see what we can do."

With those words, Arcahia flicked his wrist to show the discussion was over. He closed his eyes, took a deep breath, and resumed his meditation. Yeshua pressed his palms together, bowed his head, and backed out of the cell.

But he couldn't sleep. The marketplace with its vibrant noise, scents, and colors had tickled all his senses, but he pitied the impoverished people who had shrugged out of their way in fear. He would like to do something for them, change their lives. But how? And then he remembered the wave of pure love Arcahia had sent through him. He sighed; to reach such enlightenment, he had to free himself of all desires, including the need to save others, and even the yearning for enlightenment.

Had he set himself an impossible goal?

A week passed. Two weeks. Three weeks. Still no word from Arcahia. Yeshua meditated, performed his daily chores, and attended his lessons as if nothing had changed. He tried to be satisfied with what he had, but every night he dreamed that he was a guru who walked among the common people and taught them about God. The more he tried to quell his desire, the stronger it burned. Meditation became his only refuge, his only source of peace.

One day, in meditation, he heard God's voice as clear as any man's: "You are already holy in your heart. Serve me, and you will bring salvation to the world."

Yeshua looked up and around him in the darkness of his cell. Was someone playing a trick on him? But then his eyes filled with tears; it was the same message he had heard as a child. If studying in this temple was all that God had planned for him, it had to be good enough.

The next day, Arcahia called him aside after class. "Issa, the High Brahmin has asked me to make a pilgrimage to the holy city of Benares with three Brahmins." Yeshua waited patiently for Arcahia to continue. "I've asked that Vasanta join me."

Yeshua nodded, surprised that he didn't feel envious at all, only excited for Vasanta; a pilgrimage would work wonders for him.

"Guru Udraka, he will also join us." Arcahia paused and looked straight through Yeshua, as if waiting for his reaction.

"May your journey be safe and successful." Yeshua bowed his head and pressed his palms together in front of his heart.

"You would like to accompany us, is that correct?"

Yeshua smiled. Was Arcahia testing him? "May Brahman guard your every step. May your speech be one with your mind, and your mind be one with your—"

"Issa, we would be pleased if you joined us. It might benefit you to see how our teaching affects the common man."

This time Yeshua's heart didn't skip a single beat. At peace, he nodded his assent, just as Kahanji had taught him, aware of his own irrelevance.

Yeshua cherished walking for hours on end, sometimes without uttering a single word. He enjoyed not knowing what they would discover around the next bend and found it always looked different from expected. The Brahmins—two gurus and two apprentices—crossed the lush lands of Orissa. They paused in every village to share lessons from the Vedas in exchange for food and lodging—just like the nomadic preachers in Palestine his father so despised. Often they were met by a crowd of excited peasants who had heard about the White Brahmins who preached the word of God. But Yeshua's excitement dwindled every time the village men chased away the women and children. Udraka also shooed away the poor farmers, craftsmen, and any servants who dared approach, reminding Yeshua that only those of warrior and priestly families were permitted to learn about the Holy Scriptures.

Arcahia and Udraka took turns teaching, each in his own style. Arcahia spoke with passion and treated all strangers like long-lost friends. Udraka, despite his vast knowledge, stuttered through a dry and practiced script. If someone in the audience raised his voice either in disagreement or to express an opinion, Udraka raised his fist and ordered him to leave. Yeshua couldn't help but wonder what Kahanji would have done. Perhaps he would have hit Udraka with his stick and asked him in his gruff voice if a demon had seized him. Yeshua grinned at the thought. He missed his guru. Kahanji had been ever so hard to please, never satisfied with anything but perfection, but he had taught Yeshua practically everything he knew.

Every few days, Yeshua asked Arcahia when he could teach, but the answer was always the same: "Be patient. Your time will come. Let us make the mistakes."

Yeshua quieted his ego and welcomed the unique opportunity to study the gurus as they passed through dozens of villages. Despite his temper, Udraka could be quite funny. Once he overcame his shyness and his expressions became more animated, the crowd couldn't get enough of his stories. Arcahia's strength lay in his clarity and his positive disposition when something went wrong—like the day his class was interrupted by a small herd of curious goats or when they were caught in a downpour and had to seek shelter in a women's tent. And, Yeshua found, when they used personal anecdotes of how a passage of the Upanishads had changed their lives, everyone leaned forward and devoured each word.

During the walks between villages, Yeshua practiced his teaching silently in his head. He pictured himself as the perfect speaker—relating anecdotes in his own words and with his own gestures. He fantasized about using parables to get people involved in the narrative and make them remember it. And if they didn't quite understand the message at first, perhaps they would ponder the story until the actual meaning became clear. One day he hoped to be a light-bearer, someone who ignited fires in dormant souls and awakened them to the Brahman inside that Arcahia said was alive in every being.

After six months, the Brahmins reached the valley town of Rajagriha, not far from the Holy Mother Ganges River. That night, as the boys rolled out their sleeping mats in the yard of the local temple, Udraka called out, "Vasanta Brahmas, tomorrow you will teach."

Vasanta froze, his arms still raised to shake his mat. "Me?"

But Udraka had already pulled his sleeping cloth over his face to signal he was not to be disturbed.

"Yeshua!" Vasanta said, his face tense with fear. "You heard Udraka? What he said?"

Yeshua watched his friend, stunned. Vasanta had lived in the temple all his life and studied the scriptures since childhood, but he wasn't ready. He forced himself to swallow his pride and put his arm around Vasanta. "Don't worry, you'll do fine!"

"But I don't even know how to start," Vasanta said, his voice choking. "I need more time."

Yeshua yawned, rubbing his eyes, and looked longingly at his sleeping mat, then back at his friend. "Let's practice," he said, and took Vasanta by the hand. "And I promise, by tomorrow morning, you'll know exactly what to do."

They walked barefoot through the rice fields. The moon played hide-and-seek among cinnamon-colored clouds in a dark blue sky as Vasanta and Yeshua discussed the story they loved the best, where Krishna tells Arjuna he is an incarnation of God. Vasanta repeated the story over and over, going over passages where he stumbled until the words and gestures were etched into his memory.

Yeshua encouraged him. "Look people in the eye, pause to give them time to consider what you have said. And smile. If you lose your way, take a deep breath and continue. Remember: friendliness goes a long way."

By the time they returned to their sleeping mats, their feet were wrinkled from walking in the inundated fields. Birds were chirping in the trees. It wouldn't be long before their gurus woke for morning prayers.

Vasanta dragged his feet through the dew-laden grass up the hill to Vulture's Peak, where legend said the Buddha once had preached on a plateau overlooking the fertile valley. Eagles soared above, and rabbit-like pikas peered out from crevices in the jagged rock face. A fresh breeze promised a perfect day.

At the top of the hill, they lit incense and spread flower petals in front of the provisional rock altar. Sweat trickled down Vasanta's face as they chanted a mantra to open the lesson. He had closed his eyes, and furrowed his brow in deep concentration. At the last verse, Arcahia, Udraka, and Yeshua took a seat beside the altar, and left Vasanta alone before the crowd.

Blushing, Vasanta drew a deep breath and closed his eyes again, breathing in and out until he had regained his center.

"Friends of Rajagriha, I salute you. Welcome." His voice trembled.

Yeshua cringed. Vasanta didn't aspire to teach; he would happily spend his life meditating in a cave, isolated from the rest of the world. But as the audience grew quiet, Vasanta garnered his courage. Old or young, well dressed or in tatters, they all stared in awe at the White Brahmin before them. Yeshua's heartbeat slowed to a normal pace.

"Today I will tell you about Krishna, who came to earth as a reincarnation of the god Vishnu. He was a young…" Vasanta ran out of breath and he blushed again. He scratched his beard, drew a deep breath, and attempted a smile. "Krishna was a handsome man—very handsome—and he, he was working…as a charioteer for…for…for—"

"Prince Arjuna," Udraka supplied, "who was going to war to—" and he motioned for Vasanta to carry on.

"Um…regain the…kingdom. The kingdom…that his family had lost…"

Vasanta stuttered and staggered through the story. Udraka and Arcahia filled in a phrase here, an image there, and interrupted at times to make sure the audience understood the message: when you eliminate distress from your life, only blissful enlightenment remains.

At the end of the lesson, when the sun had reached high enough to burn their scalps, almost everyone stayed to ask the gurus questions and hear more about this incredible deity called Krishna.

Yeshua stole away to meditate. He tried to be happy for Vasanta, but there was a hole in his heart. Vasanta had failed the test. What if his failure meant that his teachers would never give Yeshua a chance?

He might never be allowed to teach.

Benares, AD 15

The silhouette of the ancient city of Benares emerged through the mist across the Ganges River, sketching the horizon with temples and domes. A light haze colored the buildings a pale rose, as if the entire city were enveloped in dreams. Yeshua shivered with excitement as they waited to be ferried on a raft across the river.

The road brimmed with the terminally ill, the aged, and the crippled, who crawled on their hands and knees or staggered forward one step at a time, determined to reach the other side of the river before death caught them. There, at last, they could die in peace, because everyone knew that dying in Benares was a sure way to Nirvana.

By the time they crossed the river, night had already fallen. In the distance, fires lit up the embankment and the wind carried the smell of searing flesh.

"Are those people cooking?" Yeshua asked, surprised that they would serve meat in such a sacred place.

Arcahia put a finger to his lips as he stared out over the water. A small black log floated past. Yeshua was about to pick it up when he realized what he was looking at: five charred fingers at the end of a scorched arm. They weren't roasting meat at the fires; they were burning corpses. People came to Benares to die. Their bodies were cremated and the remains returned to Mother Ganges.

When Arcahia saw that Yeshua had understood, he returned his focus to the prayer beads in his hand, passing them through his fingers, repeating a silent mantra.

It was well past midnight when they reached the shore. Yeshua and Vasanta followed their teachers up the embankment, past the men and women sleeping on the wide stairs, through a labyrinth of dark alleys, up more steps, around a corner, and down another alley until Yeshua had lost all sense of direction. The mud stuck to his feet, and the pack on his back grew heavier with every step.

"Master, it's late," he said. "Can we please stop here and rest?"

"It is not safe. A little bit farther, boys. Don't give up." Arcahia increased his pace with long, vigorous strides. Yeshua and Vasanta looked at each other and sighed. What was that passage in the Upanishads? "A man must free himself from the impulses that tie him to his body and become indifferent to feeling hungry, thirsty, cold, warm, or tired." Yes, that was it. Yeshua concentrated on separating from his body, like he did when he was hungry. He stayed close behind Arcahia, who sprinted up a hill as if they had just started walking.

Yeshua closed his eyes and breathed in deeply. He imagined he had just woken up, that his limbs were full of life and energy. When he opened his eyes, the fatigue was gone. The pack on his back that had weighed him down only moments before was as light as the wind. He started running, his legs almost flying away with him, and he reached the top in no time.

Arcahia winked. "You're learning, Issa."

For a moment, Yeshua let himself bask in the praise. Pride was a much more difficult animal to tame.

"Careful, now." Arcahia struck him gently with his walking stick, always aware of what Yeshua was thinking.

At last, the four White Brahmins unrolled their mats in an empty field and lay down to sleep under a grove of trees. A soft breeze cooled their overheated bodies. Before long, they were all asleep.

A troop of monkeys woke them with their chatter. They danced around the sleeping Brahmins, shrieking and pulling at their sacks. Udraka jumped up and chased futilely after them. Yeshua laughed so hard that tears rolled down his face. The monkeys were clever: as soon as Udraka chased one away, another was digging into the guru's travel sack. Udraka screamed and swore and whipped at them until the animals finally gave up and scurried away to find food elsewhere.

"They're just monkeys, Teacher!" Vasanta laughed. All his life he had seen simians from the nearby jungle steal a banana here, a naan there. "They're hungry, just like us."

"But I've got nothing," Udraka said. He turned his sack inside out for proof.

"So there's nothing to steal." Arcahia chuckled.

Udraka muttered to himself as he put his clothes back. Then he swung around with a defiant grin. "They wanted to take my loincloth! You want me to walk around naked? Is that it?"

Yeshua and Vasanta doubled over with laughter. Arcahia put his arm around Udraka to calm him. They were used to each other's quirks.

"Let's bathe in the Ganges," Arcahia said, after the laughter had subsided.

It wasn't a suggestion.

What a pell-mell: people, cows, monkeys, snake charmers, wherever they looked. Men and women stood in the river, water up to their waists, chanting. Holy men in mustard robes and turbans meditated on the stairs, their faces streaked with red and yellow dyes. Cows rummaged through heaps of garbage, poking their noses for anything edible, and children chased monkeys down the alleys. The White Brahmins of Jagannath might have stood out in their impeccably white robes, but nobody stared. In this city of God, everyone minded their own business.

On the stairs, a beggar without arms and with mere stumps for legs wormed his way toward Yeshua, pleading with his eyes for something to eat. Yeshua's chest tightened. He didn't even have a crumb of bread to share. Perhaps later, once he had something to eat, he could come back.

He smiled apologetically at the beggar and walked away.

"Why don't you bathe?" Vasanta called to Yeshua. He had already plunged his lanky body into the murky water. "Come, it will refresh you."

Yeshua dipped his toes in the river; the coolness enticed him. He stepped into the water, closed his eyes, and opened his heart to receive whatever Mother Ganges would offer. Another step, and he was up to his ankles. He inched forward, reciting the Gayatri mantra in his mind until he was up to his neck in the river. He squatted, lowered his head, and dove under the surface until he could no longer hold his breath. He sprang up, gasped for air, and swam forward. His head nearly exploded with light. He swam under and above the surface, stroke by stroke, until he was saturated with the river's blessing.

As if cast into another dimension, Yeshua sat on the bank and crossed his legs in lotus position. The world had shifted. The sounds around him were a hundred times sharper, the smells a thousand times stronger, and everything around him was enveloped in waves of energy. He wanted to stay right in that moment and never return. Nothing, absolutely nothing else mattered. The world was a perfect place, and the people around him were sublime. The white cows grinned at him with their big teeth. The cripples had come here to fulfill their purpose. A healthy body didn't guarantee happiness any more than the lack of arms caused grief. Ultimate bliss resided in the soul, the atma. The atma was God. And everyone and everything was God.

Yeshua could have stayed in trance forever, but the aroma of fried pastries and milky chai teased him back. His fellow Brahmins had spread out an assortment of foods on the stairs and feasted on spicy vegetable samosas. But Yeshua was no longer hungry. His body was satiated with spirit, and his physical needs seemed arbitrary. Instead, he remembered his silent promise to the beggar. He selected a puffed pastry stuffed with lentils, picked up a mug of tea, and returned to feed the cripple.

The man seemed to have expected Yeshua's return. How easy it was to communicate with a mute: Yeshua simply opened his heart and connected their atmas. The beggar had lived on this very spot for years. His life wasn't bad. He was always hungry but never starving. Most pilgrims were generous, and barely a day passed without his receiving something to eat. But could Yeshua please bring him closer to the river for a blessing?

The man wheezed with delight when Yeshua carried him down the stairs and placed him waist-deep into the water. He held the cripple in his arms and helped him float in the sacred waves. Quietly, Yeshua chanted a healing mantra while the cripple absorbed the sacredness of Mother Ganges.

When Yeshua placed him back on the stairs above the river, the cripple gleamed, his face twisted in a smile. And when Yeshua left him there, he knew he had done enough. Kindness was free, and it was something he had in abundance.

They settled into temporary lodgings on the roof of a local temple. The next morning, Arcahia asked each Brahmin to walk around town and bring back a recommendation on the best way to preach in this city. In smaller villages, people hungered for news and welcomed entertainment, but Benares teemed with competition; it was possibly the only place in the world where holy men outnumbered common people.

Yeshua made his way toward the outskirts of town. He sat on a fallen tree trunk to watch a farmer and his family plow a field. They pointed at him and gossiped, perhaps wondering what a holy man could want with a family of peasants. He waved.

One of the sons put down his digger and walked over with his sister. "Namaste, Brahmin," he said, and bowed. "My papa invites you for a meal, if you please."

Yeshua's stomach growled with anticipation, and he realized he hadn't eaten that day. Besides, turning down an offer of food would be an immense insult.

"That's very kind," he said, and he followed the young man and the girl across the field to their home. A roughly made mud-brick wall stuffed with hay enclosed a courtyard kitchen with three small huts: one for drying and storing crops and two sleeping quarters with worn blankets for doors. A cow seemed to be their only livestock.

"What brings you here, Your Holiness?" the boy asked as they sat down in the shade of the house, their backs against the wall. Yeshua told him how he had traveled all the way from Palestine, crossed Sindh, and made his way east to Jagannath, where he had lived with the Brahmins for many years. Now he had come to Benares on a teaching pilgrimage.

"Tell me something, then, will you?"

Yeshua hesitated. He could be punished for teaching peasants. But in all honesty, as a carpenter, he also belonged to the Shudra caste. What harm would it do?

"Very well, let me tell you a story. And please, come sit with us." Yeshua gestured to the girl who peeked at them from the doorway. He was already committing an offense by mingling with peasants; there was no reason to exclude her. And he liked the idea of resting his eyes on an attractive woman for a change. He scanned her voluptuous body as she squatted beside them. Her delicate bare feet were covered with gray mud, and her long hair was unkempt. The plump breasts that burst against her threadbare sari made him tremble. He had to think of something else—fast. He closed his eyes, tugged at his beard, and breathed deeply to quiet his pounding heart. *Think of God*, he told himself. *Think of Krishna, of Buddha. Physical desires merely separate us from God.* When a glowing light warmed his heart chakra, he knew the most difficult moment had passed.

Yeshua opened his eyes and centered his attention on the boy to avoid the girl's entrancing black eyes.

"Once there was a man who owned a large property of a thousand acres," he said. "The man had three competent sons, but only one could inherit his fortune. To test them, he gave each son a piece of land to manage in any way he pleased. The only condition was that each had to give the father a share of the profits. The oldest son, a greedy man, immediately confiscated his brothers' lands. He employed one brother as a foreman, and made the youngest a slave who would provide the labor. Thus, the oldest brother enjoyed life as a wealthy man and visited the property only once in a while to take his earnings. The middle brother earned a fair salary, while the youngest brother toiled from early morning until sunset under the unforgiving sun and earned nothing.

"When the father came to check on his sons, he was shocked to find that the oldest had made himself king while the middle son happily exploited the youngest brother. He threw the oldest son into prison. He stripped the middle son of all belongings and sent him away. Then he released his youngest son from the chains and told him to walk away in peace as a free man and never let anyone take advantage of him again.

"After a couple of years had passed, the father called his three sons to him. They all admitted their mistakes and vowed that they had learned their lessons. Thus, their father forgave them. Again, he divided his land into three equal shares and begged them to follow the laws, respect one another, and live in peace."

Yeshua paused. The young man gawked, his eyes wide. The girl gasped behind her head scarf.

"What does it mean?" the boy asked. "Why are you telling us this story?"

"It's about the castes. The father is Brahman. And please, call me Issa."

They nodded, deep in thought.

"Issa," the girl finally asked, "will God also break women's chains one day?"

"Enough already!" Her brother laughed. "Go and cook for us like a proper girl."

But the question intrigued Yeshua. He had never heard a woman speak of being in chains before.

"Wait!" he called as she turned to leave. "You're right. Brahman says all his children shall be free, even the servants, untouchables, and women. We're all children of God. Our souls are part of Brahman. So, yes, you may rise up and God will break your chains."

When the rest of the family returned home, they sat together on a blanket in the courtyard to eat. Yeshua talked and laughed and listened to the family's stories, making sure to include everyone in the conversation.

But his thoughts kept returning to the girl. He had been living with men for so long, he had forgotten how charming women could be, how enticing the swell of their breasts, and how they could communicate by a subtle raising of an eyebrow or the faintest wink. Yeshua wondered if she would allow him to touch her. He wouldn't, of course. She was the only daughter in a respectable family. Her virginity was reserved for whomever she married. And a Brahmin could never marry a peasant girl. They had no future together, unless he brought her home to Palestine. Yeshua shook his head. But he couldn't help fantasizing.

"We should preach to the Vaishyas," Yeshua suggested that night when he returned to the temple roof.

Udraka and Arcahia pretended they hadn't heard him.

"Farmers?" Vasanta asked, and crinkled his nose in disapproval.

Yeshua nodded.

"Exactly. Listen, they're starved for knowledge," Yeshua continued. "I know we've never taught them before, but——Benares is different. Hundreds of Brahmins congregate here. They're established and trusted, and we're not. Who's going to listen to us here?"

Yeshua paused. He had never dared to speak freely to his teachers before. It must have been the energy carried over from meeting with the farmer family. He meant it, though. The whole idea of castes was nothing more than a system created by some men as a means of controlling others.

"How can you even think like that?" Udraka spat out the words. "You've reached such a high level of awareness, and you still don't understand?"

Yeshua took a deep breath to calm his heartbeat. He was using the wrong approach. "I'm sorry, Master Udraka, Master Arcahia." He bowed his head to show them he didn't want to argue. "I don't mean any disrespect. It's just that as I was walking around town all day, looking at people, it hit me: the peasants. They could offer a new, a different path to deliver our message. But you're right, I was mistaken."

The teachers accepted his apology and continued eating. They had collected quite a feast: sautéed chickpeas, vegetable curry, bread, fruit—and a boy who refilled their mugs of chai after every sip. Yeshua sat back to listen as the other Brahmins spoke about their day.

Vasanta had spent the entire day by the river observing other Brahmins. They simply sat down next to people and told them stories about Brahman. Arcahia said he liked the approach but it would take too long to spread their message if they had to teach one man at a time.

Udraka had walked among the many temples to study how the locals prayed and how their teachers taught. Most temples, built of mud or stone, were dedicated to Shiva, Mitra, Surya, or Indra, but he hadn't seen any dedicated to Krishna. If they built a temple in his name, it would attract the curious. Arcahia seemed to contemplate the idea but finally said it was an impossible endeavor because they had no money. Maybe sometime in the future.

When it was Yeshua's turn to describe his day, he hesitated. He couldn't tell the truth, but lying was not an option. Arcahia would see through him like water. He had to make something up while staying as close to the truth as possible. Yeshua sent a silent prayer to God to help him sound believable.

"At first, I just walked along the streets. Oh, mighty Krishna, what a city! Such a magical energy, like an ethereal spirit." He was blathering, trying to collect his thoughts. "I stood in the shadows and observed the street life. How can they live in such destitution and stay absolutely clean? Such a miracle."

Vasanta and Udraka shifted in their seating positions. They had no idea where this was going. Arcahia watched him, a smirk playing at the corner of his mouth.

"You see, purity—that's what matters to the people of Benares. Purity of body and mind. And that's what we should preach." Yeshua clapped his hands to drive in his point.

Udraka frowned.

Arcahia stepped in. "I believe his morning bath in the Ganges washed away Issa's mind." He laughed. "What he wants to say, I think, is that the people of Benares consider cleanliness of utmost importance. I, too, walked along the shores of the river, and I saw how they wash their clothes and beat them clean: even the beggars try to keep their rags unsoiled. Issa's point is"—Arcahia looked straight at Yeshua to show who held higher rank—"we have to make sure we are always thoroughly clean when we go out to teach."

Yeshua sighed with relief. His teacher had saved him from embarrassment. No matter how much Arcahia knew, he would never judge.

"This town is overrun with preachers." Arcahia looked from one to the other of them. "We are fortunate to have this temple roof for ourselves. Not everyone will find free lodging."

Udraka had finished his meal, and he lay down on his side to rest and half closed his sleepy eyes. Yeshua peeled a mango and sucked on the sweet flesh.

"What makes us different from the others here is our experience," Arcahia continued. "We've spent almost a year walking from village to village. We have met all sorts of people and have answered every kind of question. We know how to tell a good story. Because of this, we can pick any place in town. Anywhere. And if we go back to the same location every day, people will come. What do you think?"

No one else had considered an answer that simple. Of course they could just preach. Soon enough, someone would stop and listen. Then someone else. And eventually there would be an entire crowd.

"Wonderful," Yeshua said, happy to be off the hook.

"Splendid, Issa." Arcahia licked the crumbs from his mouth. "Because you will be the first to teach here. Tomorrow."

Benares, AD 15

Sweat trickled down Yeshua's armpits, staining his robe. He knew how to speak and he knew people would listen, but he had never been appraised before. He must impress his teachers, show them he was worthy. His head spun and he could barely breathe. Teaching was what God had called him to do; it was the reason he had left Palestine and had brought such disgrace upon his family.

On a plateau above the river, among screaming children and bleating goats, Yeshua sat down to meditate and ask for guidance. He drew in the energies of everyone around him to get a sense of what they needed to hear. By nightfall, he was ready. God would guide him, and there was no reason to worry. He floated on clouds of anticipation all the way back to the temple roof, ready for a good night's sleep.

But Benares never slept. All night long, the sounds of people chanting, cows bellowing, and dogs fighting over scraps of meat lingered over the city and kept him awake. Despite a night of interrupted sleep, Yeshua woke with a grin before sunrise. This was his day. Today his destiny would come to fruition.

By the river, Yeshua waved at his friend, the cripple who lay on the stone steps at this most spiritual hour and listened to the cascade of prayers around him. The peacefulness he emanated warmed Yeshua's heart.

When the bells from nearby temples chimed to announce the arrival of a new day, Yeshua and the other White Brahmins from Jagannath immersed themselves in the water to chant their temple mantra.

Om, let us meditate on the deity whose belly was tied by a rope.
O, Universal Spirit, give me higher intellect and peace, and let
Lord Krishna illuminate my mind.

Yeshua was more than ready: safe and guided, aware nothing could go wrong. He couldn't wait for the crowd's reaction, to see their faces transformed by the light he shared. He loved nothing more in the entire world than seeing God's grace reflected in others.

The White Brahmins set up their altar at a corner where two streets crossed. While Yeshua gathered his thoughts, Arcahia lit the clumps of incense and Udraka and Vasanta spread marigold petals on the white blanket where he would speak. They chanted to alert passersby that prayer was about to start. Yeshua sat cross-legged on the blanket to prepare. His chant emerged from deep within his soul, and, focusing on each word of the mantra, he connected with God. He opened his chakras, allowing the Kundalini to rise like a coiled serpent through the energy centers along his spine and fill him with love.

Elated and completely relaxed, Yeshua opened his eyes and looked out across the square. Only two men had stopped to listen. He cleared his throat, ran his fingers through his beard, and smiled. "Welcome, my honored friends. They call me Issa. I'm a White Brahmin of Jagannath. I have come here this wondrous morning to tell you about God—Brahman—and how you can find him."

The men waited expectantly. Yeshua drew a deep breath and continued. "You may know that God cannot be found in one place; he exists everywhere. But did you know that God's meeting place with you is right here"—he patted his chest—"within your heart? If you stay still and listen, you will hear his voice like a whisper. That voice is God."

The men stared at him in silence, but Yeshua noticed a spark of interest in their eyes. Three passing adolescents stopped to listen.

"Do you ever wonder how to tell whether the voice within you is God? This is how; once you open the ears of your soul to connect with God, you'll notice the voice within you is completely different from your own thoughts: it's kind and calm and loving. All you have to do is be still, open your heart, and listen. God is waiting to speak to you."

"What does he say, then?" one of the young men wanted to know. "What does Brahman tell you?"

Yeshua blushed with delight, excited that someone had interacted with him. "He speaks of love. He asks us to serve our fellow men, to offer strangers a helping hand. Give to those who wish you harm or have nothing to offer you in return. Assist the poor and the weak. Treat others as you would treat yourself. Why? Because we are all one. If you help someone without expecting anything in return, you have served God and also helped yourself. Brahman is the sublime presence in all beings."

Yeshua paused to let his words sink in. He nodded invitingly at a few newcomers who had stopped to see why a gathering had formed at this busy junction.

"God doesn't want us to harm others. He expects kindness. He wants us to unite with him in our thoughts and actions. And when you do, he will dry your tears, quiet your fears, and fill your heart with peace."

A withered man in his last years of life asked, "But if God is everywhere, tell me—to which temple should I bring gifts? Where should I make offerings?"

"Brahman has no use for gifts. He doesn't want us to waste plants or grains in his name. The food you offer your murtis belongs in the hungry mouths of the poor, and the flowers belong in the hands of your beloved. You see, when you help someone who is truly in need, a heavenly scent of incense rises up and alerts God that a good deed has been done. It will return to you as a blessing."

Yeshua rose to walk among the onlookers. "The murtis, your holy statues," he said, "they can neither see you nor feel you. They cannot eat the food or appreciate your prayers. They are nothing but objects. God, on the other hand, is alive within you. Make your human heart your altar and offer him alms with the fire of love. This is how you may truly worship Brahman."

Yeshua looked from one stunned face to the next, assured that he had planted a seed of wisdom in their hearts.

"Master, I want to follow you." A gray-bearded man, tall and noble, in a worn Brahmin's robe approached him. "Baba, how can I become your apprentice?"

Yeshua shook his head. "I'm your brother, not a master. Listen, I'm neither higher nor lower than you." Yeshua stood on his toes and reached up to pat the man's shoulder. Then he looked out at his audience. "Love your fellow man, but praise and follow only God. He's the One."

With that, Yeshua bowed his head and sat down next to Vasanta. Arcahia stood to let the listeners know they would return the next day.

Yeshua's heart raced with pride. At least a dozen people had come to listen, and perhaps one or two had truly heard his message. He might have made a difference in someone's life. God had filled him with the sweetest nectar and had spoken through him.

"Quite sufficient," Udraka said, and patted his back. "But next time, try to incorporate a story, as you have heard us do."

Arcahia was more encouraging. "Well done! You have a way with words and you connected rather well with the listeners." He paused, and Yeshua waited for the *but* he was sure must follow. "But when somebody asks to become your apprentice, the answer is always yes."

"I was speaking about forming a direct relationship with God. I asked them to abandon their shrines and shift their adoration from deities straight to Brahman. How then can I tell someone to follow a man?"

"You're not just a man, Issa," Udraka said. "You're a Brahmin."

"Of course."

There was no point in arguing. Next time, he would use a parable and everyone would be happy. But in his heart he knew he had shown how White Brahmins were different from other gurus and had awoken their interest. Tomorrow, the crowd would likely be bigger; that was all that mattered for now.

He was right. The Brahmins' following grew so fast, they had to move their lessons to the banks of the river to not interfere with local business and trade. Arcahia and Udraka remained the principal teachers, but every so often Yeshua and Vasanta were given an opportunity to teach. Although Vasanta still struggled with fluency, he appealed to the youngest listeners. Yeshua was more confident, but found himself increasingly constrained by his teachers' interruptions. As long as they were with him, he couldn't truly speak his mind.

The solution appeared one day when Yeshua came upon a crying toddler who was carrying firewood to one of the cremation ghats. The little boy had fallen and was bleeding from an open gash in his knee. When no other adults reached out to help, Yeshua picked the boy up and cradled him in his arms. The child wriggled like a trapped rat, trying to free himself.

"Where are you going, son?" The boy wailed and squirmed, his blood smearing Yeshua's white robe. Yeshua tried to calm him, holding him closer to his chest. He closed his eyes to connect with Brahman, and placed a hand over the boy's knee to halt the bleeding.

Everyone who passed them stared and shook their heads in disapproval.

One man attempted to pry Yeshua's arms open. "Let him go. Now!"

Another blocked Yeshua's way. "Brahmin, are you out of your mind, carrying an untouchable?"

Yeshua pushed them away. What kind of world was this, where grown-ups were expected to ignore an injured child? And where were the parents? The boy was far too young to carry such a heavy load. Yeshua took the boy to the river and washed his wound. The cut was deep and wouldn't stop bleeding.

Yeshua removed his head scarf, ripped it into strips, and dressed the wound. He placed his hands over the knee and recited healing mantras to relieve the pain, and soon the child's cries softened to whimpers.

When Yeshua arrived at the funeral pyre where the toddler's father worked, he found the family gathered for a meal.

"Mai, please, here's your boy." He handed the child to his mother. "Don't worry: it's a frightful wound, but he will be fine."

The father watched Yeshua with suspicion. "You not come from here?"

"No, but—"

"Then you not know—about us."

"Yes, I do. You are children of God, like me." He touched the father's shoulder. "I also know something else: Brahman loves you."

The father frowned, staring at the bowl of thin soup in front of him. "That is a lie."

"No, it's true. He loves me. And he loves *you*."

"Why do you say that? Who are you? What do you want from us?"

"I'm a simple man, nothing more. But my destiny is to deliver God's word. To everyone."

"You are mistaken." He pushed Yeshua away. "Just go."

But Yeshua didn't leave. Instead, he sat on the mat next to the cremator's wife, tore a piece from the large flatbread, and put it in his mouth to show he wasn't afraid to be soiled.

"God watches our actions," Yeshua said. "He doesn't judge us on what we do for a living. He doesn't care if you handle corpses. He looks into your heart and sees your kindness. To him, your soul is as precious as that of any priest or warrior."

Yeshua sensed their unease but continued.

"Listen, once there was a farmer who owned a field of ripening sorghum. One day he noticed that some of the plants had broken leaves, and he ordered his workers to cut and burn the damaged plants and to preserve only the perfect ones. When the time of harvest arrived, the farmer found his field completely empty. Furious, he confronted his workers, demanding an explanation. They replied that they had followed his orders: they had cut and burned all the flawed sorghum plants. But once they were done, not a single stalk was left."

The cremator's face was blank.

"You see, no one is perfect," Yeshua said. "Brahmin, warrior, or slave. We all have flaws. But God loves us all nonetheless."

"But we are untouchables."

"You may have a broken leaf or two, but so does everyone else." Yeshua delivered the same lesson as on his first day in Benares. He showed the man and his wife how to connect with God in their hearts, and taught them how loving the people who mistreated them could only bring them joy.

When Yeshua left, his heart brimmed with excitement. He had found a way to fulfill his life's purpose, how to serve God by teaching the needy about salvation while still adhering to his teachers' rules. Every afternoon, instead of meditating, he would seek out those who hungered for the words of God: the merchants, the peasants, and the untouchables. He would be their guru.

A few months later, Arcahia stopped him as Yeshua was leaving for his "midday meditation."

"Issa, come here."

Udraka and Vasanta looked up from their mats where they lay resting.

"Have you heard anything about a Brahmin who preaches to the Shudras?" Arcahia paused.

Yeshua wanted to shake his head, but couldn't move.

"They say he wears white, like us. He has a shaved head and a long brown beard." Arcahia paused. "And light skin."

A chill ran up Yeshua's spine. "Master," he said softly, twisting the strands of his beard, hoping to forestall Arcahia's anger, "tell me again, how should we view the different castes? Wouldn't you say that in the eyes of Brahman, we are all equal?"

Arcahia clenched his jaw. "Stop the foolishness, Issa. You haven't heard, then? The local Brahmins are furious. They are threatening to kill this White Brahmin."

Yeshua had heard the rumors, but people always talked, and it was mostly idle chatter. "Master, what do you honestly think? Doesn't God love everyone the same?"

"We have been over this before. We are all part of him, but just as your head is wiser than your toes, we are not all equal."

Udraka rose from his mat to side with Arcahia, his face blotchy with anger. He raised his hand to slap Yeshua, but Arcahia pulled it down. "Vasanta, come here," he said. "Tell your friend—again—why all castes cannot be equal."

Vasanta's eyes darted between Arcahia and Yeshua, trapped between his teachers and his friend. He drew a deep breath and looked at Yeshua. "In the beginning of the world, Lord Brahma created four men. The first came out of his mouth; he was white and tall and wise. The Creator called him Brahmin and made him a priest."

Arcahia nodded with approval: Vasanta hadn't stuttered once.

"The second man was created from Lord Brahma's arms, the Kshatriya," Vasanta continued. "He was big and strong, so Lord Brahma made him a ruler and warrior and the defender of God's word."

Yeshua knew the story well. What he wanted to know was how it was consistent with the Holy Scriptures.

"Lord Brahma made the third man, the Vaishya, from his thighs, to have someone who could grow and sell food to the priests and rulers and warriors. But legs don't have ears, and therefore they cannot understand the word of God. Thus, it's useless to teach them."

Udraka had sat back down. He clasped his hands in front of his big belly, proud of his apprentice.

"At last, Lord Brahma looked down at his feet. They were cracked and soiled from walking barefoot in the mud, and he saw that someone had to serve the others. So he created the dark-skinned Shudra, who may not even look at a Brahmin. But they can work hard and perhaps in the next life return as Vaishya."

"That doesn't make sense." Yeshua scratched the floor with his big toe, noticing that his toenails needed cleaning. "Do you love your arms more than your feet? Cut them off, then. Live like a cripple by the river and depend on others to feed you."

Arcahia rubbed his forehead with both hands.

"And"—Yeshua couldn't stop himself—"isn't it written in the Brihadaranyaka that there is no diversity in Brahman? That whoever sees discrepancies in God will go from death to death?"

"You interpret it wrong," Udraka said.

"Do I? What about 'as long as there's duality, one sees the other, hears the other, smells the other, knows the other, but for the illumined soul all are dissolved in God'?"

Yeshua didn't want to argue. He loved these men more than anyone else in the world, but they were mistaken. The God he knew would never cause anyone to suffer.

"And what about the untouchables?" Yeshua's hand flew to his mouth.

Arcahia turned away, resigned. But Udraka stood up and put his face so close to Yeshua that he could see every pore on his nose. "The untouchables do dirty work. They're scum. And if you speak to one, their filth will rub off and you will become one of them." Udraka's eyes narrowed.

"Then your Brahman is not a god of justice," Yeshua said.

Udraka slapped him so hard that Yeshua lost his balance and fell to his knees. He picked himself up and stepped close to Udraka. Smiling, he closed his eyes, and from his heart projected a sphere of infinite love that engulfed Udraka, Arcahia, and Vasanta.

Udraka raised his hand again, paused, and then slapped Yeshua's other cheek. Yeshua staggered but kept his balance. His smile remained.

"My God, the one I listen to," Yeshua continued, "loves all men without distinction: the white, the brown, the black—even the untouchables."

Arcahia looked at him, his eyes clouded in thought.

"Why do you always think you know God better than anyone else?" Vasanta asked. He grabbed Udraka's hand, as if to keep him from hitting Yeshua again.

Yeshua looked at his friend, suddenly aware of how much he loved him, afraid of leaving him behind like he had once left Yakov and Dhiman. "Ha!" he said without joy. "You know me so well."

He wanted to explain how wrong Vasanta was, how he didn't think he knew God better, but what could he say at this stage to change his friend's mind?

"Man invented the castes," Yeshua continued, centering his gaze at Udraka. "Man filled his temples with dead images of stone and wood, not Brahman. I know—and you know—that God is love. Only love."

Udraka charged at Yeshua one more time, but Vasanta held him back. Yeshua backed toward the edge of the roof, to the stairs that led down to the street. He had said what he needed to say. Yet he hesitated.

"Be careful, Udraka," Arcahia said, following Yeshua with his eyes. "Nothing you say can change his mind. If he is wrong, his words mean nothing. Let him go in peace."

Arcahia's dismissal stung more than Udraka's blows. Yeshua took one last look at the three White Brahmins, in awe of how much he loved them. Maybe Abba was right after all, perhaps priests did come from a different breed and he was never meant to teach. He bowed lightly before he descended the stairs.

Where would he go now? What did God want from him?

Northeast Kushan Empire, AD 16

Yeshua walked aimlessly along a road that led north through Isipatana where the Buddha had given his first sermon, but he could not find the peace of mind to linger there and meditate. His tears flowed freely as he agonized over his fate. What if his message of a God inside each and every person made no difference in the lives of the poor? What if they viewed him simply as temporary entertainment, a mere respite from their daily woes? Had he embarked on a pointless quest?

Intuitively, he followed the pilgrimage path toward the mountainous region of the Himalayas, the kingdom of Sakya and Lumbini, where Lord Buddha had been born. At the Ghaghara River, Yeshua took a knife to his beard and let the hairs feed the stream. With a clean-shaven face, he trudged forward in Lord Buddha's footsteps. The fresh midday air allowed him to walk farther and well past sunset. During the frigid nights, he sought warmth under leafy branches propped against tree trunks. But as the days passed, his hunger and loneliness intensified, and his energy dwindled.

One morning, as he was about to give up and welcome death by starvation, he came upon a tiny forest hamlet of half a dozen wooden huts nestled under tall Bhutan pines. Overwhelmed with relief, he banged on the door of the first hut. No one answered. He peeked through the divides in the walls, where the moss between the logs had loosened, but saw only darkness. The same happened with the next one, and then the next. His throat clenched. Had all the huts been abandoned? He tried one after another until one single hut remained. Some of the wood in its walls had rotted, leaving gaps as large as a woman's arm, and a soiled carpet covered the entrance. It seemed pointless to even knock. But then he noticed the fresh scraps and buzzing flies on the garbage pile beside the hut.

Yeshua pushed the carpet slightly to the side and called through the opening. "I come in peace."

An animal grunted inside. And then, the sound of shuffling feet. A man, hefty as a bear, peered at him through the doorway.

"Namaste, sir." Yeshua bowed, aware of his disheveled appearance. "I'm Issa. I'm a pilgrim from Palestine."

The man scratched his graying beard. "Pali?"

"No, Pa-le-stine." Yeshua pointed west. "Over there, about five seasons' walk."

The man pulled back. "You walk year—and half?" He grabbed the carpet-door, ready to yank it shut.

Yeshua thought fast. He had to appeal to the man's generosity, an integral part of his culture.

"I'm sorry to bother you, sir, but I'm famished."

The giant glared at Yeshua's stomach, muttering under his breath. He peered back into the hut for a moment, but then he shrugged and held the carpet-door open, allowing Yeshua to enter. In the darkness, two huge long-haired black cows with curled horns snorted and scuffed. Behind them, a woman lay dozing on a bed of hay, covered by woolen blankets.

The man filled a small bowl with burned clotted milk and handed it to Yeshua. "Not much food for share." He motioned to the woman. "My wife, very ill."

Yeshua savored every sip and thanked God for his good fortune.

"Your wife—what's wrong with her?"

"She dying." The man sighed. Sadness furrowed his face. "Not long live."

Yeshua touched his hand. "What happened?"

"Baby die inside." The giant covered his face with his hands and sobbed.

Yeshua knelt by the woman's side. Her bones jutted through her skin like the boards of a wrecked ship. Her face was ashen. Blue veins protruded from her neck, and only a faint rise and fall of her chest confirmed she was still alive.

He cupped one hand behind the woman's neck, placed another on her forehead, and chanted a mantra to attract the Kundalini. He let his hands hover above her head, neck, torso, and pelvis to connect the chakras and to allow the energy to travel through her. Her life force was frail. Yeshua prayed harder. Sweat trickled down his face. He asked God and Krishna for guidance. Deep in meditation, he felt the spirit of his guru Kahanji appear beside him, directing his movements. The woman's body trembled lightly and a pinch of color appeared in her cheeks, but she needed more of the healing energy, and he couldn't let her go until she was safe. Yeshua extended his hands above her belly and held them still, channeling the energy through his hands and into her until his arms ached with exhaustion. When he couldn't hold his hands up any longer, he lowered them to rest right below her chest.

She wheezed.

Yeshua drew his hands away.

"Will she live?" the man asked.

"I don't know. We have got to get the child out. It's poisoning her."

The big man wailed. He knelt by his wife and rubbed her belly as if he could push the baby out.

"Is there a shaman around here?" Yeshua asked.

The man shook his head.

"A midwife? Someone who collects herbs?"

"Everyone gone. Last year, many, many water. Only we here."

It seemed hopeless. With the dead baby inside her, she would surely die. Yeshua might be able to help restore some of her strength, but without herbs…

Kahanji would have insisted she be healed through prayer, but there was no time. She would be gone before nightfall if she didn't improve. He had to find some herbs.

"I'll be back."

Yeshua left his host kneeling by her bedside. He thought he remembered having passed a tuft of herbs in the woods not far from the hamlet. With a little bit of luck, he would recognize some of them. He ran in the direction he had come from, squatting here and there to inspect plants. He tried to remember what Kahanji had taught him about the herbs and their healing properties.

Frustrated and vexed, Yeshua slumped against a tree, shaking his head and trying to free his mind. Parsley. He had seen parsley only moments ago. What else? Pansy. He remembered seeing the yellow flowers somewhere. With renewed vigor, he retraced his steps and found pansies and parsley growing close together. *How strange.* Yeshua drew a breath of relief and raised his palms to the skies in gratitude.

Returning to the hut, Yeshua steeped the herbs in warm water and then dipped a clean rag in the brew. While the woman's husband slowly squeezed the liquid into her mouth, Yeshua held his hands above her throat to ease its passage. She coughed and whimpered, but she swallowed the bitter liquid little by little until it was all gone.

"Now let her sleep. Tomorrow, we'll do it again. And the day after. And the day after that."

On the evening of the fifth day, the woman pushed herself halfway up and bellowed with pain. A foul smell filled the hut and a bloody mass stained the hay. The bearlike man picked up his wife and carried her to a nearby stream, where they let all the blood wash out into the clear water. Once the bleeding stopped, they wrapped her in a clean blanket, brought her back to the hut, and covered her with yak skins. Yeshua rolled the soiled hay into a bundle, took it outside, and burned it to send the child's soul to the other side.

Over the following days, Yeshua focused on healing her liver to help drive out the toxins. Along with a nutritious diet of berries, herbs, and milk, the three of them restored their health and faith in life together.

In less than a fortnight, she was up and moving about, and Yeshua, sensing the couple's need for privacy, resolved to continue his journey. With teary eyes and gifts of a yak wool blanket and fur wraps to protect his feet, the man and his wife sent him on his way.

Yeshua trekked across fields of yellow mustard plants and through dense forests. Some mornings the fog rose thick from the ground and transformed nature into a dream world, where majestic sal trees revealed themselves like spirits, one by one, along a path that appeared and disappeared before him. His thoughts bounded and rebounded from fear of being lost to joy at being found, from abject terror to supreme bravery, and from the pit of despair to unwavering hope.

When at last he heard human voices in the distance, he knew he had made it to Lumbini, the birthplace of the Buddha.

Lumbini, Himalayas, AD 17

Yeshua followed the chatter of voices through a garden brimming with rhododendrons and orchids until at last he came to a cluster of redbrick buildings by a pond covered with pink lotuses. Dozens of monks sat cross-legged, praying under magnificent Bodhi trees, while a group of women cooled their feet in the shallow water of the pond. Children of all ages chased each other around a tall pillar, giggling with delight. Yeshua couldn't help but giggle along, until his gaze landed on the statue of a horse that adorned the top of the pillar. The hairs on his arms stood right up. *King Ashoka's pillar.* The famous king had erected the pillar on the exact spot where Lord Buddha was born.

"Hello, friend!" A monk with a toothy grin ran up to greet him. His warmth, and the way he had casually wrapped his maroon-colored robe around him, reminded Yeshua of Dhiman. "I'm Omkar. Come sit and share this piece of bread with me."

Omkar listened intently as Yeshua told him about his travels, his studies, and his interest in the Buddha. As the morning receded into afternoon, Omkar asked Yeshua to accompany him to Kapilavatthu, a village half a day's walk away.

"It was Prince Siddhartha's—Lord Buddha's—home, you know, where he grew up. We have a splendid temple and a garden, and many scrolls of sacred scriptures. If you like, you may stay and study with us."

"But I don't speak Pali," Yeshua said, regretting his response the moment the words crossed his lips. "I mean... You said sacred scriptures?"

Omkar nodded, flashing his white teeth.

"I can learn, can't I?" Yeshua said, and he stood, ready to get back on the road. "That way, is it?"

The decision was made. Instead of staying in Lumbini, he would continue to Kapilavatthu, where he could learn the language and continue his studies. The mere thought of touching the actual words of the Buddha made him dizzy. Until this day, all his knowledge had come secondhand, from stories. At last he would have the Holy Scriptures at his fingertips!

The palace where the young prince Siddhartha had grown up was long gone, but the walls around the Kapilavatthu fortress and the palace gardens remained. Red roses, yellow orchids, and pink anemones fought for space below tall nyagrodha trees, creating an ambience as serene as if the Buddha had painted the air with his very soul. In the middle of the garden stood a stupa, a tall mound decorated with white and red stones. A long line of monks and nuns walked in a slow line around the shrine, mumbling quiet prayers.

"Our temple is farther down the road," Omkar said, and took Yeshua by the hand.

They walked through fragrant meadows toward the town center, passing temples of varying size and shape: whitewashed mud huts, rustic timber houses, and solid brick buildings. Like Benares, Kapilavatthu was overrun with holy men, but here everyone was on a quest for enlightenment rather than on a mission to spread his faith.

"Come. I will introduce you to Master." They removed their footwear at the entrance of a large rectangular tent and passed through it into a sprawling garden. A warm breeze carried the sweet aroma of jasmine flowers and the smoky scent of incense. In a pond, golden fish played among purple lotuses, producing a bubbly sound as they broke the surface. At the base of another stupa, a dozen maroon-robed monks sat in deep meditation. Yeshua and Omkar took a seat behind the other monks, crossed their legs, and placed their hands, palm up, on their laps.

Yeshua connected with the peace of the monks around him and fell into a state of tranquility and bliss.

Dong. Dong. Dong.

The clang of a gong brought him back to reality. Yeshua opened one of his eyes and peeked at the standing monk who was hitting a large bronze disk with a padded stick.

Dong. Dong. Dong.

Pause.

Dong. Dong. Dong. Dong. Dong.

One by one, the monks rose and congregated in a circle. As one, they started walking around the stupa. Yeshua and Omkar followed behind them in mindful silence. After circling the mound three times, they began to chant as they walked:

> *Iti pi so Bhagavâ-Araham Sammâ-*
> *sambuddho.*
> *Vijjâ-carana sampanno Sugato Lokavidû*
> *Anuttarro Purisa-damma-sârathi*
> *Satthâ deva-manussânam Buddho*
> *Bhagavâti.*

Yeshua mimicked the chant as best he could but stumbled on the words. Despite its similarity to Sanskrit, the Pali language confused him. All he understood was that the verses referred to the Buddha and his enlightenment.

The walking and humming continued for hours. When the blisters on Yeshua's feet broke, he lifted his consciousness from his body to his third eye, aware that his body did not truly exist. As if in a dream, the pain dissolved, his feet healed, his exhaustion evaporated, and his voice gained strength as he trailed the others around and around and around, until he lost all sense of self.

Dong. Dong. Dong.

Pause.

Dong. Dong. Dong.

Pause.

Dong. Dong. Dong. Dong. Dong.

Once again, the gong brought Yeshua back to the present, but this time his body was energized and his mind at peace. Around him, the garden radiated with a healing force, and he hungered for more.

"You want to meet Master?" Omkar put his arm around Yeshua's shoulders. "He's a bodhisattva, you know—very, very close to enlightenment. You'll like him, I think."

Inside the tent, monks rested on sleeping mats or squatted in groups and chatted in hushed voices. The master stood alone in a corner, observing his companions. Dwarf-like and plump with a high forehead and one eye half closed, he didn't resemble any other holy man Yeshua had ever seen. His good eye caught on Yeshua, and he gestured for him to come closer.

"Namaskaar, Bhikkhu!" the master said, and bowed low.

"Namaskaar." Yeshua bowed even lower. The master's energy flashed through him as they connected on a soul level and, without words, exchanged memories from many lifetimes.

"Welcome to Kapilavatthu," the master continued after what seemed an eternity of silent communication. "You shall stay and study with us. You are most welcome."

Yeshua bowed once more, having no words. He had never met anyone like this, who could read his mind. And it frightened him.

"What does *bhikkhu* mean?" he asked Omkar later as they walked together in the velvety night.

"'Monk.' Master calls us all monk to defy our ego-consciousness, our separation from one another, and we call him Master."

Yeshua nodded. It could be nice to be anonymous for a while.

In this temple, the monks depended solely on alms from the community. Every morning, the monks walked around town with their begging bowls. Not allowed to ask for food, they had to accept anything that was placed in their bowls. Sometimes they received enough food for the entire day, other times they ate only in the morning and went hungry until the next day. Material for their robes had to be donated by the villagers. If a monk received only patches of fabric, he must wait until he had collected enough pieces to sew an entire robe. Yeshua was impatient to discard his soiled white robe and to dress like everyone else in the sangha.

Omkar read him the long and complicated list of precepts that Lord Buddha had prescribed for monks who followed the righteous path. Monks were not allowed to steal or murder, of course, nor were they allowed to pretend to have reached a higher state of consciousness. Master could not say that he was already enlightened, and Omkar could not pretend to be a bodhisattva. A monk could not keep an extra robe after receiving a new one, or accept a robe as a gift from another monk. They were not allowed to own a rug made of silk or a blanket made of wool, which meant that Yeshua had to donate his yak-wool blanket to someone else in need.

A monk could not touch, kiss, embrace, or have sexual intercourse with a woman. He should not flirt, ask for a sexual favor, or arrange a marriage with her. And he absolutely must not ejaculate, unless it happened as an accident while asleep.

The rules went on and on. Yeshua wondered if he would ever remember them all. When Omkar finally came to the standards of eating, Yeshua just stopped listening. As long as he had access to the sacred scriptures, he would follow whatever rules the temple prescribed.

One afternoon after Yeshua's arrival, Omkar and Yeshua went for a walk by the Banganga river, to discuss the Vedas, the Yehudi scriptures, and the wisdom of the Buddha.

"I am very pleased I was born a man," Omkar said. "Man is the marvel of the universe compared with other creatures, is he not, Issa?"

Yeshua followed Omkar's line of vision as he gazed up at the treetops where downy bluebirds swung on leafy branches and chirped cheerfully.

"We are the only ones with minds that may be perfected," Omkar continued. "Although every living being has a soul, even tiny worms and colossal elephants, we are the only ones who can reach enlightenment. Just think about it: everything else in the world is bound by the laws of rebirth. They have to evolve over many lifetimes until they are reborn as men."

"And the women?" The question was out before Yeshua could hold back.

"The women will also become men, of course. And then men will evolve to even higher forms of life."

Yeshua shook his head, amused. "Omkar, who taught you this?"

"Master, of course—all masters. Everyone." He peered at Yeshua with a furrowed brow. "Why do you find this amusing?"

Yeshua straightened his face. "Omkar, you are a wise man. But you can't learn everything from others. You must find the truth within yourself. Everything you need to know is already inside you."

Omkar walked in silence as he contemplated Yeshua's words.

"You remember your life as a monkey?" Yeshua asked. "Or a spider? Perhaps as a butterfly?"

"Of course not."

Yeshua put his arm around him. "See? If your only proof of having evolved from a worm is that someone said so, you're simply guessing. You need to reach within." Yeshua patted Omkar's chest. "That's where you'll find answers."

"You think I can't evolve? That's a terrible thought."

Yeshua picked a yellow flower from the tall grass, sniffed it, and handed it to Omkar. "Every living being can evolve into perfection of its own kind. I know you don't believe in God, but hear me out: if God is Self and Self can't die, there is no death. There is only evolution—and perfection."

"As a man?"

"No, not as a man. As Self."

Omkar nodded. He clutched the yellow flower to his heart, as if the plant held all the wisdom in the world. On the way back to the temple, they discussed more trivial matters, like how many days it would take to gather enough fabric for Yeshua's robe and how to best dispose of his old clothes. But along the way, Yeshua thought about teaching. Omkar was a wise man, but he still had questions that begged for answers. Yeshua didn't have all the answers, but he longed to share the knowledge he had. Yet at the same time, he wanted to stay in Kapilavatthu as long as possible.

How could he do both?

One full moon cycle after arriving in Kapilavatthu, Yeshua had collected enough pieces of fabric to sew together his very own robe. Omkar helped him dye the robe maroon, as the Buddha had prescribed, and thus he became a full-fledged member of the sangha. No longer did he have to walk behind the others when collecting alms, or sit in the back during daily lessons.

When Master brought him to a sealed-off area in the back of the tent and opened the lid of a rectangular basket, Yeshua's cheeks flushed with excitement. Inside were dozens of rolled-up scrolls, etched palm leaves, and inscribed pieces of birch bark.

"Once you have learned to read, you may study these." Master's warm voice could have melted butter.

Yeshua beamed. This was the opportunity he had been waiting for all his life. Ever since he'd found out a carpenter could not study the Torah, he had yearned to read sacred scrolls. And now Master had chosen him as one of the monks who could touch the scriptures.

"Luck has no role in this play. You have established your worthiness," Master said, reading Yeshua's mind.

CHAPTER TWENTY

Kapilavatthu, Himalayas, AD 19

The Pali language was complicated, almost impossible to learn. In the beginning, Omkar had brought simple fabric scrolls with him on their walks by the river and urged Yeshua to be patient. "Think of the toddlers, how long it takes them to master speaking and know all the words. Why do you think you can learn any faster?"

But Omkar's words held no comfort. Yeshua had learned Punjabi, Sindhi, Prakrit, and Sanskrit without much effort; he didn't understand why Pali had to be so much harder. Perhaps he was too impatient, or maybe his age had caught up with him. Omkar practiced with him for hours, going over words, phrases, and bits of grammar. The process was slow and arduous, and the only highlights were sporadic glimpses of clarity, as on the evening when Yeshua realized he understood every word of their daily chant:

> *Like so is he, indeed, the Blessed One,*
> *The Holy One, and fully enlightened,*
> *He is graced with clear vision and righteous behavior:*
> *he is magnificent.*
> *He knows all the worlds; the incomparable leader of men,*
> *The teacher of gods and men, he is enlightened and blessed.*

When Omkar's language lessons were no longer sufficient to advance Yeshua's fluency in Pali, Yeshua visited the other temples to improve his reading skills. If only he could spend more time practicing reading, he could speed up the learning process and impress Master with his knowledge of Pali in no time. In Kapilavatthu's biggest, most famous temple, located at the edge of town on the road to Lumbini, Yeshua found what he was looking for: hall after hall of walls covered in flowery script. Yeshua's heart fluttered with impatience as he sat behind the other monks and pretended to meditate. Between half-closed eyelids, he scanned the walls and deciphered the verses word for word until they formed meaningful sentences.

He returned to the temple day after day, month after month, until he had read and understood them all. Then he started over again in the first hall, reading the phrases one by one until one day he could read an entire wall without stumbling. On that day, Yeshua ran back to the temple and waited for Master to emerge from his nap.

When Master finally pushed the curtain aside, yawning and rubbing the sleep from his eyes, Yeshua sprang toward him.

"I am ready!" he almost shouted, unable to control his voice. "I can read, Master. I can read Pali!"

"Can you now?" His teacher squinted at him with an amused smile. He opened the basket and pointed to the scrolls. "Come, let's see if you are truly ready."

With trembling fingers, Yeshua chose a yellowed fabric scroll from the top of the heap. He removed the string, unfurled a partition, and read out loud:

"'I listened to...Brahman's request... And out of...compassion for... all beings, I examined...the world with...the eye of a Buddha.'" Yeshua drew a deep breath and tried to still his beating heart. He could do better than this. Perhaps if he ignored Master's presence, he could read faster. He tried again.

"'I saw beings with little...dirt...in their eyes and others with a lot of dirt in their eyes...with great...skills and poor skills.'"

Yeshua paused again. He didn't dare look up; he wasn't sure if he was reading well enough to please Master. He had to read at a better pace. He closed his eyes, gathered the strength in his core, and read the rest of the scripture without hesitation.

"'With good qualities and bad qualities, intelligent and not intelligent, and some who saw only fear and blame in the world. Just as in a pond filled with blue and red lotuses, some lotuses thrive submerged under the water, whereas others rest sleepily on the water's surface, yet some rise straight up and stand tall above all others.'"

At the end of the scroll, Yeshua stopped, his gaze nailed to the text. Goose bumps covered his arms, and sweat trickled down his spine. These were the Buddha's words. The Buddha had spoken in parables, just as he did. And he, Yeshua, saw everything the same way. He saw the good and bad in people, and he didn't judge. They were all equal in the eyes of God, just different. He knew all that.

When Yeshua looked up, Master was grinning. "Go on. There are many more."

Carefully, Yeshua rolled up the scroll, bound it, placed it back in the basket, and picked up another one. He read out loud:

"'The king's minister, Ugga, approached the Buddha, bowed to him, and said: "It is magnificent how wealthy Migara Rohaneyya is, and how astonishing his riches!"

"'The Buddha replied: "But what is it he owns? What are those astonishing riches worth?"

"''One hundred thousand pieces of gold, Lord, not to mention his silver."

"''Yes, that is true wealth, Ugga. I don't say it is not. But all his property is susceptible to damage from fire, floods, taxes, thieves, and greedy heirs. Let me tell you about seven even more valuable treasures that no fire or flood can harm, and no kings, thieves, or hateful heirs can steal. Those are the ones you should pursue."

"''Which are those seven?" Ugga asked.

"''The treasures of faith, virtue, conscience, compassion, listening and learning, generosity, and right understanding. These, Ugga, are seven treasures that are not susceptible to fire, flood, taxes, thieves, or hateful heirs. Whoever possesses these seven treasures owns the greatest treasure in the world, something one cannot lose in the worlds of humans or divine beings.'"

Yeshua sat still, cradling the scroll like a baby bird in his hands.

Everything the Buddha said was true. The words opened his heart and infused it with peace. He knew without doubt these teachings were true. The Buddha had become one with God.

Master nodded and let his half-closed eye rest on Yeshua's chest, signaling that their session had come to an end.

In the months that followed, Yeshua read and memorized the verses written on scrolls and etched on palm leaves and birch bark. He discussed their meanings during lessons with other monks and listened closely when Master explained the meaning of the suttas. Most referred to sayings of the Buddha, such as, "The mind is unpredictable and flighty; it goes wherever it likes and is difficult to control. It is an excellent benefit to know how to discipline the mind. A controlled mind is a great source of joy."

Master emphasized the four noble truths that Dhiman had taught Yeshua all those years ago: all is suffering, the origin of suffering is desire, the cessation of suffering can be achieved through mind control, and only the eightfold path makes it possible to end suffering. He drilled them in the eightfold path (right view, thought, speech, action, livelihood, effort, mindfulness, contemplation) and the precepts of the Buddha that required a monk to abstain from taking untimely meals and from dancing, singing, taking high positions, and accepting gold and silver. Yeshua thought of the golden ring he still kept tied into a corner of his robe, no longer for the security it offered, but with the intention of returning it to its rightful owner one day, and decided to keep the treasure a secret for now.

The pace of life in the temple town was tranquil. No one was ever in a hurry, and rarely did anyone raise their voice or argue about petty matters.

Although physical contact with the local nuns was strictly forbidden, Yeshua enjoyed their company and thoughtful conversations. The nuns embodied the Buddha's teachings better than most monks, because generosity, compassion, and patience came naturally to them. And they moved with such grace that they were a joy to behold. One day, Yeshua told himself, he would take a wife. He dreamed about caressing a woman's body, touching her supple breasts, and longed for their tender kisses. Like Ramaa. He would never forget the ecstasy of their one night together, but more than ten years had passed, and the details had faded. Ever since they parted, he had only observed women from a distance and hadn't allowed himself to give in to his desires, not even with prostitutes. A lover would have distracted him from learning and achieving enlightenment.

On an early summer's morning, Yeshua went for a long walk along the river. He breathed in the delicate fragrance of wildflowers and listened to the drone of honeybees collecting sweet nectar, unaware that their lives would soon come to an end. How wonderful to be a bee, to live life to the fullest and always remain in the present moment. He paused to sit on a slope on the river's bank, far from his daily chores, his monastic life, and the busy town, and closed his eyes to meditate. Within moments, he had connected to the movement of the water, the feel of the gentle breeze, the bouquet of blossoming magnolias, and the hum of life around him. He was one with God. With everything.

And he was gone.

Hours later, when he returned to consciousness, a family of serfs had gathered nearby. Yeshua stood and brushed the dust and grass from his robe. He smiled and nodded at a broad-shouldered but frightfully thin man standing beside him. But the man's eyes were shrouded in sadness. Yeshua looked around. Every one of them wore the same expression of hopelessness.

"Namaste, my friend," Yeshua said, turning back to the man. "May I ask what is the matter? What has made you so sad?"

"Bhikkhu, what do you gather?" The man's voice seeped with misery. "Life is difficult. We labor in the fields all day and all night, and all we can ever hope for is more work. As long as we work, we feed our children. And if there's no work... It's hard, Bhikkhu, life is hard. Blessed be the day when I can put down my sickle and go to rest in the city of the dead."

Yeshua's stomach cramped with sorrow at his words, and his heart swelled with compassion. How unfair that most people had to struggle for their daily bread. He grabbed the man's hand.

"My friend, listen. I understand your troubles, but don't let work depress you. If you infuse love into everything you do, your troubles will feel lighter and your whole life will fill with joy. Look at the bees; they work from morning to night to produce honey for their queen. They never worry. They know that what they need will be provided until their last breath. Believe me: this—not worrying—this is Nirvana."

The man stared at him wide-eyed. "Nirvana? But Bhikkhu, how can these words offer me comfort? I will toil through endless lives before I ever reach Nirvana. It is hopeless. All we do is work, work, and work. We never find time to rest."

The others had edged closer to hear what the monk was saying.

Yeshua placed his hand on the man's shoulder. "Brother, you are mistaken. Nirvana is not far at all."

He cleared his throat and addressed the whole group:

"Nirvana is not a place of limits and borders. It's not a country to which you can travel, it's a state of mind!" Arms spread, he looked out at their worn and tired faces.

"You see, Nirvana is a place in our mind, in our consciousness, not something God created. We—you and I—are its creators. We make our own Nirvana. Like the bees make their honey."

The serfs looked at him with puzzled expressions. All their lives, they had been told they were worthless and would have to reincarnate again and again before they could ever hope to reach enlightenment. And now a stranger was telling them that they could create their own heaven?

"You must look within to relieve your suffering, not to the outside. Open your hearts and let the peace of Nirvana flow into you, like a beam of love, and bring you endless joy."

A few of them looked up into the sky as if searching for this beam.

"I promise, if you open your mind and connect with the love of God, your work will no longer be so hard."

The serfs, desperate for good news, stepped closer. Their unwashed bodies reeked of sweat from hard labor.

"Bhikkhu, tell us more!"

Yeshua flushed, glad to ignite a spark of hope in their hopeless lives. "If you sit down, I will tell you a story."

The serfs sat in a semicircle before him, watching him intently.

"Once there was a farmer," Yeshua said, making eye contact with each of the serfs, "who owned a field of stony soil. He toiled from early morning to late at night, but still he could not grow enough food to feed his family."

They listened, spellbound. This was their own story.

"One day, a passing miner stopped at the edge of the field and called out to the farmer. 'My good man, you plow and sow and reap the land with great effort. Can you not see the treasures buried just below your feet? Every day you skim only the top layer of the poor soil while you walk on a fortune of sapphires.'

"The farmer thought the miner was mocking him.

"But the miner continued: 'I promise, if you plow up the rocky soil and dig deep into the earth, you will no longer have to struggle.'

"The desperate farmer started digging. He dug for days and days until, at last, he uncovered a vein of precious blue stones. After that day, he never again had to work so hard."

Yeshua looked out at the blank faces and sensed their unspoken questions: How did the miner know what was deep in the ground? And how could they, simple serfs, find precious stones in fields that didn't even belong to them?

Yeshua continued.

"You see, like this man, you work relentlessly. You break your backs by plowing barren fields, the way your fathers did. You cannot see an end to it. But I assure you, within that rocky soil lies treasure of a kind that cannot be counted or weighed. Your hearts, dear friends, are that farmer's field. In your hearts, you will find invaluable treasure. But you must dig deep inside your mind and open the door of your hearts to recover it."

He paused and looked around. For several minutes, no one spoke, and Yeshua thought that perhaps they had not understood him.

"Teach us how, Bhikkhu," a young boy finally said. "Show us the way to the wealth inside our hearts."

Yeshua stayed and talked to the serfs until the light faded from the sky and the moon rose over the treetops. He promised he would come back the next day, and the next, until they had opened their own private gateways to Nirvana.

As he walked back to the temple, he thought of the White Brahmins of Jagannath and realized how much they had taught him. Oh, how he missed them.

Kapilavatthu, Himalayas, AD 21

During the following years, Yeshua met with the serfs most nights until their backs had straightened with hope and their eyes sparkled with joy. In the mornings, he studied the suttas and practiced mindfulness with the other monks. Master cautioned him to remain humble and warned Yeshua not to let his pride go to his head. After all, he was no different, no better, than the others.

In springtime, Yeshua joined the other monks in long walks to settlements at the foot of the Himalayas, where they stayed for a few weeks at a time and taught the villagers basic meditation to gain serenity and insight.

"You can eliminate suffering," Yeshua told them, "by focusing on something and allowing your mind to be absorbed into it." He described the qualities of suitable objects for meditation: the colors blue, red, or green, elements like earth and fire, even foul things like decomposing corpses or dead animals. He taught that the best place for meditation was a quiet, secluded spot—perhaps in a nearby cave or under a cluster of trees, ideally, sheltered from both rain and disturbing insects. And most importantly, it should be within walking distance of a teacher who could answer questions.

As the villagers learned to calm their minds, quiet their emotions, and become aware of nothingness, he also taught them how to see beyond the needs of their bodies. He told them that their minds were boundless and that both hunger and sensual desires could be controlled.

Finally, he spoke of compassion. "Everyone suffers—slaves as well as kings. One day you will understand that happiness is within everyone's reach."

Back in Kapilavatthu, Master taught Yeshua and the other monks to adapt their message to their students. Parables could be effective for those who were ready to absorb the message, whereas those not yet ready to awaken would think they had just heard a simple story. He emphasized that those who wished to follow the Buddha's path must first learn to recognize and refrain from the five barriers to enlightenment: sexual desire, laziness, restlessness, hatred, and worry, which could take years, or even an entire lifetime, to master. The monks had to be patient and guide their disciples wisely.

"What do I tell my wife?" a newlywed man asked Yeshua. "If I don't take her to bed, she will think I no longer find her pretty. I need sons. I have a farm to run."

Yeshua paused to consider. When speaking of desires, refraining from sexual intercourse seemed to bring the most resistance. He had to make sure he used the correct words.

"There's nothing wrong with taking your wife to bed. But don't let your lust consume you. Don't stare at the soft breasts of every woman you pass." Some of the men chuckled. "Yes, I know you do." They all laughed. "And don't undress your neighbor's wife in your fantasy. Yes, I know that, too." More laughter. "When you make love to your wife, make love with your soul. Unite with her under the covers; become one with her—and with God."

The younger men snickered and shoved at each other.

"I don't want to make love to God," an adolescent called out.

"Ah, but you do," Yeshua said. He approached the boy and patted his shoulder. "Because when you make love with God, you make *love*. When you become one with a woman, you've become one with God. There's no ego. No desire. No suffering. Just bliss. True intimacy is unity. Once you know how it feels, you will bring that completeness to all relationships in your life."

"You mean I need to make love to men, too?" More rowdy laughter.

Yeshua nodded thoughtfully. Master and Yeshua had practiced for hours, considering all possible questions.

"Only if you want. Once you realize that everyone in this world—your friends, your foes, strangers—are all one with God, you will understand that loving another is loving yourself. Loving your wife is loving yourself."

"But what does sex have to do with suffering? I like sex. And I like looking at breasts. I like ample buttocks. That doesn't make me suffer. It makes me happy!"

Yeshua remembered how it used to make him happy, too. He squatted next to the youth, to meet him at the same eye level. "Suffering comes from lack of satisfaction. You may have intercourse a thousand times, but it will never be enough. You will always want more. And you will suffer when you cannot have it. Anything you desire causes suffering because the unfulfilled desire reminds you of something you do not have."

"I am certainly always satisfied after lying with my wife. You should see her!"

The men laughed at the fellow, whose face collapsed with embarrassment. Yeshua patted his shoulder. "And when you wake up the next morning? Are you still satisfied?"

The man shook his head.

"So—you see? It's not the act of making love that causes the suffering; it's the desire to make love. The only way to make love and not suffer is to overcome the desire to have relations again and again and again."

Anger was another common struggle.

"But my neighbor stole my horse. Of course I despise him!"

"My wife is mean and nasty. How can I possibly not be angry with her?"

"I didn't do anything. It's my brother, he is always angry. Honestly, I have been kind to him every day of my life, and look how he treats me."

They always blamed someone else for their troubles.

When Yeshua wanted to give up, Master advised him how to manage the responses.

"Tell them their own reactions destroy their peace of mind, not the actions of others. To justify our emotions, we must first believe we have every right to be angry. Thus our fury increases. The Buddha taught that hatred is our worst enemy because it causes unhappiness and makes us ugly and miserable."

Yeshua nodded. He picked up the broom that stood in the corner of Master's bedroom and swept the clean floor, contemplating the master's advice.

"Have you asked them if they notice how good things happen when they are in a pleasant mood?" Master asked. "And when they are angry, everything seems to go wrong?"

"Of course," Yeshua said, placing the broom back in the corner. "You can't eat, you can't sleep, you get sick, and your body hurts here, there, and everywhere."

"Exactly. And that's why the Buddha spoke about loving-kindness. Approach your foes with compassion. Embrace them and respond to their attacks with love. Wait and let their rage dissipate, and then ask them what's wrong. Perhaps they are suffering a terrible loss or facing a problem. It might have nothing to do with you. But if you cannot bring yourself to meet them with a heart full of compassion, you had better avoid them. The world is quite fair. No one escapes justice. No one can hide from karma."

Yeshua let Master's words sink in, and then said, "I ask people if it really was someone else who caused their anger or if it could be that they are angry with themselves. I tell them to search their hearts and consider if they can do anything to change their attitude. Often they will find that once an issue is settled within themselves, it no longer bothers them in others."

Master closed his eyes, as if in deep thought. Yeshua waited. After a long while, when the master hadn't moved, Yeshua bowed and left Master's room.

The lesson had come to an end.

Kapilavatthu, Himalayas, AD 23

Two distinct seasons divided the year in Kapilavatthu. During the dry and clear fall through early spring, the monks left the temple for weeklong walks into the mountains to teach the word of the Buddha. From summer through early autumn, when daily rainfall turned the roads muddy and impassable, they spent their days between the local temples, discussing the suttas with elders and studying the scriptures. Yeshua's favorite part of the year, however, came at the end of monsoon season when the villages celebrated their harvest. The monks traveled from one festival to the next, carrying messages of peace and hope while savoring the gifts of abundant fresh produce.

Each community had its own customs. In one village, the men dressed up in yak-skin coats, painted their faces red, and chased the women and children around. Little boys and girls shrieked with laughter as they scurried to find hiding places in piles of hay and behind their livestock. Young couples sought refuge in vacant huts, and nine full moons later a whole crop of babies were born. Other festivals were more devout, with processions around provisional stupas and daylong chants that ebbed and flowed with the force of the wind. Yet others slaughtered their fattest sheep, roasted it on a spit over a raging fire, and feasted on the mutton with freshly harvested mustard greens. Whenever he traveled alone, Yeshua let down his guard and participated in the festivities with body and soul. With unbridled joy, he sang and danced with the villagers around each house and across the fields until his feet blistered and bled.

Returning to the temple after harvest always made Yeshua gloomy. Although he loved Master and his fellow monks, he struggled with life lived under strict rules. With every new moon, he became increasingly torn between the path of a bodhisattva and a normal life among ordinary people. Master stressed the importance of honoring one's vows, but sometimes Yeshua wondered if the Buddha's suttras may have been falsified. To him, laughing, dancing, and singing—even making love— were other means of communicating with the Self, with God. Joyful activities fueled him and connected him to others on a higher level. How could that possibly be wrong?

When he asked Master one night, after the other monks had fallen asleep, his teacher almost choked on his fermented milk. "What? Have demons possessed you?"

Master shook his head. He stood from his cushion to pace slowly, meditatively, around the room, muttering to himself.

Yeshua's heart beat nervously in his chest. He closed his eyes and sent his teacher waves of love.

"Issa," Master said after what seemed an eternity. He glanced at Yeshua with his good eye. "You do understand why the Buddha provided our rules of obedience? We are role models. If we cannot maintain our dignity, how can we teach others? You, if anyone, should understand how attachment to sensual pleasure blocks the path to Nirvana."

Yes, of course. That's what he had been taught.

"You understand that dancing and singing distracts from the Self, do you not? And it cannot connect you to the Self at all."

Yeshua sank to his knees before Master and touched his forehead to the floor. He shouldn't have asked. He should have stayed quiet, trusting his intuition. Why had he imagined that Master would understand this new thought that went against all that the Buddha preached?

"How many rules have you broken since you arrived?" Master asked. "Ten? Fifty? A hundred?"

Startled, Yeshua looked up. He thought of all the times he had masturbated in the woods, embraced a crying woman, or picked and eaten a pear from a wild tree. He thought of the golden ring he had refused to give up. What a fool he had been! Hadn't he sensed from the very first day that Master could read his mind and see right through him?

Yeshua tried to form an apology, but the words died in his mouth. He couldn't, wouldn't lie to Master.

Master shook his head. *This way of life is not for you*, he seemed to say. *Not for you.*

Outside, the vibrant blossoms in the garden glowed in the blue light of the full moon, but Yeshua was blind to its beauty. Master wanted him to leave. A child wailed inside him, the boy who had left everything and brought shame on his family——and all for nothing. He had failed once again.

Yeshua cleaned up his sleeping space, shook his blanket, and packed up his belongings. He took one last peek at the Holy Scriptures in the sealed basket. Then he woke Omkar. His friend followed him all the way to the end of Kapilavatthu, where a well-trodden road led farther north to the slopes of the Himalayas.

Without a word, they embraced.

The crisp winds of the changing season propelled Yeshua past blossoming rhododendrons that signaled the arrival of fall. Once the flowers had wilted, the weather would remain clear for three new moons before winter swept across the highlands. Far ahead, the snowcapped mountains beckoned, and beyond them——a world unknown. Long ago a merchant had mentioned a kingdom high up in the Himalayas: Ladakh. Some people called it the Holy Land, like Palestine. Perhaps they would welcome his message there. He only had to make it across the mountains before the snowstorms caught up with him.

Yeshua ran the discussion with Master over and over in his mind, wondering if he could have said something to change the outcome. But how could expressions of joy ever be wrong? And how could dancing in trance with others distract you from the Self? Dancing connected people on a soul level and made one forget who is who and who does what. Of course, the rules of the monastery might be useful for teaching young men restraint and control, but Yeshua was convinced something else, something important, was not being taught. Seclusion and abstinence were all well and good, but God had created humans for a reason. Why must he leave the world to become one with God? Living in the world while staying connected to God had to be the answer.

The ever-ascending and descending path weaved past scattered communities where villagers welcomed him as a traveling holy man and offered him food and shelter. The sun warmed his cheeks, and he hummed cheerful tunes as he made his way north. At the base of the Annapurna, the path became narrower, more treacherous. In the early mornings, a sheen of black ice covered the rocky trail, and he inched forward, careful not to slip and plummet down the narrow crevices. The higher he climbed, the more he struggled to breathe. His lungs ached from the thin air. He walked slowly, took frequent breaks, and huddled in caves at night after the sun had descended behind the peaks and he could no longer see where he was going. No communities had settled at this altitude, and he only came upon the odd family living in a cave or on a hillside, but they were few and far between. Two days had passed since he had last eaten. The wild yaks and horses he spotted in the distance were too far away to catch and fill his bowl with warm milk, and the only person he had met in the last couple of days had been a naked holy man even more desperate with hunger than he.

Yeshua's head throbbed, and his knees buckled underneath him. He sat down to rest on a cliff overlooking the mountains that still lay ahead. Should he turn back? Or should he continue, hoping to cross to the other side of the mountain—and risk dying in the process?

"Lord!" Yeshua called out. His voice echoed between the jagged ridges. "What do you want me to do?"

The words bounced and faded as fast as his hope. Perhaps he should return to Kapilavatthu, beg Master for forgiveness, and start over. Yeshua gazed across the mountains before him. The icy peaks rose like giants against an indigo sky, intimidating and warning him. Omkar had assured him the journey was grueling yet not impossible, but did he really know? Yeshua staggered to his feet. Daylight would be gone soon and he had to keep moving. Surely tomorrow he would feel better and would find some food. Any food.

His head pounded. His eyes zoomed in and out and refused to focus. The mountain spun in circles. He steadied himself with a hand on the cliff wall and, in a trance, forced his legs forward step by step. He shuffled past one turn, then another, until his legs gave out and he collapsed on the path. He closed his eyes, knowing the next breath could be his last. He might never open his eyes again.

For the first time in many years, Yeshua called out the name of Yahweh, Abba's name for God. The familiar name comforted him, and he thought of cuddling up into his mother's warm embrace, like a child. The ground seemed to shift beneath him, and Yeshua let himself be drawn into the earth, as if a root spiraled down from his tailbone and connected with the base of the mountains. The chakra at the top of his head opened and, like a funnel, channeled the energy of the universe. He floated high above his slumped body and saw himself lie too close to the edge of a steep cliff. His skin had turned blue from the cold, and the vapor diminished with every exhaled breath. Rising higher, he saw the people of the villages he had passed on his journey. He saw Master, Omkar, and the other bhikkhus meditating in the Kapilavatthu temple garden. He soared higher and higher, drifting all the way to his home in Capernaum, where he saw his brothers, sisters, and mother weeping by a sealed cave.

A grave.

Who had died? And at once he knew: his father. With the shock, Yeshua slammed back into his body, back into the Himalayas. His throat clenched with sorrow, and his gut cramped as if someone had punched him right in the pit of his stomach. His dear father had passed away. Yeshua swallowed. He couldn't breathe. He curled up into a ball as his eyes flooded with tears. Abba, his wonderful, kind, and patient father— gone. He would never, ever see him again. Never.

Yeshua wanted to scream, but all that came out of his mouth were whimpers. He tried to get up, but his limbs were glued to the ground. He wailed like a beast, the pain tearing his heart out. Never again would Abba look at him with his knowing smile. Never again would he sing the funny little songs that made the whole family laugh. Never again would he embrace Yeshua as only a father could. And never would Yeshua be able to beg Abba for forgiveness.

He screamed as hard as his weakened lungs could bear, trying to alleviate his agony. He wept and begged God to forgive him. He cried for his mother and his sisters. He whispered sweet words to the brothers he had abandoned. Oh, how he longed to be that twelve-year-old boy again, with a mother and a father, the boy who worked with his father as a carpenter—the boy who was safe.

He drifted into unconsciousness, exhausted by sorrow, unaware of the world around him, not caring whether he would ever wake up again.

Himalaya Mountains, AD 23

Darkness. Was he dead? Yeshua tried to move his arms, only to discover that something heavy covered him, held him in place. He moved his head from side to side. Soft fur tickled his nose. Someone must have brought him here, wrapped him up.

Where was he? His headache and vertigo were gone, and he was warm and dry, comfortable. He looked around, but his eyes encountered nothing but a thick veil of blackness. Yeshua shuddered. If this person hadn't taken mercy upon him, he would have died out there on the slopes. God had saved him. His eyes filled with tears of gratitude. He hadn't been mistaken after all: Yahweh wanted him to continue.

A shadowy movement caught his attention. He squinted to see better. Something—someone—had moved in the dark.

Yeshua sat up. "Hello?" he called out. "Sahib?"

The creature moved closer. Then, a wide row of white teeth: a smile. Strong hands anchored his armpits and pulled him up to sit. A warm bowl was placed in his hands. Yeshua moved the bowl to his face and sniffed: fresh yak milk, herbs. He took a sip. The liquid was sweet and frothy, and the herbs tingled his throat and stomach. He finished it in gulps.

Giggles. The sound cascaded like a waterfall.

"Thank you," Yeshua whispered. "You saved my life."

What a fool he had been, traveling into the unknown mountains alone and without packing any food. Monastic life had made him dependent on others. He had forgotten how to think for himself.

Yeshua could hear breathing near him. "Sahib, do you understand me?"

Maybe his host didn't speak Pali. Local language often changed from one village to the next. Or perhaps the being was mute. The silhouette retreated into the darkness and disappeared. Moments later, he reappeared and placed long, leafy stalks of something fragrant into Yeshua's lap.

"Eat!" The voice was soft, childlike. "Chew!"

The man did speak Pali, after all. Yeshua bit into a leaf. It tasted bitter but with a pleasant tang. Its juice numbed his lips and tongue. His eyelids felt heavy and his head swirled. His host was nudging him back to sleep. He lay back down, pulled the hides up to his face, and closed his eyes. The next moment, he was sound asleep.

As from another dimension, a falcon's shriek pierced his dreams. Yeshua rubbed his sleepy eyes and looked around, but the bird was nowhere to be seen. The sun's rays played over painted cave walls: yaks, deer, snow leopards, birds, women harvesting plants and cooking, men hunting, couples making love. Yeshua pushed himself up on his elbows to see better. These were pictures of real life: men and women—families—together.

Staring at a painting of a man working a piece of wood, he remembered that Abba was gone. Oh, how he yearned to return to an ordinary life in Palestine. He must leave. Now. But would he still have a home there? He had been a mere boy when he left. Would his brothers and sisters still know him? Could they forgive him? Yeshua thought of his brother Yakov and how, when tickled, his laughter made his whole body shake. His brother loved life. He used to skip Sabbath to play with stones in the lake because—he said—listening to stories about imaginary people was a waste of time. Once, Yeshua had smacked him because Yakov had claimed that any truth in the scriptures had been lost in a weave of lies. Yeshua remembered how angry he had been, how offended at the suggestion. But Yakov had known then what it had taken Yeshua a lifetime to learn—making people happy was nobler than preaching the Torah, because happiness equaled godliness.

He couldn't wait to meet his grown-up brother. He had to return home. There was work to do there. Real work.

When his host returned to the cave, Yeshua observed his every move. The petite man lowered the sack full of plants to the cave floor. He removed the fur skins tied to his back and the layers of woolen scarves wrapped around his head. Yeshua couldn't take his eyes off him. What an interesting face: perfectly oval with a flat nose and a delicate, graceful mouth. If it hadn't been for the short, choppy hair, Yeshua could have sworn he was looking at a girl. But only men would wear such heavy furs and those wide-crotched pants, and of course this young man didn't have breasts.

Or did he? As the man removed another layer of thigh-length robes, Yeshua saw that his hips were wide under a slim waist, his buttocks plump, and his small breasts perky. Oh, goodness. *Her* breasts.

"You. Are. Awake. Good. I Have. Food." The words came out in chunks. She grinned, revealing a row of crooked white teeth. When Yeshua smiled back, she scurried away into an adjacent space in the back of the cave to prepare the food. He watched her stoke the fire, chop the plants with a coarse blade, and put a ceramic pot on the fire to boil milk. Yeshua couldn't take his eyes off her. It had been years since he'd been able to observe a woman without feeling shame.

She squatted at his side and handed him a steaming bowl of porridge. "Now eat." Her eyes followed his every move as he tasted the food and devoured it with a healthy appetite. The porridge was foul-looking and bland, but it made him warm, and the taste reminded him of a vegetable soup Ama made.

"I'm Issa," Yeshua said, after licking the bowl clean. "What's your name?"

"Pema." The girl pointed to herself, and then reached for the empty bowl. Yeshua held it back, hoping she would stay and talk.

"You live here—alone?" She reached for the bowl again.

Yeshua hid it behind his back. "Please... Pema."

She looked at him, confused. When Yeshua put his hand on hers, she pulled it away.

"Talk to me."

Once she realized he wouldn't come after her, she relaxed but stayed at a safe distance.

"Tell me about the pictures." Yeshua pointed to the drawings on the walls.

Pema scanned the room, as if searching for the best place to start. With basic words and gestures at the cave wall, she told her story. Her family had always lived in the Himalayas. They hunted for meat, gathered plants, and kept yaks. One day, in the midst of winter, a group of starving Zhang Zhung soldiers passed by and saw the family's stores of dried meat and milk. The soldiers chased her family out of the cave and gorged themselves on their food. Like beasts. Pema and her family stayed outside the cave for days, waiting for the soldiers to leave, but they never did. Pema's parents begged them to let the small children in for warmth, but the soldiers refused. Before long, two of her youngest siblings had frozen to death. To save his family, her father guided them down the slopes to seek refuge in the villages in the valley. On the way, her father was attacked and killed by a snow leopard. Her other siblings died for lack of food. When Pema and her mother reached the nearest village, her mother caught a fever, and in only a few days she wilted away.

Pema paused and stared at the ceiling, her face blank. After her mother died, a man invited her into his hut and offered her a place to sleep. Pema thought her luck had changed—until he raped her. She escaped the next day and eventually ended up living with another family who fed her and offered her a bed of straw among the animals, but they made her serve them from dawn until long after dusk. One night, the father came to her and she let him have his way. Pema's voice trembled—she had feared the man would strangle her if she refused. Early the following morning, she returned to the safety of the mountains. By then, spring had arrived, and the soldiers had left. Her yaks came when she called them, and within days she had made a comfortable home for herself in the cave. She made a pact with herself that she would stay in this cave until she died.

"Alone?" Yeshua asked.

Pema brushed the dust off her pants and went to poke the fire. She handed him another bowl of porridge. "I have animals. And birds. Mountains. Ancestor spirits. Not alone."

"And the Buddha? Do you know Lord Buddha?"

Pema frowned.

"It doesn't matter. You said spirits?"

She shrugged and laughed. Yeshua laughed with her, happy to be in her company.

"You know spirits?" she asked.

When Yeshua shook his head, she scrunched her nose, eyes wide. "You not hear? They talk and talk. All time."

"God speaks to me. He's like a father to me."

"Yes, my father speak to me," she said.

Yeshua felt sadness burn his throat. His father was also gone. He swallowed his pain and looked at the woman again.

"Your father and your mother?"

"Yes, my mother. But father and grandfather, they speak."

"What do they say?"

"They tell truth. When I see you, I not know if you alive. I not know if bad man. They say me take you inside."

Yeshua's eyes stung with fresh tears. He had asked to be saved, and Yahweh had saved him.

"They say this meeting"—she paused—"is sacred. When I see you, I know I save you. Not only life. Save."

"Save me from what?"

Pema seemed lost in thought. Then a big grin spread across her face. "Save from death. Life is picture." She pointed at the paintings on the cave wall. "Life not real. We forget we same as ancestor spirit. And we never die."

Yeshua watched her, stunned. Could it be that simple? Did separation between man and man—and man and Yahweh—begin when Adam and Eve ate of the fruit of the garden? Was separation an illusion? Could it be that everyone was still one and united with God? This woman, living on her own, had just expressed one of the most profound messages he had ever heard. "How do you know this?"

"Spirits tell me."

Yeshua scratched his head. She talked of spirits in the same way that he spoke of God. The words of her ancestors were no less divine than the words of the Buddha. Yeshua leaned back, watching her. Not only had she saved his life, but she had changed it. When he left Kapilavatthu, he had thought there was nothing more he could learn. How wrong he was!

He brought the bowl to his lips and sipped. The porridge had chilled, and oily yak butter coated the top. He took another sip, bigger this time, and handed the bowl back to Pema.

She finished it off without pause.

Yeshua thought of his father all day long. At night, Abba came to him in dreams.

Don't cry, son. I am still with you.

When Yeshua begged him for forgiveness, his father shook his head.

You are loved, and love does not judge.

Abba's words comforted him to some extent, but he still knew he had let his family down. He should have stayed and married a rich girl. He could have brought wealth and prestige to the family and made his parents proud. But instead he had selfishly followed his own dreams. And look where they had brought him. He was a grown man, but still a student. He had achieved nothing.

Remember, son, Abba whispered, *the spirit is a bridge between time and eternity. Neither day nor night, neither old age nor death or sorrow can cross that bridge. No one but the man who becomes one with spirit, whose night becomes day, because in the world of spirit, light is everlasting.*

Yeshua woke with a stomachache. He knew what he had to do. He didn't want to seek learning anymore if it meant losing everyone he loved. First Kahanji, now his father. He wanted peace. And how could he teach others if he couldn't quiet his own suffering?

Pema nursed Yeshua back to health. During the day, he rested, and in the evening they talked of God, spirits, and life. Much of what she said surprised him, and joy seemed to be her natural state of being. When Yeshua asked about her secret to happiness, she shrugged.

"I remember only good things. People who hurt me are not real. If they do bad, is only dream in my head. When I remember bad things, I hurt. So I forget bad things. We all are same spirit. Why I want to hurt myself? Forgive is easy."

"But what if oneness is not real?" Yeshua needed to hear more.

"What if world is not real? Instead of fight world, change your thought. See world as good, people as good. You want to be right—or happy?"

Yeshua wanted to take her in his arms and embrace her. Hold her tight. She was not the prettiest woman he had ever met, but her soul was beyond beautiful.

Himalaya Mountains, AD 24

"You must go now."

Her words hit him like icy rain. Pema had returned from milking the yaks at dawn and set down the vat of milk on the cave floor. He waited for her to laugh at the joke, but she stayed silent as she stoked the fire.

"Now?" he asked.

"Yes. First eat, then go."

He had never intended to stay forever. Of course not. But he had enjoyed her company and her simple life, and had even allowed himself to think about what their children would look like. It seemed only natural after all the nights they had spent talking about God and spirits that their lives would forever be intertwined.

"Why?" Yeshua's voice quivered.

"Time to go." She chopped the plants, ground the herbs, mixed them with butter and milk, and put the pot on the fire, whistling low as she stirred. She picked something out of one jar, then another, and added it to the brew. She didn't seem to notice his sadness.

She filled a bowl and handed it to him. Then she knelt beside him and pulled a yak skin over their legs. Her eyes met his.

"You want go to Ladakh, yes?"

He nodded.

"Ladakh far away. You go now, before winter."

She was right. The paths were treacherous during fall. In winter, they would be impassable.

Yeshua hung his head and stared into the porridge, his appetite gone. Pema had been an oasis, but her place was here. And he had to return home.

"I show you." Her eyes glittered as she put her hand on his. He grabbed her hand, cupped it between his hands, and brought it to his lips. Her warmth radiated through him.

After the meal, she showed him how to dress in layers to stay warm. She wrapped his feet in skins and fastened them with long strands of yak hair. Then she pulled robe after robe over his head and hung a heavy fur on his back, which she fastened with a leather sash at his waist. When Pema tied a bundle of furs and blankets to the back of one of her yaks, Yeshua realized that this was not the end: she was going to show him the way. Overcome with joy, he wanted to pull her close and kiss her. But the look on her face told him to stay away. Still, he couldn't help but smile.

At first, Yeshua struggled to keep up with her. Pema skipped up the paths like a gazelle, unfazed by the thin air and oblivious of the steep precipices. Now and then she turned to make sure he was still behind her. Yeshua gestured toward the yak carrying their bundles as if the animal were slowing him down, although his lungs hurt and his head spun, and he wanted nothing more than to stop and rest. But he told Pema he was fine, just fine. Although they were nothing more than friends, Yeshua still wanted to show strength and be the man.

Their first point of navigation was the rounded peak of the Tisé, the seat of spiritual power and the symbol for Om. Its name meant "Mountain of Sea Water" because it was the source of several holy rivers running all the way from the Himalayas to the plains of Satavahana. Some believed Lord Shiva lived inside the mountain, but Pema's parents had insisted the mountain was the home of the sky goddess Sipaimen. Perhaps it was both.

The Tisé, roof of the world, rose high above the snowy peaks sprawled in soft blue layers that contrasted with the stark grays of the cliffs. During the day, the sun burned so hot that they stripped down and walked in their under-robes and leg coverings. But when dusk cast its shadow and the air grew frigid, no amount of furs could keep them warm.

Pema encouraged Yeshua to continue moving during the coldest hours, allowing him to doze off only once the sun had risen over the horizon. She was the perfect guide. She could start a fire using sheets of ice to catch the sun's rays and send sparks into a bundle of wool and light a fire in the dried yak's droppings. She knew which plants to eat and taught him how to smear his face with grease to protect against the cold. She let the sure-footed yak lead them along the safest paths in the dark because one single unfortunate slip could plunge them down the ravines to certain death.

Pema's wisdom amazed him. At first, she didn't say much, just listened when he talked of his plan to spread the teaching of Lord Buddha and Krishna in Palestine. When she finally spoke, she asked:

"Who is Buddha? Who is Krishna? Who is Moses? Who is Abraham? Who knew the truth? All of them?" She paused. "Truth is inside." She poked her finger into his chest. "If you go to Palestine and no one likes your lesson, you angry then—or sad? Issa, you want to be happy? Because happiness from here." She poked him again as if to push her point into his heart.

Yeshua grabbed her finger and pushed her back, causing her to tumble backward. They both laughed as Yeshua pulled her up. Everything was so easy with her.

They slept in caves or in crevices, side by side under layers of furs, near enough to share body heat but far enough not to touch. One morning, Yeshua felt Pema snuggle closer. He moved away, thinking she was dreaming. She moved nearer, and again, Yeshua inched away. She crept closer again. And again. Exhausted, Yeshua gave up and succumbed to sleep, enjoying the intimacy of sleeping next to another human being after all these years.

When they woke, Pema acted as if nothing had happened and Yeshua sighed with relief. But to his astonishment, the very next day as they lay down to sleep, Pema didn't even pretend to be asleep when she put her arm around him. Yeshua trembled at the feel of her soft breasts against his back. He thought of her cave paintings of men and women making love. He thought about sliding his hands down her body, feeling her nipple harden in his palm. But he couldn't move.

After that, Pema cuddled up to him every day. She let her hand slide a little bit lower and lower until her hand was inches away from his crotch. Yeshua could scarcely breathe. Was she playing with him? When they walked, she spoke about spirits and the universal force that was part of every being. She showed no interest in him as a man. She never gazed into his eyes or casually touched him as they spoke. She moved close to him only when they lay down to sleep. Yeshua allowed her to touch him as much as she wanted while he struggled to think of Krishna and the Buddha and all the holy men in the world who preached abstinence. He thought of her wisdom and their friendship. And still, he reveled in her touch.

One morning as they were falling asleep, Pema reached for his groin and held on to him. Yeshua swallowed. There was no point in denying her intention. Her hand grasped him gently at first, then more firmly, playing up and down the length of his penis. Yeshua held his breath. He tried to distract himself, but her movements became more determined. When he couldn't resist any longer, he lifted the fur and moved his hands up inside her robes, baring her breasts in the cold morning air. He pressed his cheek against her chest and sighed. He had waited so long. Then he opened his mouth and sucked on her nipple, tasting its saltiness, its deliciousness. Women were such beautiful creatures—why would God ever want them to live apart from men?

When Pema lowered her pants and spread her legs, Yeshua climbed on top of her. At last he could look at her face without embarrassment. She closed her eyes and moaned. He kissed her neck. He kissed her cheek. He kissed her lips. But then he hesitated: had he gone too far? When Pema lifted her hips to him, his doubts vanished. She wanted him.

He grabbed her hips and rocked her harder and harder until she screamed with pleasure. Their bodies moved together until he exploded with relief, laughing uncontrollably. He rested his head on her chest, listening to her heartbeat. How had he never noticed how beautiful she was before? Those glimmering eyes, the sun-scorched cheeks, and the perfect breasts. He lifted his face to hers to kiss her again, but she turned away, pulling down her robe. Time to sleep.

Yeshua sang through the rest of the journey, just like Abba used to on their long walks between the villages of Galilee. He made up songs that described the beauty of the nature around them and the power of God. But he never sang about Pema and their relationship, even though they now made love every day.

The Himalayan plateau was as magical as Pema. Antelope grazed the steppes against a backdrop of snow-covered peaks. Snub-nosed monkeys played hide-and-seek behind thorny bushes and between the rocks. Occasionally, hordes of donkeys or three-toed horses galloped by far off in the distance. One day, as they stopped to rest, Pema and Yeshua discovered carvings of animals and humans on the walls of a cave, and wondered how many travelers had walked this path before them. They passed rivers, lakes, and camps of nomads, and if they were lucky, were invited in for buttery tea.

Pema taught Yeshua how to survive on his own. They picked eggs from nests of water birds, making sure to leave one or two for the mother to hatch and raise. She showed him edible plants and how to find the juiciest winter berries.

When they came upon a hot spring that spurted water high into the air and painted a shimmering rainbow in the mist, Yeshua and Pema peeled off their layers of clothes and dove into the warm water. They scrubbed their bodies with dried leaves and washed their hair with mud. As they prepared to continue their journey, a caravan of Han merchants on horseback passed by and welcomed them to ride along. In gratitude, Yeshua and Pema rubbed the merchants' tired backs with herbs and transmitted healing energy from their hands. When their ways parted, the men gave Pema and Yeshua thin silk wraps, claiming they would keep them warmer than the thickest wool.

Although Yeshua was getting used to their wandering lifestyle and their early morning couplings, he knew these blessed days would not last. One day, Pema stepped out on a ledge overlooking a fertile valley and raised her hands toward the sky. She spoke to the heavens in a singsong language with words Yeshua didn't understand. She pointed to herself and to Yeshua and to the valley and bowed her head three times. Then she knelt at the ledge, spit in her hands, and drew lines across her face with the saliva. She called Yeshua to come kneel beside her and took his hands in hers, closed them palm to palm, and brought his thumbs to the space between her eyebrows.

When she released his hands, she smiled, eyes full of love.

"There," she said, and pointed at the valley. "SLes. Ladakh. Now you go."

Yeshua had prepared himself for this moment. He knew Pema would not share his life's journey, although she had been his teacher in the purest sense: she had shared her wisdom and asked for nothing in return. He stood at the ledge, shaded his eyes with one hand, and scanned the green valley sprawled between gray hills below. Pulling Pema close, he thanked her without words. Theirs had been a spiritual connection: God had sent her to save his life, to care for him, and show him the way. He kissed her cheek and then turned away. With peace in his heart, he walked down the hill toward the valley and the brown speck in the distance that was the Ladakhi village of sLes: the crossroads through the Himalayas that connected the Far East and the rest of the world.

sLes, Kingdom of Ladakh, AD 24

As Yeshua entered sLes, children rushed to greet him with shouts of welcome. Dogs barked and wagged their tails. Small, round-faced women with high cheekbones and elderly men with long braids stepped out of their whitewashed houses to see what the commotion was about, and then beamed at the pilgrim with their entire beings. With a relieved grin, Yeshua waved at the adults and pinched the children's cheeks. He sent waves of love to the growling dogs until they didn't know what to do other than sit down and watch him. He followed a path below umber cliffs pockmarked with dug-out dwellings in the direction of the village center.

When he reached a bazaar, Yeshua squatted down and leaned his back against a wall to take in his surroundings. Farmers displayed pyramids of fresh apples and turnips. Bakers laid out bundles of noodles on a blanket next to baskets of steamed dumplings and sacks of finely ground barley. Women offered healing herbs, freshly made yak's-milk cheeses, woven linen fabrics, and heaps of black yak wool. Butchers with bloodstained aprons sold dried slabs of yak, camel heads, and cured horsemeat. Traveling merchants hawked salt and spices, cashmere wools, silks, blue indigo dyes, and a sweet and sour herb for smoking called cannabis. Pilgrims moved from stall to stall, begging for morsels of food in exchange for a blessing. How familiar this was! And yet, with the backdrop of snowcapped mountains, how very different. Yeshua's soul filled with gratitude. Fresh produce meant friendly people with satisfied stomachs. There was no better time than harvest season to enter a new town.

A group of children, attracted by his contented smile, sat down beside him. They stroked his sunburned skin and tugged his beard. Yeshua hugged them one by one and kissed their foreheads. One rosy-cheeked girl hid behind the others and giggled, playing peekaboo with him. Before long, the shrieking children were chasing Yeshua around the market while the excited dogs barked and snapped at their heels.

Exhausted but happy, Yeshua finally slumped down to rest against a hut made of sun-dried bricks. He couldn't remember the last time he had felt so carefree. For the first time in his life, he was enjoying himself without fearing the consequences, without regret. What was it Pema used to say? If you are truly one with Spirit—her name for God—you cannot feel guilty because you know you are perfect. Guilt comes from separation. God is perfect, and so are you.

So am I, Yeshua thought as the children plopped down next to him, panting, worn out from their play. They held his hands as he sank into a meditation. At once, he was one with God: bodiless, guiltless, and free.

When at last he opened his eyes, the sun had descended behind the peaks, and he shivered with cold. Black ravens soared above, screeching. Yeshua watched their flight across the skies until the echo of an empty stomach reminded him it was time to find food and a place to stay. The children had long since left, but a small group of adolescent girls idled across the market square, trying to appear busy. They twirled the yellow and red silk ribbons in their braided hair and hid their eyes under pointy fur hats with triangular flaps pulled back like dismissive dogs' ears. Yeshua gestured for them to come closer. The girls looked at each other and burst out laughing. Then they approached him, their burgundy gowns swaying under the yak skins on their backs.

"Good evening!" Yeshua tried in Pali.

The girls did not respond.

"Namaste?"

Same result.

"Jule," he tried in Bön, Pema's language. When they giggled behind their hands, Yeshua knew he had found common ground. "Kind women," he said, searching for words in a language he had not mastered, "where may a pilgrim find food to fill his stomach?" He patted his belly. Still tittering, the girls led him to a two-tiered building lit by torches. Yeshua bowed to the girls and pressed his palms together in front of his chest.

"I'm a pilgrim," he said to the innkeeper who appeared from the back room, "begging for a meal and a place to sleep."

The innkeeper shook his head. "No pilgrims."

"No?"

"Pilgrims sleep with animals."

Moments later, Yeshua pinched his nose as he rolled out his sleeping mat in the dingy stable that he shared with horses, camels, and yaks. The innkeeper had brought him a bowl of noodles with stale pieces of carrots and cabbage, but despite his generosity, Yeshua knew he couldn't stay in a place like this more than one night.

Pema used to say, "What you expect is what you receive." If so, could he change his sleeping quarters if he believed he deserved better?

The night seemed endless. All the stomping, grunting, and stirring kept him awake. Every time he dozed off, the stench of urine, feces, and rotted hay woke him, and before long he gave up. He rolled up his sleeping mat, wrapped up his possessions, and stepped out in the blue light of daybreak. He filled his lungs with the crisp mountain air and stretched his limbs, pausing to say a prayer. The White Brahmins of Jagannath had imprinted on him the importance of starting each day with a prayer to set a purpose for the hours ahead.

Yeshua walked down a stony path to bathe in the river. The icy water numbed his limbs as he waded in up to his chest. He held out his arms and implored Spirit to charge his body with divine light. Pressing his palms together, he recited the mantras his Buddhist master had taught him. He asked the Blessed One to help him appreciate all he was given this day and graciously accept the lesson in everything. Nothing happened by coincidence.

Yeshua washed his clothes to rid them of the stable stench and rubbed his body dry with grass. His reflection in the quiet water surprised him; with his curly long hair and dark beard, he resembled an Israelite more than a monk. Did the men back home still wear their hair and beards long? Would he be accepted among his neighbors when he got home?

He thought of the slow, arduous walk ahead of him, wondering if he would even make it, when light snowflakes fell on his head. Winter. He had to move on soon. Pema had said the road from sLes to Parvasenpur became impassable during the cold months. Pema. His heart fluttered when he thought of her. Would she make it back before the snows? But the flash of worry dissolved as quickly as it had appeared; Pema was in command of her life. Nature obeyed her. A pang of sadness replaced the concern.

He missed her.

Yeshua hung his wet clothes on the branches of an apple tree, wrapped his new silk robe around himself, and nibbled on a fruit. He imagined himself before a cozy fire and felt the heat spread through his body. Warm and comfortable, he drank from the river until his thirst was quenched, stuffed his sack with as many apples as he could fit, and wondered how long they would last. The thought excited him: he was curious to see how the next weeks would unfold. Who would God place on his path? Smiling, he lay down under the tree, pulled his silk robe over his body, and fell into sweet slumber.

He woke to find himself surrounded by a group of children staring at him. Yeshua drew his robe tighter around him.

"Where you from?"

"Your name?"

"You speak Ladakhi?"

"You have children?"

The questions rained down on him. He looked from one open face to another.

"I'm Issa. From Palestine. Far, far away. Very little Ladakhi." He answered as fast as he could in a mixture of Pali, Bön, and Sanskrit, using words they seemed to understand. A crowd formed as other villagers gathered to see what the fuss was about.

"You think I look different from you?" he asked.

The children nodded.

"I sound different?"

"Yes, yes!" the children shouted. A couple of adults joined the shouting.

"What if I said we are all the same—in God's eyes?"

They shook their heads in unison.

"But we are. We look different on the outside, but we are the same on the inside."

The grown-ups stared at him as if he spoke nonsense, but the children were drawn in by his energy.

"You worship the mountains and the sun, yes? You pray to the rivers. What if none of those alone can protect you? Only Brahman—God—the one who made the mountains and the sun and everything you see around you can keep you safe. And God does not exist only in the things you see. Brahman also lives inside of you."

Silence. Perhaps they didn't understand, but they stayed put.

"Think about it," Yeshua said. "Who is hurt if you become angry with someone? You or the other person?"

"The other person!" someone shouted. The others hushed him.

"Me!" a little girl said, her eyes sparkling.

Everyone nodded.

"And if you help someone, do you feel good or bad?"

"Good!" Some of the older children chimed in this time.

"When we help others and think positive thoughts, we become one with God. We feel him in our hearts. And when we are as pure and good as we can be, we cannot die. And we won't be reborn. We are already one with God."

Yeshua combed his fingers through his long locks and scanned the crowd to make sure they followed.

"Like the Lord Buddha?" a young man asked. "I've heard pilgrims speak about him."

Yeshua nodded to the young man and smiled. "Yes. Lord Buddha was one of many who came to this world to teach others how to reach oneness with God."

He looked across the crowd, enveloping them in a circle of white light. "You can feel safe in the limitless power of love within you. You have no need of idols or sacrifices. They can only separate you from God. Be kind to one another, that's all you need to know. Open your hearts and share your love with your fellow men and women—and children—for you are one with God."

Yeshua glowed with excitement and love. He was drenched in sweat. Where had the words come from? His speeches had always been guided, but this time it felt as if God had entered his body and spoken through him. And they had understood him.

Eventually, the crowd broke up, and Yeshua returned to the bazaar. His stomach grumbled, but he didn't want to beg anymore. Whatever he needed, God would provide. He leaned against a wall and watched the children chase each other around the stalls, slipping and sliding in the fresh snow. What a blissful land. Even the women were free. They never lowered their eyes in conversations with men, whether the men were old or young, married or single. Some women even had two or three husbands. And why not? In other lands, men took more than one wife; why shouldn't the women do the same?

One of the girls he had met last night squatted next to him. "How was the inn?" she asked in a language that resembled Bön with a different tone. It would take some time to learn.

Yeshua shook his head. "Not inn—stable."

The girl frowned. Yeshua wanted to tell her not to worry about him, but he couldn't find the words. How could he explain he would be quite all right whatever happened? But before he could form a sentence, she darted away. Yeshua watched her run, her long gown flapping around her trim legs. He sank down to sit on top of his sack, overcome by dizziness. It had been hours since he had eaten the apples. His stomach craved something more substantial.

"Here, eat!" As if summoned, a Punjabi merchant appeared and handed him a bowl of salty barley noodles, cottage cheese, and shredded turnips. Yeshua accepted the food with both hands. He brought the hot bowl to his lips.

"Thank you kindly, my friend."

The merchant showed him to a tent where other travelers were dining. Relieved to communicate in Sanskrit, a language he had mastered, Yeshua took his time finishing his meal.

This group of merchants was traveling to Luoyang in the Han Empire to trade cottons and salts for silk, the most lucrative of all commodities. The profits could keep their families fed for several years, but Yeshua wondered if they weren't driven by less altruistic needs. As a man sporting a long, white mustache pointed out, "Why stay with an ugly witch at home when you can buy as many pretty women on the road as you want?"

The others chuckled in agreement, but Yeshua's smile faded. He remembered how he had once admired the traders, how they had seemed incredibly wise and interesting. Now he realized they were nothing but weak men, seduced by money and sex. Their wealth had poisoned them. Perhaps it was better to be poor. Perhaps the less a person owned, the closer he could be to God.

Before he could ponder further, the girl reappeared at the opening of the tent and motioned for him to follow. Yeshua wiped his mouth and thanked the merchant for his hospitality. He could hear the men snicker as he left with the graceful girl.

"I'm Stanzin," she said, and took his hand as they climbed a path along the soft curves of a low hill toward a field farther out from the village. "My family—we are nomads. My father welcomes you." Yeshua wasn't sure if she spoke in simple sentences for his sake or if the language was that basic. "I'm Issa. From Palestine."

"Pali." She beamed. Once again, Yeshua wanted to explain that he was from a land very far away, but did it really matter what culture had raised him?

On a plateau outside the village, dozens of yurts had been raised among a herd of yaks. The icy wind sent flurries whirling in the air, dancing across the grassy plain, blurring the backdrop of jagged peaks. Stanzin disappeared into one of the yurts. Moments later, a fierce-looking man appeared in the doorway. Wide as a bull and as hairy as a macaque, he peered at Yeshua from under bushy brows. A shiver ran down Yeshua's spine and he took a deep breath, but then the man's face broke out in a single-toothed smile, and he engulfed Yeshua in a firm embrace. "Welcome to our home, Issa."

Inside the yurt, Yeshua was greeted with hugs and kisses from Stanzin's mother, sisters, and brothers. Their two Tibetan mastiffs danced around him, unable to contain their excitement. The family chattered in chorus, in a language Yeshua barely comprehended, and peppered him with questions without pausing to hear his replies. A boy showed him to the men's sleeping yurt and pointed to a pile of hay covered with blankets and furs that was to be his bed. Yeshua unpacked his sack, grateful he had found a warm and clean place to stay.

Two days after his arrival, a snowstorm covered the valley and closed sLes off from the rest of the world. All caravans and pilgrims would be stranded here until spring.

Stanzin's family treated Yeshua like a member of their clan and made him guard their livestock, a grave responsibility. The yaks provided a source of milk and meat, wool for clothing, and a handsome income from the sales of newborn calves.

Every night during the darkest hours, Yeshua and the mastiffs kept watch outside by the fire, armed with a slingshot to protect the family's yaks and mules from wolves, bears, and snow leopards. In the daytime, Stanzin's older brothers shooed away any wild asses that sneaked close to eat of the dry bushes needed to feed their own animals. Every so often, Yeshua took advantage of the brief daylight to trudge with the dogs through deep snow to the village and teach anyone who wanted to listen how a person could become one with God. As his renown spread, an increasing number of villagers and travelers gathered to hear Sage Issa speak. He accepted the title with some reluctance, but as long as they listened and learned, they could call him sage or prophet or anything else they liked.

One day a woman brought her unconscious daughter to him. Yeshua took the lifeless toddler in his arms and held the girl up to the ceiling of the fur merchant's tent where he had been speaking.

"God," he said, "please save this child."

He placed the girl on a pile of furs and put his ear to her heart. When he detected a faint beat, he placed his hands on her torso, just as Kahanji had taught him. Pema's voice rang in his head: "Sickness is of the mind, not of the body. The healthy mind cannot conceive of illness, because it and everything is God. And God is without disease."

His hands traveled across her body and onto her head. He raised his consciousness to unite with God, to the dimension where everything was possible. The child coughed and convulsed with spasms under his hands, but Yeshua stayed focused. When at last the girl opened her eyes, her mother cried with relief. The little girl's cheeks colored to a bright pink and Yeshua drew a breath of relief. Pema and Kahanji had been right: healing was possible if you believed everything was already perfect.

After what seemed like years of winter, the first purple flower sprouted through the melting snow, announcing the arrival of spring. The time had come for Yeshua to continue his journey. He had already stayed much longer than planned. And though the Ladakhis had been receptive students, he couldn't wait to go home and teach his own people how to practice compassion, kindness, and oneness with God.

A long line of sLesians accompanied him to the first bend in the road to Parvasenpur. They waved their good-byes with joy in their hearts.

"Now you know that anything is possible," Yeshua said when they reached the end of the village. "All you have seen me do, you can do, too. All I am, you can be. God's gifts belong to us all, every people in every land. God is the bread and water of life."

He straddled Moshe, the mule they had given him, and raised his hand for one last good-bye. Stanzin, her sisters, and the mastiffs followed him a little farther. The girls sprinkled him and the mule with holy yak milk to keep them safe from wild animals and steady their steps on the icy path.

With a heavy heart, Yeshua pressed his palms together and bowed. They had been so kind. Leaving Stanzin's family felt like deserting his own kin. Yet again.

Would the good-byes never end?

Bactria, AD 25

For the first time since he had set out on his own, Yeshua enjoyed his journey. He had the company of Moshe, who carried him for long stretches and whose body provided warmth at night, and he felt closer to God than ever before. Surrounded by love, he was never alone. He had finally realized the meaning of life and death: everything around him was his own creation. The only time was now; the present moment was the same as the past and the same as the future. This life was an illusion. Was he really here, or did he exist only in his mind?

One night he woke from the sound of a singsong voice. Pema. She lay beside him, in the flesh, and looked at him with that broad, angelic smile. His love had come back to him! Yeshua drowned her with kisses, holding her in a tight embrace, nuzzling her neck, until he could no longer keep his eyes open and drifted into sleep.

When he awoke, she was gone. Only the honeyed scent of her skin remained. She had appeared to prove that space and time exist only in our minds. He smiled. He only wished she could have stayed a little longer.

The path to Parvasenpur led him over high mountain passes and across shaky suspension bridges, past golden prairies and dry desert valleys. He encountered caravans that had been stalled for the winter, and befriended nomads who invited him to share their meals. Ever since Yeshua had stopped obsessing about hunger, his meals had been more frequent—and tastier. Letting go of wants and needs had made his life simpler, leaving him with no needs or wants at all.

In some stretches, the alpine landscape displayed a sea of pink rocks and gray pebbles under a boundless blue sky; in others, the scenery bragged of lush oases where delicate yellow and pink flowers peeked up through high grass. He collected dry branches for firewood whenever he walked past a cluster of trees and was careful to cross streams in the early morning, as by midday the melting snow had changed them into rushing rivers.

The town of Parvasenpur reminded him of Kapilavatthu with its green fields surrounded by tall forests. It marked the end of the most treacherous leg of his journey. From there onward, the path would trail downhill into warmer climates. Yeshua celebrated his feat with a day's rest by the Dal Lake while Moshe grazed the nearby meadows.

Refreshed after a bath in the lake, Yeshua tied Moshe to a tree and went to the market to exchange his furs for a woolen coat and a lighter cotton robe to wear under his worn silk wrap. The Kushan food was spicy and delicious, rich with the flavor of cardamom, chilies, and cloves—a welcome change from the bland dumplings of sLes. But he found himself picking out the meat from his bowl. He hadn't tasted flesh since boyhood, and the mere thought of consuming animals made him queasy.

Although he was tempted to stay and rest in Parvasenpur for a while longer, Yeshua was more eager to continue homeward. When an Egyptian merchant insisted he join their caravan, Yeshua gladly accepted. The next morning, he and Moshe set off westward beside his new merchant friend and hundreds of overpacked camels and horses. Yeshua struggled to converse in the Aramaic he hadn't spoken for many years and thought he misheard what the Egyptian told him. Herod Archelaus had run Judea into ruin and subsequently had been dismissed and banished to Gaul, leaving Judea to be ruled directly by the ruthless Romans. His brother, Herod Antipas, in turn, had let power go to his head and had built a brand-new Galilean capital, Tiberias, on the southwest shore of Lake Kinneret. Yeshua remembered how, as a boy, he had wanted to join the coming Messiah in fighting the Romans and kicking them out of their country.

Was it too late to fight back?

In less than two new moons, the caravan reached Rawalpindi, where a lifetime ago Yeshua and Dhiman had bid good-bye to their fellow travelers and turned south to Sindh. Yeshua smiled when he thought of his wise friend. Surely Dhiman would be the head monk of his temple by now.

And then he thought about Ramaa, the delicate girl with large brown, antelope eyes and her shaved head. Had she remained at the hermitage? Was she even alive? If he went to fetch her now that they were adults, would she follow him? Would she marry him?

Pining for his first love paralyzed him. When the caravan left Rawalpindi, he stayed behind. Every morning, he awoke determined to return to Ramaa and save her from a life of misery, but the longer he waited to leave, the more his resolve wavered. She wouldn't want to see him. He would remind her of the life she had lost. Yet as the day progressed, he changed his mind over and back again until his head spun and he thought he was going insane. Was she even the same person? Pema would have said that Ramaa was nothing but an image of a perfect being that Yeshua had created in his mind over the years. If he went after her, he would face a woman of flesh and blood with flaws like everyone else.

Yeshua swallowed the tears he hadn't cried. His family was waiting for him. He picked up a stone by the river, kissed it, and ceremoniously dropped it into the water as a symbol of his love for Ramaa. As the stone sank into the dark water, his spirits lifted. At last, he had let her go.

Memories of his journey to Sindh as a boy shadowed him on his way back home. How young and naïve he had been, and how self-assured. To think that all he had wanted then was for people to listen to his stories, to be seen and heard and valued. Now his quest was different. All he wanted was to teach others how to find oneness with God, so they could become enlightened and spread the word to others. He was but a single drop in the ocean, yet the entire ocean was alive within him.

Walking without company allowed him to stop in every village. His open and peaceful manner attracted many listeners, including local priests. But when some of the holy men heard his message, they became outraged.

"How dare you come to our village and spread lies. Our gods have always protected us and our rituals have brought us plentiful harvests. They work! You are an ignorant fool, nothing but a troublemaker."

Yeshua spoke softly. "If the gods you worship are so powerful, ask them to strike me down right here."

He looked to the sky, as if expecting a thunderbolt. The villagers, too, turned their eyes upward, perplexed. Even the priests looked up. When nothing happened, some youngsters giggled. Soon, all the villagers were laughing. The priests glared at him.

Yeshua shushed the people around him. "All I am saying is that when you listen to that calm, loving voice inside, you will always know what is true and what is right."

In Kabul, Yeshua joined another caravan that would accompany him across Persia and Mesopotamia, through lands where the fruits were always fresh and the vegetables always in season. The golden ring still burned in the folds of his robe and reminded him that it was time to visit the Zoroastrians, who had once mistaken Yeshua for their prophet, and return their ring.

Over the years, Yeshua had heard many stories about the prophet Zarathustra and learned about his faith. The prophet had preached about a kind God called the Wise Lord and an evil being that was at constant war with God. The only way to keep evil from creating chaos and destroying the world was through good deeds. After a centuries-long struggle between good and evil, the Zoroastrians were still waiting for a savior who would release them from suffering and raise the dead for final judgment, so that the righteous could once again be united with the Wise Lord. Yeshua loved the stories, but he didn't believe there was a need to fight evil. Being one with God was enough to bring peace to everyone.

In Kandahar, Yeshua found another of King Ashoka's stone pillars, similar to the one in Lumbini, although this pillar was inscribed in Aramaic and Greek. He struggled to decipher letters he hadn't seen since he left home, and read the text out loud, word for word:

> "*The years have passed since King Piyadassi pledged to teach all men about the Buddha... King Ashtoka taught us not to eat and kill animals, not even fish... Practicing Lord Buddha's teachings has brought value to all men...*"

Yeshua smiled. The words felt familiar on his tongue, and he knew that in no time he would be back to speaking like a native Galilean.

On entering Phra, Yeshua spent the night in the ruins of a Greek citadel among the city's poorest inhabitants. They offered him a meal of maize dumplings with curdled milk, and Yeshua spoke to them about finding God within. A dark-skinned, voluptuous girl brushed her breasts against him at every opportunity, but Yeshua resisted the temptation to follow her into her tent. Once back home, he might take a wife, but until then, he had to focus on spreading the word of God. He smiled at her to show his appreciation, but explained he needed a full night's sleep because he was traveling early the next morning.

The next time a new moon rose in the sky, Yeshua arrived in Susa. A throng of men in billowing white pants and flowing head scarves met him at the gates. They guided him up the stairs of a palace adorned with wooden pillars and statues of winged bulls with human heads, to a raised platform overlooking a tiled courtyard.

"Sage Issa, your renown precedes you. Pray bestow upon us the wisdom you have acquired on your travels."

Yeshua surveyed the dozens of men and women staring at him with anticipation. Although he was weary from days of riding his mule on dusty roads, he would not let them down.

"Men, women of Susa," he said in halting Greek, "I am humbled in your presence, being neither nobler nor wiser than you."

The men and women exchanged confused glances.

"All I can do is show you the entrance to God's Kingdom."

The crowd relaxed. This was the message they had come to hear.

"My travels have brought me through many lands and empires. I have studied with the Yehudim and the Jains, the followers of Lord Buddha and Lord Krishna. I have studied the Vedas and the Bön—"

"And what about the prophet Zarathustra?" a bearded man called out.

"Yes, I am familiar with your prophet who preached about one God and the importance of good deeds. I agree with his words: you may suffer in this life, but you will be rewarded in the afterlife."

The people cheered. This was what they had been taught, also.

"Everything I have learned from all traditions can be summarized in one single truth: we are all one with God—and God is good, so good."

The listeners nodded and chatted among themselves.

"But what if I told you there is no need to fight evil and to suffer until your savior arrives to release you?"

Absolute silence.

"What if I said you could enter God's Kingdom right this moment?"

All was quiet.

The stillness shattered when two priests shoved through the crowd. "Halt this heresy immediately!" they demanded.

Yeshua opened his arms, inviting them to join him on the platform.

But they stopped in front of him, arms crossed. A priest with eyes set wide like a goat peered up at him. "Are you not aware, you miserable imposter, that Zarathustra is the *singular* man who has spoken with the Wise Lord?"

Yeshua beamed at him with love.

The priest spat at his feet. "Who are you to preach about a new God and blaspheme against the Wise Lord? Who gives you the right to sow doubts in our hearts?"

Yeshua stepped down from the platform and put his hand on the priest's shoulder. "I'm not speaking of a new God, dear Teacher. I speak about the same God, the Wise Lord who has existed since the beginning of time."

The priests stepped back as if threatened by Yeshua's mere presence.

Yeshua pressed his palms together in front of his heart. "Your ears may be deaf to my message, but the hearts of your people will hear God's voice through my words."

One of the priests grabbed Yeshua's arms and shook him. Another stepped in front of Yeshua's face to challenge him. "How dare you come to our town and soil our people's minds with your untruths? Do you expect anyone to listen? And to believe they can live without rules?"

Yeshua placed his hands on their shoulders and gently turned both priests to face the crowd.

"Before there were priests, people lived in peace. They abided by natural laws, their souls connected with God. They didn't need priests or idols to communicate with the Wise Lord."

One of the priests pushed Yeshua to the side and opened his arms to the crowd. "Stay calm, citizens! This man is an imposter. He aims to fill your heads with lies. Go home now in peace."

The crowd dispersed, all but a lanky white-clad, turbaned old man squatting in the back. His eyes glowed with the color of a burning sunset. Yeshua's heart beat faster; he knew this man! It was one of the mystics who had stopped at Abba's workshop all those years ago. Yeshua waited until everyone but the priests had left before he approached him. He untied a knot in the seam of his robe and revealed a bundle wrapped in a tattered yellow silk scarf. He squatted next to the old man and held the bundle out to him.

"I came to return this," Yeshua said.

The priests stared at him, full of mistrust.

The mystic unwrapped the scarf. He held the golden ring with the turquoise stone between his thumb and forefinger, and turned it this way and that. Then a wide smile of recognition spread across his face. He looked up at Yeshua in disbelief.

"When I was a little boy," Yeshua said, "you visited my family in Galilee. You thought I was the reincarnation of your great prophet Zarathustra." Yeshua shook his head, smiling.

The old man and priests were so focused on the ring, they didn't react to his words.

"But you see, I'm not who you thought I was, and I have come to return the ring. Praise the Wise Lord, I hope one day he will reveal to you the true reborn prophet."

With that, Yeshua left the stunned priests and the old mystic and walked down the stairs to find Moshe.

The next morning, Yeshua rose early and went for a walk in the town center where the locals went about their morning duties: sweeping the streets, begging for food, buying fresh bread, and selling eggs. The men wore embroidered jackets over leggings that fell in multiple folds and golden diadems in their long hair. The women sparkled like expensive gifts, all wrapped up in colorful clothing that covered everything but their faces. The jewelry that adorned their heads, wrists, and ankles glistened as they caught the rays of the morning sun.

Animated voices ebbed and flowed from a tent at the back of the market, and Yeshua grew curious. He pushed aside the entrance flap and saw a grown man squeezed into a child's body standing on a bench, preaching to a crowd. His hair shone red like a harvest moon, and his matching silk jacket reached all the way to his ankles.

"God's gift to man is free will. Oh yes, my friends, we may all choose our path. Have you made this most important choice yet?" The speaker wagged his finger at a youngster in front of him. "Are you following the road of deceit—or truth? Be honest! God witnesses the choices you make. Yes, yes, you don't have to confess in front of us all, but know this: the path of evil leads only to despair. Choose the path of *truth*, my friends, the path of truth. We are all God's helpers. We all have to make the righteous decision. Agreed?"

The tent shook with shouts of "Praise the Wise Lord" and "Agreed, agreed."

Yeshua nodded. The message was good, but the threat of despair was unnecessary. God had no need to torment.

The tiny preacher pointed to a fire blazing in a clay vat beside him. "See those flames? They help us gain insight and wisdom. How?" He cackled, shaking his wild red mane. "Because fire is one of the first elements created in the world, it represents the sun that gives life to all. It is a symbol of truth and learning. And like knowledge, the fire should never, ever die."

Yeshua pushed through the crowd to face the speaker. "And what about silence?" he asked.

"Silence?"

"Yes, silence. Isn't silence the best tool by which to gain wisdom?"

The preacher laughed and gestured for the crowd to join him. "Silence! Oh, Wise Lord, indeed—silence!"

"If there's no silence, how will you hear?" Yeshua asked.

More laughter. "And what can you hear, my good man…?"

"Issa."

"And what can you hear, Issa, if no one is talking?"

"The voice of God."

The preacher's grin lapsed into a sneer.

Yeshua turned to address the crowd. "Silence is where our souls meet God, the place where wisdom abides in all of us. If your life is a burden, if everything seems hopeless, seek refuge in silence. Find a quiet place to close your eyes and listen to the voice within you. Whether you call it prayer or anything else, pause your thoughts and let the Wise Lord do the talking."

The crowd gawked. Some scratched their heads.

"Open your heart and fill it with love. If only for a moment, lay aside your anger, your work, your troubles at home. Once your mind is empty, it may be filled with the divine. And in that space, you will hear God's words, God's wisdom."

The preacher raised his palms toward Yeshua, his face flushed. "This man speaks the truth! Through him, the Wise Lord's words have been spoken."

Yeshua nodded to the preacher and walked away. He wasn't entirely sure they had understood his message, but at least they had let him speak. And that was what was important—to sow that seed.

He returned to where he had left Moshe, packed up his belongings, and resumed his journey.

His work in Susa was done.

The closer Yeshua came to Capernaum, the more he urged poor Moshe forward. The road brought him through Ctesiphon, Seleucia, and Dura Europus, where the size of the towns was matched by the Roman entrance tax charged at the gates. How strange it felt to once again blend in and look like everyone else. No one stared at him. No one paid him any attention at all.

The longing in his heart turned into a stomachache. He was so close to home, he could almost smell the musk oil his mother used to wear. He fought the desire to hurry, aware that affection for his family was a sign of attachment to the physical world. Instead, he stayed in the present, making a point of stopping in every village and settlement along the way, if only to share a kind word, an embrace, or a healing touch.

Damascus, Syria, AD 26

In Damascus, memories of the young boy with pompous dreams and an inflated sense of self-importance came flooding back. The crossroads of this majestic city had been the point of no return, where he had made the final decision that would change his life forever. Here, he had given his ring to the fierce caravan leader in exchange for protection on the route to Sindh. Yeshua sat in the shade of tall poplars by the Temple of Hadad to contemplate the journey still before him. Once Damascus had blinded him with its sophistication: the tall city gates adorned by colorful mosaics, the temples, theaters, and—perhaps more than anything else—the primped ladies who left traces of rose petal perfume in the air as they walked by. As a boy, the traveling merchants had seemed both clever and worldly and the holy men infinitely wise.

Now the city seemed smaller, its treasures less impressive, the inhabitants more common, and the traders seedier. Yeshua sent a thought of gratitude to the gruff caravan leader who had taken pity on two naïve young monks, fresh off their mothers' tits. How intimidating he had appeared at first, and how kind he had turned out to be. It had been Yeshua's first lesson in not judging people based on their appearance. Oh, what a serious young man he had been, so convinced of his piety. It had taken years of study and a lifetime of experience to realize that only the joy that came from unity with God could lead to holiness. He recalled how his fellow travelers had listened to his stories about Abraham, Moses, and King David. Had they simply indulged him? It didn't matter now; their food had kept him alive through the yearlong journey across deserts and steppes, over mountains and glaciers.

The main thoroughfare led him past Caesarea Paneas along the upper Jordan River and down the hills to Capernaum. Home. Yeshua tasted the word, wondering if he still belonged in the town he had left so long ago. The road seemed both familiar and foreign. It was still covered with pebbles, but over the years the increasing amount of traffic between Damascus and Alexandria had widened the path into his hometown.

Capernaum seemed more welcoming than any other town he had lived in or passed through during his journey. Yeshua nodded to everyone he passed. Could they be old friends? Relatives? How could he possibly recognize anyone now after all these years? An entire lifetime had passed since he had left home. The scent of seaweed drifted between the sand-colored houses, along the narrow streets, and mixed with the sweet fragrance of blossoming rhododendrons. The breeze from the freshwater lake brought tears to his eyes: no other lake in the entire world generated a wind quite as soft. In the center of town, a new synagogue built with gray basalt had replaced the old mud-and-straw-brick building. Black smoke swirled toward the sky from the courtyards of the flat-roofed buildings. In every home, families were preparing to sit down around platters of grilled fish and legumes for the evening meal, the same way they did every night of every day of every month of every season. Did his mother, brothers, and sisters still save a place for him in their midst?

Overcome with emotion, Yeshua stumbled through town, intuitively finding his way down alleyways between newly built houses and older ones that sparked forgotten memories and made the hairs on the back of his neck stand up. He could have asked for directions, but he didn't want anyone to know who he was. Not just yet. First he had to know if his family would welcome him back and forgive him. If they rejected him— he didn't dare to think about what would happen if they did.

The market was smaller and more crowded than he remembered, but otherwise not much had changed. The fishermen still peddled baskets full of the tilapia, carp, and sardines they had caught that same morning.

The sandal maker's and blacksmith's wives competed with their bargaining skills, their wares laid out side by side on a blanket. Farmers from the surrounding villages hawked their lambs and calves and chicks, and traveling merchants offered up colorful fabrics and jewelry to the townsmen, who mostly ignored them. At the south end of the square was the ledge where Yeshua had first met Dhiman, and next to it, the cluster of palm trees where the exotic pilgrims and holy men had huddled, hoping for a piece of bread or a handful of grapes. Today, fortune-tellers who predicted the future using the intestines of sacrificed birds occupied that space. On the north end, prostitutes with crudely painted faces loitered, waiting for the cover of night when their business thrived. And there, right there, was a place he knew well: the stonemason's shop. The walls had yellowed and the window shutters hung askew, but the same old triple-chinned mason in his dusty apron still stood in front, hands on his hips. His skin sagged and his waistline had expanded, but otherwise he looked the same as the day he came to Abba's house to present his daughter to Yeshua—what was her name? Behind the mason's house, only five or six doors down the alley, was his father's workshop.

Yeshua's heart throbbed and his legs trembled. Bile rose up his throat, and he had to steady his hands on a wall to stop his head from swirling. What if his family didn't want to see him? He had caused them so much pain, they must despise him. He should leave, turn back, run away—escape somewhere.

Moshe, sensing his anxiety, trotted close to his side and pushed Yeshua against the nearby wall. His mule was right; he shouldn't flee. This was home. He owed it to his father to let Ama know he was alive. He led Moshe down the street, past houses made of rough stones and smoothed with clay, until he reached the familiar blue door. The paint was slightly chipped and perhaps a touch darker in color, but there was no mistaking it. Yeshua ran his finger along the Aramaic letters carved into the wooden sign: *carpenter*, and underneath, *bar Yosef*. Yosef's son.

This was it.

He tied Moshe to the hook assigned for pack animals and paused in front of the door.

Unable to breathe, Yeshua raised his hand to knock, only to lower it again. He took a deep breath. He had survived near starvation and freezing weather, evaded attacks by robbers and wild animals—and this was what he feared?

He closed his eyes and focused on what he had been teaching: the world around him was nothing but an illusion. There was no reason to be frightened, because nothing real could be threatened. Only oneness with God and all humanity was real; everything else, including all fears and threats, were but fantasies. That, in essence, was the ultimate peace of God.

He knocked and waited. Then he knocked again and pushed the door open. Inside, a carpenter leaned over a workbench, carving detailed patterns into a board. He didn't look up. Yeshua's heart raced. The man resembled Abba, with the same long limbs, scruffy brown beard full of wood chips, and bushy eyebrows, but this man was perhaps a few inches taller and decidedly more muscular. His long, artistic fingers moved with purpose and grace. Could it be Yakov? Another of his brothers? Yeshua searched for words, but his brain had come to a complete standstill.

How did you say *brother* in Aramaic?

The carpenter looked up. "Yes?"

Those vivacious eyes... Yakov! Of course. Yeshua's beloved little brother. His best friend.

"Can I help you?"

Yeshua wanted to throw himself into his brother's arms, but he couldn't move. He opened his mouth, but no words came out. Yakov took a step closer, his head tilted, eyes probing.

"It's me, Issa. I mean Yeshua. *Achui.* Your brother."

The chisel slipped from Yakov's hand and dropped to the floor with a clang.

"Yeshua?"

Before he could move, Yakov had picked him up and swung him around in a tight embrace. He kissed Yeshua's cheeks over and over again, laughing rambunctiously until tears flowed from his eyes and his breath caught in hiccups. They both fell to the clay floor, shaking with laughter until they ran out of air.

"May God be blessed, you returned!" Yakov raised himself up on his elbow. "I always said you'd come back one day. And see, here you are—— in one piece. Just like the brother I remember. Ha! You look exactly the same. Except with a beard. And taller. But what's the story with that robe? What is it—Mesopotamian?"

"Kushan."

"Look at you! Where all did you go, big brother?"

"Everywhere."

Covered in sawdust and wood chips, the brothers sat with their backs against the workshop wall while Yeshua tried to describe in broad terms how he had left with Dhiman, shaved his head, and become a monk. He told Yakov how he had crossed the Satavahana continent alone and how he had lived with the White Brahmins for many years and studied Krishna's lessons under the great Kahanji. He reminisced about teaching in Benares and how he had learned everything there was to know about Lord Buddha in Kapilavatthu. But it wasn't until he had met Pema that the teachings had crystallized. She had taught him that everything, every crumb of knowledge, had always resided inside of him.

"God lives inside us all." He patted Yakov's chest.

"Why did you come back?" Yakov's voice had died to a whisper.

Yeshua put his arm around him and clutched his shoulder. "I missed you. And I need to—want to—share everything I know with our people. We've suffered so long. Think about it: we have nothing; we're not even lords of our own land. I want the Yehudim to know there is no need for suffering. We may not control the world outside, but we are kings of our own reality."

Yakov looked lost. He spun the chisel on the floor, making it rotate on its tip.

"What about you?" Yeshua turned the conversation around. "You're as remarkable a carpenter as ever. But did you wed? Do you have a wife? Any children?"

"Of course! I have the loveliest wife, Michal, and five children, two with—and three without."

It took a moment for Yeshua to remember his brother's sense of humor. Of course. He chuckled: two boys and three girls.

Laughing, Yakov stood and pulled Yeshua up from the floor.

"Come," he said. "Dinner should be ready any moment. When did you last have a proper grilled fish with stuffed grape leaves?"

"Yeshua!" His mother threw her arms around his neck and wailed, releasing the anguish from years of grieving the loss of her firstborn son. Yakov joined the embrace, squeezing Yeshua so hard he could scarcely breathe. They stayed clustered, sealed tight, one around another, until their hearts calmed to a gentle hum. Yeshua couldn't remember the last time he had been so happy.

One by one, Yakov's children drew close to their once-lost uncle, asking him a hundred and one questions. Ama wouldn't let go of his hand. "My son, my treasure, where have you been? And by God, what have you done? You look like a hermit." She tugged his dark curls. "What's with your clothes—they're so soiled."

She reminded him of Ramaa: such a delicate physique and those large sad eyes that shone with such profound love. Yeshua caressed her soft, wrinkled cheeks and pushed her silvery hair out of her face. How he had made her suffer, and still she welcomed him back with open arms, forgiving him without hesitation.

The courtyard overflowed with people as his brothers, sisters, nieces, and nephews joined them for the evening meal in the courtyard. With kisses, stories, and cups of wine, Yeshua reconnected with the family he had abandoned as an adolescent. Shimon, a carpenter with his own workshop, had married a gentile and brought six children into the world. Iosa, a sought-after robe maker, had eluded marriage. The angelic Salome arrived with her husband and two daughters. Miriam was pregnant with her eleventh child. But his brother Tau'ma surprised Yeshua the most. Not yet born when Yeshua had left, he had grown into a near-identical image of the son his parents had thought they lost. Like Yeshua, Tau'ma had pestered the rabbi with unanswerable questions and thus had earned his nickname Tau'ma—which meant "twin" in Aramaic.

As the night wore on, the children grew sleepy and Yakov's youngest curled up and fell asleep in Yeshua's lap. Well after nightfall, when the jars of wine were empty, Yakov showed Yeshua to a padded matting filled with hay in a corner of the back room. Worn from an emotional day, Yeshua lay awake listening to the sleeping sounds of his brother's family. His head spun from the wine, and his stomach resisted the energy of the fish, the first live creature he had eaten in years. In the distance, he heard the voices of fishermen as they splashed their boats into Lake Kinneret. Somewhere, a jealous husband screamed at his wife, upset that other men ogled her in the streets. In the courtyard, Moshe brayed along with the local donkeys, and the sheep seemed to bleat in agreement.

Yeshua felt like a child again. The coarse linen of the matting scratched his skin just the right way, and the familiar scent of dill, thyme, and coriander that permeated the walls brought him comfort. He should have come home sooner. But then he would never have met Pema, his amazing woman who had taught him that all could be forgiven—should be forgiven—just as his family had forgiven him.

Being home was both strange and wonderful. Yeshua soon fell back into his role as the oldest son. He helped Ama bring produce from the market and assisted Yakov in the workshop, although it soon became apparent from his throbbing thumb and all the crooked nails that he was better suited for sweeping. He rekindled his relationships with his brothers and sisters and was amazed when learning how much they had in common, despite spending their entire lives in different parts of the world.

He accompanied his mother on long walks along the lake, listening to her memories and soothing her worries. In the evenings, he sat with her by the fire and massaged her painful limbs and healed them with his hands. But when he talked about his journey and told her all he had learned about enlightenment, compassion, and love, Ama patted his head and kissed him as if he were a child talking nonsense.

On the evening of the first Sabbath after his return, Yeshua sat next to his brothers on a mat in the back of the new synagogue. The spacious hall filled with families looking for cool shelter on a hot spring night, and now everyone sat side by side, wiping their sweaty faces with cotton scarves.

The flames from the oil lamps on the rabbi's pulpit danced in the slight breeze from the narrow windows, throwing glittering traces on the walls. Yeshua closed his eyes and listened to the voice of his beloved rabbi, the potter, whom he had idolized as a child. His teacher had grown old and had not recognized Yeshua as the child who had once followed him around. Still, the light of God shone from within him, and Yeshua found himself swept away in the story of creation. As he listened, he pictured Brahman creating the light and the sky, forming lakes and rivers that Yeshua had passed in his travels. He saw the trees and bushes and flowers that the Wise Lord had created, each with its own seeds for reproduction, and the sun, moon, and stars that had lighted his journey. He thanked the Creator for the animals and birds who had kept him company and for the men and women who had taught him how to be one with all. And last, he thanked Yahweh for the Sabbath, which provided time for rest and a day for prayer and contemplation.

The rabbi's voice interrupted his meditation. "And we welcome back our long-lost son, Yeshua bar Yosef."

The rabbi had remembered him after all! Yeshua raised his hand in a wave and peered out at his townsmen. A murmur of surprise spread across the room as everyone stared back at him.

"Yeshua, why don't you tell us about your travels." The rabbi gestured for Yeshua to join him in front of the assembly.

Yeshua rose to his feet. He bowed to show his reverence for the rabbi, but remembered that bowing to others was forbidden and quickly straightened his back.

"My friends. Galileans."

His voice broke with nerves. Aramaic. He had to remember the words. He had taught in Greek, Ladakhi, and even broken Bön, but this was different. Aramaic was his own language. They would scorn him, call him pretentious, if he mixed in foreign words. Yeshua closed his eyes, drew a deep breath, and asked God for assistance.

"Our Lord guided me through many lands and showed me the magnificence of his creation. I have seen mountains as tall as the Tower of Babel; they rise so high into the sky that even the air does not reach all the way to the top. I have traveled deserts so dry and wide that my eyes played tricks on me and I saw pools of water appear and disappear where there was only sand. I have met people with no arms or legs and priests who walk around naked. I have ridden on the backs of great gray hogs as tall as camels but with long snouts that curve to the ground. And I have studied with holy men who showed me the key to eternal life. My brothers, fellow sons of the almighty God, I shiver in humility as I assure you that the spirit of God came upon me and told me to be a messenger of his words."

Yeshua paused to look out at his family and his neighbors.

"I learned about Krishna, an incarnation of God who walked the earth, like Isaiah and Moses and many of our patriarchs and prophets. And like them, Krishna was a reincarnation of God."

Yeshua closed his eyes, feeling the fire of God's love burn within him.

"From Krishna's scriptures, I learned that ignorance stems from our attachment to pleasures. We all want to satisfy our desires. But that will never make us happy.

"I studied the teachings of Lord Buddha, another incarnation of God, who said that when you no longer consider anything yours, you will reach a place of peace. For nothing truly belongs to you. Attachment causes suffering, and only release from desires can bring you peace."

Yeshua opened his eyes. His townsmen were exchanging puzzled looks. He had to make the connection for them before they lost their patience.

"Like Isaiah, who said we should keep from doing as we please on the Sabbath, the Lord's holy day, Krishna and Buddha also taught that we may honor God by adhering to his commandments. When we are true to God's will, we accept him into our hearts and we become one with him."

The hall filled with confused whispers.

"One with God?"

"Who are these idols he speaks about?"

"He thinks he is God?"

"Do you hear what he's saying?" A man stood up and turned to the people seated around him. "There is only one God!" he yelled. "Yahweh says we should have no other gods before him!"

From the back, an old man's shriveled voice rang out. "Isn't that the son of Yosef, the carpenter?"

Yeshua turned to the man and stretched his arms wide to show modesty. "Yes, I am he, Yeshua bar Yosef."

"Who gave you the right to preach? You're a craftsman, not a rabbi."

"That's true, I'm not a rabbi." Yeshua's heart pounded as he looked at the crowd who had gathered around him. He tried to keep his voice from shaking. He focused on sending love from his very being to the men and women around him. If only they would listen, if only they would give him a chance.

One man grabbed Yeshua's robe and started dragging him outside. "You're nothing but a false prophet. Get out!"

Yeshua freed himself from the grasp and pulled away from the man. He tried one more time to explain:

"My friends, of course there is only one God. But he comes in many shapes and forms, and—"

Too late.

A crowd of men surrounded him, grabbed his robe by the neck, and hustled him out of the synagogue.

The door slammed shut behind him.

Yeshua fell to the ground, defeated. Bitter tears rolled down his cheeks. For the last two years, he had been set on returning home. It was supposed to be the end of the quest, the place where everything fell into place and his true purpose came to light. He had lived for this moment. His entire journey with hundreds of detours had led him back here; this was where he belonged. And now his own people had thrown him out, discarded him like one of the mad field preachers his father had despised.

At home, Yakov tried to comfort him. "Listen, brother, no prophet is ever welcome in his own hometown. Just as a doctor doesn't heal his own family."

But Yakov's words held no comfort. He might as well give up and become the carpenter he was born to be. He was a nobody.

He had failed as a teacher.

"I'm not going far, Ama," Yeshua said as he wrapped a couple of tunics into a bundle and stuffed them into a traveling sack. "I have to get away from here to think."

When his mother lowered her eyes and clutched her chest in sadness, Yeshua's heart ached with shame. He had disgraced the family yet again. Everywhere they went, everyone was talking about the incident in the synagogue. But despite the pain he had caused her, his mother's love still showed through.

"Yeshua, why don't you go to the temple in Jerusalem? Stay with Aunt Elisheba. Renew your faith."

Yeshua held back his tears and kissed her head. "Don't worry. I'll be back before the nights grow colder."

"And don't let me see you with tattered clothes again!" Ama called after him as he set off toward the southern shore of Lake Kinneret in his brand-new sandals.

Southern Galilee, AD 26

By nightfall, Yeshua had reached the mouth of the Jordan River and rolled out his sleeping mat on the bank. Wind whipped his face, and ominous clouds threatened rain. He reached down and splashed the water. When no bulging crocodile eyes appeared, he washed his tunic in the river and hung it in a riparian tree to dry. Relieved to be alone in the wilderness again, away from judging eyes, he lit a fire and asked Yahweh to protect him from lions and cheetahs and other wild animals. He begged God's forgiveness for wanting to go against the laws of the Torah that clearly taught that the priesthood was reserved for Levites. Then he closed his eyes and drifted into jagged sleep.

The next day he continued his journey. The farther south he walked, the more frequently he heard stories about a Nazirite who initiated his followers by immersing them in the river. Some whispered, their voices full of hope, that this Baptizer might be the Messiah everyone had been anticipating for so long, the one who would save the Yehudim and expel the Romans from the Holy Land.

"The time has come," they said. "God is angry, and only the Messiah can save us!"

Despite his sadness, Yeshua grew curious and joined the flow of people in search of the holy man.

Nothing could have prepared Yeshua for his first glimpse of the self-appointed preacher dressed in a camel-hair tunic, standing up to his waist in the middle of the river. With his long and tangled hair, he resembled a madman more than the Messiah. Hundreds of devotees sang and chanted around him. Some twirled in a wild dance as if possessed.

Yeshua sat on a boulder at a safe distance to observe him. Abba would have ridiculed this jester, but Yeshua watched him with keen interest.

One by one, the believers waded into the river, their heads hung low. The Baptizer reached his palms toward the sky and spoke in garbled speech, with words that made no sense. But just like Sanskrit mantras, the power of the words seemed magical.

The Baptizer cupped the chin of the man before him and whispered something in his ear. With his other hand, he scooped up water, splashed it over the man's head, and dunked him backward under the water before he brought him back up in one quick motion. Holding the man by the shoulders, the Baptizer yelled something to the heavens before he sent the believer off. The crowd roared with excitement.

Yeshua moved closer to better hear the words the Baptizer spoke to the next man in line.

"And God will punish all sinners. He will send his ax to cut down trees that do not bear fruit. Come, all weak and lost souls, and be baptized. Be purified in God's name!"

Some of the newly baptized wept, others jumped with joy. Out of curiosity, Yeshua joined the line of those waiting to be baptized.

When at last his turn arrived, Yeshua entered the river and lowered his head before the holy man. The Baptizer extended his hands toward the sky and shouted, "Lord, wash away this man's sins. O, most sacred Creator, let the water cleanse his wrongdoings, his misdeeds. Accept him as your son who loves you!" He took Yeshua's face in his hands. "My son, confess your sins, and you will be baptized in the name of God. Share what you have with those who have nothing. Abstain from sedatives like wine and fermented drinks. Do not eat or sacrifice animals. And—"

The Baptizer stopped midsentence.

Meeting his eyes, Yeshua noticed something familiar about the Baptizer's freckled face. It reminded him of someone he had known once. A friend?

"Yeshua?" With a guttural laugh, the Baptizer shook Yeshua's shoulders, then nudged him back to see better. "Mother of a lizard, it *is* you!"

Yeshua frowned. How did the Baptizer know his name? Who was he? Wait—could it be…Yochanan? Uncle Zekharyah's son?

Before Yeshua could speak, Yochanan swept him up in his arms and hugged him tight. Then he turned to the astounded onlookers and shouted, loud enough for everyone to hear, "This man was lost in the desert, but he has come home. Thanks to Adonai." Still grinning, Yochanan scooped up water from the river, splashed it over Yeshua's head, and dunked him. Yeshua sank willingly. He allowed the water to cleanse him, like the holy Mother Ganges once had. God entered his soul. The light in his heart spread through his body and connected with everyone on the banks of the river. *Heaven.*

His trance broke only when Yochanan lifted him from the water to the cries of "God has saved you, sinner!" all around him.

In a daze, he waded to the riverbank and succumbed to the shaving ritual. Once again, he allowed a sharp knife to cut away his past as the token of a new beginning and submission to God. He sat among the other initiates to relish the ecstasy of the already baptized and the anticipation of those still in line. God hadn't deserted him after all. God had led him here.

Yeshua stayed a few days to observe his cousin, trying to understand why someone destined for priesthood had given up a life of respect to become a wandering preacher. Had he also become disillusioned with the limitations of Yehudi law?

Though newly baptized, most of the Nazirites remained burdened by daily worries. They could not feed their families. They were harassed by the Sadducees and the Romans. Some had family troubles, an abusive husband or a wife who was sleeping with the money changer. Yeshua did his best to console them.

"Listen, the poor are the truly blessed, because only you have access to God's Kingdom," he said after hearing their woes. "The rich spend their lives worrying about losing their money and their possessions. They suffer because the more they have, the more they want. What they have is never enough. But those who have little appreciate all they have and gladly make room for God in their hearts."

"Where is God's Kingdom?" they asked.

"Right here. And everywhere. It's in every land, in every village. Some people just can't see it."

But Yochanan's followers believed that the end of the world was imminent. They waited for a magical warrior, a Messiah who would banish the Romans from their land and catapult the Yehudim to paradise. They expected thunderbolts and men walking on water, not a message as subtle as Yeshua's: that everything they saw was an illusion and that heaven could be found only inside.

Disappointed, Yeshua left the Nazirites and wandered aimlessly around the lower banks of the River Jordan. He had no idea what to do and where to go from here. One morning, after spending the night in the company of Samarian shepherds, he woke up thinking about Pema. She had found all her answers while meditating in a cave in the mountains, all by herself. The Buddha had spent forty days and forty nights alone in the wilderness searching for enlightenment. And so had Moses.

He laughed out loud. The solution became as clear as the blue sky above: isolation. All his life, he had been surrounded by others. Coming home, he had expected to sweep in and be welcomed with open arms by people eager to be enlightened. But no one was looking for enlightenment. They were quite content to suffer under Roman rule and receive only the crumbs of God that the rabbi shared. Were all his years of learning a waste? Should he return to the Parthian Empire and continue teaching there?

No, he did belong in Palestine. His mission was here.

Yeshua crossed the hills to the Samarian desert and set down his mat between cacti and rocks in a vast area inhabited by nothing but reptiles. He would stay here and meditate until God showed him the way. And although his stomach already screamed with hunger, he silenced the pain. If the holy men in Benares no longer needed food or drink to survive, neither did he.

He sat down, closed his eyes, and waited. And waited. Ignoring the protests of his empty belly, he focused on the true existence, the one so different from the world before his eyes. The moon rose and traveled across a boundless sky. Birds woke to greet him with their songs. Lizards scurried across the sand into the shadows of the cacti, waiting for the relentless sun to give way.

Countless days later, weakened by the heat and the lack of food and water, his mind drifted in and out of delirium. He fixated on a brown stone by his feet. "If you're that special," a voice in his head challenged, "why don't you turn that rock into a loaf of bread?" Yeshua shook his head to clear his mind. "Look at the world," the inner voice provoked. "Look at it!"

In an instant, Yeshua found himself floating high above his body, looking down at the rawboned man sitting cross-legged in the middle of an immense desert. He saw the land of Palestine from Judea to Galilee, the glittering sea, the mountains of Mesopotamia, the entire world. "This belongs to you," the voice tempted. "You can be the master of it all."

Yeshua crashed back into his body. He was going mad. *Water.* He chewed on his dry tongue and smacked his parched lips. He needed water. Blinded by the scorching sun above, he blinked. What was that in front of him? A cactus. Liquid. If he broke off one of its arms… But no, he couldn't give up. The Buddha had been challenged by demons in the desert—the same demons that tempted him. "I can't," Yeshua rasped. "I'm not a master. Only God can be the master."

At once a brilliant light enveloped him and he connected with God, free of body and free of his ever-doubting mind. Free of duties and free of expectations. Free of wants and needs. Free of hunger and thirst. At one with God and all beings.

His father appeared as a warm gust of wind and bathed him with love. Yeshua absorbed his presence and felt his father's approval sanctify him. And then he knew: Abba hadn't despised the traveling preachers, he had feared them. They had threatened his faith in God.

Don't be afraid, my son, Abba said, his voice caressing Yeshua's soul. *God speaks through everyone. If you act with love, God will show you the way.*

Yeshua's heart opened, exploding with gratitude. The message was as clear as the purest wind: God spoke through all living beings, not just him. Everyone played a part in fulfilling the universal plan. And at last he understood what his teachers had tried to tell him—the path of serving God was not for him alone. It was for everyone. No one had to be led away from the Torah, their faith in Yahweh, and their traditions. God did not want him to remove or disturb anyone's beliefs. His message should be simple. He would remind them about the nonviolence and compassion taught in the Torah while following the highest ideals of the Law of Moses. A smile cracked his dry lips. At last he was free of the need to change and convince others. And God would show him the way when the time was right. All he needed was to let go of his plans and let God take control.

"Never leave me again," Ama pleaded when he returned home. He took her face in his hands and kissed her forehead. But he couldn't promise anything. Wherever God led him, he would follow.

Early one summer morning, during his daily walk along the shores of Lake Kinneret, he saw two fishermen far out on the lake. They threw their net out again and again to spread it as wide as possible, then pulled it back into the boat. Sometimes the net came back loaded with fish; other times it was nearly empty. A flush of warmth spread through Yeshua. A sign. He would throw out his net to people, and whoever wanted to hear his message would come with him. Those who didn't could just swim away. If he only used the words of Lord Buddha and Krishna without naming them, perhaps people would listen.

When the fishermen returned to shore, he approached them. "You caught many fish today."

The men looked up for a moment, and then continued to unload the fish.

"Your catch was plentiful," he tried again.

"Not plentiful enough."

"But your boat is full of fish."

"Not full enough." They were simple fishermen, ignorant of the Holy Scriptures. Very similar to the peasants he had spoken to in Benares and Kapilavatthu.

"What if I told you I could teach you how to catch more fish and how to always get what you want?"

The fishermen laughed as they continued to empty their nets.

"Come and listen. I will make it worth your while."

The men shook their heads.

"I'll buy a basket of fish if you give me a few moments of your time."

They looked at each other. The market wouldn't open for a good while, and selling a basket of fish this early would give them a head start on the day's sales.

After hanging their nets over their boat to dry, the three men sat on the rocks at the water's edge, with their feet cooling in the waves.

In the months that followed, Yeshua met with the fishermen every day at dawn. He helped them clean their nets, told them stories, and taught them how to open their hearts. When their catch grew bigger day by day, they called their friends to listen.

"Ask, and you will be given," Yeshua said. "He who expects will receive." Old man Zebedee's sons soon joined the group of fishermen-students.

"God makes everything possible," he said, aware that he had made a connection. The men listened, mesmerized, as if afraid to break the spell. "In God's Kingdom, we are all wealthy. We can all have what we want. And the kingdom is right here."

"Where?" one of Zebedee's sons wanted to know.

"Here," Yeshua said, patting his chest. "You can't see it, I know, but if you believe in it, anything's possible. The Kingdom of God is like a treasure buried in a field. You can work the land for years and never know the treasure is right underneath your feet. You won't find the incredible wealth inside you until you dig, deep down."

"When will I be rich, then?"

Yeshua nodded, pleased that they were asking questions.

"There are more important things to worry about in life than what you eat and what you own. Think of the ravens. They neither plant, nor harvest, nor store their food—and still God feeds them. And don't you think that you, as men, matter at least as much to God as birds do? Believe me when I say that worrying is a useless habit. It makes you anxious and unhealthy. And worry does not solve any problem; it enhances it. Relax and trust in God. He knows you must eat. He will provide for you."

"But surely God loves the rich more than he loves us."

Yeshua shook his head.

"No, he doesn't. In fact, you—the poor—are the most blessed by God because you are much closer to his kingdom."

News of Yeshua's teachings by the lake spread through Capernaum. When people came to see, some were disappointed to find a common Galilean in a simple linen robe speaking to the poorest of people. There was nothing sensational about Yeshua. But he spoke of God's Kingdom as if he knew it well, and he claimed that its portals were open to everyone.

The local rabbis heard about his gatherings and came to see for themselves.

"What good news do you speak of? The end of the world is nigh. You had better prepare," they shouted from a safe distance.

Yeshua filled his heart with love for them. "God's Kingdom will not come because you wait for it. It's not a matter of saying 'Here it is' or 'There it is.' It's already here—everywhere."

The rabbis didn't believe him.

"Are you claiming, then, that the Messiah has already come? You believe he is the Baptizer, don't you?"

"I'll tell you a story," Yeshua continued, ignoring their questions. "Once there was a farmer who had a handful of seeds to plant. He threw them out over a large field. Some of the seeds were caught in the wind, landed on the road, and were eaten by the birds. Others fell on stones where the seeds could not take root, or got caught on thorny bushes where worms ate them. But a few seeds fell on good soil, sprouted, and grew into healthy plants that produced an abundance of fruit."

The listeners waited.

"You see, you are those seeds. Whoever has ears will hear."

Yeshua's simple lessons made sense, and although the fishermen didn't always understand his words, they noticed their lives had improved little by little. Not only did they catch more fish and make more money, but they also overcame their anxieties and became more patient with their wives and children. Once they viewed themselves as equal to both noblemen and beggars, their lives became easier. They no longer feared the Romans or the rabbis because they recognized a light within every person they met that was of God.

And they felt protected.

Capernaum, Galilee, AD 27

"Why must you leave again?" his mother cried when he announced he was taking his disciples on a journey around the lake. "Why can you never be still? You're always wandering, always looking for an answer. Can't you stay here with your brothers, marry, have children——"

"I'm too old to find a wife." Yeshua kissed her graying hair.

"Nonsense! Your father was older than you when we wed. And he was a good husband. How dare you say your abba was too old?"

"I know, Ama, he was a wonderful father. But look at you, all alone. I can't leave a wife to care for the children if I die."

"Your sons can look after your wife."

"And if I have only daughters? Who will make sure they marry into a good family?"

"That's why you have younger brothers."

Yeshua shook his head and continued packing. "They have their own families to care for, their own responsibilities. Besides, who says I'll be the first to go?"

"Iosa has no family."

It was true. His brother Iosa had never married and had no children. He made a decent income as a tailor, making exquisite garments for affluent families all over Galilee, Samaria, and Judea. He could take care of Yeshua's wife. But it was all speculative: there was no wife, and there were no children. Anyway, who would marry a traveling preacher? No man in his right mind would give away his daughter to a wanderer.

Yeshua kissed his mother good-bye and slung his sack over his shoulder. "I'll be back before you have time to miss me. Oh, and Yakov's coming with me."

He closed the door before she had time to object. In the last few weeks, Yakov had become a regular participant at his gatherings. At first, like a typical younger brother, he had questioned everything Yeshua said. But last night something had changed. One of Yakov's remarks had clarified the meaning of a parable. And when Yeshua suggested Yakov join him on a journey, his brother agreed without hesitation. Yeshua couldn't be more thrilled. Yakov's positive outlook on life and his injections of joy would be welcomed, especially among the sick and downtrodden. Yakov was his brother in flesh as well as in spirit, his equal among the others, who were more interested in witnessing miracles than anything else except perhaps catching more fish. Yeshua smiled when he thought of his disciples: they lived for those darn fish.

"My brothers," Yeshua said to the fishermen at the shore. "I know you all have mouths to feed, but listen: we are going on a journey around the lake to teach the people in the other villages. Will you come with us?"

They all agreed and rushed home to tell their wives. Three of the fishermen—Andreas, Ioannes, and Shimon—returned a while later with their belongings rolled into neat bundles. Only one man returned empty-handed, looking as if his best boat had sunk.

"My wife said no."

The others laughed. What a pitiful man who obeys his wife, they chuckled.

Yeshua looked at them, scratching his beard. "How can you see the speck of sawdust in your brother's eye and not notice the huge branch in your own? Did you not promise to come with me wherever I go? Tell me, what is the difference between obeying me—and obeying a wife?"

The fishermen shrugged and shifted their gazes from one to the other.

Yakov interrupted. "Friends, you laugh and all, but do you truly know why this man's wife needs him at home? No, you don't. Then you cannot criticize him, because when you chide someone, the judgment returns right back to you."

Chagrined, the fishermen patted the young man's back and asked him to keep an eye on their families while they were away.

The five men reached the village of Bethsaida by noon. As they rested by a riverbed, Yeshua brought out his shaving knife.

"You have a choice," he said, thumbing the sharp blade. "Would you make a formal commitment to serve God?" He combed his fingers through his hair, which had already grown to his shoulders. "Or will you stay as you are?"

The men looked from one to another. "Is it allowed?" they whispered.

But Yakov stepped forward and knelt before Yeshua, his head lowered. Smiling, Yeshua splashed water onto his brother's head and put the knife to work, carefully shaving the contours of Yakov's head. One by one, the locks of his long hair fell into the water and floated into the lake. When Yakov stood and straightened his back, bald as a newborn, he promised to stay forever clean and to always serve God. Without another moment of hesitation, the others knelt before Yeshua, ready to take the vow.

On an outcrop overlooking the lake, they shared a meal of flatbreads with cheese, honey cake, and apples. With their hunger appeased, it was time to meditate.

"It's more difficult to pray when your belly is too full or too empty," Yeshua said, and he showed them how to sit with a straight spine and allow God's energy to flow through them.

"Yawn and stretch. Relax your shoulders and move your head from side to side to loosen up. Just so. Rest your hands comfortably on your thighs, palms up. Now breathe. In and out. Focus on the breath moving in through your nose, circulating through your chest and down to the pit of your belly. Then release your breath through your mouth."

As the men breathed in and out, their wrinkles softened and their limbs settled at ease.

"Imagine a ray of light rising up from the crown of your head, reaching higher and higher until it touches the heavens and connects with God. Yes, just so. Repeat in silence, to yourself, 'I am the light,' over and over until you believe it. And then, listen inward. Still your thoughts so that you can hear God speak. Breathe in and out—and listen. If stray thoughts enter your mind, bring your attention back to the ray of light at the top of your head and connect with God again."

At last, having guided his disciples in the way of meditation, Yeshua closed his own eyes and opened his chakras one by one. He connected them, one to another, until they were in balance and his energy was one with God. So deep was his trance that he didn't notice the sun setting and the others, having emerged earlier from their meditative state, chatting louder and louder.

When at last he returned to consciousness, he was pleased to see his friends looking carefree and rested. With their bare heads, they reminded him of the monks in Kapilavatthu. Although curious about their first meditation, Yeshua did not want to break their blissful spell. He wanted them to think of meditation as something natural and uncomplicated. He didn't want anyone to become discouraged when comparing their experience with someone else's. It took time to find a personal connection with God. It had taken him years.

The night hung heavy by the time they rolled out their mats to sleep under a cluster of sycamores. Bats whizzed in and out of the trees, rustling the branches, but the five pilgrims slept serenely protected by the oneness of God.

In every village they visited—Kheresa, Hippos, and Philoteria—people invited Yeshua to heal a sick uncle, a lame mother, or a blind sister. In one village, he relieved the symptoms of a leper with a mixture of garlic, thyme, olive leaves, and red wine. In another, he used faith to help a disabled man move his limbs. In yet another, he brought a widow's son back from near death, sending God's healing energy into him.

Wherever they went, Yeshua always took the time to share a story. "A man had prepared a feast and sent his servant to invite the well-to-do men of the town. The servant approached the first man, saying, 'My master invites you to feast with him tonight.' But the man dismissed him, saying, 'I am sorry, but tonight I must meet with some merchants who owe me money.' The next guest answered, 'I have recently purchased a new house. I must stay and oversee the repairs. I cannot spare any time today.' Another said, 'My brother is getting married, and I must prepare the banquet. I shan't be able to come.' Yet another responded, 'I must collect rent from the people on my land. Tell your master I have no time for debaucheries.'

"When the servant returned to his master, he said, 'All the guests you invited made excuses and cannot come.' At first, the master was furious, but then he told the servant, 'Go to the town and bring back anyone you meet so they may attend my feast, to eat and drink with me and be merry. Since all the wealthy men and the merchants are too busy making money, I will never invite them again into my house or that of my father.'"

"Did the man invite the poor men so his food wouldn't go to waste?" one villager asked.

"Not only that. He realized that people who deal with money often prefer wealth over their friends. They are lost in the physical world, and they will never find the entrance to God's Kingdom."

"What's it like, then, this kingdom?"

"It's like a mustard seed—the smallest of all seeds. But when it falls on cultivated soil, it grows into a plant so big it can shelter all the birds of the sky."

"Where can we find it?"

"It's already here, where you are. All your lives, you have listened to rabbis who learned about God and his kingdom from scriptures. But did these teachers pause to feel God in their hearts? Have they ever listened to the voice that speaks inside them? Or have they only repeated the stories they were taught, never considering if they were true or not? You have accepted the stories because you have heard them spoken as the truth, over and over. But listen, if a rabbi says, 'The kingdom is in the sky,' you will find the birds are already there. And if they say, 'The kingdom is in the sea,' you will find the fish swimming there. Do you think God lives among the fish? With the birds? Yes, he does, but he also lives everywhere else. God's Kingdom is both within you and outside you. And when you truly know yourself, you will know you are a true son of God. You are one with God."

The farther they traveled, the more Yeshua worried that people came to see him only for healing. He yearned to empower them, teach them to recognize the light of God within themselves so that they could spread this awareness. If only they would listen.

Galilee was his home. These were his people. Then why did he feel at odds with them? What was missing? He understood their resentment toward Herod Antipas, the shameless tetrarch who had built his new city Tiberias on the site of a Yehudi burial ground and then married his niece, his half-brother's wife. He sympathized with their grievance toward the Roman prefect Pilatus, who had turned the holy city of Jerusalem into a Roman town. Why wouldn't they hear his message? All they wanted was an easy resolution to their woes.

"Heal me, Yeshua!" they cried, and they latched on to him, demanding his help. But whenever his treatments didn't succeed, they called him a fraud. Everyone just used him for their personal gain. And if the healing *did* succeed, they left without listening to his message. They weren't interested in hearing that healing the body was pointless because the body was nothing but a reflection of the inner being. What needed to heal was the spirit, the soul. If only he could make them understand—*truly* understand—that everything around them was an illusion created by their minds, they could teach others, who in turn would teach others, until the world was filled with people spreading the good news.

"I just want them to wake up," Yeshua said one night as he slumped down next to Yakov, "and all I find is people intoxicated with the cheap wine of simple wants and needs. No one is thirsty for enlightenment. They're drunk on the proof of God's power I just showed them, but when they sober up, they'll realize they have missed their chance to attain eternal life through oneness with God. My soul cries for them. They're blind in their hearts."

Shimon, the quiet fisherman who had been one of the first to comprehend Yeshua's mission, put his hand on Yeshua's shoulder. "Don't worry. Your light shines brightly. Those who are ready will understand. The rest, well, perhaps their time will come later."

"You're like a rock, Shimon," Yeshua said, and patted Shimon's hand, "so stable and secure." He smiled. "From now on, we will call you Kephas, the Rock."

Yakov laughed. Kephas blushed, but laughed, too. It was a good name, an honor.

Later that night, Yeshua lay awake, thinking. If he stopped healing the sick, people would suffer. If he continued, his message would be diluted, if not ignored. The Upanishads taught that "Like the waves in great rivers, there's no turning back of that which has previously been done. The soul is like a lame man—bound with fetters made of the fruit of good and evil." Perhaps the sick and weak were paying for deeds committed in a previous life. Maybe his healing took away their opportunity to learn from their mistakes. Was he hurting people rather than helping them? Perhaps forgiveness was the greater lesson? If they could forgive themselves, they could also heal themselves.

He almost laughed out loud. From now on, he would no longer heal every sufferer—he would instead teach them to heal themselves. Yeshua looked at his sleeping companions. They would understand. Of course they would.

CHAPTER THIRTY

Lake Kinneret, Galilee, AD 27

As the days grew colder, their pilgrimage changed from a journey of healing to one of teaching love and forgiveness. Holding the lessons in a large tent they carried with them, the gatherings attracted hordes of people who passed by, seeking warmth, but then stayed to hear the uplifting message. By the time they reached Tiberias, they had initiated several men and women into their group.

"He who drinks from my mouth will become like me," Yeshua said to those who had come to listen, "and I will become he. When this happens, everything hidden will be revealed. If you have ears, hear me." He scanned the crowd, making sure everyone was paying attention. "There is nothing that is hidden, and no secrets that will not come to light. Spread this message to others. Shout it from the rooftops. For what use is the lighting of a lamp and letting it shine under a cover? Share the light; place it as high as you can so that everyone who enters your courtyard will see it and rejoice."

Not everyone appreciated this new practice. Those who had come to see miracles or to be healed were disappointed when all they found was an ordinary man with a foreign accent who told confusing stories. When they left, muttering obscenities, Yeshua sent them love from his very being and continued to speak to those who stayed.

"Once there was an honest farmer who sowed good crops in his fertile fields. But one night, his neighbor sneaked in and planted weeds among the wheat. Soon, both the wheat and the weeds sprouted. When the servants realized what had happened, they became frantic. They told the farmer they would pull out the weeds so that the harvest wouldn't be destroyed. But the farmer refused. He said, 'If you pluck the weeds, I fear you will also pull out good wheat with them. But don't worry; at harvesttime, the bad weeds will stand out clearly amidst the good wheat, and then you can easily pull them out.' The servants left the field alone. The wheat grew strong and healthy, and in the end the bad weeds met the destiny they deserved. You see, the good wheat is love. The weeds are envy, judgment, and fear. Love will always grow strong and prevail if you treat each other with kindness and love."

By now, Yeshua's group of disciples had grown to several dozen men and a few women. They wandered from village to village along the shore and set up their tent camp by the lake, where they took purifying baths and prayed together. Yeshua taught them that eating fish or animal flesh was detrimental to the spirit, and that immersing themselves in the water at dawn cleansed their souls better than any animal sacrifice. Every evening, after the daily lesson, they relaxed by the fire and shared anecdotes, much as Yeshua had done when he traveled by caravan. Now, however, he sat back and listened to his companions' insights and dreams.

One day, a friendly Pharisee named Abimael invited Yeshua to dine with him in his home. Yeshua accepted gladly, hoping he would be served something other than the stale bread and cheese he consumed most every day.

Seated on soft cushions around a low wooden table in Abimael's fancy dining room, Yeshua politely declined the stuffed chickens with mint sauce. Instead, he happily devoured the lentil stew, carrots cooked with cumin, honey-baked figs, and fresh pomegranate juice.

While Abimael's wife cleaned away the empty platters, Yeshua lounged back on the cushions and took the opportunity to learn more about his host.

"My dear friend, tell me about your teachings. You and I worship the same God, do we not?"

Abimael rubbed his beard and took a sip of wine. "Certainly, but *we* are the true believers. You understand? The true!" His sentences were exclamations, as if every word teemed with revelation. "We, the

Pharisees, are the disciples of Aaron; he taught us to bring mankind closer to the Torah. Not like those foolish Sadducees who are imprisoned by the exact letters and words of the scriptures!" Abimael laughed so hard at his clever words that his belly bounced against the table. "Such brutish men, how can they not realize that ignorant men cannot be—will *never* be—saintly. No, *we* are the wise, you and I. We listen to the Lord and we understand him very well."

When Abimael lifted his cup to propose a toast, the door flew open with a bang. A woman in tatters, her nakedness barely veiled by a threadbare tunic, threw herself at Yeshua's feet and covered them with kisses, letting her long, tangled hair sweep the marble floor.

"Get up, you whore!" Abimael banged his fist on the table. "Out, woman!"

She ignored him and continued bathing Yeshua's feet in kisses.

Abimael scrambled to his feet and yanked her up by the hair. He shoved her toward the door. "Get out of my house, filthy witch."

Yeshua grabbed on to Abimael's arm to calm him. "Sit down. Let this poor woman be. Please."

Abimael hesitated for a moment before letting go of her hair. Reluctantly, he sat down again, staring at the woman at Yeshua's feet.

Her eyes were damp with sorrow as she lowered her head and used her long hair to wipe her tears from Yeshua's bare feet.

"Don't let that harlot touch you," Abimael cried out. "She's... repulsive!"

But Yeshua didn't see a fallen woman; he saw a lost girl who was humbling herself at his feet.

"Let me tell you a story," Yeshua said. He raised his cup to his host.

"I will gladly listen." Abimael smiled, but a false note betrayed his irritation.

"Two people owed a moneylender a lot of money. One owed him several hundred denarii, the other fifty. When the loans came due, neither could pay him back. The moneylender—who was a good and honest man—decided to forgive the debts of both men. Now tell me, which of the two men do you think loved the moneylender more?"

Abimael scratched his beard again, holding his gaze high to avoid looking at the woman crouching at Yeshua's feet. "The man who owed more money?"

Yeshua reached over and touched Abimael's hand. "Exactly."

He cupped the woman's chin and raised her up to stand before him. "Look at this woman. When I arrived, you didn't bring me a bowl of water to wash my dusty feet. But this worthy woman, she wet my feet with her tears and dried them with her own hair. You didn't offer me a kiss, but she has been kissing my feet from the moment she entered. Whatever sins she may have committed in the past, they are forgiven because she has shown me love. You say you know God better than the Sadducees? Then you will know that God is love. If you love only a little, you'll be forgiven a little. And if you love a lot…"

Abimael turned away from Yeshua and gulped down his wine, too angry to look at his guest.

Yeshua smiled at the girl.

"Go," he said, and gently pushed her to the door. "Your faith has saved you. Leave in peace."

The woman closed the door behind her and walked away, her head held high.

Magdala Nunayya, Galilee, AD 28

By the time they returned to the northwest side of Lake Kinneret, Yeshua was tired of everyone expecting him to be perfect all the time. Some days he simply wanted to be Yeshua, not a teacher or a leader.

In Magdala Nunayya, a half day's walk from Capernaum, he told the others to pray by the lake while he went into the village. He wandered through the market, looking at the same dried fruit, salted fish, eggs, goats, chickens, textiles, and ceramic jars as could be found in other dusty towns. The same fat merchants, busy wives, and grouchy husbands. People were the same everywhere. In fact, if he squinted, this market could be in Palmyra or Susa, in Jagannath, Benares, or Kapilavatthu. People had the same basic needs everywhere, and most were content as long as their stomachs were full and they had a roof over their heads. Yet in every corner of the world, priests lured them in with false promises, persuading them to follow their particular version of the truth.

Yeshua watched the crowd until his head swirled and his stomach pinched with hunger. Time to make his way back to the others.

"Rabbi!" A boy with an entire ocean contained in his eyes appeared by his side. "Come. Please come."

How could the boy know him? They had arrived in Magdala only that same morning.

"I'm sorry," Yeshua said, trying to rid himself of the boy, who was tugging at his mantle. "I'm not a healer. I'm a teacher. I can show—"

"Please, Rabbi!" The boy's eyes filled with tears. "My sister, Rabbi. Please..."

Yeshua looked toward the lake where his companions were waiting, and then back at the boy, whose voice quivered with desperation. Yeshua sighed. *Just this once*, he told himself. Just this once more would he succumb to pleas.

He followed the boy down an alley to a house at the back of a dead-end street. The boy banged on a sturdy wooden door three times his size.

"Father, it's me, Tavi!" When the door creaked open, the boy ran ahead through a rose garden to a modest house. "Come!" he called again.

His father, a gray-haired man with the same aquamarine eyes, followed them. "My daughter, Rabbi," he said. "Her husband died four months ago, and now she is also dying."

In a room lit by a single oil lamp, five women wailed by a bed where a woman lay wrapped in white sheets. They parted to let Yeshua through, to allow him a better look. Her skin appeared gray in the dim light, her eyes rolled backward, and her hair was soaked with perspiration. Yeshua lowered his ear to her chest and listened. She was alive, but barely. He placed his hands on top of her head, then on her forehead, and at last on her feet.

"Bring me a jar of cold water," he said to the boy. "And honey." Yeshua lifted her arms and massaged her armpits. Cradling her head, he centered on oneness with God and transformed himself into a channel for healing energy. He let God's love flow through his hands into her, reaching every corner of her body and every dimension of her soul. He visualized her as a perfect being, united with God, one with himself and with everyone else. He filled her with God's light until there was no space for illness. And thus he sat with her, holding her hand, touching her head, and massaging her feet until the fever broke.

Yeshua was still connected to her when she opened her eyes and stared at him in awe.

"Who are you?"

"Yeshua."

"I saw God."

"I know."

He washed her face with cold water and fed her drops of honey. He watched as her spirit pervaded her body again, resting by her to make sure the malady had vanished for good.

When Yeshua left the house, dusk had already fallen. Locusts hummed. A wolf howled in the distance. He was so tired he could barely walk, but his soul had filled with euphoria.

Something had shifted; healing the girl had awakened a buried sensation. He could barely remember leaving her house. The whole day had disappeared in a mist. No doubt, he had brought her to the other side where they had united with the Eternal Spirit. She said she had seen God. He had seen God, too.

And it was marvelous.

When he reached the encampment, he touched his finger to his lips to signal silence. He wanted to be alone.

He walked along the shore away from the others and lay down on his mat under an olive tree. The stars glistened high above the lake. The waves slapped against the rocks. Yeshua pressed his hands together in prayer to thank God for inviting him into his kingdom.

"It's impossible for a man to ride two horses," Yeshua said as he spoke to a crowd a few days later. "Just like it's impossible to stretch two bows at the same time. Or for a servant to serve two masters—for he would be faithful to one and neglect the other."

He looked out at his listeners.

"Only God can be your true master. Neither I, nor the priests, nor even your fathers may command you. To enter the heavenly kingdom, you must make oneness with Yahweh your only goal."

Yeshua gestured to a mother feeding an infant. "Look at that baby. Only beings like him will enter God's Kingdom."

"Are you saying that only children can enter God's Kingdom?"

"Not at all, but you must make yourself as innocent as a child. Notice how his skin is as fresh and smooth as his unblemished thoughts. Like him, one day you will no longer notice the difference between heaven and earth and between male and female. When your thoughts are that pure and innocent, you will enter the kingdom."

"Will we see God's face in everyone?"

A woman's voice. Yeshua scanned the faces in the crowd to find her. "Yes, exactly." He shaded his eyes with his hand and saw a familiar face grin at him. His heart jumped. Tavi's sister, the young widow he had healed a few days earlier.

"Just so," he said, smiling at her before he forced his attention back to the sermon. "As I have said before, love your enemies and bless those who curse you. Pray for them. If someone slaps you on the cheek, offer him the other cheek as well. If someone steals your coat, let him have your tunic, too. Because we are all one single spirit. Help anyone who asks you. Treat others like you want to be treated. It's that simple: when you are kind to another, you are also kind to yourself."

His final words echoed in his head. Sometimes he forgot to treat himself with kindness, as if spreading his knowledge had a time limit he couldn't ignore. By now he knew that only a handful of listeners would understand his message. He accepted that. The ones who did made it worthwhile. They would be the torches that spread light around the world.

Tavi's sister had pushed her way forward. She looked so different; her indigo eyes were bright and her cheeks rosy with a healthy glow. Yeshua pressed his palms together to show the sermon was over and walked toward her.

"Rabbi, do you remember me?" she asked. "I'm Mariamne."

"I'm glad you came."

She tilted her head and blushed.

Yeshua's heart pounded in his ears. Why was he reacting like this?

"I came to thank you," she said. "But now that I've heard you speak, I would like to know more of your words."

Yeshua's cheeks burned. He had taught hundreds of women in many countries, yet no one had affected him this way. She was attractive in the most common way: tall and slender, milky skin, and eyes the color of the Bay of Bengal. Her sleek hair fell in soft curls under the turquoise scarf that framed her face perfectly. Her full lips reminded him of Ramaa's, plump and succulent. Yeshua ached with the desire to kiss her.

She left him speechless.

"Master, if you don't mind, I'd like to hear more. May I join you? I promise I won't be a burden."

Yeshua swallowed.

He should say no. She would distract him from his mission. But then again, didn't she also have the right to seek enlightenment? He nodded curtly and turned away, anxious to leave her alone and recover his senses.

At a safe distance by the lake, he once again found solitude beneath the tree where he had slept a few nights earlier. With a deep breath, he closed his eyes, placed his hands in his lap, and meditated on his heart.

"Release me," he pleaded. "Free me from this yearning."

"How fortunate are the humble," Yeshua said to his growing group of followers when they had settled back in Capernaum, "because the Kingdom of Heaven belongs to you. And how fortunate are those who mourn, because they will be comforted. Those who hunger for fairness will be satisfied, and those who are pure of mind will see God. My brothers and sisters, you are the peacemakers who will be called the sons of God."

His disciples listened attentively, their eyes ablaze. Three among them, his brother Yakov, the fisherman Kephas, and Mariamne of Magdala, shone like fireflies in their own right. Another six were on the brink of enlightenment.

A woman pushed her way to the front of the tent. "Your mother and brothers are waiting outside. They're asking for you."

Yeshua nodded to her, and then turned to address his students. "Who is my mother—anyone? And who are my brothers? You are. Because anyone who answers God's call is my brother, father, sister, and mother. You, the people who live by God's words, you are my family."

He looked up and saw the hurt look on Ama's face. Yeshua's heart sagged. She had entered in silence and had heard his harsh words. When she turned to leave, Yeshua hurried after her. "Ama, you came."

His mother's cheeks were streaked with tears. "I came. And I heard." She tried to push him away, but Yeshua held her in his arms and wouldn't let her go.

"I'm sorry. I only meant to say... Of course, you will always be my mother." He looked at Iosa and Tau'ma, who stood by her side. "And you will always be my brothers. But these people are my brethren, too. Won't you stay? Please."

His mother wiped her tears on her sleeve, then sat next to the other women, who made room for her on their mat.

Delighted to have his family present, Yeshua continued:

"As you well know, you cannot harvest grapes from thorny bushes— or figs from thistles. In the same way, a respectable man will produce high-quality goods, whereas a wicked man will deliver only poor ones. We all act according to the wealth of our hearts. That is, we react either with love—or with fear." He glanced at his mother to make sure she was listening. "You see, the Kingdom of Heaven is like yeast: a small amount mixed with flour produces several large loaves of bread. Accept the yeast of love into your heart and watch how the dough rises within you. Then divide the dough into loaves and share it with others, who will take it into their own hearts. Now, hear me well, if you have ears."

Yeshua's mother's eyes glowed; she had already forgiven him.

After the lesson, Ama and Yeshua took a walk along the crumbled town wall and sat on a boulder by the shore. Ama caressed his hand.

"Who are these people who follow you from village to village? Have you made sure they're trustworthy and decent?"

Yeshua put his arm around her frail shoulders. "Ama, some of them are like children who have settled down to rest in a field that belongs to someone else. When the owner returns, they will rise and leave. They don't always understand why they're here, and some of them are too easily impressed. I tell them to be on their guard, to be like the master of the house who knows a thief is coming, so they will be armed against deceit."

His mother caressed his cheek. "Are you coming home tonight?"

Yeshua lifted her chin to face him and pushed a strand of hair from her face. "I am home, Ama. This is my home now."

Capernaum, Galilee, AD 28

Yeshua's only distraction was Mariamne. As much as he tried to avoid looking at her, she always caught his eye. Her shaved head only enhanced her beauty. She reminded him of Ramaa, and like his first love, she brought a special light and joy to the group. But however hard the women worked, some of the men were still opposed to having them around.

"It isn't fair for Mariamne to follow us," Andreas, the fisherman, said a few weeks after she had joined them. "You are wasting her time."

Yeshua squatted next to his friend to hear better. "Why do you say that?"

"Why do you think? A woman can never reach eternal life. Why mislead her?" The envy in Andreas's voice was palpable.

Yeshua patted his shoulder, wondering if everyone had noticed the attention he awarded Mariamne. "I would not worry about her. Won't you help me teach the women how to be perfect, like men? Because you don't believe women are unable to learn, do you?"

After that conversation, none of the men raised the subject again, and Mariamne and the other women remained as equals. They slept apart from the men, but during lessons, they were both seen and heard as they sat among the men and partook in discussions.

Despite Yeshua's efforts to avoid Mariamne, she seemed to be everywhere. When he went off to pray alone, he would find her sitting in the exact spot where he had planned to go. When he walked to the market, she would be standing in front of him, beside him, behind him. She was everywhere.

One morning before dawn, as Yeshua finished his prayer in the lake, he found Mariamne waiting for him on the shore. His heart beat so fiercely he couldn't speak. He grinned like a lovestruck boy and settled down next to her. She leaned her head against his shoulder, buried her nose in his neck, and gently sniffed his skin. Then she kissed his chin.

Yeshua froze. He wanted to be transported away from her, leave this situation, escape. But this time, God didn't listen. Mariamne moved her hands across his back and stroked his damp hair. Yeshua held his breath. He closed his eyes, hoping she would stop, but she didn't. Instead, she turned his face toward hers and kissed him. The salty taste of her mouth startled him. Before he realized what he was doing, he opened his lips and let his tongue meet hers. Oh, she was delightful. Mariamne brushed her face against his cheeks and nibbled his earlobe.

Yeshua broke away to look at the wondrous being in front of him. He could no longer deny it. He loved her. He traced the line of her face down to her neck and let his hand slide under her tunic where her skin was as smooth as the softest peach. He kissed her cleavage and licked the bare skin between her breasts. He didn't even notice how the clothes came off, but there she was, naked as a child before him. Her large breasts hung heavy, inviting him to taste her. Yeshua kissed her nipples, her stomach, her belly button. He forgot all about God and his kingdom as he gently pushed her down and united with her, gasping with forgotten passion and pleasure. As if from another dimension, he heard her moan as he thrust himself into her again and again, harder and harder, until they both exploded with ecstasy. Then he lay still with his eyes closed, present in the moment.

This was paradise. This woman had appeared out of nowhere and had given him exactly what he needed: love, companionship, and understanding. What more could he ever wish for? He rolled over to rest on his side, admiring the divine being beside him. Mariamne smiled. She raised herself up on her elbow, leaned over, and kissed him with an insatiable hunger. And thus they lay kissing in the grass by the lake until the sun crept over the horizon and colored the sky the sweetest shade of gold.

Within days, everyone had noticed the intimate looks between their teacher and the young woman from Magdala. When the more conservative followers complained it was unlawful for an unmarried man to court a widow, Yeshua quieted their concerns by summoning a rabbi and marrying the woman with the deep-blue eyes.

"Be compassionate," Yeshua reminded his students, "just as God is compassionate with you. Fear binds you to this world and makes you judge others. Compassion will set you free."

Meanwhile, an inner circle had formed of those who genuinely understood the teachings. It had started with Yakov, Kephas, Mariamne, and Tau'ma, Yeshua's youngest brother and so-called twin. Before long, the group included a couple of other Capernaum fishermen and their treasurer Yudah, the only Judean among them.

When Yeshua first noticed that these seven disciples spent a lot of time together, he grew curious. One night before dinner, he pulled Mariamne aside.

"What matters are you discussing? Are you studying together?"

Mariamne took his hand, as she always did when sensing he was distressed. "My master, haven't you noticed that the harvest is colossal but the laborers are few?"

Yeshua smiled at the image.

"Kephas, Yakov, and I have spoken of ways to send more laborers into the fields."

Yeshua nodded thoughtfully. She was right: these seven were ready. They were far better suited to spreading his words than anyone else.

The next morning, he assembled them to send them off.

"Brothers, sister, I see a grapevine has been planted outside my house, and the time has come to see if it will thrive. If it's flawed, we will soon know, and it will be pulled up by the roots." He laughed at his joke before he turned to kiss them, one after the other. "Go, my friends. Spread the good news."

He watched his wife pack her belongings and get ready. It hurt to see her go, but he had no right to hold her back. She must find her own way, like the Buddha who had left his wife and child to search for enlightenment. And he belonged here, in Capernaum, with those who yearned to embrace God's Kingdom but weren't yet ready to let go of the material world.

As they were leaving, Yeshua offered them a last piece of advice. "In every village, search for an honest person and ask to stay at their house. Remain there until you leave. Don't go from house to house. As you enter, bless the house and share what you have with them. Eat and drink whatever they offer, because they have worked hard for what they serve you. But if you enter a town or a home where no one welcomes you, shake the dust from your feet and leave. Trust that your presence has already blessed them."

Without Mariamne to distract him, Yeshua focused on those who had stayed behind. But life had lost some of its shimmer, as if the sun had disappeared and left only clouds behind. Her smooth lips and delicate touch had brightened his world. Without her, his confidence wavered. Was he wise enough to bring his listeners to a greater understanding of God? Yeshua thought of his teachers and the techniques they had used.

"If everything else fails, repeat, repeat, repeat," Arcahia used to say. Honoring his words, Yeshua told the same parables over and over again. He planted the same seeds of knowledge day after day, hoping one day they would sprout, until he noticed hints of awakening in their eyes. His teachers had been right. He had spent too much time on the advanced students and had forgotten that even the blindest stone can grow moss if the rain continues long enough.

One day, to break up the routine, he joined a few of his fishermen disciples on their boat. Although black clouds hung threatening over the lake, the fishermen assured Yeshua there was more than enough time to go out and return to shore before the storm caught up with them.

But they had barely cast out their nets when the sky turned as dark as night and gusts of wind hurled the boat from side to side. Waves as high as a man rocked the boat up and down, so hard it almost capsized. The seasoned fishermen clung to the sides and cried out in panic, "Lord, save us! We're all going to die."

Yeshua hung on to the mast and shouted as loudly as he could, "Have faith! If you believe the storm will die down, it will."

"We're drowning! Oh, Mother, save me!" the men screamed, their faces white with terror.

"No! You will not die. Close your eyes. Do it! Envision a calm sea."

If only they would trust him on the water as they did on land.

"I can't! I can barely hold on to the stern."

"Close your eyes. Now!" But the wind muted his voice, and they couldn't hear him.

Yeshua held on to the mast, closed his eyes, and visualized a quiet lake with gentle waves lapping against the boat. He imagined a tranquil scene with all the details, scents, and sounds until he believed it was real.

A soft breeze touched his cheek. The boat rolled less and less until at last it quieted completely. When Yeshua opened his eyes, he saw the fishermen still clutching the sides of the vessel, still begging for their lives to be spared. Then, one by one, they realized that the storm had passed.

"Master, how did you do that?"

Yeshua wiped the sweat from his forehead.

"You must have faith, that's all." He looked from one to the other. "With faith, you can accomplish anything."

After dragging their boat onto the shore, the fishermen rushed to tell everyone what had happened. The crowd gathered around Yeshua as he helped store the empty nets, their awe of him renewed.

Good, Yeshua thought. *Maybe now they'll listen.*

In the height of autumn, Mariamne and the other disciples returned, rife with enthusiasm. They spoke of their adventures and the miracles they had performed. They told Yeshua how people were hungry for the good news, and that many wanted to come to Capernaum and hear him speak.

Everything was going according to plan, until one day, Yakov and Tau'ma came running into camp, their eyes wide with alarm. "They've arrested Cousin Yochanan, the Baptizer!"

Yeshua took his brothers aside. "Who has arrested Yochanan?" he asked.

"Herod Antipas," Yakov said, his perpetual grin replaced by horror. "We just heard. He's gone absolutely mad."

"But why? I mean, what did Yochanan do?"

Tau'ma covered his eyes with his hands to hide his tears. "Antipas heard that Yochanan was using him as a bad example, that he said that only the most miserable sinner could marry his half-brother's wife."

"And for that they arrested him?"

Yakov pressed his palm against his forehead. "For that they noticed him. And saw what an extensive following he has. I don't know; maybe they heard all those whispers of a coming Messiah? It wouldn't surprise me if those fools thought Yochanan was a rebel in disguise, waiting to lead the Yehudim in revolt against the Romans."

"But he's a Nazirite, a man of peace. He wouldn't hurt a spider."

Tau'ma looked at Yeshua. "It was his stepdaughter, the daughter of Herodias. She asked for Yochanan's head on a platter."

Yeshua flinched. Would they execute Yochanan on the whim of a girl?

"Antipas threw a lavish party, as he likes to do, to celebrate his new marriage. And he invited all the prominent Romans. That filthy fox probably just wanted to show off his stepdaughter, make his guests drool. Of course, they adored her dancing and all." Tau'ma closed his eyes and shivered at the thought. "That imbecile! Antipas was so drunk with pride he told his stepdaughter she could have anything she wanted as a reward. Anything in the world."

"And that's what she asked for, Yochanan's head?"

Yakov nodded.

"Surely Antipas won't go through with it."

"Then you don't know the chief of Galilee—he's a snake. He even pretends to be a Yehudi, just to fit in. He celebrates Pesach, Shavuot, and Sukkoth—all our holy days. He can't be trusted." Yakov shook his head. "Yeshua, he made the promise in front of everyone. He won't take it back."

Yeshua's heart pounded. "I'll go and demand his release!" He reached for his bundle of clothing, determined to set out toward Tiberias that very moment, but Yakov held him back.

"It's too late; he's gone."

Yeshua's knees buckled beneath him. He couldn't not do something. Tears welled up in his eyes. Frustrated, he kicked a pebble into the lake, barely missing a waterfowl. Yochanan had never harmed anyone. Why did this evil woman want him dead? What kind of person was she?

"Forgive her." The voice in his head rang as clear as morning dew. "Fear and anger imprison you. Forgiveness sets you free."

But he couldn't forgive—not yet. He doubled up in pain and sank to the ground. A whimper rose up his throat. Yochanan, his dear cousin, was going to be killed because of a false rumor, because of a frivolous young girl.

Yeshua had to get away. He didn't want to speak to anyone. He didn't want their pity. And he definitely didn't want them to see his anger and the numbing sadness that crippled him.

Alone by the shore, he allowed himself to weep. He cried, screamed, and spoke to God, raging with fury, asking for forgiveness, until all tears were gone and a feeling of peace settled within him.

His disciples had followed him at a safe distance. They believed in him. They knew he would forgive. Yeshua took a deep breath. Yes, he would. He would forgive not only Herod Antipas but also his stepdaughter. Yochanan would find his place in God's Kingdom, and he would guide his flock from there. There was no doubt that Yochanan had agreed to his fate. Everything happened for a reason, exactly the way it should.

Darkness had fallen. A couple of bonfires lit up the sky where his followers had set up a temporary camp between Kheresa and Hippos.

"What shall we do?" Mariamne asked when Yeshua finally joined them. "We didn't bring anything from Capernaum. We don't have enough to feed everyone. Perhaps we should send someone to Kheresa to find some food. Surely someone will give us some bread or fruit."

Yeshua caressed her cheek. "No, my love. What we have is enough."

"But there are more than three dozen of us, and look—we have only one loaf of bread."

"Stay calm, my love. Let me show you."

Yeshua took the loaf of bread from her and raised it to the sky.

"Lord, thank you for the plentiful meal. Let each of us go to sleep tonight both full and satisfied."

He divided the bread into small pieces and walked around to his followers, handing every person a small chunk of bread. "Eat this," he said as he placed the food in their hands. "This will fill you up."

Everyone stared at him. They usually ate well at night and wondered how a small piece of bread could be enough. But Yeshua was patient. If they trusted him, they would notice their hunger waver and dissipate.

"How did you do that?" Yakov asked after everyone had eaten.

"Easy. You create your reality. How do you make love and produce a child? How do you plant a seed and grow a tree? How do you think of someone and the next moment have them appear by your door? Anything is possible."

"Anything?"

"Yes. Anything."

Yeshua looked out over the crowd. These men and women had given up everything to follow him and learn all he knew. Just like Yochanan's disciples. What would happen to them now? Had they learned enough to survive on their own?

"Among all men," Yeshua said, choking back tears, "beginning with Adam, there have been few as wise as the Baptizer. Yet if you become as innocent as a child and discover the world that exists beyond what your eyes can see, you will be as wise as he. When you understand that light and dark, life and death, right and left are one and the same. Inseparable. Life is not life, and death is not death."

Yeshua left the group, unable to speak further. He took Mariamne by the hand, and together they walked away to seek privacy. The moon stood full above them, casting long shadows as they sought a place to lie down along the pebbled shore.

"Did we meet because we believed?" she asked.

Yeshua kissed her, inhaling the sweet scent of jasmine in her hair. She was his guiding star. She shone with the light of both Ramaa and Pema. And if she left, her spirit would appear in yet another woman.

The news of Yochanan's arrest and death stirred Capernaum. The Pharisees and Sadducees used the event to correct anyone who veered from Yehudi law and took every opportunity to harass Yeshua for his unconventional teaching.

"Why do you not obey the laws of our ancestors?" they asked. "How dare you not respect the Sabbath? And people say you no longer fast during Yom Kippur."

Yeshua broke bread with every person who came to complain. If he could explain why his disciples acted one way or another, surely they would understand and leave them be.

"I haven't come to abolish the law but to fulfill it," he said. "I aim to remind my brothers and sisters to love God and one another. Because it's what's in your heart that makes you righteous or impure. An unhappy heart breeds immoral thoughts, and those thoughts can cause a man to slander, lie, or even murder. Those are the things that matter. But whether you nourish your body or fast on a holy day—it doesn't change the way God views you."

The local tax collector also found reason to bother them. "Have you paid the temple dues?" he asked.

Yeshua scratched his head. Everyone knew his group didn't have an income. They lived in simple tents and never visited the temple.

"Very well," Yeshua said after a long pause, and he nodded to Yudah to bring the treasurer's pouch. "Why don't we give Caesar what belongs to Caesar." He took out a bronze coin and gave it to the tax collector. "Now you must give God what belongs to God."

"But I do not serve your God. I serve my country and my emperor."

"Yes. Indeed. But isn't it written in the law that you must love your neighbor as you love yourself? Many of your brethren, sons of Abraham, are dying from cold and hunger. Every night you return to a warm and comfortable home filled with fine goods, and you give nothing to the needy."

Yeshua invited the tax collector to sit with him on the raw linen cushions filled with straw. He handed his guest a cup of pomegranate juice.

"You see, my friend, the Kingdom of God is like a wealthy merchant who found a pearl of immeasurable value in the market. He was clever. He knew what he had seen was more precious than all his belongings combined, so he sold everything he owned and bought the pearl. Like this merchant, you must abandon the worldly treasures and seek the precious wealth inside you that neither moth nor worm can destroy."

"I don't seek prosperity—"

"If you aren't searching for God's treasure, you're only holding on to what is old and worn and will one day wither to dust."

Yeshua patted the man's shoulder as he got up to leave. "I always keep a jug of fresh juice handy. Whenever you're in Capernaum, why don't you stop by?"

The tax collector did come back. In the beginning, he pretended to come for taxes, but after a while he no longer cared to feign the purpose of his visits. He came to hear Yeshua's message.

Some of the newer members protested. "Master, how can you invite a sinner into our midst? We have done everything we can to become worthy to enter the Kingdom. And now you treat a greedy man who has sold his soul to the Romans as our equal?"

Yeshua called them close. "If you respect only those who act in accordance with God's will, does that make you a good person?"

The new initiates blushed. Everyone had turned to watch them.

"If you embrace only your brothers and sisters, does that make you better than a tax collector? If you lend money only to those who will repay you, what credit is that to you? Even the most dishonorable people give money to their own kind because they expect something in return.

"If we treat everyone well, both friends and foes, our reward will be greater than you can ever imagine. God lets his sun rise on the evil as well as the righteous. And he sends rain to both the just and the unjust. He loves us all."

Yeshua put his arm around the tax collector's shoulders.

"Those who put themselves on a pedestal are easily humiliated. Only those who humble themselves will be blessed."

Lake Kinneret, Galilee, AD 29

Yeshua and his closest disciples continued their visits to the villages around Lake Kinneret, where they taught simple lessons to anyone who was ready to receive. Now he understood why Arcahia and Udraka had been reluctant to let their students speak during their first months of the pilgrimage to Benares. A teacher had to use the correct words and speak with authority, because listeners decided in a blink whether they believed Yeshua and his companions were messengers of God.

One afternoon they returned to Capernaum to find a crowd assembled outside their camp. A man had brought his son to be healed, but a couple of Pharisees were blocking them from entering the main tent.

Yeshua placed his hands on the Pharisees' shoulders. "What, may I ask, are you arguing about?"

"Master, help me," the man pleaded. "My son is possessed."

In his arms, he held a writhing boy, whose eyes had rolled back in his head and who snarled like a demon. Foam gathered at the corners of the little boy's mouth.

"I brought him here to be healed, but it seems no one can help him."

Yeshua gestured to the Pharisees to step back. "Give him to me," he said, and cradled the boy. He turned to Mariamne. "Make a potion of lobelia, valerian root, and chamomile."

He removed his mantle and laid the shaking boy down, placing his hands on top of the child's head. Then he filled the boy's soul with healing energy. Slowly, the seizures subsided as the energy replenished his strength. And after a few sips of the healing liquid, he drifted into deep and peaceful sleep.

One of Yeshua's disciples approached him, his chin quivering.

"Master, we tried everything. We did exactly what you taught us. I don't understand why we couldn't drive out the demon."

Tired from the long walk, Yeshua sat down, took off his sandals, and rubbed his feet. He looked up at the freckle-faced adolescent.

"Where is your faith? Even if it were as small as a mustard seed, you could tell a mountain to move—and it would. How can I help you understand you are one with God?"

The youngster blinked uncertainly. Yeshua picked up a child who toddled nearby and set him on his lap.

"Unless you become like this little one, you will never be able to heal others. Forget everything you think is real. You must look at the world through a child's eyes and believe that anything is possible."

Some of the other disciples had also tried to heal the boy and had failed. Yeshua feared they would become disillusioned and lose faith, so he called the most discouraged together for a special lesson.

"Believe me when I say you are all powerful beings. You are sons of God. Why do you still doubt this? The spirit of God exists within you— he has always been there. Follow him."

"How?" one of the skeptics asked. "We obey the laws of the Torah, we follow your teachings, and we use healing energy, but still we couldn't heal the boy. Is it because we are sinful?"

"No. And forget about sin. What sin means is that you are so attached to the physical world, you don't realize that what you see before you is an illusion. You believe you are separated from others, from God. If you look at the world with the eyes of your soul, you will see that we are all one. It's this separation that is the sin. Once you awaken and understand that nothing you see with your physical eyes is real, the hidden will be revealed."

Despite the frosty mornings, Yeshua still took cleansing baths and meditated by the lake before the rest of the camp awoke. Some days Mariamne joined him; more often he relished the solitude. In prayer, he connected with all the teachers who had influenced his life: Abba,

Cousin Yochanan, Kahanji, Arcahia, and Pema. Like five trees of wisdom, they remained as alive and active within him as if they had been there in person.

Your purpose in life is to teach as many as possible, he heard them say. *Open their eyes and show them the path to God's Kingdom. When you are gone, your light will shine on through them.*

Walking back to the encampment after speaking to his teachers, Yeshua always felt filled with new determination. By now his flock had grown to nearly fifty and many of his followers had already glimpsed the Kingdom; they had become gifted healers and teachers in their own right. They believed in his message, and once Yeshua taught them how to suppress hunger and to trust that food would appear when needed, they embraced the ascetic lifestyle.

Above all, Mariamne spurred him to continue. Her luminous smile still made his knees weak. After days of walking, helping fishermen clean their nets, teaching, and answering endless questions, he cuddled up with her in their tent and all the troubles of the world vanished. She was everything he needed, and so much more. She never complained about the time he spent with others. She didn't blink if he walked off with another woman. She trusted him completely. And she understood what he was trying to do. Sometimes Yeshua wished she were a man so he could send her off to preach on her own; it would double their effort. But if she were a man, he couldn't kiss her and make sweet love to her.

She was perfect just the way she was.

In the Galilean villages, Yeshua still mostly spoke in parables to appeal to as many as possible.

"Teacher," a Pharisee asked one day, "what must I do to attain everlasting life?"

Yeshua smiled, always pleased when priests partook in his lessons. "You study the Torah. You must know the answer to that question."

"Well, the Law says I must love God with all my heart, body, strength, and mind. And to love my neighbor as dearly as I love myself."

"That's true, my friend. Do that, and you will never face death."

"But Master, if you will, who are those neighbors? Are they the people of my village? Or is a 'neighbor' anyone who lives in Galilee? Surely it cannot be the Romans or the gentiles."

"Let me tell you a story," Yeshua said. "A man was traveling from Jerusalem to Jericho when a band of robbers attacked him. They stripped him of his clothes and belongings, beat him, and left him for dead. A passing priest saw the man lying lifeless on the road and became frightened, so he crossed to the other side and continued on his way. A little while later, a man from the tribe of Levi walked by; like the priest, he crossed the road and looked the other way. But when a Samaritan arrived at the scene, he took pity on the dying man. He hauled the man up onto his donkey, took him to an inn, bandaged his wounds, and anointed him with wine and oil. When the Samaritan left the next day, he gave the innkeeper a few coins and asked him to nurse the patient back to health."

Yeshua asked the Pharisee: "Which of these men do you think was a neighbor to the poor man?"

"The good fellow who showed him mercy, of course."

Yeshua nodded. "Exactly. You see, spiritual love is like perfume. A man who anoints himself with fragrance also allows those around him to enjoy the scent. The Samaritan used nothing but wine and oil to heal the wound, and it worked because love heals any wrongdoing. Now, go and treat everyone you meet like a neighbor."

One day, after a lesson on the slopes behind Capernaum, a merchant on his way to Damascus approached Yeshua.

"Teacher, your word is good, but I bring you a message of caution. I recently passed through Tiberias and heard Herod Antipas threaten to execute all rebels and vagrant preachers who cause disturbances. He mentioned your name."

Yeshua frowned. Antipas, the man who had ordered the beheading of Yochanan.

"You must leave Galilee before it's too late. His soldiers could already be on their way."

Yeshua shrugged and forced a smile. Surely the merchant was exaggerating. Why would Antipas want him dead? He patted the man's shoulder to reassure him that the tetrarch was not a threat.

But fear had taken root.

"Why don't you go on a journey, my love?" Mariamne suggested when he told her. "Take some time. The fear of rebellion will have diminished by next spring, and then you can return in peace."

Yeshua kissed her softly and enveloped her in his arms to repress his worries. He didn't want to leave her. But perhaps she was right. Yeshua opened her robe and nuzzled her naked breasts. He needed to think about something else for a while.

Once again, Yeshua gathered his closest disciples to travel with him. Dressed in simple tunics, warm woolen mantles, and head scarves for protection from the cold winds, they hurried south along the eastern shore of the lake. This time, they didn't stop to give speeches or heal the ailing. Instead, they moved as fast as they could to leave the territory that Herod Antipas governed.

When at last they reached Samaria, they set up camp for a few days. Yeshua lay awake at night, contemplating the canopy of stars above him as he had so many nights before. Why did God always keep him on the run? And if the body was just an illusion, why did he fear death? Abba and Kahanji had appeared in his dreams many times, as had Yochanan the Baptizer. They had convinced him that death did not exist. So why was he afraid?

Although he yearned for Mariamne's touch, he couldn't allow himself to be distracted, and he had commanded the women to sleep apart from the men. He had a destiny to fulfill, and time was running out. He looked at his sleeping companions. How peaceful they looked in the lavender light, innocent as lambs. What right did he have to bring them on this journey and place their lives in danger?

Yeshua strolled down to where the creek eddied into a pool. The moon cast long shadows on the ground and painted the water with eerie patterns from the date palm trees and thornbushes. He lowered himself into the pool and splashed his face with the cool water. Pema always said he could change his destiny and stay safe. But what about the others? He had to trust that God would protect them. Mariamne wanted to teach, and they all possessed enough knowledge to continue on their own. Was he unwittingly keeping his disciples from evolving, the way he had grown only after Kahanji had passed?

The hour had come to share his last crumbs of wisdom. He should leave Palestine soon. Alexandria could be an interesting place to visit. Or perhaps Thessalonica, where the winds were said to always blow fresh. Perhaps Mariamne would come with him. They could live simply, like normal couples. Have children…

Jerusalem, Judea, AD 30

The temple in Jerusalem rose majestically before him. Blinding white and shimmering like gold, it stretched toward the sky in a solid testament to God's power. Yeshua paused as a shiver rose up his spine. The magnificence of the temple still made him dizzy. As a boy, the temple had changed his life forever. His first visit had confirmed his life's purpose—to serve God, to study and teach. What had seemed impossible then had come to pass: he had spent his life learning. And now he was sharing his knowledge with his disciples. The circle was complete.

How wonderful they were, the men and women who accompanied him on this journey. Their faces glowed as they gazed up at King Solomon's temple. Few of them had been in Jerusalem before, and nothing they had ever seen could compare, not even the grand fortress of Tiberias or the Herodian winter palace in Jericho.

In awestruck silence, they walked the path up to the eastern side of Jerusalem toward the temple hill. When Mariamne left with the other women to take their baths of purification, Yeshua's heart trembled with affection. She bound him to this world.

Leaves and moss floated on the surface of the mikveh. Green and brown algae covered the plaster walls, as if the flow of living water was clogged and the pools had not been scrubbed in years. Yeshua hesitated before he stepped down the narrow stairs into the dark water. Submerged up to his shoulders, he splashed water on his face and neck while trying to ignore the stench. When at last the temple priest nodded his approval, Yeshua climbed out, wrung the water from his tunic, and stood in the sun to dry. Once, this ritual had felt sacred. After traveling the world, it seemed unnatural and forced.

"What's the point of washing the outside of the cup?" he whispered to Yakov. "Don't they know it's inner cleanliness that matters?"

Refreshed and purified, Yeshua and his men made their way up the broad staircase into the outer courtyard where the women waited. But something was not right. The once serene temple court had turned into a raucous slaughterhouse. Hundreds of unblemished lambs, goats, oxen, and birds waited to give their lives in sacrifice for someone's salvation. Merchants hawked the terrified animals at inflated prices, while money changers haggled over shekels, staters, denarii, and drachma in a bizarre spectacle. Yeshua's heart pounded so hard, he thought it would explode. His inner voice told him to stay calm. He took a deep breath, but he couldn't stay still. Instead, he darted up to the closest merchant and knocked over his cages that were piled one atop of another. As they crashed to the ground, the bars shattered and dozens of doves escaped into the sky.

"How dare you dishonor God's house like this?" Yeshua cried. "This is a house of prayer, not a temple to Mammon!"

He rushed about the courtyard, knocking down tables, growling at anyone who tried to block him, and pushing people out of the way. His fury propelled him, made him move faster, made his body stronger. Like in a dream, he moved with the force of wind while everyone else stood still.

Then he stopped cold, panting, his head lowered while he caught his breath. Everyone stared at him as if he were insane. But he was not the one who had gone mad. They had.

His voice shaking, he addressed the crowd:

"What is this? Didn't God tell you his temple should be a house of prayer?"

Yeshua gestured to the vendors and dealers. "You have made his temple a palace of blood. Of suffering."

His companions closed up around him.

"Get out," he shouted at the merchants, raising his fist. "If you have any respect for the Lord, leave this temple. Now."

Yakov yanked him aside. "Yeshua, what is happening? I have never seen you like this."

Mariamne forced him to sit down in the shade of the colonnades and handed him a waterskin.

Still quaking, Yeshua gulped down the water, trying to calm his mind. He had never been this angry before. Bothered, yes, but not full-blown furious like a madman. He closed his eyes and listened to the voice inside him. Instead of yelling at the traders, he should have forgiven them. After all, were they not an apparition of his mind? They mirrored the part of him that was still bound to the material world—his yearning for fame and—more than anything else—his love for Mariamne.

At last, Yakov cleared his throat and said, "Salt is good, is it not?"

Everyone nodded.

Yeshua looked at his brother, full of love, and blessed him in his heart. His question was a cue for Yeshua to teach the daily lesson. Yakov gestured to him to continue, and Yeshua picked up the thread: "But if salt lost its taste, how would you restore it?"

"Do you mean salt is wisdom?" one of his disciples asked.

"Exactly. If the salt is diluted or mixed with sand, it will lose its flavor. And then it cannot be used for anything."

Yeshua saw they understood his apology for having confused his love for God with attachment to the world. His anger had come not from his spiritual, godly self but from his selfish, worldly self.

"You see, this world is such: a married couple had to move from one house to another. In the process of moving, they dropped a couple of jars, spilling their contents. But the wife didn't mind the loss because many flawless jars remained. Like this couple, we must all learn to ignore that which is not perfect in our lives and celebrate what is complete. Keep your salt pure and nothing else will matter."

His listeners breathed easier, recognizing the teacher they knew and loved.

"My brothers and sisters, you must always support those who stumble. Extend a hand to anyone who is sick. Feed the hungry and offer a place of rest to the weary. Awaken those who wish to arise, and shake up those who are sleeping, because each of you holds the wisdom of God."

Mariamne moved to stand next to him, and Yeshua's heart beat a little faster. He dropped his hand to his side, gently touching hers.

"Your inner being is what is important, not matters outside you. Forget about sacrifices—God purifies you through good deeds, not the killing of innocent animals. Don't dwell on the past, and don't encourage the demons of selfishness and materialism, because you have already banished them. What stands in your way will collapse on its own if you don't give it attention. And always, always follow God's commandments, because you are one with him."

Other pilgrims had joined the small group and leaned in, trying to hear what was being said. Yeshua waved them closer. Maybe they wouldn't understand all he said, but the intention would enter their hearts and kindle the light of God.

The next morning, after a night under the stars near Bethany, Yeshua returned to the temple with his companions, eager to immerse himself in joy and be kind to one and all. The merchants and moneylenders had reappeared, once again shouting their prices for all to hear, but today it didn't infuriate him. Instead, he smiled at them and he forgave them.

As Yeshua brought his disciples close for the daily lesson, a priest pushed his way into the crowd, his face flushed with anger. He grabbed Tau'ma by the shoulders and shook him. "Who granted you authority to lecture in the temple?"

Yeshua approached the priest and gently placed a hand on his shoulder.

"Teacher, I believe you are looking for *me*."

The priest glanced in confusion from Tau'ma's face to Yeshua's, and back again, as if wondering which one of them was the radical who had raised hell in the temple the previous day.

"Yes, you," the priest said, regaining his composure. He poked his finger into Yeshua's chest. "Who granted you authority to tell people that God has no need for animal sacrifice?"

"Your holiness, forgive me, but it was God. Yahweh gave me the authority."

The priest's face darkened, and beads of sweat formed on his brow. "It was God? Blasphemer! Who do you think you are—a priest? Leave my temple now. Get out!"

Just like Yeshua had raged at the merchants and money changers the previous day, this priest wanted to throw him out of God's abode. Yeshua closed his eyes and centered on his heart chakra, sending waves of love and forgiveness toward the man before him. Of course the priests were furious. The sacrificed animals fed the entire priesthood. Remove the tradition and they would go hungry. He opened his eyes, looked straight at the priest, and said, "God granted you a special role with his people. Don't you understand that the only way to earn their respect is by showing them the same respect? Treat them as equals."

Yeshua turned to face his disciples.

"Some of you have wondered about the difference between this world and the Kingdom of God," he said, fully aware that the priest was listening. "It's simple. All parts of this world—all elements of nature—are interwoven. Everything is of God. What is composed will decompose, and one day everything will return to its origins."

A few children had approached their group, and the disciples shifted to make space for them.

"It is the attachment to physical things—and people—that creates passion, and that passion causes problems between your mind and your body. That's why you should always stay harmonious. When you feel out of balance, close your eyes and listen inside. Your true nature will inspire you, if you have ears to hear."

More people approached, and Yeshua waved them in.

"Peace be with you. *All* of you," he said, nodding at the priest. "Let serenity rise in you and fill you up. But stay cautious; don't be misled by someone claiming 'Here it is!' or 'There it is!' You don't need anyone else to show you the truth. All the wisdom you need is inside you. God is alive inside all of you."

With a smile, Yeshua nodded at the priest and turned to leave the temple, followed by his disciples and dozens of new listeners. He would continue the lesson on the temple stairs outside.

"Be wary of the Pharisees and Sadducees," Yeshua said when he resumed the lesson in a tranquil place away from the crowds. "Some of them don't understand that the law has been distorted for the sake of tradition. Forgive them in your hearts, but stay aware that although they pride themselves on their knowledge of scripture, they will do anything to call attention to themselves. See how some parade around in flowing robes and demand to be greeted as holy men. They take important seats at banquets and in synagogues. They tie heavy loads onto people's backs and then do nothing to help. They don't know that the most valuable teacher lives within each of us. He who praises himself will be humbled, and he who humbles himself will be praised."

The new listeners nodded in agreement, and Yeshua's heart filled with gratitude. These people were hungry for a new message. Though they had spent their lives looking for God, they remained empty and unfulfilled.

"Look how the priests shut the gate of God's temple in your faces. Because they don't know how to enter God's Kingdom, they want to make sure no one else enters." Yeshua smiled. "They are like blind men with blind hearts leading the blind."

But later, sorrow clouded his heart. Why could he never be quiet? He shouldn't have insulted the priests. They held considerable power in Jerusalem and had connections to Herod Antipas. What if they took their anger out on his disciples? Or what if they harassed Tau'ma again, thinking he was Yeshua? How far would they go?

That night at dinner, Yeshua noticed that Mariamne kept her distance. Ever since they had entered Jerusalem, young women had tried to catch his eye, winking at him, drawing near to him, even touching him. Yeshua had tried to treat them with the same respect as any of the men, but Mariamne must have noticed.

All he wanted was to reach out and kiss her. It had been weeks since they had made love, and he missed the smell of her hair, the feel of her dewy skin, and the way she pressed her soft curves against his body.

Tonight, he decided, he would take a walk with her after the others had gone to sleep. Perhaps they would find a place to lie down together. He needed her more than ever.

Yeshua took a sip of pomegranate juice and stood up to speak. His time with this group of disciples was coming to an end. In one or two more days, he had to move on and leave them to continue his teachings elsewhere. The room seemed to spin at the thought of what was to come, and he had to hold on to the edges of his mat to steady himself.

"My brothers and sisters, I have told you many things, but I want you to remember this: God's Kingdom is like a head of grain in the field. When the grain ripens, the wind scatters its seeds all over the fields. The seeds sprout, and the next spring, the fields are filled again with many new heads of grain. And so it is that every seed you sow will multiply into dozens, then hundreds, then thousands of enlightened beings. Will you, please, always continue to plant and harvest the grain so that God's Kingdom may be shared with others?"

Kephas grinned at him, his mouth askew, as he always did when he was close to falling asleep. A bubble of saliva played between his lips.

"As sons of God," Yeshua continued, "your words will reach far into other lands. But wherever you go, never allow God's Kingdom to dry out and become a desert within you. When your light touches others, treat them as I have treated you, with love and devotion."

The sounds from nearby Bethany stirred in the cloudy night: clattering of hooves on stony roads, boisterous singing, drunken brawls, and ardent prayers. Yeshua observed his faithful companions with a love that knew no bounds; they were the reason he could leave his homeland once again. Tonight, he would ask Mariamne to travel to Alexandria with him. One more day teaching at the temple, a final dinner with his disciples before Pesach, and then he would start walking. Again. His life had been one of steady movement. Why stop now? Why not spend the remaining years of his life in a place where nobody knew him? He had fulfilled his duty and served his Heavenly Father every day of his life. Perhaps now he could take up carpentry again and make his earthly father proud.

Everyone had relaxed after the long day and the disturbances in the temple. Some had fallen asleep. His brothers Yakov and Tau'ma were making up silly songs like Abba used to. Others were discussing how to win an argument with a temple priest. Andreas and Yohannah had stolen away, hand in hand. And why not? They also deserved happiness.

"Isn't the magic of love delightful?" Yeshua whispered to Mariamne. His fingers traced her face as she nibbled on a fig. "Without love, the world wouldn't exist. Just think of the power of intercourse…"

She blushed and covered her face with her shawl, giggling. Yeshua drew her close and kissed her. "My love. My dearest love."

He took her hand and led her away from the others, down a path away from the village and out of sight of the Roman soldiers. She didn't resist. In the darkness, they found a cluster of blossoming almond trees and lay down underneath them. Yeshua caressed her hair and kissed the tip of her nose. She closed her eyes. He slid his hand under her tunic and studied her face. Mariamne's smile betrayed her; she wanted to be taken. Yeshua caressed every inch of the body he knew so well. She quivered and moaned at the touch of his fingers. Gently, he pulled her tunic over her head, trembling at the perfection of her body. She lay on the ground, as God had created her, legs spread, waiting for him. But he didn't want to hurry. He licked her toes, the soles of her feet, gliding his tongue up first one leg, then the other, and tracing the valley from her navel to her neck. He sucked her fingers, one by one, and kissed her palms. She shuddered, unable to contain her pleasure.

At last Yeshua touched his lips to hers and explored her mouth with his tongue. As she kissed him back, he raised his tunic and lowered himself into her. He moved slowly at first, matching the rhythm of his body to hers, entering deeper and deeper. With a surprised gasp, he climaxed too soon. He hardly dared to meet her eyes, afraid she would be disappointed. But her satisfied expression reassured him.

Lying side by side in the afterglow, they watched the pale moon peek out from behind silvery clouds. It was now or never. He had to tell her. Yeshua drew a deep breath.

"Mariamne. Love."

She turned to him, smiling, but when she saw the serious look on his face, her smile faded.

"I must leave."

She turned her head away. "I know."

"Come with me. We can go anywhere. To Alexandria, or perhaps east. We can stay with my friend Dhiman in Sindh, or with the monks in Kapilavatthu. We can raise a family, have babies: a little baby Yeshua and a baby Mariamne."

She took a breath and slowly let it out.

"We can be safe."

She turned back to look at him, her large eyes flushed with sadness. "Can we?"

He gasped with pain, as if someone had torn his heart out. Yeshua pulled her close. "Of course we can. I love you, Mariamne, more than I've ever loved anyone else. I need you by my side. We can teach together, be happy wherever we go."

Mariamne shook her head. "Forgive me, but I can't."

"Why not?" The words came out with more force than he had intended. He didn't want to continue alone. He was tired of being lonely. If Mariamne wouldn't come with him, he might as well stay.

"The women here need me. They look up to me. Because of you, I give them hope. They wouldn't go on teaching without you, especially Yohannah. And the others, the men—they don't respect me, don't respect women. Some even curse behind your back because you treat me as their equal." She held his hand to her heart. "My dearest love, you mean everything to me. You are my world. But I must stay here for the women."

For a moment, Yeshua cursed himself for having taught her so well. He always said that everyone was equally worthy: men and women, rich and poor, educated or ignorant, sinners or believers. And she was right: the women of Palestine needed her more than he did. But that didn't make it easier. His love for Mariamne made him suffer. He needed her, couldn't imagine life without her, but he had no right to hold her back. He had to let her go her own way.

Was he prepared to start over again? Walk from village to village, give lessons and gather a new group of followers? He was tired. He didn't want to start over. He looked up at the glittering stars and the full moon that had once again emerged from the clouds. Could he run from his problems, or would he encounter the same resistance wherever he went? And what if he stayed put and let fate run its course? There was comfort in the thought. If the Romans arrested and killed him, he would simply move to another dimension.

His heart filled with a strange peace as he watched Mariamne's lovely face, asleep on his arm. That's what he would do. He would welcome death. And, from the other side, he would prove once and for all that life in this world was an illusion, that life continued, even without a body.

He kissed Mariamne's hair and covered her naked body with his tunic. She was right. She belonged here.

Jerusalem, Judea, AD 30

The next day at the temple, thousands of people gathered in preparation for Pesach. The courtyard that had been half empty only a day earlier swarmed with worshippers from Palestine, Babylon, and Alexandria, even as far as Britannia. Yeshua looked at the faces of the men and women seated around him. They all had placed their faith in his message.

"Let no one tell you that one person is more important than another," he began, nodding toward the Sadducee priests who walked around the Court of the Gentiles, blessing pilgrims with words from the Torah. "They view themselves as higher beings, and believe they are the only ones who can communicate with God." Yeshua shook his head with compassion. "They are caught in the illusion of the physical world. They have forgotten that we can all become 'higher' by entering the room inside our hearts and speaking to our Father who lives in that sacred space within us."

People who had heard Yeshua speak on previous days took a seat among the disciples. Others, too, drew closer to catch a word or two from the Galilean preacher.

"God's light shines in every man and woman, a light so bright it illuminates the entire world. Connect with the light inside you, sense its power, because only then can you reach absolute peace. Those who won't allow the light to shine from within will always live in darkness. Whoever has ears will hear me."

Yeshua mused at the glow radiating from his listeners.

"Some of you may wonder what this light looks like. The truth is, you will never see God's light with your eyes. The light that illuminates us can be seen only with our souls. But if we allow the physical world to seduce us, we will never become one with the light."

A couple of temple priests drew nearer, shaking their staffs at him in warning. Yeshua kept an eye on them but continued speaking. His message was too important to silence. He had to reach as many people as possible and teach them to trust their inner voice.

"Always be kind to others. Never cause anyone grief, no matter if they are important or meek, sinner or believer."

One of the priests was now standing right behind him, but Yeshua held steadfast and kept going. People needed to hear this.

"Help those in need, not only the ones who can repay you. The wealthy may threaten you and demand that you give them everything you own, but you must resist them. Instead, give to the most deserving, even if it infuriates the greedy."

Another priest now joined the other. Yeshua's heart beat so hard, he could barely steady his voice.

"Knowledge is freedom. Don't be a slave to ignorance, because only truth can set you free. If we recognize what is genuine, the seed of truth will grow within us and bring us fulfillment."

One of the priests put his hand on Yeshua's shoulder. "The high priest wants to see you."

Yeshua didn't turn around. He kept his gaze on his listeners.

"Caiaphas can wait. I've come to deliver my Father's message to these thirsty men and women. If Caiaphas is thirsty, I will certainly bring the jar of knowledge to him. But later, once I've shared it with these humble people before me."

"Thirsty? Are you out of your mind?" One of the priests lifted his staff to strike, but the other pulled his hand down. Yeshua relaxed. It would be foolish for them to attack him in front of a crowd.

"I plead with you—cease the sacrifice of animals," he continued, looking at his listeners but addressing the priests. "God wants mercy, not suffering. If you understand what this means, you will no longer condemn innocent creatures to die for your sins or for food. It's written in the scriptures: God provided us with every plant upon the face of the earth. We shall have them for food, and let the animals live."

The priests walked away, their heads close together, conferring.

Yeshua watched them go. So the rumors were true: Caiaphas had heard about him. That couldn't be good. The high priest was known as the self-adoring ruler of the Yehudi supreme council, the Sanhedrin, and a pawn of the prefect Pontius Pilatus. It was common knowledge that the Yehudi authorities and Roman rulers helped each other stay in power. If one side of the scales tipped, the other, too, would lose its balance.

Yeshua swallowed the bile that rose in his throat. Perhaps he should have humbled himself before the priests. But his message was important. And if he couldn't stand up to the priests, how could the newly awakened be expected to have courage?

The crowd before him grew restless, eager for more kernels of wisdom. Yeshua took a deep breath to calm his nerves and mentally shook the worries away. He had to finish what he had been called to do. No matter what tomorrow brought, the people deserved to hear the truth.

As the sun began to set, Yeshua ended the lesson. The priests had swarmed in and out of the crowd all day to eavesdrop, but hadn't approached him again. Their dark spirits hung like heavy fog among the enlightened souls. Yeshua knew to expect the worst. He had faced disapproval before. But in Benares he had been more of an annoyance, not an actual threat to the Brahmins' power. And once he had left, they had not pursued him. Here, hundreds of men and women had gathered to hear him speak, and there was no place to hide. The priests were furious. If he didn't stop speaking, they would make him. He should have left last night. But he didn't want to leave. He belonged here among his disciples, his successors, who would take over and spread the good news to as many as possible after he no longer could. He had to stay here until the end, if only to prove that life continued even after death.

Yeshua asked Yakov and Kephas to accompany the women to prepare the evening meal at the home of a local merchant who had invited them to his house. It would be a perfect setting for the traditional meal on the eve of Pesach: festive, yet private.

When they had left, Yeshua called Yudah, his bravest companion, to walk with him in the gardens of Gethsemane at the foot of the temple mount. They strolled side by side in silence while Yeshua gathered the courage to ask his friend for an impossible favor. A warm wind tousled his hair, and in the distance, the voices of drunken Roman soldiers broke the peace of the quiet evening. The soldiers had been called to Jerusalem to keep the peace while thousands gathered here for the holiday. Yeshua put his arm around his beloved disciple.

"Yudah, you have learned well about the mysteries of God's Kingdom, have you not?"

His friend nodded thoughtfully.

"And you understand that to reach salvation, you must deny the material world and the body that binds us to it."

"Of course, Master."

"Please don't call me——" Yeshua stopped in midsentence and chuckled. "You have learned well."

They continued walking in silence, stopping only here and there to smell the fragrant blossoms of the olive trees.

"My time here is done, Yudah. I don't know how to tell you this, but I'm afraid I have become a symbol for change in Palestine that neither the Romans nor the priests can accept. The Romans think we're another group of rebels trying to overturn their power. And the priests are afraid of losing their privileges with the Romans."

Yudah's hand went to the dagger at his belt. Yeshua exhaled with a mix of relief and sadness; he had chosen the right man for the job. Yudah was as brave as he was wise. He wouldn't let him down.

"My message is lost on them. They view me as another ignorant Galilean stirring up trouble. They don't realize that we are all on God's side, and that it's not me, but my message, that will bring change. When I'm gone, you and the others will continue to spread the good news. I'm but one of a thousand. You and I are just two out of ten thousand. But if you all stand together as one, like a castle built on a mountain and fortified by a strong wall, you cannot fall."

Yudah stopped walking and turned to him. "Where are you going?"

His eyes teared up. "Master, I had a dream—"

Yeshua took Yudah's hand.

"I dreamed that the other disciples stoned me. Persecuted me. Hated me. They said I had killed you. But I could never harm you."

Yeshua's heart grew cold. Perhaps he was asking for too much. "Come," he said. "I will show you what needs to be done."

He pointed at the Roman soldiers idling by the garden entrance. "Look. They're watching me. They're afraid I'm some rebel who will cause an uprising. And they fear that if Caiaphas can't keep the Yehudim under control, the Romans may lose their power over the people."

"What do you want me to do?" Yudah asked.

"If they come for me, if they decide to arrest me, this is what you must do." Yeshua explained his plan.

After a warm embrace, he held Yudah at arm's length before him.

"I know what I'm asking isn't fair. But it will be an act of God. For God. My message has been lost. You call me Master, the Son of God, but I am a son of man, like everyone else. You raise me above yourselves when all I want is to show you how to enter God's Kingdom. And only by dying can I prove that this world is not real. I want everyone to understand that this world is nothing but a corpse, and that life is God's Kingdom, which resides within each of us. When I leave this world, you will all understand. Please help me. I'm afraid that if I don't surrender myself, you will all be arrested and tortured. And Tau'ma, my dear, sweet brother—people will think he is me. And he is innocent. You are all innocent."

Tears streamed down Yudah's face. He slumped against the garden wall. Yeshua reached for his hand. "Don't despair, my dear friend. Fortunate is the man who knows when the enemy will enter so he may stand up, muster his courage, and arm himself before they invade."

Two dozen of Yeshua's closest disciples congregated to celebrate the Eve of Pesach in a spacious dinner hall with marble floors and high ceilings. The women had arranged low tables in a long line, decorated them with spring flowers, and puffed up silk cushions all around. Yeshua took a seat at the end of the long table, between Tau'ma and Mariamne, and rested his hand on his wife's lap. The women served platters of vegetable stew, carrot and leek salad, and stuffed dates. And then Yakov blessed the pomegranate juice in place of wine, which they had sworn off at initiation. They ate in silence, mindful of every bite.

When everyone had finished their meal and pushed the platters away, the room filled with laughter and song. Only Yudah sat quietly at the table, watching his teacher, his eyes laden with sadness.

Yeshua lifted his cup to signal he wanted to speak. The room stilled as his disciples turned their attention to him.

"My dearest friends, thank you for joining me, in days of feasts as well as days of starvation. Words cannot describe how much I love you—each one of you—and how blessed I am that you have chosen to walk this path with me. Wherever you go, never forget to love your brother and sister as you love yourself. Care for each other like the pupil of your own eye. Because we are reflections of one another. We are all one."

His companions beamed with joy as they lifted their cups to cheer him.

"Remember my words and everything I have taught you. Because when one of you betrays me—"

"Master, surely you don't mean me," his nephew Taddai blurted out.

The others looked around the room in confusion, searching the faces of their companions.

"It won't be me. I love you so."

"Or me. I could never…"

Yudah hung his head.

"None of us would ever betray you."

Yeshua forced a smile. "When one of you, someone who is dipping his bread in this stew, betrays me, remember to forgive him, because God's will has been done."

The disciples, Yudah included, looked from one to the other with horror and disbelief.

"Why would any one of us do something like that?" Tau'ma asked.

Yeshua shuddered at the worry in his youngest brother's eyes—his reflection. How could he explain? He stared at the juice in his cup, took a sip, and scanned the faces of his companions.

"Why? Well, tell me, Tau'ma—and Yakov, Kephas—everyone, compare me to someone and tell me who I'm like."

Kephas stretched his hands toward Yeshua. "You're like an angel. A righteous angel, an angel of the Lord."

Everyone laughed. Yeshua laughed, too, but shook his head.

"You're like a wise philosopher," another suggested.

Yeshua smiled, but again shook his head.

"Master," Tau'ma said in his most tender voice. "My brother, you're all that. But you are not like anyone else."

Yeshua leaned over and kissed his brother's forehead. He looked around the room, from one of his companions to the next. "Whoever I may be, I am not your master. The time has come, and you must remember everything I've taught you, because from now on, *you* are the masters."

Yeshua drained his cup, placed it on the table, and pushed it away from him. There was no need to say more. Ever since Herod Antipas had killed Yochanan the Baptizer, they had known he ran the same risk. Not only was he a Galilean, whom the Judeans generally viewed as patriotic troublemakers, but his actions in the temple could only have added to any suspicions of rebellion. The Romans would never allow a common Yehudi to threaten their authority.

Mariamne placed her hand on his thigh. "If you should leave us, my master—I mean, my love—who will lead us?"

Yeshua squeezed her hand. His most beloved Mariamne. His wife. She deserved to be their new leader. She was the wisest of them all. If only she had been a man.

"Each of you has your own star to follow," he said. "From now on, you must become your own masters. Walk on, and proceed with courage, love, and a heart full of hope. And when you encounter difficulties, remember that I am always with you, wherever you go. You'll never walk alone."

The confusion on their faces filled Yeshua with sadness, but he knew he was doing the right thing.

"I have taught you all I know, and from now on you must teach others. Believe me when I say I have faith in you. But if you're ever in doubt about what to do next," he added, "go to Yakov, my righteous brother. He will guide you."

"And how will this all end?" Mariamne asked. Yeshua caressed her thigh under her tunic, seeking comfort in her warm flesh.

"Have you found the beginning, then, that you're looking for the end? Remember, the end is the beginning and the beginning is the end. Whoever understands this will not experience death."

The disciples were slumping at the table. The shock of Yeshua's announcement had exhausted them.

"I want you to know that if you should abandon me, I'll forgive you."

His words startled them awake.

Kephas banged his fist on the table. "Yeshua, we will never leave you! None of us."

The others, too, declared their eternal support. Kephas stood up, his face bright red. "They'll have to arrest me first. I'll fight them to my last breath. I'd even die for you!"

Yeshua shook his head and gestured for him to sit again. "Kephas, calm down. Everything happens as it must. I will leave you with the gift of peace. Do you understand? Don't let anything worry or upset you or frighten you. And soon you will find that everything I've taught you is true."

Kephas sat down, but now Yakov came and kneeled beside Yeshua and put his head in his lap.

"I don't want you to go."

Yeshua stroked his brother's hair. "But I won't be gone. Just because you can't see me doesn't mean I'm not still here with you. You already know that everything you see before you is a lie, and that God's Kingdom lives within you, and that's where you will find me. There will be days when you'll look for me in vain, but on those days you'll simply have to try harder. Remember what I've told you. Live your lives as someone who is only passing by."

At last Yeshua stood, wiped the food from his mouth, and brushed the crumbs off his beard and robe. He took Mariamne by the hand and led her to a private room in the back. He needed one last moment alone with her.

Too shaken to make love, they lay down and held each other. Yeshua buried his face in her hair and wept for the fleeting illusion of a life that would soon come to an end. Mariamne cradled his head and kissed away his tears until he had exhausted his sadness and fear. Tomorrow he would be strong. His words had sprouted as seeds, and one day the harvest would be rich. But first the shell of the kernel must disintegrate and return to the soil. Just like Moses. Like the Buddha. Like Krishna.

Jerusalem, Judea, AD 30

By the time the women had cleared away the food and swiped the floors, it was too late to return to Bethany. Instead, Yeshua and his followers decided to spend the night in the gardens of Gethsemane where many other pilgrims had rolled out their sleeping mats under the open skies. Yeshua kissed Mariamne and left to meditate alone. He needed to withdraw inside and connect with the Eternal Spirit. Only there would he find peace.

"Father," he whispered, tears straining his voice, "let me live. I know anything is possible. Please take this bitter cup away from me."

But his inner voice reminded him that the agreement had been made long ago, before he had even come to this earth. The script of this life had been written, he had acted out all the scenes, and now the end was nigh. Everything was happening as it should.

Like Kahanji had once taught him, he breathed deeply and opened one chakra after the other, joining them along his spine as he freed the Kundalini life force. Light flickered behind his eyelids, and his heart filled with warmth. His breath became shallower and his heartbeat slowed to a quiet hum. From his crown chakra, he reached high into the heavens and became perfectly, absolutely one with God. The world disappeared.

When he came out of his trance, Yeshua found Yakov and Kephas in deep slumber only a few feet away. He shook them awake and whispered:

"My friends, why are you sleeping? Couldn't you stay awake for even an hour, waiting for me?"

They stirred, embarrassed, but relaxed when they saw his grin.

"Come," Yeshua said, "let's go find the others. The sun is coming up."

Returning to where the others slept, Yeshua found Mariamne and kissed her awake. Her lips tasted sweet, like honey. Would she kiss other men after he was gone? Would she find comfort in Tau'ma, who looked so much like him? Jealousy stabbed him like a jagged knife but dissolved in a heartbeat. She had been his muse. They had shared wonderful times, and he was thankful for their time together. But she was not the key to his happiness, just as she knew he wasn't the key to hers. And he loved her for that.

Under the golden skies of early dawn, the sun cast its first rays over the hilltops. Yeshua sat down to wait. A few yards away, Tau'ma curled up, asleep like an innocent child, his chest rising and falling with every breath. He could not allow the Romans to arrest Tau'ma by mistake. Strangers could never tell them apart. Yeshua rose and walked toward the gate, quietly humming a Buddhist mantra. His hands shook, but he was ready.

A group of soldiers approached, stomping as if to emphasize their importance. Mariamne shrieked. Rubbing the sleep from their eyes, the other disciples rushed to form a shield around their teacher, but he waved them away.

"Yeshua, no!" Mariamne threw herself at his feet. "Don't go. I'll follow you anywhere!"

He pulled her up and held her trembling body close. The soldiers marched toward him, their faces obscured by their bronze helmets and their hands holding firmly on to the daggers that hung off their belts. They stopped a few feet away to allow a man through. Yeshua swallowed and pushed Mariamne to the side. Yudah, his loyal friend, was following his instructions perfectly, despite the pain it must be causing him.

Yudah advanced toward Yeshua and their eyes locked. Yeshua fought the urge to run. He stayed still and accepted Yudah's kiss that left traces of saliva on his cheek. Time seemed to stop as the soldiers grabbed him and pushed him to the ground, facedown in the dust. One soldier straddled him while another tied his hands behind his back. When they yanked him back up and dragged him away, Yeshua hung his head low. He turned only once to see Mariamne crying and a few of his disciples fighting the armored soldiers. Others stood over Yudah, kicking him, as he lay doubled up on the ground, vomiting. Yeshua opened his mouth to shout out, tell them to leave Yudah alone, when a blow to his head forced him to turn away.

Where were they taking him? It didn't matter. There could be only one outcome in this, the last phase of his earthly life. Yeshua took a deep breath and separated himself from any physical emotions, and ascended to a dimension where he felt neither pain nor fear.

The soldiers pushed him down the narrow alleys, through the tall gate of Herod's palace, and threw him into a dungeon below the fort, slamming the door shut. The stone walls seeped with moisture, and the green moss that covered the ground made his feet slide from under him. Yeshua pulled his mantle closer for comfort. The scent of death made the cell even darker. Smaller. How long would they keep him here? Wails from adjacent cells told him he was not alone. The Romans had been busy, arresting anyone they suspected of stirring up trouble.

How long would this take? Pesach would begin at sunset. Surely they would want to settle this matter before then. If not, they risked offending the Yehudi people and causing an uprising. The Romans were barbaric, but they were no fools. Yeshua wiped his running nose on the side of his head scarf. Were they planning to banish him from Palestine? Or would they really—kill him?

Death. Yeshua shivered at the thought. Now that the steps were set in motion, he was overcome by doubt and fear. Would they cut off his head, like Yochanan? Stab him with their swords? Stone him to death—or crucify him like a zealot? Whatever they decided, he prayed the end would be quick.

Yeshua lay down on the cold ground, pulled his knees to his chest, and fell asleep, drained from the events of the long night.

His fate was out of his hands.

When the soldiers returned, the sun already stood high in the sky. They yanked him to his feet and dragged him through damp stairwells to a brightly lit room in the upper levels of the fort. Yeshua breathed deeply to calm his racing heart. He was famished. Exhausted. Frightened. But he knew why he was here. Caiaphas must have brought the Romans' attention to him. If only the temple priests had been willing to listen, perhaps they could have learned something, might have used his message to help others find peace. But they were hopelessly married to this world, blinded by their possessions and positions.

The soldiers left Yeshua standing barefoot on the cold mosaic floor with only a guard for company. Heavy brocade drapes covered high windows that nearly reached the vaulted ceilings. In an alcove at the back of the room, water splashed from a spout into an ornamental, semicircular basin. Six thronelike chairs stood pushed against the smooth red walls in front of him.

With a clank, the door swung open, and a short man in a full-length white robe entered accompanied by two soldiers. Yeshua knew him instantly: Pontius Pilatus, the prefect of Judea. For some reason, Yeshua had expected him to be taller and more imposing, maybe even handsome. With his broad face, mushroom nose, and large teeth that pushed out between closed lips, the man resembled a hyrax. He walked around Yeshua, examining him from every angle.

"So you were planning an uprising, weren't you? You are a traitor."

Yeshua let out a bitter laugh. Caiaphas had no shame. Or had the word come from Antipas? A slap across his face silenced him.

"Silence! How dare you laugh at me?"

Yeshua bowed his head. What was wrong with the man? Did he need to use physical violence to get his thoughts across?

"Are you going to answer the question?" Pilatus struck his legs with his staff.

Yeshua waited. How much power did Pilatus have? Was he a friend of the Herods? Did it matter?

"You believe you are the king of the Yehudim?"

Yeshua looked up. What king was he talking about?

"Answer me!" Even his voice sounded like a hyrax.

"Those are your words, not mine," Yeshua said.

"And you? What do you say?"

"I'm a son of man. I'm here to bear witness to truth."

"Truth?" Pilatus laughed. "Holy Jupiter, then speak the truth. You say you are the king, the leader of the Yehudim. You corrupt the feeble-minded with fanciful ideas about a new kingdom. Power, is that what you seek? Do you seek power?"

Yeshua stared at the tiny man in front of him. What kind of interrogation was this? Why was he alone in this room?

"I never said I was king of the Yehudim—or of anyone," he said at last.

When Pilatus stepped close enough for Yeshua to smell his foul breath, he winced. Insulted, Pilatus raised his hand to slap Yeshua but was interrupted when a group of Roman soldiers burst in and grabbed Yeshua. They tied his hands behind his back.

Pilatus grinned. "You have been sentenced to die for rebellion, king of the Yehudim." He peeked through the window at the high sun, then nodded to the soldiers. "Let us finish this matter before sunset."

Yeshua's knees buckled under him. This was not the way he had pictured his end. Did he have to give his life for this fool over a Yehudi holiday that Pilatus didn't even celebrate?

The soldiers dragged him into a bare room and stripped him naked. They bound a loincloth around his waist and shoved him around between them, laughing as Yeshua stumbled from one soldier to another. Why had they left him here with a group of juveniles who amused themselves by causing pain? Why not just kill him?

When a senior soldier arrived to take charge, Yeshua almost cried with relief. But the comfort didn't last long. Outside, in the stark sunlight, the soldiers bound a heavy wooden beam across his upper back, and fastened it with ropes around his wrists.

They were going to crucify him.

Yeshua staggered and tripped under the weight as the soldiers forced him down the rocky streets, behind two other prisoners who struggled under similar beams. Rebels, he heard the soldiers say. Masterminds of a planned uprising. Of course. Only traitors to the empire would be subjected to the torturous, humiliating death by crucifixion. A warning to all zealots and other Yehudi patriots. Caiaphas must hate him. And for what? Because Yeshua reminded him that God didn't care about riches or power or sacrifices? A true servant of God was humble and kind, generous and forgiving. Caiaphas was none of those. He was ambitious, vain, and cruel.

Yeshua tried to shift the beam up to straighten his back. The ropes around his wrists cut into his skin. He wanted to fall to his knees and give up, let them beat him to death. Instead, he separated his consciousness from his body and willed his legs to continue walking.

As he struggled along the path, he recognized the faces of Yakov and Tau'ma in the crowd that was standing by, watching. And there— Mariamne, her eyes swollen with grief. At her side, his dear friend Kephas, and all the others, too. Everyone except Yudah. Yeshua's heart dropped into the pit of his stomach. What a terrible price Yudah would pay for his favor to Yeshua. Didn't they understand that without Yudah, others more innocent and less ready might have been arrested and tortured? Tau'ma, his dear little brother, might have been hung in his place for the simple crime of resemblance. But poor Yudah, he would never forgive himself. Where had he gone?

Yeshua glimpsed the tearful eyes of his mother. She must have hidden among the crowd at the temple and listened to him from a distance, covering her face so that no one would recognize her. And yet, here she was by his side, although he had forsaken her. A mother's love—more powerful than any other. Oh, how he wished he could have given Mariamne a child, someone to love when he was gone.

On top of a hill, a band of executioners had gathered to nail the three prisoners to their crosses. The young soldiers who had mocked Yeshua earlier kept the onlookers at bay with their spears, in fear of a revolt.

A temple priest had arrived to ensure Yeshua received the punishment he deserved. What did he expect? That Yeshua could talk the Roman soldiers out of his execution? One of the executioners offered Yeshua a cup of vinegar and wine to calm his nerves, but he pushed it away. He had sworn off all numbing substances and wasn't going to break his vows now. The other prisoners gulped down the sour liquid without hesitation. They trembled with dread, unable to look at the executioners who stood ready with their sledgehammers and those long, thick nails, commonly used for the doors of wealthy homes. Yeshua's heart didn't even race. He could probably leave his body now, if he chose to; he just didn't know how to actually die.

When the executioners shoved him down and positioned his torso on top of the crossbeam, Yeshua closed his eyes. He sought the place inside where he was one with God.

An inhuman cry of pain jolted him back to reality.

The man beside him wailed as the massive nails slammed into his wrists. The poor man's face turned white as he watched the blood drip from his punctured wrists.

Another nail pegged his feet to the cross. By then, his cries had faded into agonizing moans. The other prisoner threw up, seeing the fate that awaited him.

Yeshua closed his eyes again.

"Holy Spirit, please remove me from this place," he begged. He didn't fear his own pain. What he couldn't stand was to hear the others suffer. He wanted to reach out and tell them about the Kingdom of God within. Convince them that physical anguish was an illusion. But his voice had left him. And could they even hear him through their fog of torment?

Grunting under the weight, the executioners raised the first cross, then the other, in deep pits, securing them with large stones. The soldiers cheered. What kind of men would rejoice over another's pain? Yeshua didn't even want to know. He had to focus on forgiving. Whatever they did to his body, they could not touch his soul.

At last it was his turn. One by one, the ropes around his wrists were tightened. The executioners nailed a plank below his feet and another under his buttocks to keep his body from sagging under its weight and to prolong the process of dying. Yeshua felt the tip of a nail press into his skin. And then, slam! The pain burned like fire. He gasped and tried to separate from his body. In his mind, he repeated over and over, *It's only my body, only my body, only my body.* But before he could remove himself, another nail pierced his wrist. The pain was so fierce, he convulsed and leaned forward, vomiting the remains of the previous night's meal. The soldiers laughed. Someone kicked his head.

Our Father, glorified and sanctified be your name...

Yeshua went inside, released himself from his physical body, and begged the Eternal One for relief. He found the sacred place just before they drove a nail into his ankles.

He didn't even wince.

May you establish your kingdom speedily and soon...

For effect, the executioner drove another nail into his feet, but Yeshua didn't react. He was with God.

When they finally raised the cross, Yeshua caught sight of the crowd who had assembled to watch the spectacle. Judean women who lamented the sacrifice of innocents, curious Alexandrian traders with their camels, a cluster of boys of the age when spilled blood excited more than horrified, and a centurion in full armor. At his feet, the soldiers chatted and laughed as they rolled sheep's knuckles like dice on the ground to pass the time. None of his disciples had dared come, unwilling to risk meeting the same fate.

The weight of his body caused the nails to rip the flesh of his wrists. He tried to push up against the plank under his feet for relief, but his feet slipped and his legs could not bear his weight. How long could he last?

Through the afternoon mist, an angel appeared below him, illuminated by a dazzling light. Mariamne. Yeshua's heart swelled with love. His faithful wife. He grinned through the delirium. Oh, those ignorant Romans, they could never imagine his rescue by a woman, and had allowed the wives, mothers, and sisters of the prisoners to approach the crosses. What fools. They did not realize that Mariamne was more powerful than any man.

Yeshua smiled down at her.

She didn't smile back. Her hand rested on her rounded belly. Yeshua's heart skipped. Was it true? Why had he not noticed the glow on her face earlier? Was there a budding life inside her?

"Let me take you down, Love," she whispered. She curled up by the cross and kissed his bleeding feet. Yeshua shook his head. He had accepted his fate. He hung there for all to see, a warning to others who threatened to overthrow the empire. They had made an example of him. Do not stir up trouble in the temple. Do not upset the priests. And most important of all, do not threaten the power of Pontius Pilatus.

But Yeshua had shown them they could strip him naked and nail him to a cross, and still he would be at peace because he was with God. The material world was an illusion, and he was the proof.

A yellow butterfly landed on his shoulder. It fluttered its delicate black-tipped wings as if to fan him. Its large black eyes seemed to stare right through him. What a gorgeous creature. And he recognized the spirit within. The butterfly had come to give him hope, to assure him that his disciples were ready to spread their own wings.

Yeshua drifted off. The world disappeared into an abyss.

And then his mother and his sister Miriam were there beside Mariamne. His mother threw herself at the soldiers' feet, begging them to release her son. But they just kicked her away. Yeshua wanted to tell her not to worry, tell her he was all right, but his voice had dried out. Mariamne pulled his mother into her arms, embraced her, and wiped away her tears. Yeshua had never loved her more. If only his mother would understand that although her son hung dying on a cross, he did not suffer.

"Lord, forgive them." Yeshua's voice cracked.

The chatter stopped. Everyone, even the soldiers, looked up at him, shielding their eyes from the setting sun that had broken through the clouds. Mariamne smiled, at last.

With a final push, Yeshua nodded at the soldiers. "Forgive them; they don't understand what they are doing."

Yeshua's chin dropped to his chest. He drifted in and out of consciousness. Only the moans of the men beside him kept him in the present. Unable to move his body, his spirit reached out and touched their souls to comfort them. Soon after, their whimpers ceased, and they hung motionless on their crosses.

The air grew colder as the evening drew near. The thin, layered clouds turned orange against the dark blue sky. The crowd melted into an inseparable mass. The soldiers became one with the observers, the executioners, and his loved ones—and then with him. The oneness he had taught about was real. He loved and forgave them all. They were all reflections of him. And at last he realized he had also forgiven himself.

Above him, a ray of brilliant light appeared to call him home. In the glow, he recognized the radiant faces of Abba, Yochanan, Kahanji, and Pema; they beckoned him to follow the light of the celestial doorway. God's Kingdom. It was right here, as he had always imagined.

Below him, the three women he had left behind—Mariamne, his sister, and his mother—wept in one another's arms. They caressed his feet, calling to him as if he could return.

Floating high, he watched one of the executioners step closer and poke his body with a stick as it hung lifeless on the cross. But he had already left his physical body, like so many times before, only this time the silver cord that attached him to his earthly self had snapped. There was no going back.

Heaven embraced him like a hot summer breeze, enveloping him with pure love. Home. Yeshua looked once more at the three women at the cross who loved him so. They were ready, too. He had given them all he could. From now on, their fate was to continue without him.

His father called him, Yochanan reassured him. Pema presented him with all the love of mankind. Kahanji invited him into the tunnel of light that continued into nothingness.

And Yeshua followed.

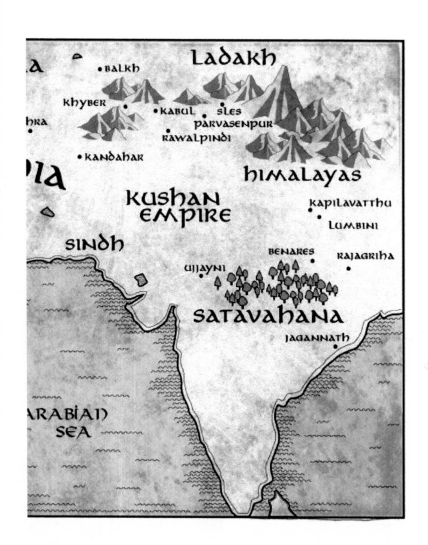

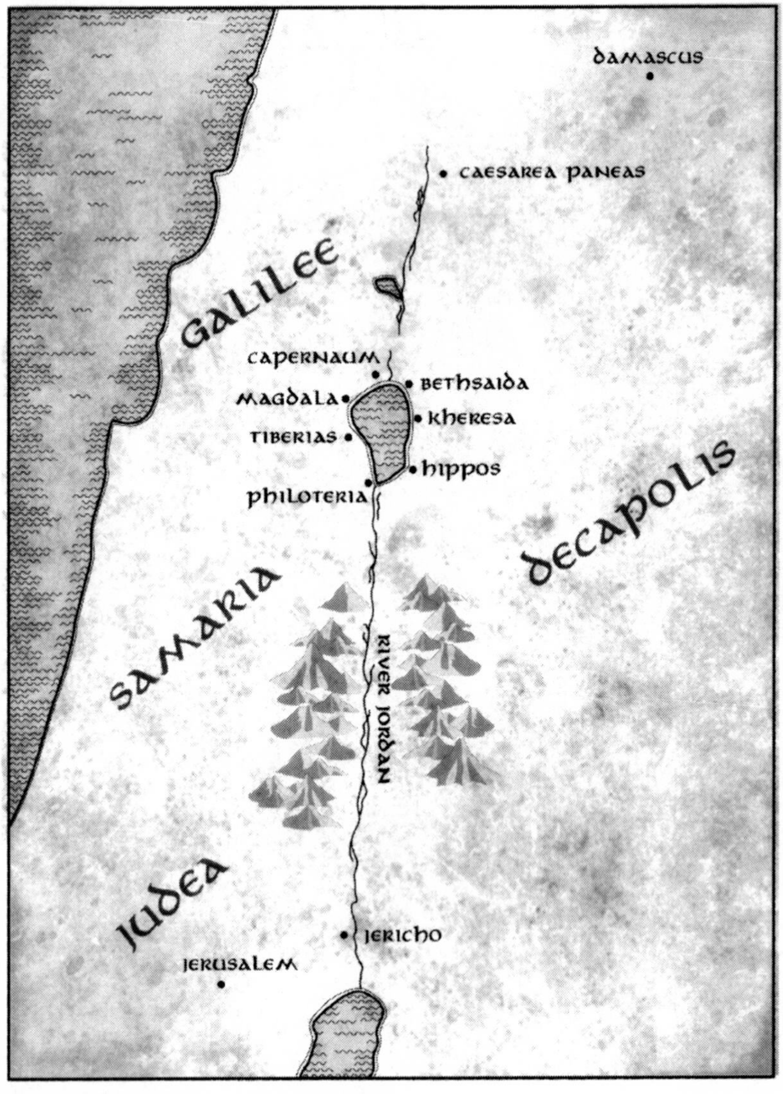
DAMASCUS
CAESAREA PANEAS
GALILEE
CAPERNAUM
BETHSAIDA
MAGDALA
KHERESA
TIBERIAS
HIPPOS
PHILOTERIA
DECAPOLIS
SAMARIA
RIVER JORDAN
JUDEA
JERICHO
JERUSALEM

Author's Note

We don't know much about Jesus. None of the books of the New Testament were generated during his lifetime. None of them, except possibly the Epistle of James, were written by people who had met him. Most of the New Testament books originated decades after Jesus's death and are based on stories the authors had heard from people who knew people who knew people who had once heard Jesus speak. Imagine retelling an event to a friend, something you heard happened to someone else forty years ago. How much of that story would be accurate? Would you know the exact words that were spoken? Would the story have "grown" and become more interesting? Did the fish he caught weigh five pounds or fifty? And when it comes to Jesus, did he feed fifty people or five thousand with five loaves of bread?

I've focused on the most authentic sources for this book, trying to establish who Jesus truly was. What did he look like? Where did he spend all those years not mentioned in the Bible—from age twelve to thirty? What really happened? At the same time, I've dismissed large parts of the New Testament and the common story line portrayed in movies and books.

Why? Because the books we know as the New Testament were selected by Emperor Constantine and the Roman bishops during the First Council of Nicaea in AD 325, three hundred years after Jesus died. At the time, there were more than eighty versions of the gospels floating around, and the emperor decided to establish a consensus of what Christ stood for and what Christianity should mean. The oldest existing documents are tiny fragments of second-century scrolls, written generations after Jesus and his disciples lived. We don't know how much of the Bible texts were changed during the previous three hundred years, nor do we know why the emperor and bishops deemed certain books "authentic" and others "fraudulent." We can only assume that any books that didn't proclaim Jesus as the Messiah and the only son of God were discarded. Around AD 380, Pope Damascus announced that the (cherry-picked) books in the New Testament were inspired by the Holy Spirit, and subsequently any questioning of the authenticity of the Bible became a punishable crime.

The closest we come to actual first-century sources are the thirteen letters of Paul; however only seven of them are unanimously considered authentic by experts. But Paul of Tarsus never met Jesus; he never knew him. Paul only had a "vision" of Jesus a few years after Jesus's death. In his letters, Paul recounts his quarrels with Jesus's disciples and complains about how they rebuffed him. Although he begged the disciples to accept him as one of their own, even bribed them with food during the Jerusalem famine of AD 47, Jesus's disciples would not oblige, because the stories Paul told were completely different from what their teacher Jesus had taught. (Galatians 1:7–21, Galatians 2:11–21, 2 Corinthians 11:22–24, 2 Corinthians 12:11, Philippians 3:1–3, etc.)

Therefore, we can deduce that Paul invented his own story line about a mythical creature called Christos, the Greek word for the Messiah. Paul was a Roman Jew who lived among non-Jews far away from Palestine. Thus, he had to attract followers by speaking about a god they would recognize. He based the characteristics of Christos on Attis, a dying and resurrecting god also called "the Good Shepherd," and drew inspiration from other popular deities such as Horus, Adonis, and Apollonius (death and resurrection) and gods born from virgin mothers (Marduk, Perseus, Immanuel, Pharaoh, and even Caesar). He also added events such as Osiris's last supper (Osiris was betrayed at this supper by the evil god Set).

The only credible, relatively unbiased author from the time is Josephus Flavius (AD 37–94), a first-century Roman-Jewish historian.

In his books, Josephus described all the contemporary spiritual influences and trends in detail, but didn't mention anything about Jesus or the Christian communities. There is a passage where "Christ" is mentioned, but it is considered by all experts to be a later interpolation. Furthermore, Josephus mentions a whole slew of pseudo-Messiahs, prophets who behaved as though they had been chosen by God and who caused disturbances in the eyes of the Romans. Thus, if Jesus did exist, he was not the only healer who preached God's word along the roads of Judea, Samaria, and Galilee. And Jesus's followers were not Christians; they were simply followers of a man called Jesus. The first mention of Jesus as the Messiah appears forty years after his death. However, although Jesus wasn't widely known during his lifetime, his message of peace and love did have an effect and influenced people to carry it forward for centuries to come.

Sources used for *The Transmigrant*

I don't pretend to know the whole truth (nobody does and nobody ever will), but I have tried to get as close to original, authentic sources as possible, those that have not been distorted over the years. Therefore, I've largely dismissed the canonical gospels (the Gospels according to Matthew, Mark, Luke, and John) and have used only parts of Mark (written around AD 70) and Matthew (written between AD 80 and AD 150). I have not used any part of the gospels of John and Luke, which were compiled by a variety of authors between AD 90 and AD 110, as I consider them to be unreliable and hearsay at best. I have completely dismissed the Acts of the Apostles, which was written around CE 95 by followers of Paul, not followers of Jesus. Instead, I've relied on *The Lost Gospel, the Book of Q (Quelle)*, which is believed to be the original but lost source of the canonical gospels. I've used the *Nag Hammadi Library* codices, a collection of more than fifty texts, that were discovered in upper Egypt in 1945 and include texts that were thought to have been destroyed during the early Christian struggle to define Christianity. I've also relied on Nicolas Notovitch's *The Unknown Life of Jesus Christ,* which includes *Life of Saint Issa,* Buddhist scrolls about Jesus's life in India, which were discovered by the Russian adventurer in 1887. I've assessed the sources based on logic: if Jesus was a man of God, he would have been kind, curious, nonjudgmental, inclusive, and loving. It's this person I've tried to portray in this novel.

Did Jesus grow up in Nazareth?

There is no proof that Nazareth existed in the early part of the first century AD. If it did, it would have been a small cluster of perhaps half a dozen huts. Archaeologists have discovered remnants of houses in the area, but most likely they were built by zealots who fled to the countryside after the uprising and destruction of the Jerusalem temple in AD 66. Nazareth is not mentioned in any scriptures of the time, not even in Josephus's list of all sixty-three communities of Galilee. In addition, if Jesus had grown up in Nazareth, he would likely have said he came from Sepphoris, the Galilean capital only three miles from today's Nazareth, just as people today say they are from New York rather than Staten Island, Paris rather than Vincennes, or London rather than Barnet. It's more probable that the "from Nazareth" epithet derived from the word *Nazirite,* a member of an ascetic Jewish sect, someone who had sworn off wine and meat and was initiated into the faith by shaving their heads and then never cutting their hair again. If Jesus lived among Hindus and Buddhists, the Nazirite faith would have made a lot of sense to him. Given that all we know about Jesus's adult life in the New Testament revolves around Capernaum and the Sea of Galilee, it's fair to assume he grew up and lived in that area.

Did Jesus flee Bethlehem and go to Egypt after the Slaughter of the Innocents?

Only the Gospel of Matthew mentions the flight to Egypt. At the time, Bethlehem in Judea was a tiny village of no more than a few hundred inhabitants, and it's not clear whether Mary and Joseph ever lived there.

Neither Mark nor Paul, authors of the oldest New Testament books, mention Bethlehem. Also, there is no known record of a mass infanticide ordered by Herod the Great. Historians believe that the "Slaughter of the Innocents" refers to Herod's killing of his own sons in 7 BC, not Jewish boys in Bethlehem. If Herod the Great had called for all boys under the age of two to be killed, the story would appear somewhere in historical sources, but it does not. It is more probable that the author(s) of the Gospel of Matthew created the story of the slaughter and the flight to Egypt to match the quote from Hosea 11.1, "Out of Egypt I called my son," to support the claim that Jesus was the awaited Messiah.

Did he have brothers and sisters?

Theologians have debated this question for millennia. Some read the text of the New Testament where Jesus's brothers and sisters are mentioned and conclude that yes, he did have siblings (Matthew 13:54–56; Mark 6:3). Others believe that Jesus's mother was a virgin and stayed a virgin all her life. They claim that Jesus's "brothers" and "sisters" referred to cousins, because the Hebrew language doesn't distinguish between the words for brother and cousin. However, the gospels were written in Greek, and the word *Adolphos* can only mean blood brother.

The Gospel of Mark (considered the most authentic of the canonical gospels) never suggests that Jesus was in any way a supernatural being. In fact, the only books in which Mary, his mother, is portrayed as a virgin is in the Gospel of Matthew, where the author desperately tried to force a connection between Messianic prophecies and Jesus, and the Gospel of Luke, written more than sixty years after Jesus's death. Moreover, the virgin story was unknown to the original Christian community and didn't flourish until the fourth century when Emperor Constantine created a Mother Goddess Mary as a Christian substitute for the popular Mother Goddess Isis.

Did he really travel through Asia?

Again, we don't know, and unless we invent a time machine, we will probably never know for sure if the scrolls Nicolas Notovitch found in Ladakh in 1887 were authentic. According to Notovitch and the others who followed in his footsteps, the scrolls have been locked in cabinets in the monasteries around Tibet, which now cannot be reopened until the Dalai Lama returns to his homeland. Over the years, many historians have dismissed Notovitch as a fraud on the basis that no one else has ever seen the Ladakhi scrolls. But that's not true. In 1922, the Indian Swami Abhedananda saw the scrolls. In 1925, the Russian professor Nicholas Roerich saw them, and two women, the American Mrs. Clarence Gasque and the Swiss Madame Elizabeth Caspari, saw the same scrolls in 1939.

Several facts support the theory that Jesus spent the bulk of his life in Asia. When you look at the similarities between Hinduism, Buddhism, and Christianity, it makes sense that Jesus's beliefs were influenced by Eastern religions. A comparison of the travel times mentioned in the Ladakhi scrolls during which Jesus was said to have traveled from one point to another match Google Maps' estimates of the time it would take to walk those distances. In addition, there are several places along the assumed route that may have been named after Saint Issa, like the Yuz-Marg meadow and the sacred building Aish Muga, both within a day's travel south of Srinagar. One must also wonder, if Jesus stayed in Galilee all his life, what kept him occupied between the ages of twelve and thirty? Did he change from an incredibly well-spoken child to an adolescent who focused solely on carpentry for the next eighteen years only to one day discover he wanted to teach again? Not likely.

Did Jesus have twelve disciples?

When I started writing the story, I realized that the names of the disciples listed in the Bible (Matthew 10:2–4, Mark 3:16–19, Luke 6:13–16) do not match. My doubts deepened when contemplating why Matthias had to replace Judas after Jesus's death to once again have a group of exactly twelve disciples (Acts 1:12–26). Why would Jesus care about the quantity? Why twelve? Wouldn't it make more sense to select *all* your best students, whether they numbered eight or twelve or eighteen?

In the first century, the number twelve was considered a magical, complete, or perfect number. In fact, the number twelve occurs 187 times in the Bible. There were twelve tribes in Israel. Jacob had twelve sons. The New Jerusalem that descended out of heaven had twelve gates made of pearl that were manned by twelve angels. There were twelve loaves of permanent offerings on the golden table. Solomon had twelve administrators in his kingdom. The book of Chronicles contains twelve great priests. And so on. We can deduct from this that Jesus did *not* have twelve disciples; it was just a good number to use to emphasize his holiness. The first time that twelve apostles are mentioned is in *The Teaching of the Twelve Apostles*, a sectarian Jewish document written in the first century AD but later adopted by Christians who altered it substantially and added Christian ideas to it.

Did Jesus marry?

Nowhere in the Bible does it say that Jesus was celibate. A normal marital status, on the other hand, would have been assumed and would not need to be mentioned. In the first century, Jews were strongly opposed to celibacy and the Romans enforced fiscal penalties against it.

Could Jesus have been homosexual? Yes, it's possible, but it's more likely that he was married, and that Mary Magdalene was his wife. She's always the first woman mentioned among women in the Bible. In the Gospel of Philip, one of the gnostic gospels written around the third century AD and discovered in the caves of Nag Hammadi, Egypt, in 1945, we can find the following references: "Magdalene, the one who was called his companion" and "[... loved Mary Magdalene] more than [all] the disciples [and used to] kiss her [often] on her [lips]." In addition, the so-called *Gospel of Jesus's Wife*, a fourth-century papyrus fragment copied from a second-century scroll and presented to the International Congress of Coptic Studies by Karen L. King of Harvard Divinity School in 2012, includes the lines "Jesus said to them, my wife," and "she will be able to be my disciple."

Did the Romans make Jesus wear a crown of thorns at his execution?

Although three of the canonical gospels mention that Pilate's soldiers dressed Jesus in purple and put a crown of thorns on his head, the story is probably a myth. It's extremely unlikely that thornbushes grew within the walls of Jerusalem and that the soldiers would take the time to hunt through the hills for thorns just to mock and ridicule a common criminal. Neither would they spend the time to dress and undress a prisoner. This legend was most likely superimposed to portray Jesus as the King of the Jews. However, it must also be noted that the historian Josephus Flavius uses the word *king* as a designation for any leader of a band of insurgents. Subsequently, there were many criminals labeled "King of the Jews," and the term had nothing to do with the awaited Messiah.

Didn't the Jews kill Jesus?

Not so fast. The story of Jesus's trial is highly suspicious and clearly tries to placate the Romans while defaming the Jews. At the time, the Sanhedrin (the Jewish Supreme Court) had only limited jurisdiction over capital punishment. The penalty for blasphemy was stoning, not death by crucifixion. If the Sanhedrin had, contrary to all logic, sentenced Jesus to death on a day when they were forbidden to congregate, there would have been no need to bring him before Pontius Pilate for confirmation. The Romans were generally reluctant to interfere in conflicts among Jews, especially any religious controversies. And Pilate, who viewed the Jews with utter contempt, would never have allowed a mob of Jews to influence his decision and pronounce a death sentence against his will.

In fact, only rebels against the Roman occupation of Palestine were sentenced to death by crucifixion, which was the most shameful, most humiliating death imaginable. Therefore, the eve of Pesach, when

Jerusalem filled with Jews from all over the Roman Empire, would have been an ideal time for the Romans to flex their muscles and deter anyone who tried to revolt against them. As such, Jesus was arrested by the military and the final judgment was passed upon him in a court-martial proceeding as an agitator, not a blasphemer. The Romans were in charge, not the Jews.

However, it is possible that the temple priests, the Sadducees, might also have seen the increased Roman presence as an opportunity to rid themselves of a troublemaker by warning them about Jesus. The Sadducees were known to work hand in hand with the occupying power in the interest of political tranquility.

Furthermore, in Josephus's works, where he describes every political crime and sentence of the first century, there is no mention of the sensational double trial before the Jewish Sanhedrin. Although he mentions all revolts and disturbances and any just or unjust death sentences of any political importance, he does not mention the trial of Jesus. One more crucified Jew made no difference to the Roman procurators and emperors, or their historians.

So why do the gospels claim that the Jews killed Jesus? Over the years, as the tales of Jesus spread from one man to another, the story line changed to appease the anti-Jewish sentiment among the Romans, especially after the outbreak of the Jewish War in AD 66. The Gospel of Mark, for example, is believed to have been composed by a Roman soldier in Rome. In this anti-Jewish fashion, the gospels also turn one of the disciples into the traitor who betrays Jesus. The eternal Jew, with a name that would forever be associated with Judaism, Judas became the devil and all Jews the devil's offspring.

In the end, it made more sense for the new Christians to portray Jesus as a powerful Messiah who was derided by the Jews and to characterize Pilate as an innocent man who had acted only under pressure from the Jews. Thus, they successfully convinced the Romans that the Empire had nothing to fear from the new Christian religion.

If you're interested in learning more, I suggest you read *The Court-Martial of Jesus: A Christian Defends the Jews Against the Charge of Deicide* by Weddig Fricke, an excellent book in which Fricke explains why it's unlikely that the Jews were responsible for Jesus's death.

To get an idea of what the original gospels were like, you can read *The Lost Gospel: The Book of Q & Christian Origins* by Burton L. Mack.

For more information about my research, please visit my website:
www.kristisaareduarte.com

Acknowledgments

I would like to thank all the historians, theologians, researchers, bloggers, journalists, adventurers, and authors who came before me, whose works I've studied, and whose findings have either strengthened my theories or made me question them. In particular, I owe an incredible amount of gratitude to Nicolas Notovitch, Weddig Fricke, Elizabeth Clare Prophet, Marvin Meyer, Burton L. Mack, Ben Witherington III, Robin R. Myers, and Reza Aslan. A complete list of books, websites, and videos used for research can be found at my website, www.kristisaareduarte.com.

I couldn't have reached this point and completed the novel without my beta-readers, who poked, dissected, criticized, and questioned the manuscript when it was far from polished and complete. Susan Norkin, without your comments and corrections about Judaism, I would have stepped on toes and certainly earned some sneers. Mercedes Bassani, your detailed remarks and your passionate but sober insights into Catholicism helped me better understand its intricacies. Kaie Pugi, your sweet support and confirmation of facts regarding the Eastern religions helped keep me on track. Petra Bergstrand and Anthony Giovanni, your plot tweaks, questions, and invaluable enthusiasm strengthened the story and kept my engine going through the many times of doubt. I'd also like to give a shout-out to Nathan Paul, who answered my questions about Judaism and Hebrew terminology.

I owe a huge thanks to my amazing editors. Sarah Aschenbach and Julie Klein helped clarify my direction, pointed out many structural errors, and helped make the copy both clearer and crisper. I'm also indebted to Laurel Robinson, my excellent proofreader and copy editor, who made sure all the t's were crossed and i's were dotted before publication.

I would not be the person I am without my parents. Their passing, far too early in life, taught me the importance of saying the words "I love you," and to live every day as though it may be my last.

I'd also like to thank my sisters, Anne-Pii and Tiina, for always being there for me. Even though we live far apart, you are always in my heart and in my thoughts.

And last but not least, my husband, Eduardo, who supported my passion throughout the many years of writing *The Transmigrant*, who believed in my success, and who always allowed me the time I needed to write. You're my soul mate and my best friend, and I love you more than words can say. Now can I have a dog?

KRISTI SAARE DUARTE, author of *The Transmigrant*, has spent her life traveling the world and chasing adventures. Always open to change, she has lived in Sweden, England, Estonia, Spain, and Peru, where she has studied languages, art, and acting, and has had careers in health care management, advertising, and finance. She is also a Reiki healer and spiritual channel. Currently, she lives in Harlem, New York City, with her husband, Eduardo.

If this book moved you, please leave a review on Amazon.com or Goodreads.com. Just two–three words are better than nothing: Loved it. Liked it. It was OK.

Thank you!

@KristiSaare
www.facebook.com/KristiDNYC
www.kristisaareduarte.com

CPSIA information can be obtained
at www.ICGtesting.com
Printed in the USA
FFOW03n2101090717
37501FF